Between
Light
&
Shadows

Between Light

& Shadows

ARIN L. BLACKWOOD

Published by Under the Blackwood Tree
Buffalo, NY 14075
Undertheblackwoodtree.com

Book Design: Arin Blackwood
Map illustration: Arin Blackwood
Cover: Arin Blackwood
Art: Heather Menz
Chapter Art: Isabelle Salem

ISBN: 979-8-9944056-0-4
Printed in the United States of America
1st Printing

Books by Arin Blackwood:

<u>Fyrala Chronicles</u>
Between Light and Shadows
Bound in Ash & Gold Coming Soon

<u>Atlantis Rising</u>
Lost Throne

<u>McKlean Mysteries</u>
Published under A.L. Blackwood

Blood of the Rose
Dust to Dust Coming Soon

Your mental health is important. This story is a fictional fantasy, but any good story has real-life elements. This book includes the death of characters, intense violence, off-page loss of a child, and an abusive relationship, as well as themes of grief and loss. It also includes depictions of emotional, physical, and/or sexual abuse and may be disturbing to some readers.

To those on their healing journey. I see you.

Fyrala
Shadow Court
Court of Bloom
Silver Springs
Duse Court
Court of Flame
Dawn Court
Troll Village
Amber Fields
Swamp
Court of Thaw
Witch's Hut
Nether Court
Court of Frost

Prologue

"HE KILLED HER," I SCREAM as loud as my aching lungs would allow. "He killed her!"

I gasp desperately for air, a loud sob escaping my tight throat. My mouth fills with a salty mixture of tears and mucus that runs down to my chin like acid, searing through me and cutting off the sounds I am desperately trying to make.

I can't tell the difference anymore or won't. I don't know. I am at a loss. My mind has gone completely blank, and the few words that manage to stumble out of my lips feel like hammers pounding against my temples. I want to say something, anything, but I can't seem to find the right words. Words that are strong enough. The chill of despair creeps up my spine, gnawing at my heart until I think it might burst. I pant for breath, but all I can feel is the icy pain that threatens to tear me apart from the inside out.

The hands gripping my arms tighten and pull me away. My legs strain, the soles of my shoes leaving blackened lines on the pavement in their wake. The ashes of my happiness and love leaving a trail for anyone to follow.

"Her grief is making her delusional, I'm afraid. It's not her fault, really. Please don't blame her," he says; those soft vowels and dulcet tones had once lulled me into bliss and now serve as blades in my ears, piercing down deep inside where no one else can reach. Endless flames in the darkness that has devoured me.

"She needs your help, desperately. I should have called sooner, reported her sooner, before it came to this," he adds, placing his hand, the hand I know to be stained with blood, with her blood, on his forehead, hiding those eyes—those treacherous eyes of ice and cold.

"I swear to you on her grave, on her eternal soul, that he killed her. I saw it myself. Please believe me! I know he did it. Please, you have to believe me," I beg of the men behind me, holding me. I don't even know what they look like; their masses shimmer behind my eyes in blotches of peach and black, or maybe it was blue.

"My darling, you weren't even here for the accident," he coos at me. "Her grief makes her see things; I don't understand it myself. The psychiatrist I hired, Dr. Allen, calls them bereavement hallucinations or something of the like," he says to them as I pull from their grip just long enough to spit in his face. The spittle drips down his cheek and he doesn't even flinch, simply swipes it away with one hand as he continues to talk to the officers holding me, dragging me away.

My chest screams and burns with an intensity I have never felt before—I can feel the flames of my anger licking at my entire being. It even seems to loosen their grip, their hands burning on my skin, even if only for a moment. The ice enters my left bicep, right in the muscle there, and an overwhelming chill races down my arm, into my chest, my mouth, and my head. All that is left is smoldering ash and darkness.

Chapter One

"Wearing Sorrow Like a Cloak"

I'VE GOTTEN PRETTY GOOD AT filtering her words from my hearing lately. Her voice, so irritatingly familiar it's like my brain automatically detects it and puts up a shield against it. I do like the view from Dr. Allen's new office, though. There are far more windows overlooking the city and the gardens to get lost in as she goes on and on about my 'condition.'

I almost start to believe her; the things she says about me, about my mind. That is my mistake. Even when she brings up when I almost died at that hospital, when the nurse gave me the wrong medicine. I still wonder how that orderly figured out that I not only was given the wrong medication but in a dose that would have quickly brought an elephant to its knees.

I never did see him or the nurse again, not that I'd seen them before either. They all assumed I was catatonic because I stared out the window and barely spoke. I knew, and I heard everything. They slip up when they think you're not listening, and that's exactly what Dr. Allen did.

She almost had me, almost succeeded with her subtle picking at my mind, but the moment she mentioned the word 'kind' and his name together in the same sentence, it all stopped. My brain puts up its shield, and her words hold very little power anymore. He's paying for all of this 'treatment,' and therefore it means nothing. She's probably sleeping with him.

Some of her words filter through as I watch the birds flit about outside. This office faces the east and a little garden with an antique, white metal bench like those you see in period films where the woman in her Victorian gown sits primly for her afternoon tea. The bright green blades and stems of the spring bulbs popping up against the still brown vegetation only add to the scene. Even with the distraction and imagery, words like 'delusional' and 'hallucinations' filter through.

"Elora, for this to work, you actually have to listen and contribute to the session. I can't sign off on your progress if you don't."

"I can't help what I know I saw, Dr. Allen. Nothing you say will convince me otherwise. I've said that, and yet you keep trying." I keep my gaze fixed on the garden, barely glancing at her with my answer. The little birds hop along the edge of the bench. You'd think that would hurt their little feet.

"You could pretend, I suppose, instead of wasting both of our time." This does draw my attention just in time to see her lips curl downwards like a wilting flower as she speaks, her voice rising in exasperation. Her eyes flash with resentment, and her fists are clenched at the sides of her thighs, pressing into the cushioned arms of her chair.

"That sounds like some excellent medical advice, Doctor," I say, the usual bland tone behind my words. It's hard to put emotion into your words when you feel nothing. I embraced the numbness that night—my emotions don't help me. Nothing helps me. I simply await my inevitable demise. I know it's coming, and I know he's bringing it—he promised.

"I would love to fill these slots with a client who wants to be here and actually accepts my words with the strength of education and expertise that lie behind them. Your continued insistence on these delusions that your husband—"

"Ex-husband, please do keep up."

"Your ex-husband is trying to kill you…"

"He is, and he killed her too. We've been over this," I say, fully yanking my gaze from the safety of the garden, the birds flitting away along with my sanity. The nauseating feeling in my stomach that comes with looking her straight in the face is worth it to make my point.

"Elora, for pity's sake, you weren't even there when she died." She thrusts her hands in the air, her papers fluttering to the floor as she raises her voice. "There is no feasible way, no physical way, for you to have seen what you claim you saw." Her yellow legal pad then tumbles from her knees and lands on the threadbare carpet with a soft thud.

There's a perceptible twitch at one corner of my lips. Although my face remains impassive, my shoulders begin to relax, and my head tilts a bit to the side. I watch for any other sign that it's working.

As she furrows her brow in obvious frustration, the woman's makeup cracks into a spiderweb of gray lines about her eyes, mouth, and forehead. Her hair, which was once a brilliant red, is now highlighted with a rainbow of gray and silver streaks at the roots. Someone needs to go to the salon. Her lips pull thin and tight as she notices that I noticed. Nostrils flaring, her breath comes faster and faster with each word.

There is a perceptible twitch on my part. "Let's agree to disagree, shall we?" I ask.

"You will never have any peace or contentment until you let go of these fantasies. I could brand you as a danger to yourself and others. Do you realize that?"

I shrug my shoulders at that declaration and turn again to the garden, saying quietly, "You do what you have to do."

A rather fitting moment for the little alarm on her desk to beep, signaling the end of our session. A blissful sound, that alarm, like music to my aching ears.

"Well, that's all for now," she starts.

I couldn't help the '*no duh*' that came to mind in that moment. Maybe I should take that as a sign that I'm really okay, mentally anyway. At least where she's considered.

"Don't forget that last week's group session was rescheduled for this Friday, and you are required to be there," she snaps with extra emphasis on the required bit. I flit my hand in her direction as I race for the door.

As I walk away from yet another session in hell, my head fills with discouraging thoughts, and I can't shake them off. What do I expect? That she would believe me? That she would take me seriously? As much as I want to silence these doubts, they only seem to get louder and more overwhelming.

My stomach clenches in dread as the sudden realization hits me like a ton of bricks. Group sessions might actually be worse than being alone with her in her office.

At least in the office there was just me and her, but in a room filled with a bunch of people all staring at me, judging me...I can't even. All eyes on me, dissecting my every action, every word, trying to figure out what my problem is. I hate them.

I tried avoiding group sessions before—after all, it was easier said than done to just face up to all those eyes on you—but eventually I had no choice but to go through with it. Now as I prepare for another round of humiliation, I feel myself shrink further down into my inner despair.

The thoughts of these group sessions make me feel helpless and exposed; every inch of my skin crawls with nervousness and discomfort. How could I possibly make it through without having a breakdown right there in front of everyone? To her prodding and venomous words, I am helpless.

I TREASURE THE walks to my apartment from the psychiatric center. The quiet solitude and atmosphere are the only pleasant experiences I still have in life. The one freedom. Nothing and no one press on my time, not on this walk.

Today, I decide to take the long route through the wooded park. The weather is finally improving, the sun's rays warm on my face. The temptation to close my eyes and absorb the warmth and energy almost overcomes my need to leave this part of town. It overpowers the chill that centers in my chest whenever I come here. The pain in my right toe after it picks a fight with a metal, green trash bin, however, reminds me to keep my eyes on the path and the steps in front of me. A good way to live your life, I suppose. That's if you didn't already know that your days are numbered.

I know he will find me eventually. I can only hide for so long. I change my route home constantly, never taking the same one twice in a row, never traveling in any sense of a pattern. Whatever path I choose must always be random. Never take the same exact path in a row, and I've managed just that for the last three months. My apartment, I pay for with my parents' trust. Thank God the judge honored that court order and didn't entrust that to him, too.

The only way he has to track me is through my treatment program that he magnanimously pays for. But attacking me there is too obvious. He apparently figured that out in the hospital.

I don't live anymore—I survive. There's a difference. A difference I feel every single day. From everything I've read, one day, maybe it's happened already, but my energy will run out. We're not designed to simply survive. We can't maintain that kind of effort day in and day out.

I can't figure out when it all went so wrong. When did life shift from blissful happiness to chaos and death versus survival? What did I do to deserve this life? What great sin did I commit that placed me in a living purgatory of endless pain with no breaks of happiness? No amount of prayer ever did me any good, so I stopped bothering. I have been abandoned on all fronts, and I accept this.

Today's path is one of the longer ones I take to my tiny apartment. By the time I approach the edge of the wood, the sun quickly drops behind the taller buildings to the west, the soft rays peeking around the brick-and-mortar, setting the roads ablaze.

That eerie feeling pricks at the base of my spine again, as it often does; the small hairs rising up my back and trailing down my arms until the tingling starts to cramp the muscles of my hands. I know this feeling well, and it usually ends with a pair of golden eyes. There's an animal in this wood, a big one, yet another truth that no one else will hear. As I reach the end of the dirt path, right as the sun sets completely, its eyes stare at me amongst the trees, hiding in the shadows. Two angled orbs in the distance, always watching, always waiting, unblinkingly...but for what?

While I love the invigorating walk through the woods, despite those golden eyes, I hate, no that's too strong, I greatly dislike the end. The alley I need to cut through to my street passes by the local pub owned by a despicable man named Jadis who happens to be the current bane of my measly existence. Okay, again, despicable may be a little strong.

Good looking by any standards, and he knows it, his regular propositions would make a prostitute blush and give a nun apoplexy. I think he means well, or I should say I hope he means well. I think....no, I believe it's all talk. Maybe women make him nervous, and being a cad and a rather explicit one is his coping mechanism.

Either way, I never seem to remember to not dally in the woods so that I have a higher chance of finding an empty alleyway instead of what I'm facing now: a dark-haired rake with his flannel sleeves rolled up impeccably muscled arms shifting the crates and boxes from his latest delivery through the side door of his establishment.

I'll readily admit my mouth gets overly wet and my cheeks heat at the sight of him. What? I'm not dead, yet. I can still appreciate some eye candy. I'm only human and a woman who used to have a rather healthy sexual appetite. I don't have time for that now. No, strike that, I don't have the stomach for it. I have to be honest with myself. While my body may react to his physique and that quirky way he smiles, my mind is repulsed. I can't even think about anyone touching me after *him*. I won't open myself to that vulnerability ever again. My body is mine and mine alone, and no one will take that from me ever again.

It's just me, myself, and I, and that's how it's going to stay. I'm a danger to myself and others after all. The others part might actually be true.

"Offer still stands, sweet cheeks," he purrs as I approach the idling truck that vibrates the air through half the alley. His eyes aren't gazing over the reddening ones on my face but those covered by my snug jeans. "The nights are still chill. I'll warm you right up with a single finger," he adds, wiggling his pinky in my face.

"In your dreams, Jadis," I say and nothing else. Just keep walking.

"Oh, always, love—always," he retorts and surprisingly turns back to his work.

I can't help but glance over my shoulder, as surreptitiously as possible, at the unexpected ease to the end of that conversation. He didn't spare a second glance in my direction. Why am I disappointed?

My tiny apartment stands right around the corner. The lively music from *The Bleeding Wolf* often lazes through my ears as I lay awake at night, until final call around 4 am. After that, I am alone with my thoughts, and that's a dangerous place to be. Sometimes I think I might flood my bed. Only in the dark do I let loose the chains over that hollow in my chest, letting the shreds of me twist and pull.

I found this quaint studio apartment for pretty cheap once I was released from the hospital. The weekly stipend from the trust manages to pay for that and my meager groceries easily enough. I can't get a job. That's too dangerous. Too many variables to keep track of, too many ways for him to find me. I knew my career was over long before it came to this. That fact, and the hurt that came with it, faded some time ago.

A small kitchenette along with an equally small chair, table, and a bed surrounded by grey walls. That's all I need here. What more is there to need? It's where I eat and sleep. I have no family left, no friends to entertain. It's me and my thoughts, and they don't take up much space, at least on the outside.

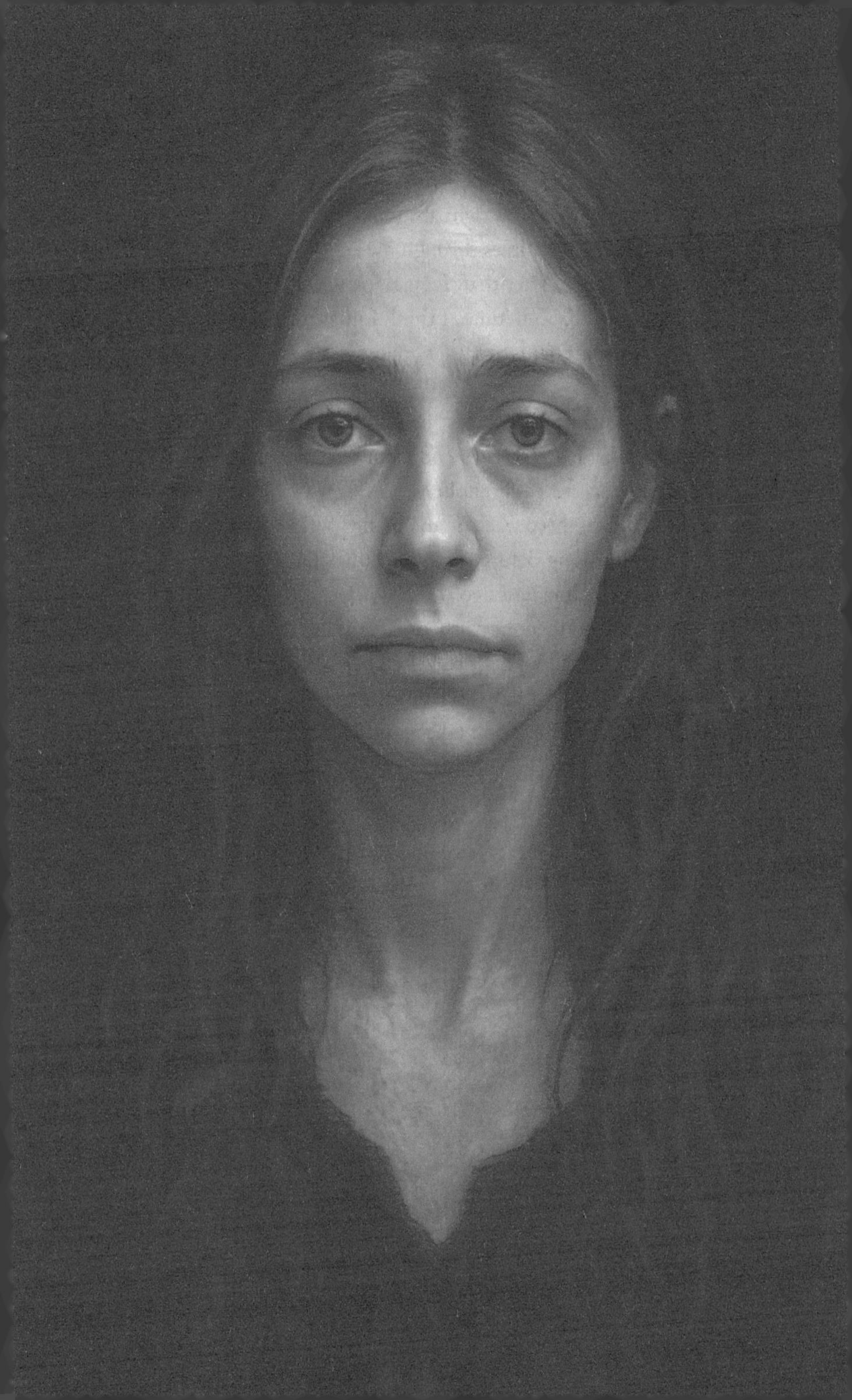

Chapter Two

"A burden shared is a burdened halved...usually"

RIDAY COMES FASTER THAN I'D like. It always does. It seems that I end one session with the vitriol vixen and walk right into the next one. I know there are good counselors and therapists out there, don't get me wrong, she's just not one of them.

The group sessions aren't terrible in the same sense as the private ones, despite my obvious reservations. I don't mind the other members of my group, not personally, minus the judgment. They need to be there, and I feel something for them, not pity, but empathy perhaps. I understand what their grief does to them, having felt that pain myself. I know why their minds broke. I am simply not one of them, despite Dr. Allen's claims to the contrary.

My grief is strong, but instead of building a fantasy in my head, it built a fortress. The only essence to get in or out is the pain and tightness I feel at the center of my chest when my mind wanders back to those times. That, and the hot tears that meander across my temples into my hair as sleep evades me.

This session isn't like the others, though. She has this look in her eyes, a conniving, thrilling look that sends a shiver up my spine. She speaks words addressing everyone in the room but only locks eyes with me. Even when others speak, she keeps her gaze on mine, and it takes all my concentration to keep my chest moving even and slow. I will not give her the satisfaction of knowing she's putting me on edge.

'Elora, don't you have something to share tonight?" She coos this at me with a slight tilt to her head, the corners of her thin, bright red lips curl up slightly as she pauses for my answer.

"No," I reply, my hands folded primly in my lap, the right one lying atop the left lightly but enough to hide my clenched fingers.

"But you had so much to say at our last session earlier this week. Why not share with your friends?" I can feel their eyes on me and imagine the quirked brows popping up on several faces.

"They aren't my friends," I say, looking around our little circle. "No offense," I finish off quickly with a small shrug. Most of them shrug in response, but Mindy, poor Mindy, starts crying, her cheek wets, and a coil of snot dangles from her nose as she sniffles and chokes.

"Look what you did," Dr. Allen says, shaking her head with pursed lips. "You need to apologize to poor Mindy. Don't you think she's been through enough?"

"I'm not a child, stop treating me like one. Mindy is always on the verge of tears; her grief is so present and raw. She's already told all of us not to concern ourselves, and she's not taking anything personally." As I speak my truth, Mindy nods, pressing a tissue to her nose, assuring me that she agrees, but Dr. Allen isn't finished.

"Yes, Mindy has a reason to be how she is. Your grief isn't as raw, is it?"

I didn't dignify her poke with an answer, the glimmer in her eye tells me she's just starting on tonight's entertainment, and apparently, it's my torment. I've never seen her like this. She's been nasty but not this vindictive and cruel. Not only belittling me, but the others. I'm not about to let her take it out on them.

"Elora here likes to claim that her husband is a murderer," she says, and a couple of gasps grace the circle, "the husband that so graciously pays for all her treatments despite her constant efforts to sully his good name. A husband who bent over backward for her all those years and tried so very hard to make it work, despite her obvious mental illness. He loved her anyway; he still does if you ask me." Her eyes flash as she spits out the words, her jaw clenching in anger. Her lips curl back into a sneer, revealing bright, white clenched teeth, and an unfamiliar aura of hostility surrounds her. If I didn't know any better, I'd say she's pissed off that my *ex*-husband might still love me because she's in love with him. Take him honey. I don't want him.

"I didn't ask you," I reply ever so bluntly, "ex-husband, I respectfully remind you, yet again. Ex. We haven't been married for some time. He is a murderer, and I will prove it one day. He pays for my treatments to maintain the control he'd like to have over me. Nothing else. He doesn't love me, never did—he wanted to control me, and I'm not the meek and obedient type, not anymore. So, if love is verbal, emotional, and physical abuse, then you can fucking keep your love, Dr. Allen, I don't want it."

"You will watch your language! This is a safe space, and you will not sully it." Her face burns crimson as her glare bores into what is left of my shattered soul.

My eyebrows fly up my forehead, and I laugh. Not a gleeful laugh, but one of those that comes from deep inside when what you've just heard or seen is so obscene and ludicrous all you can think to do is laugh.

"Safe space?" I sputter through the laughter. "Safe space? What kind of safe space are you running? I...I'm pretty sure. You just broke all kinds of rules just now, in front of witnesses, where you broke our confidence. Isn't confidentiality the golden rule of you people?"

"How dare you," she starts, rising from her seat.

"I'm pretty sure that's my line. I'm sure the judge will love to hear about how you spilled information told to you in confidence to an entire group of people without my written consent."

"Get out," she seethes, fingernails tearing into the arms of her chair as she flops back down. "Get out!"

"Gladly," I return. As I push myself from my seat, it does dawn on me how crazy I probably look this evening to the others, but you know what, I don't care. Normally, I would have been concerned that she would tell the judge I wasn't following the orders placed upon me for treatment, but I don't think she'd open up that can of worms tonight. She can't possibly silence eight other people; *he* can't possibly silence eight other people. Right?

Dr. Allen sits firmly in her chair, relaxing back against the backrest as I walk out of the room, smoothing her hair back into place and asking Mindy what triggered her tears. No one answers her, though; they all watch me go, many of them fighting the smiles that dare to crack their faces.

LIKE MOST PEOPLE, I don't like walking home after dark. It's never a pleasant feeling, and I especially hate it after attending group sessions. These sessions usually start at 7pm and end at 8pm, making it almost pitch black outside by the time I leave. Maybe that's the real reason I hate these group sessions so much. They are always at night, to accommodate work schedules.

As I trudge up the street, I can feel my heart racing and my steps quickening. My hands are shoved deep into the pockets of my long coat as I walk faster and faster. I feel like everyone and everything around me is watching, waiting, and I am the only one moving. The darkness seems to swallow me up and make it feel like I am walking through a tunnel.

I try to keep my head down and my eyes focused on the path in front of me, but every noise makes me jump. I try to blame it on my mood. The click of a door or a whisper of wind make me startle, and I can't seem to shake this feeling of being watched. I feel like I'm walking through a thick fog, and I have to keep pushing through until I reach the sanctuary of my apartment.

I try to write off the prickling sensation at the base of my spine. I try to convince myself it's the emotions continuing to swirl inside after the debacle of a therapy session, but it's more than that. The deep-seated feeling that I'm being watched, combined with a looming sense of doom, sends my imagination on a flight of fancy.

I always take one of the faster routes back after these night sessions, no delays in the woods. I don't want to see those eyes after dark. It's bad enough this path takes me right by the exit where those eyes always appear.

My rapid footsteps pound the pavement as I walk briskly past the trail, and every step reverberates off the trees like a deafening gunshot. I quickly look across the street at the windows of the storefront, desperate to see if anyone has followed me. The rubber soles of my shoes are silent, yet somehow my pounding steps still echo in the night air.

I glance again in the glass of the window to try and catch a glimpse of whoever follows me, but my stalker isn't close enough to be seen. I tell myself that it's all in my head, or just someone passing by on the street. But try as I might, I cannot dispel the feeling that he's managed to find me.

My steps quicken. I have no control over my feet as the panic sets in. If I can get to the alley, he's always there when I don't want him there, maybe he will be there when I need him to be.

My own footsteps sound like thunder on the sidewalk, reverberating with urgency as I run. Panic swells in me, and a chill runs down my spine as I notice figures moving quickly from window to window, one keeping pace with my own reflection. I can feel their presence looming closer, louder, and larger than me with every step they take. It's only a matter of time before they catch up, ready to swallow me whole.

The mouth of the alley comes into view as I hear the whispers of their pants rustling together, growing louder with each step I take. They come so close. My breaths are shallow and fast. The fear paralyzes me until I get a sudden surge of energy, propelling me into a fast sprint.

As I cross the threshold into the dark, narrow strip. I find the button on my watch and press it rapidly three times, the alarm audible to anyone nearby as it warns it's about to call emergency services.

The light flickers above the side entrance to the pub, but no one stands in the dim yellow beam. The light spreads into a bright circle on the dirt-strewn pavement and the empty crates that have been haphazardly tossed out into the alley.

"Emergency services, what's your emergency?"

"I'm in the alley next to the Bleeding Wolf Pub on Mason Street. Someone is following me, please hurry," I spill out as quickly as possible as I reach the golden beam like a safety net.

The hard palm on my shoulder spins me around with ease, and I receive a solid punch to the gut.

A WARM, TRICKLE feeling spreads down the side of my stomach, and my shirt sticks to the skin where he punched me. These are the only feelings to precede the cold sweat that breaks out over my skin.

I had long enough to see that it wasn't who I expected facing me. That's all I registered, that it wasn't my ex, before the cold, burning pain starts and my right hand moves to grip my side. The blood on my hand looks unnaturally orange in the pale yellow light as I pull it away from my stomach.

I hadn't noticed he pulled my other hand up until I heard the frantic voice from my watch saying, "Hello? Miss? Can you hear..." before ending abruptly as he shuts down the call.

She tries to call back. That's nice of her, even if I can't answer, the burning cold flame holding all of my attention. He pulls me further out of the light and into the darkness where he resides. Tobacco, I think I smell pipe tobacco. I can feel my knees buckling beneath me, giving way to the cold, hard ground below.

A bright light burns my eyes, swaying this way and that until it moves beyond where I lay, traveling further into the darkness before it turns around and back to me. It flashes down on my side, the pale yellow t-shirt now bright red under my coat, right where I thought I'd been punched, the upper part of my blue jeans now a deep brown.

"Hey, what's your name?" he asks, his flashlight jerking as he shifts position over me. He sets it down on my opposite side, the light reflecting at odd angles off the badge on his chest.

"Elora." My voice comes out hoarse and shaking, the force of every syllable struggling to escape my tight throat.

"Elora, pretty name." He speaks, and I hear the distinct sound of a metallic slide snapping after a round is chambered.

My scream is choked off abruptly as he clamps down on my mouth with a vice-like grip, his fingernails digging deep into the flesh of my cheeks. His right knee bears down heavily on the wound in my side, while his left hand holds an agonizingly cold pistol hard against my chest. The sheer force of his presence and the intensity of his gaze tell me all I need to know before he utters a single word.

The hard metal digs into the soft flesh at the edge of my left breast as he leans down and whispers so quietly, intimately into my ear, "Your husband sends his regards."

I slam my eyes shut, my shoulders tensing up into my ears, waiting for the noise. I didn't think I'd feel anything, but it never came. A sudden lightness comes over me as all the weight leaves my body and a mass of fur flies over me, following his flying person.

I hear growling, fierce snaps, and a muffled cry. Then...nothing but a pair of golden eyes in the shadows. The deafening silence lasts only a moment before sirens break it, the darkness peppered with blinding blue and red lights like unending fireworks.

The metal door slams open against the brick wall as the officers exit their vehicles nearby, just outside the alley. Jadis looks at them first before glancing in my direction, first at my face and then at the growing stain on my shirt. How can he see me in the darkness? His hands are on me, pressing into my wound as I hear a muffled, "By the Gods..." and my vision tunnels, leaving me with emerald eyes and then nothing.

Chapter Three

"Mad as a hatter"

THE STEADY BEEPING THAT FILLS my ears grows more irritating by the minute. I pry my sticky eyes apart and squint against the fluorescent light that burns through my foggy vision. My tongue feels thick and cottony. I don't know what I expected to see when I open them, but my heart weighs heavier in my chest as I survey the empty, incredibly sanitary room I now find myself in.

The sound of a throat clearing comes from the doorway, followed by a deep voice. "Well, look who's decided to join us," he says with that usual hint of amusement that comes with that overused phrase. The man it belongs to leans against the doorframe, his arms crossed over his chest, and a smirk playing on his full lips.

I shift in the stiff bed from one side to the other, trying to move, to sit up, but the searing pain quickly flattens me on my back once more.

"Nah, don't try to move yet. You got yourself a decent stab wound, missed all the really important stuff, but painful nonetheless," he says as he walks over to my bedside. He's wearing a pair of blue scrubs that are obviously two sizes too small, making the material strain against his muscular chest and arms. The cuffs of the pants stop just above his shoes.

Lifting the gown at my side, he says, "Just gonna take a peek." His face contorts. I don't know why I'm focusing on his face as he's looking at my practically naked body. I need coffee...something. He drags his lips in a downward grimace before adding, "That looks like it hurts a bit."

"Your bedside manner is impeccable," I drawl out, closing my eyes at the ceiling. "I'm really impressed with your medical knowledge. How long do I have to stay here?" I peer out from under my eyelashes.

He raises his eyebrows, one of which is sliced by a thin scar, and leans back in surprise at my sudden request. His face returns to a mask of more controlled emotion, but I can see his jaw tightening as he answers. "You want to leave? I can make that happen."

"Yes. I want to leave. What do you think that question meant? I'd rather not have to stay here too long, *Doc?*" I wanted to continue and tell him exactly what I thought of his disguise but am interrupted.

"Who the hell are you?" A tall man asks as he strides into the room and grabs the clipboard at the end of the bed.

"A friend," my guest answers without hesitation but avoids eye contact with me and shifts his weight ever so slightly. He flashes a faint, awkward smile as if to silently ask me to go with it, and he'll explain later. That's what I'm going with anyway.

"Hmm, well I'm guessing you're in pain," the doctor in the white coat says while keeping his gaze on the papers in front of him, flipping back and forth from one page to the next.

"Little bit, yeah," I answer, my voice dripping with sarcasm.

If he noticed, he didn't let on. "There's only so many options I have to help relieve that," he says, looking down his nose at me. He narrows his eyes and adjusts the clipboard.

"I'm not an addict," I deny.

"Your medical history says otherwise," he retorts, tapping a pen against the paper.

My heart stutters in my chest as I search for the words to fight his claim. 'Sometimes people lie to get what they want," I finally stammer out.

"Exactly."

Well, that didn't work.

"I can give you an anti-inflammatory for the pain. Any other complaints?"

"No. When can I leave?" I ask him.

"There's an officer outside who wants to talk to you, but otherwise there's not much else I can do for you. Follow up with your PCP over the next couple days," and with that he walked out. I really find it hard to believe that this counts as standard hospital care. Either I'm paranoid, or someone wants me under less security faster than normal.

"Friendly fellow, that one," my other visitor says out of the side of his mouth. I'd almost forgotten he was there...almost.

"Explain."

"Well, he was pretty short with you and didn't seem to care at all," he answers, one corner of his mouth curling, his blue eyes bright as a lock of wavy brown hair falls down over his forehead.

"You know exactly what I mean," I hiss back.

"Not here," he replies, and a flash of gold glimmers over the cerulean blue of his eyes. My heart stops. "Come on, let's get you dressed and out before that cop waltzes in here and ruins everything."

I can't move. My body refuses to listen because my mind is whirring a mile a minute as I stare into his now familiar eyes. His hands, rough from maybe years of manual labor, large calluses lining below his fingers, grip my arms tightly. Panic rises within me. I push him away and shout, "You, you're, no...no. Stop touching me!"

"I don't mean to alarm you, but we need to move. You know as well as I do that you're not safe from him here. He knows exactly where you are and probably plans on finishing the job that the officer started last night." He surrounds the word 'officer' with that universal quotation gesture.

"The 'officer,'" I mimic him, "didn't accomplish anything. He was going to shoot me. He's not the one who stabbed me...I don't think—wait. Why should I trust you?" My brain finally kicks in telling me to stop arguing with this crazy bastard.

"Simple. I could have killed you while I waited for you to wake up. The nurses check in on regular intervals, one every forty-seven minutes like clockwork. It's pretty impressive, actually. I had the opportunity, but you're still here and breathing."

"You could be waiting until you get me out of the hospital, where there are less eyes," I counter. I managed to roll over to the other side and then shift into an uncomfortable seated position. A bag sits in the chair to my right, and he sees my gaze and nods. "That would be pointless. I've been seen with you. First suspect." He counters back. He grabs the bag and tosses it into my lap. "I brought you clothes. I'll turn my back and watch the door. You get dressed. Fast. I have a distraction coming soon and we'll miss our window if you fight me more on this."

The more he speaks, the more a slight, smooth accent seeps into his words. He's right, though; I'm vulnerable here. That's why I want to leave in the first place. If the officer wasn't a real officer last night as he seemed, then what's to say that the one standing outside wishing to speak to me isn't the same? One empty needle and I could be gone easy as pie, no one the wiser. No matter what conclusion I come to, I need to get dressed and get out, with or without this guy in his obviously stolen scrubs.

I am surprised to find that he never turns his head, or tries to peak in any fashion, as I change. I find myself shocked that the clothes he brought fit exceptionally well even though they are brand new and not from my dresser. What surprises me the most is the voice that bellows in the hallway that apparently serves as the distraction.

Jadis stands a head higher than all the staff and the plainclothes officer that steps away from my door in the commotion. "I want to see her, and someone is going to show me where she is. She was gutted outside my pub, and I have the right to make sure she's okay."

It works like a charm, to my shock. The plainclothes officer runs to the aid of the nurses and staff standing in his way, one hand on his sidearm and the other on Jadis' large pectoral.

My 'friend' and I peek out into the hallway that apparently is now clear, and he pulls my arm in the opposite direction as I catch a wink from Jadis. He starts to bellow once more, "Elora, my love, where are you?"

"Don't you think he's going a little overboard?" I ask my companion as he pulls me along the hallway.

"Jadis never does anything half-heartedly," he answers, not even slightly breathy as we dart around one corner and the next, blasting through the door to the stairwell.

My breathing, on the other hand, is labored and my legs feel like jelly after starting down what will be six flights of stairs. Yet, all the while he keeps an effortless pace beside me. "Stairs? Really?!" I stammer out the words the best I can between heavy breaths. He looks at me with amusement in his eyes. Amusement! He's not even slightly winded from our sprint. "And I know I got stabbed and all, but how are you not even a little out of breath?"

"I'm not a weak human," he shrugs, shifting over against the wall.

"Excuse me?"

"I'm not human, you're inherently weak and fragile. We don't have time for you to take a breather here. You're going to have to push through this the best you can."

"Wait...what? No," I protest, but he grabs my arm in a vice-like grip and pulls me down the stairs. Now, I finally wonder why my brain decided to trust him.

I can't protest, that requires too much breath, but I plan on giving him a real piece of my mind as soon as we reach the bottom. I didn't have to wait that long. He does stop on the landing between the second and third floors as my feet start to fumble beneath me and coughing racks my body, forcing a cry of pain from my throat.

"Yes, I know, weak human...oh dear God, listen to me," I cry. "I have actually lost my ever-loving mind. Maybe they were right this whole time. Maybe I'm broken because I sure as hell am hallucinating that you have the same eyes that have been staring at me for weeks from the woods and in that alley last night. But they belong to an animal, a wolf maybe, and you? You're a man." The words come flying out of my mouth between heavy breaths as fast as I think them. No brain to mouth filter today.

"I prefer male, as man references the male form of a human," he says with a quick shrug of his shoulders.

"Yup, I'm certifiable as my hallucination is arguing with me over proper pronouns in a hospital stairwell. If it didn't hurt so damn much, I'd wonder if the stab wound was real. Or maybe they're that powerful? Maybe this is all in my head and I can manifest pain, and that's why they seem so real," I say to myself, grabbing at the sides of my head as I slide my back down the nearest wall.

"As much as I 'm sure you're having a moment of panic right now, we don't have time for this meltdown. We need to keep moving. I have to get you to safety or it's my arse on the line. You need our protection."

"Funny that I suddenly need your protection now. Protection from what, pray tell?" I ask from the floor, glaring up at the *male*.

"More of a who."

"What?"

"Protection from whom? I thought you'd figured this out, and that's why he put you in the asylum?"

"Carter?"

"Nope, Cartwell, but one and the same, yes."

"So, you're telling me, that after all these years of suffering at the hands of my ex-husband, *Carter*, you've suddenly arrived to protect me? How can I possibly believe that after everything he's done?"

"Certain things were set in motion, recently, that have forced our hands," he says reluctantly shifting from one foot to the other, inching closer as he does.

"Like a stabbing you mean?" I growl out the words.

"Perhaps," he answers, grabbing for my closest hand.

"This...no, it's not happening. Can't happen. No. It's all in my head." I wrench my hand from his grip as fast as possible and launch to my feet. I push through the pain and race down the stairs, stumbling past him. I'm sure I hear a growl tear from his throat, but I ignore it all. If it's all in my head, then he can't do anything to me.

At the next landing he grabs for my arm, and I push against him with all I have left, knocking him backward, his skull bouncing off the edge of the last cement stair.

I don't stop to see how long he lay there. I race for that metal door with the little rectangle of reinforced glass that calls to me at the bottom. My hand graces the cold, hard metal bar that stands between me and my freedom and collide with rock, hard flesh with folded arms.

"Ms. Morwen, I'd really like to have a word with you about the events of last night. I was going to chat in your room, but if you're in this much of a hurry to leave, then perhaps we can do this down at the station?" The plainclothes officer states with practiced formality. "Otherwise, I'd be happy to escort you back up to your room."

I glance behind me quickly, a flash of motion and blue scrubs blur past the corner of that rectangular window into the hidden shadows of the base of the stairs and I say, "Sure, Officer, let's go to the station."

Chapter Four

"The proof is in the pudding"

NTERROGATION ROOMS ARE NOT THE most comfortable of places, but I don't think they're as intimidating as the officers like to think they are. Sure, they're isolated, but I don't mind alone, quiet, and dark. Detective Peters seems nice enough. He never once asked a question on the way here, helped me, gently and professionally, in and out of the passenger seat of his car, not the back, and even brought me a coffee and an ibuprofen when we arrived.

My thoughts did stray to the possibility that he's trying to lull me into a false sense of security, but my gut fights that idea. Maybe I'm hallucinating again, I think to myself as I cradle my aching head in my hands.

"Who were those men at the hospital?"

"Sorry?" I say, looking up fast enough that my head spins a little.

"The men at the hospital that helped you leave without being discharged, who are they?" He asks me again as he takes the seat across the table.

"Oh, the tall one, the one that bellowed and called me his love? He's the owner of the pub next door to my apartment," I say, taking a sip from the now cold coffee cup, needing to do something with my hands.

"Jadis, yes, the Bleeding Wolf, correct?" he responds, flipping to a page in the little spiral notebook he pulls from his pocket.

I smile behind my little cup at the old-fashioned nature of his note taking and decide, in that moment, that I like this man. "Yes, the Bleeding Wolf," I say, my smile falling as I realize the connection between the pub and my most recent 'non-human' hallucination.

"And the other, the one that snuck you out of your room?"

"Him? Him, I don't know. He never told me his name. I've never seen him before today," I lie. I might like the man in front of me, but I'm not going to reveal my psycho all at once.

"You don't know him or his name but left your hospital bed against medical advice with him anyway?" he asks, one dark eyebrow raised.

"I know, stupid. I was desperate and in pain. The doctor said there was nothing more they could do, so...It seemed like a good idea at the time and very quickly developed into a bad thing." It never dawned on me that he actually saw both Jadis and the other mystery man, until this moment. Either I wasn't hallucinating, or the man sitting across from me was also something my mind made up. Which would explain why they were all so good looking...I must be hallucinating, there is no way on God's green earth that that man wasn't human and actually some animal, human thing, whether God abandoned me or not. It's simply not possible.

"Ok," he says simply, folding the worn notebook closed and setting it on the table.

"Ok? That's it?" I question, finally pulling my face from behind that tiny styrofoam cup. "You know these are really bad for the environment? You could at least use paper, better if you use the bamboo ones. It's a highly renewable resource."

"That's it on that for now. I'll recommend the change to the chief, but I doubt bamboo cups will fit in the budget," he says, smiling softly at me.

I can't tell if he feels pity for me or actually appreciated my care during a stressful situation. "Everyone thinks I'm crazy, so I'm not sure how I can be of any service to you here."

"Are you crazy?"

"I don't think so, but don't most crazy people think they're sane?"

"I don't know a lot of crazy people, so I can't answer that one."

It's my turn to smile. He is good, I'll give him that. My shoulders slowly sink into a relaxed position as my back settles neatly into the soft cushion of the seat beneath me.

"What happened last night, Ms. Morwen? Walk me through the evening, please. Start with what you were doing before the incident."

"By incident, you mean when I got stabbed?" I question.

"Partly, yes."

"I had group therapy last night," I start, and his questions commence already.

"Where?" he asks, flipping open that notebook again, this time leaving it on the table so he can write my answers in impeccable block lettering.

"At the Lotus Rejuvenation Center on Lia Lane. It sounds fancy but it's just another psychiatric center. I think they try to make it sound nicer to entice people to pay to go there."

"That's a good distance to walk after dark, alone," he says, but I just shrug. "Is this a regular meeting, with a regular time that you go in and out?"

"Normally, yes. This one was rescheduled from last week. I don't know why it was canceled last week. I also left early."

"Why? Can you do that? Just leave early," he lifts a quizzical brow as he meets my eyes. I think it's genuine curiosity rather than part of his actual questioning.

"No, technically. I said something she didn't like, and she kicked me out."

He nods quietly to that and keeps jotting down little notes in his book. "What happened after you left?" He's leaving it be. I knew I liked him!

"I walked to my apartment."

"What route did you take home?"

I explained to him how I change my route regularly. How I have several ways to get back to my apartment, but I always pick the fastest ones after dark. My shoulders begin to climb again as I wait for his judgmental words or body language as my paranoia seeps into the conversation.

"That's pretty smart, changing your routine. Makes you less vulnerable to predators," he smiles at me.

I smile back, my muscles releasing again, "Exactly."

I tell him the roads I walked last night and in what direction in remarkable detail. I watch his eyebrows go up and down as he reacts to the information. Asking questions like "Your footsteps echoed?" And "So, someone was walking behind you and matching your pace?"

"Maybe. I thought it could be a coincidence. There are several neighborhoods and complexes that could be accessed off that road."

"And when did you determine it wasn't a coincidence?"

"Who says I did?" I ask, my defensiveness surprising even me.

"Your 911 call. You state very clearly that you're being followed. Not that you thought someone was following you, but that you were being followed."

"I see."

"Why go into the alley?"

"It's faster, despite the creepy darkness. Jadis is sometimes outside in the alley, and I think I was hoping he would be that night, to, you know, scare the guy off."

"And he wasn't last night?" He asks, very interested in Jadis all of the sudden.

"No. Unfortunately. Probably the only time I ever hoped that Jadis was actually there," I mutter to myself. I think it's to myself, anyway.

"Why don't you usually want Jadis there?" he asks proving I didn't actually keep that to myself. He closes his notebook, though, like we're finished.

"He can be kind of crass and vulgar. Annoying mostly, but harmless, I suppose."

"Then what?"

I lay out the rest of the sordid tale, and he nods, the only encouragement I get to continue. I tell him how it felt like I was punched, the pain taking a while to register. My breathing quickens as I fall into the memory of last night. I want to stop talking, know I should stop talking, but I can't. I tell him about the blood on my hand and how he hung up the call. "And then he came."

"Who?"

"The officer. I remember being surprised that someone responded to my call so quickly. I think...he chased the other guy down the alley and then came back to check on me... wait no that's not right..."

"What did he look like?" he asks, opening that damn notebook again.

"I don't know. I remember his flashlight, it was blinding. He set it down at my right side, and it shined off the metal shield on his left breast pocket. That's how I knew he was an officer. He asked my name...but he wasn't an officer, was he?"

"Why would you say that?" He asks now, staring into my watering eyes with an intensity I hadn't noticed in him before.

"Because he was supposed to be helping me?"

"Yes, an officer should be helping you," he encouraged, setting a warm palm on my hand.

"He put his knee into my side, where I'd been stabbed," I say, the panic bubbling into my chest, my throat. "I heard metal slide against metal and a click, that was his gun, wasn't it? He cocked his gun?" I ask, meeting his gaze, the shimmer of my tears clouding the edges of my vision, centering my focus on his kind face and the little scar at the edge of his upper lip. "He pressed it here," I say placing my fingers over the still tender flesh over my heart, "hard."

"May I?" He asks, gesturing with one hand to the location where my fingers sit. I nod, and he ever so softly moves the fabric of my shirt to the side to look at the skin, the bruise dark and well formed with sharp edges outlining a very specific shape. "And what happened next?"

I hesitate, but he waits patiently, his gentle eyes not prying, just waiting. "He leaned down and whispered in my ear, 'your husband sends his regards.' Then he was off me."

"How? Did you push him?"

"No."

He waits again. I pick at the skin next to my thumbnail and gnaw at the inside of my lower lip. I don't want to answer. This is when he decides I'm crazy. This is when the world that I held on to for the last six years shatters in my face.

"Some animal, maybe a dog, pushed him off me into the darkness. I don't know what happened. That's when I heard the sirens and then Jadis came out of the pub. Everything went black."

He nods. Nods. "Thanks for filling in the missing details Ms. Morwen."

"That's it? You just believe my story like that?" I say, snapping my fingers together, the sharp sound practically echoing in the small room.

"Yes. The man that stabbed you, we don't know anything about yet, but the fake officer, with a body, that's much easier. After we ID'd him, we got a hold of his financials and found a rather large, and recent deposit. We traced that back to one of your ex-husband's foreign companies. While the start of your journey should check out easily enough, the events in the alley were recorded on a security camera from the pub. Jadis was very cooperative and gave us the footage without hesitation. The only thing we didn't know is what the man whispered to you. I'm not surprised what it was, though."

"What?" That's all I could muster, my mind disintegrated.

"It was all on camera. He was identified early this morning as a former employee of your ex-husband," he repeats in simpler terms, thinking I'm confused.

"No, I mean, you found money from Carter? Can I see it?"

"The money?" he asks, taken aback.

"No. The footage...from the security camera."

"I'm not sure that's the best idea."

"Please," I beg. I actually beg to see a video of someone trying to kill me.

He leaves the room but comes back a short while later with a thin laptop under one arm and a cup of water in the other hand. "Drink this first. You look a little shocky. I should probably be taking you back to the hospital right now."

As I drink the water, the cool liquid surprisingly soothing as it traces down my dry throat, he taps a few keys on the keyboard and turns the screen to face me. "Do you know where your ex-husband might be?"

I shake my head. I didn't even know he had foreign companies.

"We haven't had any luck bringing him in for questioning. He's not at home or any of his local businesses. We have sister precincts checking his other homes and businesses, but I'm not holding my breath. He seems like a man who's good at hiding."

"You have no idea," I say quietly, finishing the last of the water.

"Press the space bar when you're ready."

It played out just as I remembered, even the snarling I heard in the darkness off-screen.

"I think it was a wolf, by the way. Too big to be an ordinary dog." Detective Peters says, sipping at his own foam cup.

I looked over the top of the screen at him, and my world went black again.

"DR. MORWEN...Dr. Morwen?" The oddly familiar voice repeats in my ears between the thrumming of my pulse. The sensation of a hard surface against my back comes next, replacing that feeling of the soft, smooth vinyl that pressed there a moment ago. Maybe this wasn't an interrogation room after all. I don't think they give perps soft chairs. That was a moment ago, right? Yes, I was answering the officers questions, no detective, I think he's a detective.

Wait, no I was watching a movie—a video...the stabbing! The sudden and ugly fluorescent lighting compared to the darkness behind my lids shocks me out of whatever stupor my mind placed me under this time, and my thoughts whirl around as my prone head comes upright a little too fast.

"Whoa there, slow down," he says, placing a warm, tender hand on my shoulder stopping me from lifting myself further. "You had a bit of a fall from the chair there. I was about to call an ambulance if you hadn't come to," he says to me, waving his phone a little in his other hand. "I didn't think that video was a good idea. It was too soon...should have listened to my gut."

"Why didn't you? Listen to your gut, I mean," I say, resting my cold palm against my hot forehead, trying to get the spinning to stop.

"I don't know. I think it was the look in your eyes. Under the obvious terror or maybe it's disbelief, there seemed to be a need. Like you needed to see. You needed to know. I get that."

"You called me Doctor," I say, finally meeting his eyes again, focusing on slow, deep breaths while we talk.

"That's your title, right? You earned your doctorate a while back." He says this so matter-of-factly I don't know how to respond as he shifts his weight back onto his heels to guide me to my feet. I teeter a little from one leg to the other, bumping my shoulder into him as his grip tightens on my arm. "Still not sure I shouldn't call an ambulance."

"I'm fine, really. I just want to go to my apartment and lay down."

"I'll drive you home, but promise me you'll call an ambulance if you start to feel worse." He pulls car keys from his pocket and holds the door open for me. His eyes are wide and pleading as he waits for my response.

He smiles and adjusts his glasses, letting the silence hang in the air as a polite reminder, maybe, that he asked me a question. "If I may, why don't you call it home? I mean, instead of the more awkward 'my apartment'."

"Because that's what it is, my apartment. It's not really a home."

He doesn't respond with anything other than a lift to his left brow, wrinkling his forehead.

HE DID AS promised, drives me to my apartment, and even escorts me upstairs and over to my bed. I think he's left until a glass of water appears on the side table with a "Promise you'll get help."

"I promise," I mutter half-heartedly. I stay in bed for what feels like an eternity until I hear the door latch shut with a hollow thud. With great reluctance, I slowly lift my aching head off the pillow and stumble to the door. I double check all three locks and slide each of the bolts into place. My heart is heavy as I check that each of the windows are still firmly locked.

The medicine cabinet hides behind the mirror over my bathroom sink. I look like shit. No wonder he worried about me needing an ambulance. My long, honey-brown hair doesn't shine at all under the lights like normal and flies about my head like I had a war with static and lost. The purple marks under my eyes take away any golden luster in the dark irises. I look like I've been through hell, which I suppose is appropriate considering, but I wonder if I looked this bad before the stabbing.

Who am I trying to impress? No one.

The cabinet holds two things: toothpaste and a very large bottle of ibuprofen. My liver most definitely did not appreciate the chronic mystery pain I feel, especially on the bad days, which today definitely tops the list of bad days.

I pop two more pills and sit down at the small table in the kitchenette. I never eat here; the table ends up littered with my pencils and notebooks. Drawing calms my frantic thoughts; it's a hobby I returned to after—well, after everything. For whatever reason, putting pencil to the stark white paper and creating something brings me a sense of calm that nothing else can accomplish. Not even all the chemicals they pumped into my system at the hospital. All they did was calm the physical manifestations of my mind, not my mind itself.

I often have no idea what result will come when I start. I just start and see what happens, and today is no different. The pencil rests lightly in my hand, the grip of my fingers over the hardwood light and peaceful, contradictory to the racing hardness of my mind.

Time ceases to exist. Thought ceases to exist. Feelings cease to exist. All that remains is pencil and paper. I embrace the nothingness, the dark emptiness that flows through me. I don't fear the darkness at all. I like it—I crave it often. Perhaps more often than I should.

The image that reveals itself an hour later doesn't surprise me, not if I'm being honest. The golden-eyed wolf stares me down from the upper right corner of the page. I know those eyes glowing with ethereal sunshine despite the shades of grey that represent them now. It's the man at the center of the page that I find—disturbing. Not his image itself, but what it represents. He said he isn't human. Maybe it's simply the stress of the attack that made me see those golden eyes flash over his deep azure gaze. I want to, no, I need to know who he is. I need to settle this once and for all. I need to prove, if only to myself, that I'm not crazy. How do I find him?

I'm not sure how long I stare at the page, waiting for some sense of an idea of how to proceed with this new sense of purpose I found. Like staring at his face there, will make him talk, and tell me how to find him, or perhaps summon him to my door.

"How do I find you?" I mutter to myself and slump back in the hard chair, flinching immediately at the sharp pain that launches through my side and down my left leg. Tapping my right index finger on that cursed drawing, I force myself to breathe through the pain until my eyes catch the mark that flashes as my finger moves up and down.

I hadn't paid that much attention, at least I didn't think I did, but on his left arm stands a familiar tattoo. Had that recently been there or was it wishful thinking on my part. I knew that symbol; not in the sense that I knew what it meant, but I'd seen it before, many times. I'd seen it in the same location on the well-muscled, tanned skin of my neighborhood rake.

Chapter Five

"In the blink of an eye"

I did manage to remember to run my brush through my hair before leaving, that's as far as I got with any attempts to look the least bit presentable. Looking appealing is a hopeless cause anyway.

It's early. That means the pub should be quiet, and I'll have a better chance of getting my information without too many prying ears. The fewer people hearing my insane theories, the better.

I pat my back pocket, feeling for the faint outline of that folded up sketch paper I stuffed in there on my way out the door. That's as far as I got. The door to The Bleeding Wolf reminds me of the quintessential Irish pub you see on postcards; dark green painted wood surrounding a large stained-glass window with the name of the establishment. It's the golden-eyed wolf staring at me from under those letters that stops me in my tracks, hand raised to grab the polished brass handle.

I smell the pipe tobacco on his jacket before I see the gentleman that slips past me as I gawk. He grips that handle without hesitation, the door opening and ringing a tiny brass bell overhead. There it is, open and surprisingly inviting. He clears his throat with a raised, greying eyebrow as my mouth gapes almost like the door.

"Oh, thanks," I say and step over the threshold.

The interior proves oddly relaxing, the warm, low hanging lights illuminating the tables and the few people that were already seated for the evening. The early diners or drinkers, depending on who you look at, are the older crowd, settled into the soft leather benches and stools talking quietly with each other. The quiet murmur of voices is sporadically interrupted with a guffaw of laughter that fades back into the subtle conversation. I momentarily wonder why I haven't come in here before, that is until his voice rings out over the din.

"Why I'll be! This is a sight I never thought I'd see. Finally come to accept my offer, sweet cheeks?" He hollers from behind the bar in his rolled sleeve glory, that tattoo stark against his tanned skin in the dim lighting. The room hushes, I stiffen, and all eyes turn to mine, standing in the doorway.

I hide my face behind my raised shoulders as I swiftly move over to the bar, "Would you quiet down, they're all staring and, no I'm not here to accept anything!"

"They'd be staring whether I hollered or not. You look like shit. Didn't you get any sleep? You should be in bed. You were stabbed," he whispers over the bar, inches from my face. I thought he'd smell of beer and whiskey but it's pine and leather that waft across the space between us and...pure man. God help me and my lonely ovaries.

I pull the paper from my back pocket and unfold it so forcefully that a tear starts along one of the creases. Slamming it on the counter, I spin it around with stiff fingers and slide it closer to him. "Who is this, Jadis?" I demand, poking at the mystery man's two-dimensional chest.

"No pleasantries, I see. Near-death experience didn't change you much, did it?"

I don't respond. My finger remains on the page, and my eyes never waver from his own bright green orbs.

"What makes you think I know who this is?" He asks, grabbing a rag in one hand and polishing the bar next to us.

"Seriously? You're going to try that one after your declarations at the hospital this morning? You arranged to be the distraction he needed!"

"Pure coincidence, I assure you."

"Do I look stupid?" I snap.

"Is that a trick question?" He retorts, the shit eating grin splits all seriousness from his face.

"I want to speak with him and need you to call him and get him here, now."

"What makes you think I can do that?" he says, a nod to someone over my shoulder. He grabs a clear glass, flips it on end and starts filling it from the tap. "I told you I don't know the gent." He leans in closer and mimics my finger on the chest of my drawing.

"You know what's funny? Combine your orchestrated distraction with the exact same tattoo, on the exact same arm, in the exact same location and even my confused mind finds that hard to believe," I say, pressing a finger into the offending tattoo as I speak. "And don't you dare say coincidence again."

"Fuck," he swears in a hushed tone and throws that rag on the ledge hidden behind the bar top. "What do you want with him?"

"I have questions and I want answers and I'm not going to stop until I get them."

"Now that, that I believe. Come on." He nods his head in the direction of the other end of the bar and starts walking. I follow, two of my steps to every one of his and meet up with him as he exits that alcove and heads for a door labeled private.

He holds the door open, motioning for me to pass him. "Upstairs," he commands.

"Why?"

"Because I plan on ravishing you as I promised," he says, wiggling the dark brows over his meadow green eyes.

"My patience is really running thin..."

"Relax. Stars above, you're wound tighter than an antique clock. This is not a conversation I'm having down here amongst prying ears."

"Amongst?" I ask and he tosses his hands up in the air, dropping them back to his head in a movement that is obviously well practiced, the gentle wave to his dark hair follows the trail of his fingers through it. "Since when do you have an accent?"

"Just get up the bloody stairs, will ye," he follows, turning the gaze of several patrons.

I feel their eyes burrowing into my back like parasites and climb the flight of stairs with more energy than I thought I had left.

The upstairs loft glows with the light of the dying sun; giant windows line the entire west wall. Being on the second level, my eyes never trail up to see all the windows above the pub. The open plan of his kitchen and living area is surprisingly inviting, or maybe I shouldn't be surprised. All the women he must bring up here after hours, or maybe during hours—I'm sure there's someone else to cover the bar.

"Sit, or not, I don't really care. What could you possibly want to know from him?" he asks, flopping on the soft cushions of the couch and mussing his dark waves again.

"That's a conversation between him and me. Now, him? Doesn't he have a name?" Sitting across from Jadis seems too intimate, but the days are starting to catch up with me, my legs wavering a little, my body and vision swaying in response. My eyes scan the room, keeping my movements slow despite the racing beat in my chest and the frantic thoughts flipping through my mind. I spot a support post to lean against instead.

"A conversation that you seem keen on dragging me into. He has a name and it's not my place to tell it to you."

"No. I simply need you to get him to me and then you can leave...then you will leave." My arms cross my chest. I don't know if it's because I feel defensive against his tone or if I'm trying to hide the racing inside me.

He shifts slightly, leaning to one side, stuffing his hand behind him. His phone had been in his back pocket, and he angrily taps at the screen that illuminates his face with unnatural light, the sharp planes there accentuated. His bright, green eyes glowing, the narrow nose, the hollows under his cheekbones shadowed, and the dimple in his chin, one I didn't know was there before, stands out as a crater on the moon even under the hair of his light beard.

"This is going to take some time. You look like shit, like you're about to fall over. Relax a little up here. Take a bath, maybe?" He offers all of his opinions while shooting up from the couch, stuffing the phone back into his pocket, the muffled ping of a response already dinging away.

I don't get to answer, to refuse his generous offer. He leads me straight across the room, grasping my crossed arm as he passes and whirling me around towards what I assume is the bathroom door.

"You have a clawfoot tub?" A considerable time had been spent designing this bathroom. The Italian mosaic tile floor with its shimmering blues, whites, and silvers lit up the antique metal tub with the perfect spotlight effect on its polished chrome feet.

"That's a grand idea. Take a bath while we wait," he says.

"I didn't..." I try to say, but he's all over the place, completely oblivious to anything I'm doing.

"Here, bubbles and everything," he interrupts, placing a glass bottle with some viscous purple liquid on the stool that sits adjacent to the tub. He rips a towel from a nearby shelf, toppling several more to the floor and leaving them there with a shrug. "It's going to take time and I don't need you scaring the customers with your scowls. Relax up here and I'll come get you when he's here," he continues, turning the silver faucets this way and that, feeling the water and adjusting some more. He pauses longer the last time, perhaps making sure the temperature is right, yet he closes his eyes.

My eyes are gritty and swollen from strain, and my back is as stiff as a wall. I haven't truly slept in who knows how long, my body has shut down for self preservation, and now it screams at me with each breath I take to do something about the madness. The weight of everything hangs hard on my shoulders, and now, an invisible cloak of responsibility weighs heavy on my muscles and I can feel that muscle in my one shoulder tightening that always leads to another part of my body going mad, as angry nerves rake up my neck and behind my right ear.

He pours some of that purple stuff into the stream of water and my eyes see stars shimmering like the twinkle of the setting sun on ocean waves. I blink hard trying to clear my vision, but nothing works. Maybe he's right. By the time I give up on clearing my vision, Jadis is gone. All that remains of him is a ghost of warmth on my left shoulder.

"STILL IN THE bath, I see."

Water and bubbles fly everywhere as my jellied limbs flail and my backside slides out from under me, my head slipping under the water.

One moment I'm enjoying the warmth and a sense of relaxation in my body that I don't think I ever felt in my life, much less these last few years, and the next I'm sputtering bubbles at that man who is very quickly becoming the bane of my measly existence. A man who's currently bent over, bracing himself with one hand on the sink while his wild guffaws echo throughout the porcelain room.

My racing heart climbs up my throat, and I choke on water and bubbles. I feel the heat climbing my back and the acid burn climbs my throat, the saliva filling my mouth more rapidly than I can gain any traction in the tub with my feet under the water.

I press my lips firmly together and hope that it's enough to buy me more time to climb from here and race to the toilet across the room, past him. The tell-tale cramp in my stomach says I better hurry.

I make it...barely. Heaving my insides into the equally pristine porcelain bowl, he finally stops laughing as I wretch again and again, the sounds bouncing around my ears, so I don't hear his footsteps.

I jump out of my skin again at the rough touch of the towel over my sensitive shoulders, turning my head between wretches and glaring with every ounce of energy I have left. "Don't scare me like that!" I yell, breathily, as the air strains hard in and out of my aching chest.

"Lesson learned. I swear." His hands proffer in surrender after releasing the towel. In hindsight, placing a towel over my naked body was kind, but that's not the point. "Breathe nice and slow, not too deep either."

"Don't tell me what to do," I snap, but do it anyway, turning my head back to the toilet and laying my cheek on the smooth, cool seat. I roll my eyes at the sudden thought that he puts his ass right here, pretty sure there's a smirk on his face right now. If that can cross my mind, it must be over.

"Well, he's here, as you can probably guess. So, when you're ready, go ahead and get dressed...if you like...and come on downstairs."

Yup, definitely a smirk.

HIS DEFINITION OF a long time is obviously very different from my own. What was the point of crawling into that bath to just relax for a moment, blissful as it was, and then be sent into a panic attack triggered only by my lack of control?

Staring at my reflection shows the short bath did no good in that department, not that I really expected it to. I have no brush for my now wet hair, so up it goes in all its messy glory.

The door to the stairwell stares me down with long, rectangular, dark eyes. This is what I asked for so why am I suddenly scared to descend to the answers I want so badly that I walked into this bar?

What was it that my advisor once told me? Right, 'Stop being so pathetic and take the world by its balls.' While originally stated during a completely different situation, it applies. It's time to stop letting fear control my life, real or imagined! But how do I do that? What's the point of mental and self-growth epiphanies if you don't know what to do with them?

God, I wish I'd gotten a longer bath. The sun is almost to the horizon now, with the color glowing outside. That seems oddly early.

I peer around the large main room. He must have a clock somewhere. The mantel, that's where people keep clocks—and there it is. The analog clock strikes half past six just as our eyes meet.

"That's not possible," I say to myself and the clock that's still staring me down. "six-thirty means I was in that bath for two hours." I place a hand on the mantle, one on either side of the offending clock, like I can intimidate the thing into changing its mind.

The water was still warm when he set me off, wasn't it? Did I fall asleep in the tub? No, not a chance. "What the hell was in those bubbles?"

The door opens to the stairs. If done by my own hand or the door itself, fleeing in terror, I didn't know, but down those stairs I fly.

He's right there sitting at that damn bar smiling and laughing with Jadis like they're best friends. Somewhere, hidden deep inside those smiles, something taps into some energy that propels me to the stool next to him, slapping a hand on his back.

"You have some explaining to do, buddy."

Both their smiles fall from their faces like fog exposed to the sun's warm rays. Jadis gives him a quick nod and slides down the bar to a patron as my target slides from his stool.

"Not here. Let's take a walk."

"I'm not going anywhere with you until you tell me your name," I state, my spine so rigid my hands pull into fists at my side.

"Mik."

"Mik? Seriously? That could be any number of names. I'm gonna need something more than that."

"I'm not giving you my full name. If you want these answers, you're going to have to deal." He turns his body to face me, his breath warm on my forehead, he stands so close.

"He gave me his name a long time ago," I say with a nod toward Jadis down the bar. He turns at that moment and gives me a wink. I return the expression with my best, most venomous scowl.

"*His* full name isn't Jadis."

"What?" My shoulders fall as his one statement takes all the wind out of my sails.

"Are you coming or not?" he asks, not giving me time to answer or even process what he just told me before walking out the door.

I didn't think about it. That's my problem lately, I don't think. The brain-to-mouth filter is broken, and apparently the brain-to -feet filter is broken too, because I follow. I'm such an idiot.

He leads me up the alley. I haven't dared to walk there since the attack, not that it was that long ago, and my blood still stains the ground near the side door. The faint white outline down the alley shines in the darkness where my second attacker apparently fell...and died.

"This was you, wasn't it?" I say as we pass by.

He grabs my hand as I linger there, my head pivoting behind me to watch the chalk lines. "Not here."

"If not here, outside, then where?"

"The woods. There are less ears in the woods."

Great, just great. I'm now wandering into the woods with a man named 'Mik' like some Australian outback tour guide, who insisted to me he isn't human. That sums up the limits of my knowledge. Oh wait, and I convinced myself that his eyes match the animal that has been watching me in those exact woods we're walking toward.

"I also told you I'm not a man. I'm a male."

I'd said that out loud. I've devolved to not knowing when I'm thinking and when I'm speaking. When will all of this end?

The thing is, though, the only part of my verbal diarrhea that he corrected was that I called him a man. Nothing else, not the non-human bit, not the animal bit. So, he's maintaining those statements, or my hallucination is well set in and I'm walking in the woods with someone my mind created...after dark.

Neither of us says anything more until we pass the end of the trails and travel even further into the wooded area. I hesitate at the edge, and he turns, not releasing my hand. "It will be easier to explain if we go deeper, closer to the veil."

"The what?"

"The veil," he repeats and turns around like that's supposed to make any sense to me.

Oh, what the hell. If this doesn't kill me, Carter eventually will...apparently, so, what the hell?

This section of the wood turns eerily quiet. The woods are quiet at night anyway, but this section holds a complete lack of sound. Until the humming begins. It starts deep in my ear and becomes loud enough I feel it in my chest.

"What is that?"

He turns to reach out and tenderly touch my arm, his eyebrows furrowed in an expression of deep worry. "You feel it?" he asks. "Shit, Jadis is right. It's started."

"What's started? What are you talking about, and how the hell does Jadis know?"

"Your powers are waking up. It wasn't supposed to happen until we triggered it, but it's happening anyway," he says, pulling his phone out of his pocket, the bright screen blinding even under the light of the almost full moon. He sends off a text message, not even trying to hide it's to Jadis, before putting the phone back in his pocket.

"What did you say again?"

"Which part?"

"Stop fucking with me, Mik," I say, carefully enunciating each letter of his name.

"Stand here," he orders with a sigh, holding my shoulders with each hand to tell me where here is. He takes a few steps back and in the span of a single blink, a large grey wolf sits before me with those golden, yellow eyes. The yellow shimmers for a moment and, as his fur seems to settle, they fade into a very familiar bright blue.

My body turns away and I start walking back the way we came.

"Hey, wait! Where are you going?" He asks, a human hand grasping my left bicep trying to turn me back the other way.

"The hospital," I say, and pull away.

"Why? Are you not feeling well anymore? What's wrong?" He grabs for my bicep again, first searching my face and then down, moving the edge of my jacket to look at the shirt over my stab wound.

"No, that's fine. I'm going to the psych hospital." My frankness even surprises me.

His face holds genuine concern, the gold glimmers across those eyes again as he searches my face for the answers he wants. I don't have them.

"I've obviously lost my mind, just like everyone told me. It's time I face the music and get help. If there is help for this. I'm very obviously in mental distress."

"No, yer not, I swear it," he says, slipping his hand down to hold mine gently as he speaks in that newly accented voice. His brows pull even tighter together, if that's possible.

"You just said I have 'powers'." I use my free hand to make those air quotes, "and then I saw you turn into a wolf. That's not possible, and the fact that I believe it, or that I want to believe it, is deeply concerning."

"You want to believe it?" Is his only response.

"Who doesn't want to believe in magic in this world? Life is hard and magic gives a sense of hope that we can't find anywhere else. Of course, we want it to be real."

"So, why not let yerself believe?"

"Because." I choke on the words and turn my face away, "because it can't be real. If it were, then...then something could have been done, and it wasn't...or I wasn't worthy...or she wasn't worthy and I can't believe that."

"I'm sorry. I'm sorry that she died. We didn't know...we didn't think even he was capable..."

"What..."

Just wait, we'll get to all of it, I promise. We have to. It's progressing too fast." Mik looks around the trees nearby, finally settling my palm on his chest over his heart. "Ye feel that?"

"Your heartbeat?"

"Yes, would a hallucination have a heartbeat?"

What a bizarre question. The warmth of his skin seeps through the flannel of his shirt, and I press my palm firmer against his chest. "Well...no...probably not. I don't know, maybe."

He rolls his eyes and holds my hand firmly against his chest, hard enough that my fingers dig into the firm muscle there. His vice-like grip is telling me I'm not going to like what he does next. The hand over mine shifts, I watch the fingers change, the nails turning into dark claws, the fingers shortening, growing hair, the warm palm on my skin into the rough, warm pads of a wolf. As the change progresses, the hand moves up and his paw rests on my arm, my hand still on his chest, his soft, furry chest, with the same heartbeat pulsing through my fingertips.

I gently run those fingers through the fur, and he shivers a little, the new, thin black lips stretching into one of those dog smiles showing all the bright, white teeth of a powerful predator.

I drop to my knees, and he follows suit, sitting on his haunches.

I don't notice the change back until he speaks again, "You okay?"

"Yes...no...I don't know. How can I be okay?"

"It's a lot to take in and there's more..." he starts to explain as fiery, hot pain rips through my left shoulder blocking out any further sound.

MY EYES STILL work, the snarl on Mik's face looks like he may have growled like an animal, but my ears ring so loud, I still hear nothing else. He pops to one knee, placing one arm across my back while the other forces its way under my clenched legs and behind my knees, pulling me against his chest.

We move through the trees with an agility I don't think is possible. The dark trunks whiz past so quickly it all turns into the same dark, rough wall. I can hear his racing footsteps over the deadfall on the forest floor as the ringing subsides, but that humming in my chest gets worse.

"Stop, please," I beg, the arrow pointing out of my shoulder moving around with every step he takes. The pain, lightning flames traveling down both my arm and left side, exploding out the fresh hole made by the knife only two days ago.

He slows his pace, eventually setting me down, as gently as possible I assume against a tree large enough to cover my entire person from behind.

"This thing hurts more than that damn knife," I hiss, squeezing my arm into my armpit in a vain attempt to keep my shoulder from moving. I make the mistake of staring down the arrowhead that stands dangerously close to my face.

"Anyone ever tell you that for a lady you have the language of a gutter snipe?" He breaks the shaft off a hands width from the metal head.

I scream, the sounds tearing at my throat. He covers my mouth with his large, calloused hand. "You keep doing that, they'll find us again in no time and before backup arrives," he hisses.

"Then warn me next time instead of insulting my language!"

He squeezes his brow in answer noticing the strange color on the metal arrowhead, mixed with my blood. He sniffs at it and says, "Shite." Mik pulls out his phone and apparently dials a number as it goes to his ear next, holding it in place with a shoulder.

"I'm two minutes out," yells Jadis' voice on the other end.

"I'm pulling this out now, it needs to bleed," Mik says to me, flicking a quick nod with his eyes before pulling me forward with one hand, without disrupting the phone, and yanking the shaft out the back with the other.

I feel the warmth flowing down my back before it begins to darken the clothing up front. "I didn't scream this time," I say through clenched teeth, flicking raised eyebrows at him.

"Aye that, well done." I can hear Jadis yelling at him through the phone's speaker. "Aye, Jadis, faebane on an arrow through her shoulder. I'm taking her across now, there's no time. Aye, usual place." He tosses the phone into the bushes and pulls me up into his arms again.

"What's faebane?" I huff out through the pain and the heavy breathing I think is from bouncing in his arms, but it feels like I've been running alongside him.

"A nuisance for Jadis and I, a fast and deadly poison for you mortals. I have to get you across if there's any hope to stop it."

Poison. Deadly. Carter wins.

"You fight it, do ye hear me? Fight it hard. We're almost there. Someone will be able to help on the other side," he orders me before adding, "I hope," in a barely audible voice.

The humming in my chest becomes unbearable before I can ask 'across what?' Until it just stops. That was it. Was this the end of it all?

Chapter Six

"*Naerin lorynor thalzak*"

When the moon whispers, the shadows listen

AN UNBEARABLE CACOPHONY OF SOUND fills my ears; a hundred voices talking and laughing, the chirps of hundreds of birds, and the scraping of squirrels' claws on branches. The eyes that I can't quite open meet sunlight so bright it stings. The air tastes sweet but dry, as though the moisture has been sucked out by a powerful force.

Mik's voice rises desperately but my ears are filled with a deafening roar. My vision is blurred, overshadowed by multicolored halos that surround everything in sight. I can't comprehend a single word, the buzzing consumes me so that all I can do is watch helplessly as Mik's mouth moves. A wave of nausea threatens to overwhelm me, and I have to turn away for a moment.

My heart races as I march towards Mik, my throat tightens as I think I scream, "What's going on?" But I hear nothing emerge. My neck clenches and I feel my steps falter, yet no words escape me. As my foot hits the ground, I stumble in a mix of confusion and fear.

My legs tremble and buckle until I am crouched on the leaf strewn moss beneath me, my stiff right arm the only thing that breaks my fall. The world spins around me like a carnival ride and my fingers sink into what looks like green, feathery moss but every single strand cuts into my skin like a thousand blades. Yet, I can see no damage done. My body feels heavy and, for the briefest of moments, I know what it is to be crushed under the weight of stone and stillness.

I hurl, barely able to miss my own hands beneath me. The sound of my own retching breaks through the gnarled mess in my ears alongside yelling and some sort of melodious vibrations. The vibrations send waves of stillness through my skin and deeper inside, an almost metallic ringing that taps into a primordial part of me, shaking the contracting muscles of my stomach back into submission.

I focus on that sound, trying to trace where it comes from, moving my head slowly to keep my surroundings from spinning too much. Just over a dead log a few feet in front of me stands a small patch of orange mushrooms, glowing like tiny beacons in the dark forest. The beams of light shake in the same pattern as the metallic tones that still ring in my ears with some more shouting.

The mushrooms are singing...

I feel a sharp burning sensation as my left arm goes numb, quickly followed by an excruciating pain. A force pulls me up with such suddenness that I can't even scream until I land on my feet.

When the world slows its spinning, Jadis' face finally settles into view, his forehead creases sharply as his eyes sweep over me, measuring every detail.

"The mushrooms are singing," I say as he steadies me with firm hands on my shoulders.

"They do that sometimes," he shouts, my hands flying to cover my ears. He moves to grasp my hands in his, the rough callouses of his palms like gritty sandpaper on my sensitive skin.

"Why are you shouting at me?"

"I'm not shouting, Elora."

"Elora?" Another male voice shouts from behind him, angrily. He stands a head taller than Mik, towering over him with a stiff spine. I imagine he'd been looking down his pristinely angled nose at him before my name caused a distraction.

"Why is he shouting?"

"He's not shouting either," Jadis shouts at me, although his face remains soft other than the deep creases that continue to climb his forehead. "You're the only one shouting right now. Focus on my voice," he says, my hands still grasped in his hovering just by my ears.

I move to free them and something catches his attention on my left arm. Shifting his grip to my wrist, he uses one hand to hold me and the other to push up my sleeve. Trailing down the soft skin of my underarm were several black lines where faint purple and blue lines of veins used to be.

Jadis' voice bounces off the surrounding trees, commanding, "Mik! Fetch Margwin now!" He never shifts his gaze from my arm as he speaks. The intensity of his stare makes me feel like I've been pinned down by a hawk eyeing its prey.

"Vyn sylor thael ael naelir thyrilinor ilyrinil," shouts the tall, blond one, taking steps toward Jadis as he speaks. The tightness and manner of his face matches the sounds in my ears. I don't like him.

Jadis doesn't speak, only shifts my arm over gently for him to see the lines. I swear they've trailed farther down in those few moments.

"Brandis, think how close to her heart they must be if they're that far down her arm," Mik calls, his voice begging.

"Ryval," comes the blond's terse response.

"Why are you all yelling?" I ask again and Jadis grips my shoulders pulling my attention to him alone.

"Elora, focus on my voice. Bring your senses in closer."

"I can hear squirrels scratching in the trees and everything is blurry and shiny at the same time. Why are the mushrooms singing? What are those lines on my skin? Where are we? Who shot me? Who's he? What's going on, please tell me what's going on."

"Thalzakir lirinil? Zythal thael'nael thyril thalzakir?" Brandis shouts, his face growing red as he strides even closer. His clenched fists shake at his sides.

"You...you stay right there. Don't come any closer." I attempt to take a step backward for each of his. Jadis keeps his vice grip on my shoulders, keeping my right in front of him.

"Faebane arrow to her shoulder, Brandis," he says, not removing his eyes from my face. "Elora, focus on my voice. Did you like the mushroom's song? I like it when I'm sleeping out in the woods."

I nod my head, the motion slow like I'd imagine walking through jello would feel like. "I think they were calming my stomach so I didn't vomit on them." I thought I'd whispered that but the snicker from over Jadis' shoulder suggests otherwise. "But I also think I've lost my ever-loving mind."

"They probably did settle your stomach. Their song is designed to relax. I don't think they would have minded having extra food though," he smirks as he obviously tries to calm me down. This is a side of him I'd never experienced before.

As he speaks, his voice settles into a quieter volume, his fingers tracing little circles against my shoulders. "Your senses are trying to adjust to the new surroundings and are a little sensitive. Focus on my voice and it will get better, I promise, love."

"Jadis, here, arda," Mik says as he comes up behind Jadis with a clump of small green leaves.

"You're supposed to be..." Jadis starts to say, his jaw tightening.

"Ran into Tirin, he's flying, he'll get there faster." Mik hands off the plant with one hand and raises the other in placation.

With a stiff nod Jadis turns back to me and hands me the stems with their tiny bright leaves and even tinier white flowers. "Eat this, now. It might buy Margwin more time."

"Who's Margwin?" I look at the plant, turning it over in my palm and then smelling it. It's smells something like fresh cut grass with a faint hint of mint, but there's a subtle floral sweetness at the end.

"Would you please, for once, do as you're told, and I will continue to answer your questions. Do you not understand what the faebane could do?"

I shrug. "Mik said it kills mortals so aren't I just waiting for it to take me anyway? Carter wins, game over."

Jadis loses composure at this point and looks to the sky above. Blue slivers peaking through the heavy canopy of trees, swaying gently in the breeze. "Margwin is an excellent healer. You're not going to die."

"Thael naeloth mortalis," Brandis adds smugly, at least I'm assuming the blond is Brandis since he's the only other person here, "nael sylor thyrinor."

"She is mortal. She hasn't completed the change, Brandis. It only just started. Speak mortal tongue, she doesn't understand Fyrala Liorin'ae"

"What? Then why in the shades is she back here? That's not how this was supposed to play out. Someone explain, now, and where is Margwin."

"Wha…" I start to ask but Jadis points to the plant and then to my mouth. I oblige.

He places a thumb across the ends of those trailing black lines on my arm and continues answering my questions as promised. "Mik brought you across the veil after they hit you with faebane. That was your only hope. They can't fight faebane in your world."

"My world?" My words are slightly garbled around the latest clump of incredibly bitter plant that goes in my mouth, trying not to gag again. I'm not sure the taste is worth it…

"Yes. Haven't you noticed some physical changes in Mik and myself?"

"Mik turned into a wolf. Right in front of me…a wolf and I believe…I'm in a coma, aren't I? I never woke up after the stabbing. This is just some dream my mind has come up with while in a medically induced coma, some strange coping mechanism concocted by my overwhelmed mind."

Jadis rests a hand against my cheek, his gaze locking firmly with mine. "No. This isn't a coma dream. I swear it."

"Stabbed? Was she shot or was she stabbed?" Brandis cuts into our moment. The skin of his face is only growing brighter shades of red, his fisted hands now crossed over his chest.

"Both," Mik and Jadis answer him simultaneously.

Jadis looks down at my arm and the pointed ends of the lines sit just above his thumb now, receding slightly on their path. He releases an audible sigh and let's go of my arm.

"Someone needs to start explaining what the starflame went wrong now, or blood will start flying I swear on…"

The area to our right swirls and shimmers with an odd light, somehow manifesting a small woman with dark hair that shines with red and gold. The upper portions of it pulled back over the crown of her head in intricate braids that swirl over each other, only reflecting more light. More light than I think there is in these woods. The tips of her pointed ears peak up over the small braids that hang there.

Darkness starts to creep in from the edges of my vision, seeping into my skin like ink on dirty paper. My legs no longer want to work. I fight to keep them moving, but gravity's pull is too strong, and my feet keep dragging me down deeper into whatever hell hole I've gotten myself into.

"VAELIR, MYANIEL, SYLNATHIL naelithil, sylor lir," she says, hooking a strong hand under my right elbow, slowing my fall.

"She says take a seat, sweetling," Jadis translates for me

"That's not exactly what I said, but close enough." Her voice holds this warmth, like mulled wine at Christmas. It touches deep inside at my center, and I feel suddenly at ease. "There you go, now place your head between your knees and breathe nice and slow."

Not as patient as Jadis, she pulls my head down for me with one hand, the other grabbing at my one knee to make room for me to follow her instructions. As I breathe slowly, the light starts to return and the world finally slows its spinning. She pulls at the collar of my shirt but it won't give her the best view of my shoulder. I hear the rip of fabric right before the cool air touches the wound there and pulls me back to reality.

"It was ruined anyway," she shrugs, "the shirt. I didn't think you'd mind."

I shake my head and finally gain the gumption to look at the wound again. I almost forgot about it in the chaos; the burning fire abated into the background. I'm not prepared at all for what I see.

I'm assuming this beautiful woman is Margwin since she's tending to me, her dainty long-boned fingers hold considerably more strength than I expect. They poke and prod at a faint red circle, the diameter of a pencil. That's all that remains of the hole that once passed through my shoulder only moments ago. The black lines emanate from the pink mark like cracked glass, radiating in all directions.

"Alright Jadis, stop your fretting," she says looking at the tall, dark man that paces at our sides. "You are correct. The change has begun and her healing capabilities kicked in the moment she crossed the veil into this world." A broad grin stretches her face, not one of glee or happiness but of comfort and reassurance. "The wound is closed and the faebane is already starting to break down. She's going to be fine. Aren't you sweetling? Feeling better?"

It's odd having a woman squat there and talk to you like you'd imagine your grandmother would and yet she looks at least as old as yourself if not younger. Despite the bright, amber shade of her eyes, there's a spark there, a hint at the wisdom that lay behind them, a wisdom that only comes with advanced age. Yet, she sits here before me as spry and youthful as a young mother. A mind-boggling juxtaposition that leaves me speechless. Nothing here fits together in any semblance of a meaningful way.

"You poor sweetling," she coos, cupping my cheek gently in her hand. "Let's you and I head back the quick way, hmm? Get you inside out of the chill, a nice, hot cup of tea perhaps? Let the others settle their differences on the way back without you."

Margwin places a strong, muscled arm around my waist and steadies me as I rise to my feet and then she gestures to an open area nearby. The world shimmers again in that spot, like a heat mirage on the horizon, and she walks me towards it.

I pull back.

"It's just a portal, Elora. Some fae can open them for faster travel. That's how I arrived here." She traces a thumb over the back of the hand she holds.

"She knows that, Margwin. Stop treating her like a mudbrain." Brandis continues to scowl like a little boy stuck in a corner.

I look around me until I find the only familiar things here.

"It's safe," Jadis says, the moment I find his eyes, the pressing question apparently written all over my face. "It's like taking the slide off a playground instead of climbing down the stairs."

I nod. I think.

"Go ahead with Margwin, she'll take good care of you. You don't look the best, love. We'll be right behind ye on foot. You need her talents right now, not mine." He eases me closer to her with a wink. He takes a small step and I take an equally small step away, back toward her and the portal.

Can't you come too, I think to myself and again my question must have been written all over my face. "I need to stay this time. I, uh, have some explanations to make to your brother."

He barely finishes the last syllable when the woods slip past me morphing and changing into grey and white walls of a large bedroom.

Chapter Seven

"Vaelithil thalna, myrran lorynor"

The frost melts, and the earth whispers

"OKAY, SIT DOWN, RIGHT THERE behind you." Margwin grips my arms just below the shoulder and eases me back until a soft cushion catches my not-so-slow descent.

"He said bro…"

"Yes. He did. Not the best timing I think." She stops to brush the piece of hair that had fallen into my face away and gently tucks it behind my ear. "How about that cup of tea?"

"I suppose tea can't do any harm…right? Does the tea sing too?" I second guess myself, my fingers digging into the rich upholstery on the arms of the chair. "You don't have strange tea that will jump out and drown me of its own accord or something right?"

She laughs, an unexpected and bright sound. "No. Just regular tea like I'm sure you're used to. The only difference might be the potency of the therapeutic nature, but that's all."

I nod, my fingers slowly releasing their grip on the edge of the chair. I have nowhere to go and nothing to do. Everywhere I look, I feel like a caged bird unable to fly away. My feet itch for movement, but no destination seems right. What do I do now?

A fire crackles in the fireplace across the room, the logs popping occasionally breaking into the silence. Margwin seems unfazed by the lack of conversation and busies herself with the pot and teacups that I never saw arrive.

She brings a cup and saucer and places them in my hands, then takes the seat across from me. She settles so gracefully, blowing over the brown liquid in her own cup, watching me across the porcelain as I watch her.

"Brandis is my brother?" I test a small sip after my question, the scent of tannins fill my nose.

"Yes. He is your brother and I really shouldn't answer any questions beyond that. You really should have this conversation with him if you'd like to know more."

"I don't want to."

"What? Know more or ask Brandis?"

I shift my weight in the chair, relaxing into the back and resting a shoulder, the uninjured one, into one wing. "Ask him."

"Why not? He probably has better answer than I do," she too, rests her body in a similar fashion to mine.

"He's an ass."

The timing of my comment was nearly perfect as she sputters into her tea, spraying small drops up over her own face. She sets her tea on the small side table and stretches for a cloth to dab her face with. "He is that," she admits, nodding. "Just relax a few moments, they'll be here shortly."

I hear her clear as day and yet her lips never moved. I'm hallucinating again.

"No, you're not." This time she takes a sip from her cup as the words seem to cross my ears. *It's mind speak, all fae can accomplish it if they trust each other.*

"Trust?"

"Yes, you have to let them in your mind and that can be very dangerous to do with the wrong person, Elora."

"So, what? This means I suddenly trust you?"

"No, this means you don't know how to keep people out."

"How do I keep people out of my head?"

"Don't invite them in. Now, they're coming, and Brandis doesn't know when to stop, despite his age. When it becomes too much, and it will become too much, you let me know, in your head, and I will send them all away."

I didn't have time to nod before tea spills all over my lap as I jolt when the door bangs against the wall.

When I turn my head, Brandis' face is contorted into something unearthly, and I feel my legs pull me to my feet of their own volition. He stalks into the room and I back away faster until the backs of my calves and knees hit something low that stops me.

"Thyrel thalzak lir ilynor thalneth?" he bellows at me like I'm supposed to know. His bright, blue eyes searing like ice. There is no wondering who he's addressing with that tone.

"Wh...What?" My voice quivers, betraying me.

"He asked 'how the shades did this happen?'" Margwin clarifies.

"Brandis, again, she does not know our tongue, speak mortal tongue." Jadis crosses his arms over his chest, staring down the blond tyrant.

Said tyrant waves a single hand in the air, tracing a fast circle around. "This, all of this. How? You were supposed to stay put until the spell changed you and beckoned you to return. You're still mortal, partially, I can smell it. What happened? Why are you so, so...why are you acting like a scared little cub?"

"I don't know what you mean?" My hands clench and unclench, restless with the rising tension. I'm not going to let anyone talk to me like this again.

"What started the change? Your thyrinels? Are they the ones to defy the magic?"

"My thyrinels? What?"

Brandis pinches the bridge of his nose. "Oh, for moon's sake, your guardians. Is she really this slow?" He looks over his shoulder to the one person I thought I could trust.

"That's not fair, Brandis, and you know it." Jadis moves from around his back. "I told you she knows nothing of this world or the plan. Make your questions more specific and she might be able to answer you."

"I mean I only just got her to believe that magic even existed right before dragging her through the door. She took that bolt to the shoulder right then," chimes in Mik from his hiding spot in the doorway.

"You didn't know about magic or the fae before they brought you back here?" Brandis turns back to me and seethes his words through a clenched jaw, the muscles near his high cheek bones twitching. "You know absolutely nothing? Your own language, nothing?"

"No. I didn't know about magic until right before. I thought I was crazy actually, for almost a year now, still think I might be. I did not know about fae until just now, whatever fae is." I squirm out from under the grip of the invisible something that was holding up my lower legs and stand tall before Brandis as Jadis slides in at my side.

"Your guardians failed to educate you properly, as instructed. Where are they? They will face the consequences of their disobedience."

"What guardians for crying out loud? I don't know who you're talking about. In case my constant 'whats' aren't enough for your slow brain to figure that out."

He sighs. Sighs! Like I'm an annoying child who should know better and he's tired of trying to make me understand, sighs. "Two members of my co...this territory were sent to protect you and educate you properly, as a high aelorin of this territory should be, and prepare you for your return and your destiny."

"Whoa there, stop, destiny? Nope. I'm noping right out of that one for one, Two, do you mean my parents?"

"No, *our* parents were already with the stars."

"I'm assuming that phrase means dead. So, wait, they weren't my parents?" I grasp the locket around my neck through my ruined shirt, squeezing the two pictures contained inside, all of them gone now.

"No. Finally we agree on something." He crosses his arms over his chest, leaning slightly forward with a crooked smile. "Now, where are they?"

"Is death a proper punishment for their 'defiance'? Is that how you dispense justice here?" I lift my chin defiantly, hoping he doesn't notice the slight tremble in my hands.

"Answer the shading question!" His hands move to the nearby chair gripping the back until his knuckles turn white.

"For someone who apparently is upper class your language seems to be rather crass if I were to guess." I look to Mik, "and you commented on my language choices?"

Brandis takes a large step forward and while I maintain my ground despite the quake in my chest, Jadis takes a small step angling between myself and my brother who then backs down.

"They died in an accident about a month after my seventh birthday." The open revelation really takes any edge I'd managed to keep in my voice and of course, he ruins it.

"That's impossible. You were almost thirty when we sent you across the veil."

My breath hitches, and a high, shaky laugh slips out, unbidden and uncontrollable, like a string snapping under too much tension. I clap a hand to my mouth, eyes wide, but the sound has already escaped, fragile and absurd in the heavy silence. "I was a child."

"Of course you were a cub, that's why you had guardians. We are not barbarians sending a cub out to fend for themselves in a vicious world. If they died, then who raised you?"

"No one really. I went from home to home in the foster system until I turned eighteen."

Brandis at least looked to Jadis at this point, raising his eyebrows, I assume asking for a translation.

"It's a government run system for orphans. Families volunteer, good and bad, to raise children that have no parents or bad parents, for a fee. Eighteen is when mortals consider themselves adults, she was ninety at that point."

I stare at Jadis' profile, eyes wide enough that the heat of the room and the breeze from the chimney started to dry them out. *One year in the mortal realm is five years here.* I heard his voice in my mind.

"I see," Brandis says, wiping a hand down his face, pulling at the delicate skin, and yes, his skin looked delicate. "And how the hell did you end up marrying Cartwell?"

"Cartwell?" I asked, my mind indeed slowing with exhaustion. His eyes widen and his neck starts to blotch as a wave of crimson spreads evenly up his throat and cheeks. I can sense the intensifying pressure in the air as he takes a deep breath, ready to pin me with more questions and belittlement.

"Carter," Mik clarifies from his little hiding spot, his shoulders crawling up to his ears.

"Carter was kind and sweet. He swept me off my feet. I thought I was in love..."

Brandis lets out a cynical chuckle while holding my gaze as if to emphasize the point even further. It feels like a sharp blade has been thrust deep into my chest and twisted hard. His words are like cold water on the face. "Cartwell couldn't love his own mother much less you, foolish cub."

"I know that now, thank you."

He gasps as if the air had been punched out of him, his hands clench into fists and his face contorts in disgust. "The fact that you married him is bad enough," he spits through gritted teeth, "please tell me you didn't...please tell me you didn't give yourself to him."

My throat goes dry and my heart flutters in my chest. Fire licks up my neck as I lock eyes with him. He seems to look right through me, and I find myself suddenly fixated on the floor, trying to suppress the heat radiating off my cheeks. "That's none of your damn business."

When I dare to look up again his nostrils curl up with the corners of his mouth as if he can smell my shame. "And the result of this coupling?"

I stare at him, the disgust twisting my face and then at Jadis, but only meet his stoic profile. I'm on my own. I should have known.

"A daughter...Emmaline." I finally answer, my voice a hush.

"I have a niece by Cartwell, damn the mother for the cursed child. Our bloodlines are now linked for eternity. I will kill the bastard for that alone."

"Had," I force, my teeth creaking against each other, the bottom edge of my vision swimming, my breath shaking my lungs.

"Excuse me?"

"You had a niece, she's dead," the last word tumbles with the tear that escapes its prison and runs down the hill of my cheek.

Jadis steps back at this point and presses against my side, the heat of him, the smell of him, woods, moss, and clean leather caressing my lungs like a long stroke down the back of a cat.

"She's dead already? How?"

Surprisingly, he actually sounds like he cares. This is the moment I have been dreading, the moment when I have to reveal what no one else knows. The truth that makes me feel as if my heart is tearing into a million tiny pieces and all the life and joy has been sucked out of me. Yet still, I force the words from my lips, "He killed her." The sob leaves my chest without permission, and I wish more than anything that I could take it back.

"Who?" he asks, his face softening into some dumbstruck position that makes me want to slap him.

"Carter! Carter snapped her neck like a little twig!"

"Cartwell?"

"Carter! Carter...I married Carter and Carter killed her, her own father. I don't know who the hell this Cartwell is. I married Carter!"

"Alright, I think that's enough for today. All of you out," Margwin says, shooing them all towards the door.

Jadis remains at my side, pressing the length of his arm against me, his elbow halfway down my upper arm. I focus on the heat there and sway with my own breathing.

"Jadis?"

"Yes?"

"You said once that you were watching me, guarding me, you and Mik..."

"No, I said that," Mik answers from the door.

"Jadis, how long were you watching me?"

"Elora, I..."

"How long, Jadis? Before or after he killed her? Were you there when he decided to take her away from me?" I barely get the words out.

"After, I came after that. I chose the location of the pub after you settled into your apartment."

"You were there that whole time, watching me waste away to nothing. Watching me suffer and question my own sanity and you did nothing."

He pushes in closer, his gaze intense and his hands move firmly to my shoulders. "What was I supposed to do? Tell you everything? You wouldn't have believed a word I said." His voice is low and emphatic. His breath is warm on my skin as he lowers his head to look me in the eyes.

"You could have forced me here, just like you did today. You could have stopped it. All of it."

"Elora..." he begs, his green eyes flaring brightly in the dimly lit room.

"Get out," I whisper and turn away.

Chapter Eight

"*Laralith thalna, thyrenor sylrin nor thalanor*"

Leaves fall, but the tree endures

MARGWIN REMAINS AS THE DOOR clicks shut. Jadis' warm scent still haunting the space around me so heavily I need to move. I need to escape it but doing so starts that hollow pulsing again, threatening so loudly I can't breathe.

As I grasp and claw at the center of my chest, Margwin starts to guide me to a small door that peeks out on the other side of the room. I realize we had portaled into a small bedroom, the little side table in the living area still held our now cold tea. The large bed being what stopped my backward steps moments ago.

The walls shine like marble or a similar stone, those that didn't hold the door or fireplace were lined floor to ceiling with tall windows whose panes were held by intricately carved vines in circular and weaving patterns. The curtains, chairs, and bedclothes all shades of soft greens that bring out the tiny veins of color in the stone that surrounds us.

The small door leads to a large bathroom, the curtains there are drawn revealing a door to a large patio covered in pots overflowing with bright green vines and foliage, some with large red and orange flowers that compliment the now setting sun. A large sunken bath takes up most of the room, the water flowing from the faucet the moment we cross the threshold.

"A hot bath, a full stomach, and a good night's sleep are in order and in that order please," Margwin says helping pull my torn shirt off my shoulders and down each arm. "I think you can handle the rest, yes?"

I nod. No words would form.

She gestures to a small stool off to one side where I can sit, next to a small dresser. She pulls a few large, white towels from inside and folds them on top. I mindlessly pick at the laces on my boots, slipping one off and then the other.

When Margwin next enters my vision, she carries three glass bottles, one of which holds a familiar viscous, purple liquid. She lifts that one first, "This one's for stress to help you relax. This one's for preparing for sleep," she adds, lifting the next bottle with a similar blue liquid inside, "and this one's for frayed nerves," she says resting the last bottle of green in the line. "Perhaps all three might be a good idea this time," she adds, pinching her brow in concern. She walks over and runs her fingers through the loose hair at my one temple. "It will get better. I promise you. All of it, just be patient."

I manage to force another nod and she leaves the room.

I leave the remainder of my clothes and the now offending locket in a haphazard pile near the stool in my haste to feel the water that beckons me so loudly. The blissful heat radiating off the bath leaves an instant sheen on my skin as I add all three bottles Margwin left me. I needed all the help I can get.

Somehow, it knows the perfect temperature. Somehow Jadis knew the perfect temperature, the bastard. Thoughts of what he did still stung even though my conscience argues with itself that he was right, that I never would have believed him...that I needed to take this journey on my own time. I know I'm being irrational, but I don't care.

You know your muscles are tense, you can feel it, but I didn't quite realize how tense I had become until that water melted me from the inside out. It's not the heat of the water that makes baths so relaxing, you can get that heat in the shower too. What makes baths so wonderful, at least in that moment, is the weightlessness. The water holds some of the weight of the world for you as you float slightly above the seat, your arms and legs suspended around you, at least until the water grows cold. That's the thing with baths; when they're over, when the water loses that therapeutic heat, the world comes crashing back as the water drains away, leaving you to once again hold yourself up, crashing back down to earth feeling heavier than when you began. The rest and relaxation are as fleeting as the heat.

And yet, time ticks by, the sun falls below the horizon and the sconces on the wall sense the darkness and fill the room with their warm, soft glow, but my water remains perfectly warm. The breeze from the open doors and windows tickle the small hairs on my neck as the light fabric of the drapes wave hello to the evening. Steam wafts up from the warm water as the air around me cools giving rise to scents of warm vanilla, lavender, and jasmine.

I can't hear anything around me. Outside the world seems utterly silent and I wonder how many people my bastard of a brother rules over. It can't be that many if his world remains so silent this early in the evening.

The sounds of the soft breeze remain interrupted only by the trickle of water off my hands as I move. I watch droplets fall from my wrinkled fingers, sending ripples across the calm surface before me. I sigh.

Well, I can't stay in here forever, as much as I'd like to, I think to myself and the pop of the drain breaks the silence, followed by the sound of water spinning down a pipe.

"That was easy," I say to the empty room.

The air sends bumps all over my skin as I wrap the somehow warm towel around my torso, tucking the ends in to hold it in place. Picking up my shirt, I look at the torn collar and the splash of now dried blood. I don't want to put my soiled clothes back on.

I figure there must be a dresser or something with clean clothes somewhere, and venture in my towel back into the main room. Even if they were men's clothes...male's clothes, they'd be clean.

The pale, warm lights glow in the main room as well, bouncing off the near white walls making them shimmer like gold now instead of the silvery touches of daylight.

The small table has been cleared and the chairs placed neatly back, arms tucked just under the edges. Like I'd never been there. I wonder how long they'd leave my apartment and the few things that remained there. The rent was automatically taken from my account and I have no friends. I wonder how long they'd wait to check in on me and discover I'm gone. Surely that Detective...Peters, surely he would come looking for me and find no trace, no trail to follow, no footprints in the snow, no trails of blood. I'd be just another missing person.

At the end of the bed lay a neatly folded set of nightclothes, their buttery soft fabric feels incredible against my fingers. As I pick up the shirt to dress, a soft knock sounds at the main door.

"Come in." I retuck the end of the towel to make sure it stays secure. That's all I need is to flash some poor person who has no idea who I am.

It isn't some poor innocent person that comes through the door though. Jadis walks in with a tray in his hands, the scent of warm meat and fresh bread trails in ahead of him and my mouth waters. His eyes lift and trail down my towel clad body. "I brought you some dinner. I hope that's alright. I mean, that I brought it. You'll have a maid in the morning, to help you. They weren't really prepared for your arrival, so I thought I'd help out since you know me...."

"It's fine," I say, gripping the towel above my breasts like a vice. He notices. He tries not to look, but I catch the furtive glances out of the corners of his eyes starting at my feet and moving upwards. That's where the heat starts too, damn my treacherous body. Despite his faults, his now lightly pointed ears, and my anger with him, he's still a good-looking man...male, a stunning male. Pointed ears mean he's not a man, he's a male. Who am I kidding, he's drop-dead, ovary exploding gorgeous and I simply don't know what to do with that.

"I brought these too." He's holding a small flat parcel that he's been balancing under the tray of food. "It's paper and pencils...for drawing. I thought you might need them, or want them. You like to draw right?"

I nod. Yup, exploding ovaries. Control, breathe, I can handle this.

"I could pose for ye?" That telltale smirk returns to grace his full lips.

And there he is, reproductive explosion averted. I quietly return his comment with my usual unamused expression.

"You're missing out, I promise," he says, winking and I even think I see a flex of a bicep. "There's a guard outside your door." I stiffen at this and he instantly follows with "For your safety. He's not allowed to set foot inside this room without your explicit permission. I made that very clear. If you need anything, just open the door a little and let him know."

I don't trust my voice at all, and he needs to squirm a little still, I think. I can't forgive him too quickly. I nod again, breathing heavily through my nose but as quietly as possible. The sound is still too loud in the quiet room.

He nods too, running a hand through his loose hair, hair that has somehow grown down past his shoulders in a matter of hours. "Goodnight, Elora." With that, he walks out the door.

Before he closes it, I say "Thank you, Jadis."

I'm not sure he hears me until he turns and meets my eyes with a curt nod and a little curl starts at the edge of his lips, bringing out the smallest dimple in his cheeks. I might actually like that dimple. I try not to think about how he knew I liked to draw. He obviously knew I could; I showed him my drawing of Mik, but how did he know I liked to, or that I need to?

I almost missed his crass come ons...almost.

Chapter Nine

"Fioneth lorynor syloriniel"

The river hums a new song

THE INCREDIBLY DELICIOUS FOOD HE brought didn't last long, either for me to eat or in my stomach. The first round of night terrors brought it up with a vengeance into the toilet in the next room. At least I made it there.

They'll pass, the nightmares, they always do. I'd at least learned that by now. A few days of ruined sleep that seem interminable, end with a night of the living dead, where I spend hours into the next day sleeping off the stupor that consumes me. That's the cycle I've lived with: trigger, trauma, emotional vomiting, and then night terrors with real vomiting. So, when I woke again in a panicked sweat just before dawn, the sun's light peaking faintly enough to grace the tops of the trees outside my windows and add a wisp of pink to the sky above, I know it's pointless to try and go back to sleep. I, instead, return to the bed dangerously deep in my own thoughts.

This silent but terrifying meditation is rudely interrupted by streams of blindingly bright light shooting out of windows that I know I had curtained again. I had been so deep in my own mind I didn't hear her enter, much less pull back the drapes which she now tied off to the side of the giant windows. She's a young female, perhaps slightly younger than myself. I'm not sure if I can actually tell their ages, but then again, the concept of my actual age is now in question. She's beautiful, youthful with a round face and long honey hair that cascades down her back in a pristine braid.

"Vaelyrin, thael ithariel! Vyn naeloth sylnael thael, ithrin thael naeloth sylnor my lir. Margwin sylnor thael sylvaen lorynal, cael thael sylor ithiel ithatriel cael thyraen lir. Thael vyrnalith vaelrin ilyrin noril aelrin sylorin vaelrin, cael tharl noril lir? Thael sylor aelrin myrrin caelin fioniel myrrathil lir cael vyrinalith. Ilythar ilyrin cael vaelys myriniel, fioniel thaloraen silor vaelys, cael..." She chatters away as she turns to a wall and presses it with one hand. Where there once had been a solid wall, a door now opens, made of the same stone.

"Um, I'm sorry, I don't understand you."

"Oh my! My apologies. I was surprised you were awake because you didn't answer my knock. Your meal to break your fast is coming and you should dress for the day. There are some lovely dresses in here that are the perfect color for your eyes and hair..."

I will never get used to this place. "No dresses," I croak out, my voice sore from my night's activities.

"But...that's not proper. You're a high fae female, a princess."

"No dresses, no frills, no long hemlines. I don't do dresses. Not anymore." I cross my arms over my chest to help make my point clear.

"Alright." She draws out the word as she studies me from across the room. "Well, there's some hunting clothes in here, that's trousers and a tunic. They aren't the best choice for everyday wear but that's all I can offer right now. Not saying I can't find some other options for later..."

"Fine. But, I can dress myself, you don't have to do this. I mean, come here every morning. Just show me how to open that and I'll be fine." I wiggle my fingers at the magical wardrobe.

She looks as if she might cry, her lower lip sticks out a little more than it did a moment ago. She sucks it into her mouth and bites down gently. "You don't want a maid?"

"I don't need a maid. I'm fine. I'm sure you have much better things to do other than hover over me."

"No...not really." She plops herself into the nearest chair, yards of fabric flying up in the breeze she makes.

I suddenly feel terrible as I watch her try to maintain her composure and fail miserably. "I don't need a maid, but I could use a friend, I think. I don't talk much, and I don't think I'm good company but..."

"Oh, I'll talk more than enough for the both of us, everyone says so." Her spine shoots up to its former impeccable posture, her bright brown eyes glittering.

"Good. I can use someone that knows about this place and can answer my questions as they come. A friendly tutor, I suppose."

"What could you possibly need to know about your own home?" She tilts her head to one side with a half-toothed smile.

"Right, stupid mortal."

"You're not mortal, silly. You're Elora Aurelius, high fae daughter of the Day...former Day Court and the Deliverer. We've been waiting ages for you to come out of this room where they've been hiding you—over a century. I've lived here for years now and never once saw you or heard a single peep until they asked if I'd be your maid."

"Wait, the Deliverer? What am I supposed to deliver exactly?" My mind quickly strays from the original conversation, this was a rabbit hole I definitely want to go down. I can't even think on the century bit right now.

"Us, of course. All of us."

"And how am I supposed to do that?" I slip to the end of the bed as our conversation gets more intriguing. I need to be closer.

Her large eyes widen, and she takes an involuntary step back, her voice rising in disbelief. "You don't know?" Her hands fly to her hips, fingers curling as if she needs something to hold onto. "Because I don't know. I don't think anyone knows honestly. How do you not know?"

I sit up straighter, my hands twisting nervously in my lap. "I grew up in the mortal world," I begin, my voice faltering as a flush creeps up my neck. I can't look at her with this confession and focus instead on the edge of the bedspread as if it holds all the answers. "I'm a mortal," I add quickly, my fingers tightening around the fabric of my nightclothes. "Or at least I was. It's all a bit confusing. I have no idea where this place is, much less anything about it or how to deliver it. In case you didn't notice, I don't even know your language."

My confession must have been a mistake as her eyes widen to a point where I can clearly see the large pupils and the specks of gold and silver that had been hidden in the honey brown irises.

"Maybe we should keep this between us." She nods slowly in response, her eyes still so wide it reminds me of those nocturnal animals I saw on the Discovery Channel.

She doesn't move from the pose for quite some time as we stare at each other. The hard rap at the door the only thing to shake her back to reality. She bustles over to open it and take the proffered tray.

"Your morning meal," she presents on the table with a flourish of fluttering hands that move saucers, bowls, and plates into their proper location adjacent to a single seat by the table.

"What about yours?" I ask this as I stand and practically race to the table, my stomach growling in surprise. My seat is obvious being the one positioned directly in front of the steaming food.

"I already ate, downstairs. That's what maids do, we eat before we work." She cocks her head at me again like I'm some strange oddity in a museum, and maybe I am.

"Well, can you eat with me from now on? I'll get myself dressed and we'll eat together and chat about our day, and you can answer any questions I come up with?"

She thinks on this for a moment, her long, graceful index finger and thumb tracing lines along her small chin. "I think I can make that happen, it might take some sneaking, but it's doable."

AFTER SITTING DOWN to the delectable breakfast she'd laid out for me, the accompanying silence grew more and more tense, at least on my side. My little maid simply puttered around the room.

"So, you never told me your name," I mumble around a mouthful of buttery bread, much like a croissant of my world.

"Oh! How funny you should ask." She squeaks a little from the other side of the bed as she tucks in the soft sheets I used last night.

"Why is it funny to ask the name of someone that I've just met?" I'm sure my own confusion is written all over my face. Even when I'm quiet, my face still has subtitles.

"I'm the maid, Milady. It doesn't suit..." Her voice trails off the end leaving me to try and comprehend the point she's trying to make.

"But how would I call you if I need you or want to talk to you if I don't know your name?"

She laughs at that and skips lightly over to the tasseled ribbon I hadn't noticed hanging along the wall near where I am currently sitting. "You pull this when you're needing me and a bell rings wherever I am in the manor. Once I was assigned to you this morning, the ribbons in your suite were assigned to me and will find me for you."

"Magic..."

"Yes!" She then bounces back to her apparent duties, leaving me to my meal.

"Your name?" I ask for it again, which earns me a sigh from the other side of the room.

"You know it's unkind and rude to ask anyone's name? It's against our customs. Names are important, they hold power."

"And yet everyone seems to know my name." I say this under my breath, but it's obvious she hears me anyway. "I'm sorry. I didn't know, I promise. Well, I sort of did, but Jadis didn't go into details. I meant no offense." I hold my hands in front of me in defense. When she relaxes, I slump low into my chair, my shoulders slouching into a posture that feels far more comfortable, not only in the predicament my mouth just got me into, but also the energy I feel leaking out of my body at a rapid rate. "Can you tell me what other people call you, then? If not your name."

"Oh, of course. Call me Tressa." She acts like I should have asked for that in the first place.

"So, your name isn't Tressa, but everyone calls you that?" Her spine shoots straight as a flag pole causing me to divert my thoughts, "instead of your name, I mean."

She eyes me a little and then, with a slight shake of her head, says "Tressa is part of my name. Just not the whole thing."

"Oh." I say it like it makes sense, but it doesn't. The conversation dies back to that uncomfortable silence that I simply need to fill. "So, you're a fairy?" I try to strike up some semblance of conversation. The sudden silences as she stands there and watches me eat is stealing the small appetite I'd managed to dredge up.

"Aelorin, fae, yes. So are you, technically, well you should be. We prefer the term aelorin, now. Fairy used to be an acceptable term until the mortals ruined it." The new conversation seems to be acceptable, breaking her from the trance-like state she'd been in moments before. She makes her way to the closet and picks through the items there as I prod for more information.

"The mortals ruined fairy?" I ask around a bite of warm brown bread, unable to suppress the slight moan that escapes as the nutty, buttery flavor caresses my tongue. I can get used to all this home-baked bread.

She sighs. "Yes. The lore and pictures created by the mortals, that interacted with our kind over the centuries, have bastardized the term to the point where it only really includes the beings we call pixies." Her soft voice meanders its way from the closet that her head is currently stuck in.

"And what are pixies?"

She shifts to peek at me from around one of the large, lined doors, a single eyebrow raised quizzically over her unearthly honey eyes.

"Raised a mortal, remember?"

She nods at the reminder and resumes her search of the closet. "Pixies are small, winged beings directly connected with nature. Good for the land but get their dust everywhere inside. It's deucedly difficult to clean up and they know it." Her voice changes in volume, harder and louder. I'm not sure if it's the effects of her moving about in the hidden wardrobe or her growing frustration over discussions of pixies. "Just watch. If you ever upset one, they'll cover you in dust that will make you shine for weeks and maybe even follow you home and scatter it over every surface you touch. You'll never escape it then."

"Speaking from experience?" I ask, pushing my plate away and resting a warm hand on my very full stomach.

"Starflame, yes," she says and then sucks in a breath. I can't see her expression fully behind the hand she has covering her mouth under the pained eyes, but I'm getting the impression she thinks she said something wrong. It's my turn to raise an eyebrow.

Her voice returns at a bare whisper, "I do apologize profusely, milady, for my crass words. Terribly unladylike. It won't happen again. I swear it."

"Which one? Starflame?"

She nods quickly, her cheeks reaching an intense rosy glow. It's not like I hadn't heard that one out of Brandis' mouth already.

"Look at that, you're a great teacher. I now know a fae swear word and that Tinker Bell is, in fact, a pixie, not a fairy, all in a matter of minutes. The start of a great friendship, I think." I think she starts to smile, the corners of her mouth twitching at the mention of fae curse words, but that sours the moment I mention pixies again.

She throws the armful of clothes she has gathered on the end of the bed and makes a hard turn back to face me, her tight fists resting on her hips. "She is the worst pixie they could have chosen to make famous. Her arrogance knows no bounds. I hear her ego has grown far too big for that little island now."

I stand during her declaration and her fists shift to gesture at the tunic, shirt, and leggings she had tossed on the bed. I assume she means I should dress. "Wait," I say, walking over to her side, "She's real?"

"Unfortunately, yes. A thorn in our side to say the least. You'll find many of the tales you've heard as a child in the mortal world are ours, leaked out to mortal ears at some tavern somewhere over the centuries. Her friends in the stories aged, but not like mortals because they are fae. They aged much slower."

"No shit." I grab the shirt from the bed. The fabric is soft, not as much as the sheets and nightclothes, but enough that it glides across my skin in a gentle caress as I throw it over my head. As my eyes peek through the wide collar, I can see the gentle tilt of Tressa's head, with a questioning eyebrow in my direction. "A mortal swear word. Crass word for feces in my world. Is it the same as starflame?"

I didn't think I could shock this poor girl more than I already had, but her eyes burst wide and her cheeks flamed, the color climbing down her neck. "No, not exactly."

"Oh." I realized what is might be equivalent to. "Perhaps starflame references a more intimate action then?" Her intense blush from her ears to below the neckline of her dress is all the answer I need.

TRESSA INSISTED THAT, despite my abhorrent taste in clothes, she fully intends, or rather demands, that I let her tame my hair. I don't like being waited on. I never have. Even in restaurants, Carter always questioned why I stacked the plates for the waitstaff or made sure the napkins were on the plates along with the silverware instead of leaving them on the table. I'm an independent woman and don't need anyone doing anything for me, plus they worked hard for very little money. I can do that little to help ease their day. However, I feel bad for what I put Tressa through already today and decide to concede—today.

Concede is a word that flits about in my mind the moment she starts running her fingers through my hair. Before that thought could cross my mind again, my head leans into her fingers of its own volition. I had no idea it felt this good to have someone brush your hair or something as simple as run their fingers along your scalp. I didn't want it to stop. Tressa is good at her craft, adeptly twining pieces of my hair into intricate braids joining along the back of my head in a way I can't see in the vanity mirror, the silver-backed glass held in a delicately lined frame with tiny pastel flowers popping up here and there.

I grab the paper and pencils Jadis left me the previous evening and study Tressa as she works, moving my fingers and the charcoal tips around the paper in my usual fashion while my eyes study my subject in the mirror. I desperately want to capture the cute way she holds her mouth as she works and how, sometimes, the tip of her pink tongue escapes her lips just in the corner as she concentrates.

"You're very good at all these braids, but don't you think the braids and the flowers are a little over the top considering my clothes?" I raise an eyebrow at her reflection as my gaze travels up over my sketchbook.

"No matter what you wear, plaiting your hair sends a good message to those around you," is her curt reply, not looking up from her work for a moment.

"And what message is that?"

"Knot magic."

"Knot magic?"

"Yes. Knot magic. Plaiting is a type of knot work and the perfect way to subtly tell people around you that you're trustworthy. Knotwork as part of you being means you won't lie or deceive. It's a symbol of the ancient oath taken by all fae."

"So, you're telling people that I won't lie to them?"

"No, you're telling people that you can't lie to them. That you're choosing to be magically bound to the truth through knot magic."

"And you assumed I wanted that magical binding on my person then?" My feathers are obviously ruffled considering the tone that slips out. It's not that I like to lie, but after what my life has been like, I honestly want to have the option of a little lie here and there for my own personal protection, especially in a world that makes absolutely no sense to me. The choice has now been taken away from me and I find that far too controlling for my taste.

"Milady, firstly, you can't lie even if you want to—"

My charcoal nub stills over the page, hovering as her words sink in. I glance up at the mirror, catching her eyes in the reflection. "What do you mean I can't lie? Is this some rule here? Some law? How in heaven's name can you possibly keep people from lying to each other? Mind control?" My voice is sharper than intended. My fingers begin to tap against the edge of the pages in my lap as I try to wrap my head around her statement. "I've lied, but you insist I'm fae too." I tilt my head, the sketchbook slipping slightly in my lap as my focus shifts entirely to her.

"You've lied? But you are fae..."

"I mean I don't make a habit of it, but sometimes it saved my ass. I don't know what this has to do with being fae, but I'm not fae remember, mortal world."

"You were born fae, so I assumed that the same rules applied to you. We fae cannot lie, magic prevents us from doing so. You can tell when someone wants to lie in the not so subtle way their words will cut off their tongue. Most will mince words instead. Keeping meanings subtle and open to multiple interpretations. The knot magic means that you won't even mince words. The more intricate the knots, the more meaningful your oath. I thought, perhaps since you say you do not know much about the ways here and this realm, the knot magic oath may help you not have to constantly explain the strange things you might say or do. Help others trust you better."

I turn to meet her eyes instead of the reflection, gauging her words carefully behind me and her fingers loosen from my hair and twirl a small flower with fragile white petals. If what she says is true, then she means what she said. Her words are clear to me. I can't think of another way they could be interpreted. But, if what she says is true, then Carter is a fae and he lied to me plenty. Maybe it's different in my world and the same rules don't apply.

"Oh, thanks." My words fall flat and I find myself fumbling for something to say to recover. I finally settle on, "and the flowers?"

"You didn't let me put you in a dress, so I'm doing my best to show you as the lady you are with what you left me."

I laugh at that. A good full laugh that even surprises me and her eyes clear a little as she joins me. She then weaves the last of the little white and blue flowers into her design on my head and I return to the last touches on my sketch of her doing the same. We settle into a longer period of silence, the questions burning in my mind would no longer wait for another time.

"Tressa?"

"Hmm," she hums through her tight lips.

"Can fae not lie at all?"

"The ancient magic makes it very difficult and most listen to the warnings that make the words hard to say."

"That's an experience I have yet to feel myself. Words have always been easy, even if they were a partial lie. "And if they don't? Listen, I mean. Can they actually lie?"

"Yes, but the punishment is severe."

"And what is that?" Carter had no issues lying, he's proven that time and time again, so what punishment could magic have inflicted on him when he's still walking around seemingly unaffected.

"Why? Are you considering resisting the magic?" She deflects my question with one of her own which is highly suspicious. But the concern wrenching her dainty brows together and creasing her forehead settles my nerves a little.

"No. Like I said, I never make a habit of it anyway. I just...he...I mean Carter..."

"Ah, yes," she says, obviously figuring out my question without me actually voicing it myself. "Cartwell fought that magic long ago. It changed him, the magic, turned his mind. No one truly knows what it did, but he wasn't always this dark—or so I'm told."

"So, he can lie, then?" I ask, the lump in my throat making the words difficult to spit out and once they leave my tongue, the thundering beats of my heart make it difficult to hear her answer.

"Yes. He's the one fae who lies. No one knows how he survived the magic of the oath."

"I see," is all I can manage.

Tressa finishes her skilled work on the intricate braids and brings out a small mirror to show me what she accomplished with the mess I call my hair. It has to be an illusion, because I don't recognize a single, silky lock on my head, and I tell her so.

"Aye, your hair has seen better days indeed, I'm sure. No matter, I wove a little magic in there to help it heal."

Before I can respond or even thank her, a gentle knock sounds at the door. Tressa places a light hand on my shoulder as I make to rise, telling me to stay put while she saunters over to answer. Quiet words are exchanged with whoever called and she eventually opens the door wider for them to come inside.

It's Jadis. He walks in, his green tunic bringing out the intensity in his eyes as he takes in my hair and then accentuates the slight rise in his brows as he moves from my hair to the tunic and pants. I can swear I see a twitch of a smirk start at the corner of his full lips.

"Elora," he says my name in a way I've heard cowboys address a frightened horse on TV, his reassuring tone continuing from the night before and I'm instantly on edge. "Your brother requires your presence at today's council meeting. However, I'm of a mind to keep ye here for myself if you insist on wearing those trousers."

Tressa gasps and then hides her mouth behind a hand as she turns to tidy the sheets on the bed that already look perfect.

"Why in God's name would he want me, of all people, at a council meeting?" I ask, returning my attention to him. "I have no idea what's going on, where I am, and he obviously thinks I'm an idiot."

His eyes soften, a glimmer of sympathy shining from within. "I suspect he sees an opportunity to solidify his power in the realm by showing off that his sister, the Deliverer, has returned to his court."

"So, I'm a game piece designed to further his own agenda then," I return, the disdain dripping from my voice as I rise from my seat at the mirror. "Yeah, no thanks." The sketchbook falls from my lap and scatters pages at his feet.

Jadis bends down and grabs the first few pages before I can snatch them myself and studies my drawings. I step back, watching the subtle changes in his face as he looks over the dark lines and shading sitting starkly against the pale brown paper. A small smile tips his lips as he looks over at Tressa and then hands the sheets back to my now trembling hands.

"I don't like being used," I say as I stuff the sheets back into the leather case.

"Then don't be." His voice is filled with caution in contrast to his words. "I fear he intends to, he's known for his cunning and ambition. He sees power as a means to an end, and desires to return the realm to the old ways. He sees you as a part of the intricate game he's playing. You don't have to be a part of that game. You can make your own rules. And I can guess you probably will be making yer own rules and your own moves."

"Your voice changed. You never had an accent before, did you?" I obviously hadn't focused on the conversation at hand at all.

"Aye, I hid it at the pub. It's less I have to try and explain if people should notice and ask."

"Because you can't lie?"

He shifts his eyes quickly to Tressa again who had moved on to tidying the hidden wardrobe. She apparently felt his gaze because her head moves deeper into the closet where she can't be seen. Maybe she'll pop out in Narnia…it's deep enough. "I see you've been learning a thing or two."

"I don't plan on walking around here a complete imbecile. I'll take whatever information I can get to keep myself safe." The words even shock me, a sudden change from simple survival to something closer to drive and ambition.

"You're safe here, Elora. I won't let anything happen to you."

I give a simple and quick nod in answer. I know he can't lie, but that doesn't mean I trust anyone here, especially someone who hid the truth from me for so long. He never came out and said he was at the pub. Never approached me and even attempted to explain anything to me about any of this. There was mincing of words on his part. How many others minced words with me, keeping everything from me when they knew I was in danger? That doesn't sound like someone with my best interests in mind at all. I can depend on me, and me alone and it's better this way, in the end. Simpler.

"I'll find my own way. I'm not going to let myself be used as a pawn again. I will not be manipulated by anyone, much less a brother I don't even know and may not want to. Especially one who has made it abundantly clear that he couldn't care less about me and my feelings."

Jadis inches closer, his hand becoming a comforting weight on my shoulder. Even the thick jerkin can't shield me from the warmth of his touch. My heart stumbles and then slows its erratic pace as I watch him absorb my heavy words.

"You have my support, just be careful. Brandis can be…volatile. You're not in this court alone. Because of the prophecy, people will be looking to you. If you don't want to be his puppet, then don't. Many will share your sentiments but will fear to express them personally. Brandis is powerful still in this realm, despite the fall of the courts. Understand, I will stand by your side, no matter what oath I have taken to your brother. In the end, the oath is to your family and that includes you."

My whole body had felt weighed down for some time now. A heavy lead that settled from my chest to my toes. I hesitantly remove my shoulder from under his gentle hold. I know there is no way to avoid the inevitable, even though I want to try. "Okay," I say half-heartedly, which is more than I actually feel. "Let's just get this over with."

Chapter Ten

"Vragil zakir vaelzak"

The storm burns in the shadows

ACH BEAT OF MY HEART seems louder, an insistent drum as I cross the threshold of the council chambers with Jadis. The room is so full of nature and calm in contrast to every feeling in my body right now.

The council chamber radiates a natural beauty that's still over the top, thanks to the sunlight streaming through the tall windows. It casts a warm glow across the polished wood floor. Tapestries of blooming gardens and graceful fairy creatures hang on the walls. Vines twist along the ceiling, their thin wisps wrapping around chandeliers, adding a touch of nature to the room. All I can do is stare in awe. Even the architecture here supports just how lost I am.

At the center of the room stands a grand oval table, its surface made from a rare oak that was enchanted when constructed, Jadis tells me when he notices my staring. The table seems to pulsate with a gentle glow, as if it's a living thing mimicking the beating hearts of those in the room. Around the table are equally spaced seats, each carved with motifs of leaves and flowers and, those at the head of the table, mythical creatures like unicorns and dragons.

Jadis takes extra care to get as close as possible as he speaks, his whispered words stirring the tendrils of hair across my cheek. He explains all the details and how the fae love to blend nature and craftsmanship. I'll see that everywhere I look, their attempt at harmony with nature, or at least the look of it.

As council members take their seats, the table pulses again with a gentle light, as if welcoming them. The arrangement of the seating reminds me of Arthur and his knights, except slightly less equal. The oval shape allows one seat to stand out, subtly from the others. That chair is larger than the others and almost gives the appearance of being elevated. It holds an air of authority and, of course, currently holds the arrogant ass of my darling, and scowling, long lost brother.

I don't give him the satisfaction of keeping my attention and instead look at the large chandelier that takes up the space above the pulsing table. Its delicate crystals reflect the sunlight, casting shimmering patterns across the room. It almost resembles a frozen waterfall.

I soon realize this room is designed to give an illusion of safety, security, and equality.

Apparently, the former Day Court manor we stand in uses light to decorate, both natural and enchanted. Those that lived here before 'The Fall' had a natural affinity for light magic. The daylight that streams through the windows is proof of this and the antithesis to the cold that radiates off all the people present.

"Before," Jadis whispers in my ear, "the light was to represent the beauty of nature and soften the weight of responsibility, or some such thing. The room was designed to enhance the voices of the council members, and weave them together like the branches of a great tree as they shape the destiny of the realm."

I get the distinct impression that he doesn't believe a word of what he says.

Brandis calls Jadis from my side and whispers something in his ear, waving a hand of dismissal in my direction when he finishes. When Jadis returns to my side, his expression sour, he speaks quietly so only I can hear. "Brandis demands your presence at the head of the table. I'm to wait here at our seats until you return, which means I'm not going to like what he has to say." The low murmur of his words brush the shell of my ear, every syllable vibrating through me, leaving no room for thought until those words finally sink in.

I glare at Brandis, Jadis' head still tilted over my shoulder. Brandis' frustration simmers beneath his composed exterior, but I can see it there even if no one else can. It's there in the slight tightness of his jaw and the way his fingers tap impatiently on the table. "Of course he does."

Jadis squeezes a tight hand on my shoulder in encouragement. I take it more as a reminder to watch my tongue and that he's here to protect me. But can he really protect me from the brother that he's also sworn to? That remains to be seen.

The others still have not noticed my presence, preoccupied in their own conversations. I smooth down my jerkin and pants even though they're stiff enough to not need any smoothing. Still, my hands pull at the lower seam to straighten it out, again. With a deep, settling breath, I approach my darling brother's side as instructed.

His eyes narrow on me as I get closer, searching from the top of my head down to my toes and back, judging, criticizing, and I realize as he stops at my eyes that it's my attire that caught his ire more than some kind of faux pas I happened to commit already.

"What are you wearing?" His voice is cold. He doesn't even bother to rise to meet me but leans over in his chair in an attempt to keep our conversation quiet.

"What I'm comfortable in."

"This is not the mortal realm," Brandis continues, refusing to acknowledge my answer, "You are expected to dress as a lady of your station here, not some common bumpkin."

"Whether you like it or not, I'm a lady no matter what fabric covers my body, and I will dress however I please." I cross my arms tightly over my chest and take a step back.

He leans forward, his chair creaking under the weight of his movement. His broad shoulders stiffen, his expression hardening with barely contained frustration. The daylight streaming through the high windows does nothing to soften the sharp lines of his face. His fingers tighten around the edge of the table, the tension in his grip visible to anyone paying attention. "I expect you to dress appropriately the next time you leave your chambers."

"Yeah, whatever." I feel like a teenager but that's all that comes to mind as I turn my back to him, abruptly ending this one sided conversation.

Jadis stands near the outer chairs, a single hand resting lightly on the back of one. As I approach, he wordlessly pulls it out, his open palm gesturing for me to sit. I arch a brow, giving him *the look*, but lower myself into the seat anyway. He responds with a slight smirk, then pushes the chair in with a steady hand, his touch lingering for just a second before stepping back.

I feel my heart sink as he sits down next to me. His intuition is spot on, and he drapes a hand over my thigh in an all-too-familiar way. I try desperately to suppress a shiver as his long fingers begin to slide up and down my leg. I want to move away from him, but I feel rooted to the spot, a silent battle between fear and familiarity.

A heavy weight settles on the now cold council chamber, the warmth of the sun can't touch my mood, especially when I'm surrounded by unfamiliar faces and strange decorations. Everything here is so different from what I'm used to, yet there is something oddly familiar about it too. I try to remember who I am and why I'm here, but the more I search for answers, the less clear they became.

Lost in my thoughts, I miss Jadis leaning closer to my ear once more, his sudden voice making me jump and barely suppress a squeal. "I know three ways to make six inches disappear."

"What?" I snap and get a glimpse of the enormous smirk twisting his lips. "Ugh, you're a pig." I whisper and pull my thigh from his trailing fingers.

Of course, this would be the moment Brandis catches us, his disapproving glare landing on me before he turns to address the room. The meeting officially begins, and I try to focus on what's being said but self-conscious nerves take over again. I realize it's not only that I don't know the language, but I also know nothing about any of the people, places, or events they might speak of. I'm already tense with Brandis' attitude and the frustration of his demanding my presence when I have no idea what's going on, but some of it I can follow without the detailed context but still made no sense to me logic-wise. It's made all the more difficult by waiting for Jadis to quietly translate what everyone is saying. I can't stop the glare that creeps onto my face as the other fae speak. They talk of regaining their land, reclaiming their power, and reinstating their status—as if those who have since settled there don't belong, as if history hasn't already moved forward without them.

Brandis takes this line of talk as the perfect moment to reveal my identity, changing to the mortal tongue for my benefit, I'm sure. "Yes, and those lands and the status will be returned to you soon enough as my sister, the Deliverer, has resumed her rightful place in my court. Just as the prophecy says she would. It's time now and she'll use her Gods given power to bring our realm back to what it was, just as it was foretold."

"Why would I do that?" The words escape before I even realize I've spoken them, my tongue moving faster than my thoughts. It feels as though something inside me has broken loose, a dam bursting, releasing everything I've held back for too long. There's no taking it back now.

I don't know if I'm stepping into someone new or rediscovering the person I used to be—maybe both. The weight of my past mistakes crashes down on me, pressing against my ribs, tightening my throat. I fight to keep my composure, but deep down, I know the truth.

I am on the verge of losing control.

This realization terrifies me, but part of me welcomes it with open arms. It means freedom from all the lies and half-truths that have kept me shackled for so long. Yet, at what cost? As I grapple with these thoughts, a voice in my head screams for me to stop before it's too late.

But it is too late. The floodgates are open, and nothing can stop the wave that is about to crash on us all.

Brandis' heads snaps to my face, the seething look there actually terrifying. Jadis' warm hand returns to my now bouncing thigh and stays there, the heat permeating all my limbs calming the frantic movements.

No one speaks. All eyes rest on mine. Some are wide with what I presume is shock from Brandis' revelation while other seem wary or even upset by my question.

"Because that's what you're supposed to do, Elora. You were blessed by the Gods and your fate is to return the realm to its former glory. That's what you're supposed to intend to do now that you're home, correct?"

Brandis' tone leaves no room for guess work. That's what he intends for me to do, and it would be his version, no, their version of the realms former glory. I'd already shoved my foot in my mouth. I might as well go for gold, and piss him right off for thinking I will bend over and be his little puppet just because he says so.

"From what I've heard, it would be better to return the realm to the time before the courts came to power—" Mind you, I don't know what exactly that means or entails. I'm assuming that the courts didn't always exist. Several strong gasps interrupt my statement. "Why would any of you want to return to a state and a system that failed so epically. Isn't that why you are where you are now, anyway? Seems foolish to tread down the same path just to repeat history all over again. There's a saying in the mortal world that those who ignore history are doomed to repeat it. I'd say that's exactly what you folks are trying to do."

Those that didn't continue to look at me in shock, turn their gazes to Brandis, with, I assume, equal expressions of shock. One gaze keeps mine, on the other side of the table, in the chair next to Brandis. His ice blue eyes burn into mine, narrow and searching for who knows what.

"Elora, darling…" Brandis starts and then decides to address the rest of the council first. "You must understand that despite the whispers in my court and the lands surrounding, Elora spent these last years in the mortal world." He turns back to look at me accusingly, the corners of his lips twitching. "She doesn't know anything about this, or the matters being discussed here. She doesn't understand our world as Cartwell dug his claws into her and corrupted her mind."

My jaw clenches and the anger I feel bulldozes through all of my caution. "Carter." I spit out his name like a mouth full of acid. My fists pound the table in front of me as I meet his eyes with a glare, "didn't do shit to my mind to make it so I don't understand how foolish it is to return to a ruling system that failed in the first place. I might be naive when it comes to the fae realm but I'm not an idiot."

His glacial gaze meets mine, the temperature in the room seems to plummet again as our heated standoff continues. His rage flows off him with shockingly eloquent words. "I beg to differ. You were idiotic enough to marry and procreate with the realms greatest threat, my dear sister." These words fly across the space between us, a shock wave that hits everyone gathered at the table, drawing every eye to turn in my direction. Disdainful stares instantly replace their previously intrigued looks. "Perhaps you should consider these poor choices before opening your mouth about things you obviously don't understand."

I get it. I undermined him in what he obviously believed to be his meeting, his position of power. But that doesn't mean he gets to degrade me so easily. I slam my hands into the wooden table once again and a glow starts on the enchanted surface. Its light spreads outward, illuminating Brandis' face as he raises his palms in shock. As if he actually suffered an electrical shock. "Allowed to speak my mind?" I ask with only a hint of the indignation I currently feel. "I may not have grown up here, but as your sister, don't I still have the right to speak?"

Brandis glares at me. He expected me to shut up and bend, but I refuse. "You're just a child," he says, "You don't know what you're talking about."

I can feel my face burning, the heat climbing my cheeks and into my ears. I curl my fingers into fists as I growl, "And you're a fucking bastard that thinks he can use me as a puppet to further his own ambitions." Fury twists my mouth into a sneer, and I spit out the words with all the venom that has built up inside me since Carter.

Brandis' knuckles turn bright white as he balls his hand into a fist and slams it against the oak tabletop, causing a vase of flowers to teeter. He stands, towering over the seated group of his colleagues, and lets out a deafening roar. "That's enough." The impact of his bellow reverberates through the room, threatening to split it from floor to ceiling.

I am powerless to take back my harsh words, even if I wanted to, as Brandis erupts in a fit of rage. His fury manifests into a dazzling golden light that fills the entire room, searing through my vision like a flashlight in the dark. All I can see is the piercing lines of his face and eyes that go wide and soft after an eternity, or what seems like an eternity, before a punishing force smacks me hard in the chest. My body flies backward, slamming against the wall that's ten feet behind me. The impact shatters my chair into pieces, shards of splintered wood embedding deep into my arms.

I can't move. I can't even feel my body to do so. A blinding white light consumes me, leaving the shimmering chandelier and luscious vines of the ceiling behind. An eerie silence cloaks the room, or at least my ears until they decide to work again with a soft whisper of my name. My lungs feel like fire as I frantically gasp for air, but before I can take a full breath, Jadis has wrapped an arm under my shoulders and another under my legs. He lifts me with ease from the bitterly cold floor. The deep baritone of his voice echoes in my ears like a haunting melody as he calls my name again.

When he turns, Brandis is right there, his face tight with guilt and regret—not that I care. His gaze drops to the deep gashes along my arms, where thick beads of blood still seep from the wounds. He hesitates, inching closer, his hand hovering as if he means to touch me. "Don't...touch...me," I wheeze, halting any forward movement on his part.

He drops his eyes to the floor and wrings his hands. His voice is so low it's barely audible as he says "Elora... I'm sorry. I shouldn't have—I let my emotions take over. I lost control, and that's on me. It won't happen again."

Anger burns within me, or maybe it's still the burn from his magic, but my pain fuels the realization that our relationship is marred significantly in the few hours I've known him. His unchecked verbal assaults and now a physical attack, so damaging to any chance at a familial bond. "Losing control seems to be your specialty, doesn't it, brother?" I'm bitter and hurt and it's clear in my voice.

Securing my now crumbling facade of strength, I spit out words to Jadis, demanding he set me down. He complies quickly, and my quivering legs are finally free to carry me away. I've recovered some measure of control, but the hopelessness of my situation is inescapable. The expectations loom over me, taunting me. I must find a way to assert myself and claim back my freedom, but without sacrificing everything that matters to me. If I want to be seen as something more than a pawn in Brandis' game, I will have to stand strong despite every threat. I need to control my own temper or look as poorly as he does to those in power. What am I even thinking? Did I seriously just consider staying here?

Chapter Eleven

"Ithrin vaelrae fioneth thalnor ryvith."

Sometimes the slower river finds the way faster

HOBBLE OVER TO THE main doors, practically running out, as best I can. My mind races with a mix of anger and embarrassment as my traitorous stomach lurches forward and recoils just as fast. I hurry down the hallway, which looks so long it may be endless, desperately seeking an escape from the suffocating tension that resulted from the council. My stomach lurches forward again and then empties itself in the nearest plant pot along the wall.

Once I rid myself of that lovely breakfast I'd eaten, I take a moment to catch my breath and my hand rests on my sore stomach, the other gripping the edge of the pot like a vice. A soft breeze filters through the long hallway and stirs the air around me. The walls are decorated with more tapestries, depicting colorful forest scenes this time. One shows a stag among a gathering of does, its rack glimmering in the morning sun. Another depicts two lovers embracing beneath a starry sky near a lake, the woman's face as bright as the moon above.

The plant that happens to now hold my partially digested breakfast, towers over me. The glossy emerald leaves form a magnificent canopy, spreading outwards like the wings of a giant flying beast. Each leaf is edged with delicate yet deadly looking serrations.

The sweet smell of nature fills my nostrils as I breathe in deeply. The scent is of damp, dark soil and something else, a wildness that I can't quite place. A part of me wants to examine the strange plant more closely but an inner voice tells me I better mind my own business.

Jadis gives me space. I can hear him breathing softly on the other side of the hall, behind me. To my surprise, his aren't the only breaths I can hear. My rumination are interrupted by a soft, deep voice, "Are you alright, miss?"

A tall, wiry man with a gentle face and weathered hands stands a few feet away. The green tinge to the skin around his fingernails and the dirt on his palms and the thighs of his pants suggest that I just vomited into one of his charges. I try to speak, but my throat is raw and nothing comes out. Instead, I nod to the gentleman, feeling the tears I don't want to shed prick at the corners of my eyes.

I didn't think it was possible, but his kind face softens even more as he approaches and pats my back gently. He switches to soft circles with the palm of his hand. "Don't worry, it happens to the best of us. I've seen many a fae leave those chambers in the same condition."

I gesture to the plant, my voice raw and now filled with mortification. "I...I'm sorry for...you know," I stammer, my cheeks now burning. "I'll clean it up right away."

The gardener's weathered face cracks into a gentle smile, his eyes twinkling with amusement. "No need to fret over that, lass. That plant there is a carnivorous beauty, always eager for a little extra nourishment. I reckon it'll enjoy the unexpected treat."

I find that both reassuring and disgusting. I glance at the plant once more, marveling at its majestic and yet, now dangerous allure. From its size, I wonder what this particular plant eats. Then again, maybe I don't want to know. I doubt it would be satisfied with a few blue bottle flies.

"Thank you...Ronan," Jadis says reluctantly as he steps forward. He takes my arm in his possessively and looks into my eyes, as if to communicate something that lay beneath the surface. I have no idea what he wants. Unsettled by the gesture, I allow him to lead me away, not knowing what we are walking towards, again.

I HAVE ALWAYS been one to push myself, to prove my strength and independence, until recently anyway. In the aftermath, the drive just hasn't been there. But now, my steps falter, my breathing comes out ragged to my ears. Jadis' hand holds me upright, a forceful anchor amid the swirling chaos of the halls we walk in. His touch is warm around my shoulders, as always, a boon against the chill of the stone beneath our feet. His other hand brushes tendrils of hair from my face. I lean into him, grateful for his strength. The weight of the still new day presses down on me like a barbell, and we haven't even sat down to lunch yet.

I'm not sure how we arrive at my room door through the labyrinth or corridors, but I recognize the guard outside from this morning. "Why did the guard stay at my door when he knew I wasn't in there?" I ask Jadis as soon as I notice. By the time we crossed into this hall, his arm had slipped from supporting my shoulders to wrapping around my waist.

"To make sure no one entered other than your maid. I told you I'd make sure you are safe," he says as I lean further into his strong torso. His voice sounds strained so I turn to get a peek at his face but I can't make out what it means. His face is pained, but a soft type of pain, almost concern maybe? His well-worn hand clenches the bronze door handle, its detailed etchings catching the light. As he shifts to open the door, I feel a sharp pang of pain in my side, one of my reminders of what Brandis had just done to me. I may have earned it...No, I definitely earned it. I acknowledge my part in it all, even if he went over the top.

The door closes with a soft click behind us, enclosing us in a sanctuary away from prying eyes. Those tears start to prick at the corners of my eyes again and I fight them, looking away from Jadis as he settles me into my chair. I thought he might push, but he moves away and pulls the ribbon on the wall.

Blood stains my shirt and Jadis frowns at me as he tears open the sleeves from wrist to shoulder. The sound of hurried footsteps echo through the outer hall, getting louder.

Tressa comes in a flurry of movement, her usually formal manner gone. Her dark eyes widen at the sight of me, and she claps a hand to her mouth. I must look pretty bad. She completely drops her professional air and speaks my name with genuine worry. I can't help but smile at the breach of protocol. Maybe I did make a friend.

"I'm alright, Tressa," I assure her, a weak smile the only attempt I can make to ease her concern. "It looks worse than I feel, I promise."

"Liar," Jadis whispers so quietly I have to read his lips to fully understand.

"But Jadis, fae can't lie, can we?" I whisper back, my hand surreptitiously covering my mouth.

"You're not full fae again now, are you?" He raises that single eyebrow while that infuriating dimple graces his cheek.

Tressa stands face-to-face with Jadis, her nostrils flaring and a fiery rage ignites in her gaze. I can practically see the flames in the reflection on their surface. She jabs the air between them with a long, thin finger as she speaks in a low growl. "And where were you? Hmm? Didn't you promise to keep her safe only a few hours ago and then the next time I see her, this is how she looks, all bruised and bloody?" Her voice rises several octaves as she gestures wildly toward the cowering figure of her friend. I'm in awe.

"Tressa, please, Jadis couldn't have predicted that Brandis would act this way when I opened my big mouth. He did the best he could—" I find myself defending him despite being so angry with him only hours ago.

"Brandis did this, hmm? Why does that not surprise me at all. And you very well could have predicted an outburst from him, and you just let him send giant splinters into her arms?"

"While we both understand Brandis' temper, Tressa, I didn't think him capable of losing so much control that he'd send his own sister flying ten feet across the room."

"Hmpf, then you're a fool." This harsh statement precedes her stomping out of the room.

"Where's she going?" I ask, bracing my hands on the arms of my chair to rise up and follow her.

"To fetch the healer I would imagine," Jadis tells me in a barely audible whisper. His eyes are intense, and his face etched with worry, regret, and sadness. As he steps closer, the air between us seems to crackle.

"Elora, I am sorry," he whispers, his voice barely above a breath. "I never wanted any of this to happen. I should have prepared you better for walking into that room with him. She's right. The first time my promise is tested, I let you down." He doesn't even look at me, or can't, his eyes firmly planted on the floor between us.

I tilt and dip my head to force his eyes to meet mine, the bright green dimmer, missing their usual spark of life. Forcing this makes my entire body hurt. "You couldn't have known that Brandis would react like that." I thought I made that clear defending him to Tressa. I couldn't avoid my frustration leaking out. "I'm tired of being treated like I'm clueless. I do have a PhD for crying out loud. I'm capable of critical thinking and problem solving, even with the little information I have. I may not have grown up here, but I'm part of it whether you like it or not. I deserve a little more respect than I received in that room today.

I've realized that despite the persona he likes to play, Jadis is a gentle giant. But maybe my intuition is way off. My gentle giant's voice is layered in a thick accent when he's upset like now. He crouches down in front of me. Those grass-green eyes are still shadowed with concern. "Ye do deserve more respect than you got in that room and yer brother knows it...deep down somewhere anyway. The words set him off an' he doesn't have much control over his temper. Seems to be a family trait." He finally lifts a brow at his own jab, bringing back a little of the Jadis I'm more familiar with. "But, if it gives ye any peace of mind, I think he thought for a moment there that he killed ye. Poor lad still looked shaken when I left."

His effort at levity fails miserably. I pull my lower lip between my teeth, trying desperately to hold my tongue, and fail. "Which words exactly set him off? The ones where I said I thought he was wrong? Or, the use of fucking? Does he not like it when "a lady" swears?"

He laughs at that. Actually laughs, and I don't find it funny at all and tell him so with a stark glare. "I don't think he even knows what fucking means, Elora. Yer brother knows about as much about the mortal realm as you do about this one. Nay, it was the bastard reference. He's a little sensitive about that word. There've been whispers for years that he's only yer half brother and therefore not the legitimate heir to the court seat. It's a touchy subject."

"Well, that's the understatement of the century." It does explain a lot though. I know nothing about him, but having that hanging over your head, true or not, can be debilitating. Maybe he's an ass because he feels he needs to rise above, make up for some kind of imposter syndrome. He goes over the top so no one suspects there may be a weakness hiding underneath it all.

The door's hinges screech as Margwin steps in, followed by Tressa who wrings her hands tightly in a knot and holds them close to her chest. Margwin's bright presence fills the room and I slump back against the chair, my tense muscles relaxing at last.

Margwin's proximity comes with a faint golden light emanating from her hands, like they're excited to get to work on me. Her voice is delicate despite her presence taking over the room, as she calls my name, her eyes aren't as calm, but filled with concern. "Elora," she says gently, and I get the impression it's nowhere near the first time she tried to get my attention. "It seems you had a bit of trouble with your brother?"

I extend my arms out revealing the punctures and cuts where the shattered chair sent slivers into my flesh and she tsks. I'm not sure it's at the wounds in my arms or the face I'm making.

"Well, before I can heal these, we have to remove the splinters. So, you'll take this tincture for the pain, and we'll get to work. Tressa, fetch some warm water and a rag from the washroom and a pair of strong tweezers if you please."

Tressa says nothing, just spirits away on her mission. She seems happy to be given something to do. It appears the walk to fetch Margwin settled her temper and now she can't meet Jadis' eyes.

"Jadis, I know this is not your typical task but perhaps our lady here could use a hot cup of tea to calm the nerves? Don't you think?"

He nods in response and turns to walk out the door.

"I hate when he hovers so. He's never done it before and it's driving my shoulders straight up through my ears." She says to me as she returns her attention back to the wounds on my arms. "So, lass, tell me what happened so I know what I'm dealing with."

I start firmly with, "I called Brandis a fucking bastard—"

She snorts, her fingers suddenly squeezing a little where they were feather light before. "In front of the entire council?"

"Yeah..." I say, sucking my upper lip into my mouth. I fill her in on his reaction and the bright light and how I flew backwards, along with my chair.

"I see." Margwin tuts under her breath, her fingers deftly checking my other arm before moving to the laces of my jerkin. She loosens them with practiced ease, lifting the hem of my shirt just enough to inspect my stomach. Whatever she's looking for, she must find it, because after a brief pause, she lets the leather and fabric fall back into place with a satisfied nod.

Tressa returns and Margwin hands me a blue glass bottle with a pale liquid inside. "Drink up. It works fast but doesn't last too long."

She holds the bottle to my lips and tilts the sweetness down my throat. It drips along my tongue like the honeyed clover nectar I used to suck out of the flower petals as a child. I didn't realize how much pain I'm in until it's gone, fading to a pale light at the end of a tunnel as my body relaxes further into the soft seat of my chair.

Margwin works quickly, taking a hold of my arm and examining the skin around the splinters. She starts pulling them out one by one, using tweezers to pluck the little pieces of wood from under my skin. Tressa stands nearby with a bowl of warm water and a cloth, ready to cleanse each surface as Margwin works. I watch in amazement as the raw skin seals itself together in seconds after each splinter has been removed, leaving nothing but a pale pink mark.

When they finish, Tressa works at cleaning up the mess and Margwin turns to me again. "Alright, shirt and jerkin off."

"Excuse me?" I'm completely taken aback. Not that I mind removing my clothes in front of her very scientific and work-focused demeanor, it's just how random and frank she says it.

She raises her brows at me, flipping her one hand around as if to say 'hurry up,' and I'm wasting her time. "You said you flew back into the wall. There's no chance that the impact didn't do any damage, so show me. Why did you think I sent Jadis from the room? Now, hurry up before he comes back."

The laces of the jerkin are loose but not enough for me to remove it entirely. My fingers fumble with the ties as Margwin stands nearby. The act of lifting the tough material over my head tells me she is precisely right. My back screams at me. It must be written all over my face as, when it came to the shirt, Margwin moves closer to help me lift it more forward over my head so I don't have to raise my arms again. I wrap my arms over my ample breasts. It doesn't cover much, but enough to give me some semblance of modesty. Good thing too because as Margwin lay the shirt on the adjacent table, the door opens quietly as a hand supporting a tray of cups and a tea pot is followed into the room by Jadis.

As he clears the door and gets an eyeful, I see his eyes fling wide just before my own follow the curve of the room as I turn, giving him my back, peeking over my shoulder at him. I can feel my cheeks flame.

He pauses, his mouth hanging open as if to say something, probably something smart ass. A sharp breath leaves his lips, and he mutters "Shite...Gods, Elora, I'm sorry" under his breath as he watches my back retreating away from him. His apology is almost inaudible.

I bite my lower lip and hug my arms tighter over myself, the heat only flaming hotter in my cheeks. "I covered myself...I mean we're both adults...it's not like you haven't seen a naked woman before, right?" I say, huffing out a nervous laugh as I risk another glance in his direction. I just as quickly avert my eyes to avoid contact with his.

I'm feet away from him, and I can feel his face heat up. His voice shakes as he stammers, "Nay...that wasn't...I mean....the bruises." He glances down at the floor while he speaks, also avoiding meeting my now turned eyes.

It's Margwin that answers my unspoken question since I have no idea what he's referencing. "Aye, she's right purple from neck to arse and it's still growing. Certainly painful, let's clear this up before it gets worse. I'd wager you're still bleeding on the inside. Damn mortals and their slow bodies."

I want to find answers, but I know there are none. I am somehow both fae and mortal, an impossibility that defies all logic. No matter how much I try to understand, my mind races with confusion. I have no choice but to stay quiet despite my swirling thoughts, unable to challenge her statement.

"The continued fever worries me though, the bags under your eyes. The fact that your body healed the burn, as superficial as it probably was, but not the internal bleeding from the impact concerns me. How's your head, dear?" She asks me directly, I assumed she was either talking to herself or Jadis.

It's Jadis who speaks first as I struggle to comprehend the question in order to answer. "Aye, I felt the heat through her clothes earlier."

"Before or after the incident with Brandis?" His comments apparently distract her from the fact that she asked me a question.

"Before. I felt it as we walked to the council chambers. There was a shake to her hands as well."

"My hands weren't shaking. What are you talking about?" I round on him with a glare, trying to remain composed even though my body is melting from the wave of heat radiating from Margwin's healing spell. I can feel it stretching down my spine and taking hold like a comforting embrace. My eyes flutter shut as a sound of contentment slips from my lips.

"Aye, they were. I noticed as you grabbed the handle on the door and then when you touched the one archway you admired on the way there."

I can feel the tightness as my brows furrow, as I try and make out the source of this shaking. Was it something I had done? But no, nothing comes to mind as I ruminate over the council meeting that had kept me so preoccupied. Yet still, my hands trembled again as if they are trying to tell me something I refuse to listen to.

"Aye, that worries me. I think we need to get your body back into shape and nourished before we let the change continue." Margwin says, taking a steps back.

"You want to stop the change?" Jadis' voice holds almost a plea. "She'll be more vulnerable than a newborn cub. A mortal can't survive here for long." A heavy silence hangs between them.

"Calm yourself, Jadis. Elora has some healing capabilities already. Stopping the change won't take away what's already started. Now, how's your head, dear?"

I turn to face Margwin and Tressa pops out of nowhere offering up a new, clean shirt. Making sure, with a glance over the one shoulder that Jadis isn't looking, I take the shirt and quickly drop it over my head. "I'm covered now, you can turn around," I say to him softly before answering her question. Jadis seems eager for me to answer the question as well. "Now that you ask, there has been a constant thrum behind my one eye all morning. I thought it was just the stress of it all."

"Is it the same or worse after the blast of magic?"

"Worse, actually."

She nods her head at that and makes her telltale tutting sound. "Sit here, enjoy your tea with Jadis and I'll be back with the potion to halt the change. Your body's not ready for it yet and the symptoms could get worse, deadly even."

"Yeah, as much as I've thought about my own death recently, we should probably not tempt fate too much." I sit down in the nearest chair. Well, more like flopped into the nearest chair. Jadis glares at me as he settles into the other and starts to pour out two cups of steaming tea. What the hell did I do now?

"You sure you want to give her that without consulting with Brandis first," he questions Margwin as he sets the pot back down a little harder than warranted.

She lifts her chin and looks me in the eyes, not him. Her voice is unwavering as she counters. "Not his body, not his choice." I can feel my own conviction hardening with a smile. Even without saying a word, I stand in agreement with her answer.

"Just checking. I know how much you hate tickling his bad side and he's not going to like the delay. I don't disagree with the decision mind you. It's your decision, Elora, as she says."

"Yeah. And I say let's stop it until Margwin thinks it's safe. Brandis has made it clear he doesn't care about my well-being. I think I've had enough change for a while anyway. It would make more sense to understand it more mentally before I have to deal with it physically."

"Then there's nothing more to say on it," Margwin says with a flourish as she strides across the room. She opens and closes the door with an echoing thud that reverberates around me. With wide eyes I watch her go before nestling in with my cup of tea, still warm with steam rising off the surface.

Chapter Twelve

"Ithoryn caelaril fion, thyrelis sylorin noril."

Wisdom lights the path, knowledge leads the way

E SIT QUIETLY, BOTH OF us completely captured by the subtle steam rising from our cups. The delicate aroma of chamomile and lavender waft through the air, calming the senses without having to actually take a sip. Each breath carries a note of honey and the smallest hint of citrus.

I use the silence to study my room further. So much happened over the last few hours that I never really took it in. It is a truly tranquil place, despite my constant nerves. The delicate floral patterns that cover the tapestries on the walls are complemented by soft pastel hues that infuse a sense of serenity. Sunlight gently filters through the sheer curtains, casting a warm glow over the space, while potted plants add a touch of life with their vibrant greenery.

The tea set is also exquisite with the elegant porcelain pot decorated with hand painted flowers. Jadis settles into his cozy armchair, cradling the small cup in his now overly large looking hands, a juxtaposition that brings a small smile to my lips. Those large hands settle around the tiny cup. I watch the tension leave the joints of his fingers until he brings the cup to his full lips, his green eyes staring at me over its fine edge.

He looks at me with a deep seriousness that is countered by his gentle demeanor. His face conveys both concern and empathy as he carefully chooses his next words. "You wanted to die?"

The question hangs in the air, an almost tangible weight, and it feels like he speaks slowly, cautiously, so as not to frighten me away, like a stray dog that has never felt human touch.

"It's not like I was intending to kill myself," I say, pausing to take a sip, collecting my thoughts into something more coherent. "I...I suppose I've been in survival mode for six years now and I'm just tired." My words hang in the air as he waits quietly for me to elaborate further.

I sigh. "I knew Carter wanted me dead. That's why I was hiding the location of my apartment, why I had different routes home, so I wasn't predictable. Why I decided to walk down the alley that night, hoping you were going to be outside like always." The last part makes me look to him pulling my lower lip into my mouth as I finish. For some reason I want him to understand that despite my animosity towards him, I still knew and know that he will protect me. As I speak, my voice grows smaller and more fragile with his silence. I can feel my throat getting tighter as a wave of conflicting emotions race through my tight chest.

"I ran out of energy to fight, you know? I was tired of always looking over my shoulder all the damn time. I guess I decided that if death wanted to take me, then I'd let it. I'd welcome it. I wouldn't put myself into a dangerous situation on purpose, but I wasn't going to work so hard to protect myself anymore. What was left to fight for?"

He glances at me with suspicion before giving a brief nod, his eyes lingering on mine for a moment longer than necessary before focusing back on his cup. I feel uneasy and wonder what thoughts are running through his mind.

I FEEL BETTER than I have in a while. The pain and the headaches left me shortly after I drank Margwin's potion. In the week since the council meeting, I hadn't seen hide nor hair of Brandis and things were looking up.

During one of our many morning conversations, Tressa mentioned that the Day Court manor held the second largest library in the realm, and I immediately decided that's where I would be spending my days for the foreseeable future. If there was one thing I was exceptionally good at, it was research.

What I didn't understand was how overwhelming that decision was going to become. Luckily, the library also held a lexicon for Fyrala Liorin'ae, the language of the realm that Tressa grabbed for me before I ever crossed the threshold.

The library of the Day Court, well former Day Court, stands truly as a testament to knowledge and enlightenment, or so I'm told with the translation of the ancient language over the doors. As I enter through the grand double doors, I'm immediately captivated by the sheer magnificence of the space. Towering walls, with more ornate carvings depicting scenes of nature and wisdom, stretch upwards toward the vaulted ceiling. The room is expansive, with three levels connected by multiple spiraling staircases of light polished oak.

Sunlight creeps in through the tall arched windows and streams down from above. The rays hit the floorboards like fingers that stretch across the expanse, illuminating it with a golden glow. Toward the middle of the room, where sunlight was able to stream in unimpeded, an almost palpable warmth settles over everything in its path. A gentle breeze stirs through the interior and brushes against my cheek. It carries the scents of the outdoors: warm grasses, flowers just blooming in their full glory, and the delicious fragrance left behind after a fresh rain.

Shelves upon shelves stretch from floor to ceiling, housing an extensive collection of ancient tomes, scrolls, and manuscripts. Each shelf is meticulously organized, showcasing the past knowledge contained within the library's walls. Leather bound books with gilded spines stand side by side, their titles a mosaic of languages and subjects, waiting to be explored.

The air carries the faint scent of aged parchment and ink as you move along the shelves, mingling with the stronger fragrance of the fresh flowers that sit on the tables and in alcoves. Small nooks tucked away in corners offer cozy reading spots, with plush armchairs and delicate wooden tables, inviting visitors to lose themselves in the knowledge contained in the pages around.

What can I say? I love books.

As I traipse up the spiraling staircases closest to the doors, I marvel at the intricate artwork on the walls. Elaborate murals depict scenes of what I call mythical creatures, ethereal landscapes, and what looks like might be fae scholars engaged in the never ending pursuit of knowledge. It's a visual tapestry that celebrates everything I believe in.

On the uppermost level, a magnificent stained glass window dominates the wall, casting colorful splotches of blues, greens, and golds on the floor. The window is of a majestic tree that towers over the landscape, its branches twisting and curling in a magical display of knots. Its roots burrow deep into the ground and extend like tendrils towards small animals playing in the leaves. A single sliver of golden light shines through its ancient trunk. Knot magic maybe? I'd have to ask Tressa if this counts.

In the past week, I have gathered an appreciation for the strong bond between nature and the fae. It's obvious in their buildings as well as their loyalties. This library is not only a depository of books but also a shrine to knowledge and a respect for the living things around them.

As I stand and stare at the bright colored tree in the window, one I feel the urge to visit regularly, surrounded by a gentle embrace of light and the whispering voices of countless stories, I know that this space is where I'm going to find answers and my path. That's if I can manage to tear my eyes away from this compelling window. It means something, deep down I know it's significant, but I can't get past the mere feeling into something more substantial.

THE HISTORY SECTION is the easiest to find—look for the dustiest, oldest looking tomes and there you have it. My claims about the council earlier are only further substantiated by the fact that it's obvious that these books have been ignored for quite some time. Tressa is going to have my head with how dirty my clothes get as I wipe my dusty palms over my legs.

With titles like "Chronicles of the Aelorin: A Comprehensive History of the Realm of Liorin'ae" and "The Everlasting Dance: A Saga of Aelorin Dynasties and Intrigue," I think I'm in for a rough afternoon.

The language is relatively simple. Jadis explained it rather simply. Most words favor the softer consonants and vowels that flow off the tongue easily. The harsher sounds are reserved for specific contexts, usually something negative. It follows English grammatical structure for the most part which makes it easier for me to translate, a little anyway, with subject-verb-object.

Opening the creaky leather cover to "Chronicles of the Aelorin" first, I'm surprised how similar their books are to ours. Considering my conversations with Tressa and how much the fae have actually been involved in my world, maybe I shouldn't be. It's probably the fae that taught humans how to write books 'properly'.

Whether that's the case or not, it's easier to follow because it's familiar. What does surprise me is that the book is written by what seems to be a rather famous fae historian. If they have historians that are held in such high regard, then why do they ignore the past so much? Little did I know that the answers to that question are contained in the first few pages.

The "Chronicles of the Aelorin" covers the myths and legends that surround the birth of the fae that allow them to trace their lineages back to the primordial forces of nature. At first it seems like it will give me a meticulous history with an account of their evolution and societal structures. The concept that they left no aspect of fae history untouched isn't entirely true though. The pre-court history is glazed over with only a few brief words before moving into the now fallen court system. It's like either they don't want to remember what came before, or, they no longer know.

In the ethereal dawn of time, when the cosmos breathed life into existence, the first fae beings emerged, shimmering with otherworldly grace. Born from the essence of nature itself, they embodied the boundless magic that coursed through the veins of the world.

It sounds to me like they lost some power over the years. Fae hold magic, but is it really that strong and linked to the world around them? You wouldn't think they would struggle so against someone like Carter if they were intrinsically linked to nature and the world around them. Perhaps trying to manipulate for more power means they lost the natural gifts they were given?

As ages passed, the fae flourished and crafted magnificent civilizations that spanned across these enchanted lands. However, the passage of time witnessed the rise and fall of these ancient civilizations. Wars and conflicts reshaped the fae realm and created the unified court system.

And that's all I get in regard to the pre-court history in this book. Not that the court system information isn't helpful, but I want to know what came before. It sounds like what came before was around significantly longer than the fallen courts.

From the radiant splendor of the Day Court, where golden rays dance upon the emerald meadows, to the enigmatic depths of the Shadow Court, where twilight whispers secrets, each court boasts its unique beauty and enchantments.

The Court of Thaw, a realm of blossoming petals and vibrant hues, blooms with eternal youth and the promise of renewal. Meanwhile, the Court of Bloom exudes warmth and vitality, its majestic halls resonating with the symphony of laughter and celebration.

As the seasons turn, Court of Flame takes its place, adorned in rich tapestries of amber and crimson, where wisdom and melancholy coalesce in perfect harmony. The Court of Frost, nestled in the realms of eternal ice and snow, hold an ethereal charm, its inhabitants adorned in glistening crystals and delicate frost-lace.

And in the first light of dawn, the Dawn Court revels in the delicate balance between night and day, representing the eternal cycle of beginnings and endings.

However, the passage of time witnesses the rise and fall of these ancient courts. The court system that was once an emblem of unity, begins to crumble. The courts, now fragmented and fractured, struggle to maintain their former glory.

The Day Court, once a beacon of wisdom and enlightenment, now yearns for its former brilliance restored. The Shadow Court, cloaked in intrigue and mystery, holds secrets that are only now whispered in the shadows. The Courts of Thaw and Bloom, once vibrant and resplendent, face the weight of faded glory. The Court of Flame, is filled with nostalgia and faded memories, longing for the days of old. The Court of Frost, its icy majesty thawing, mourns the loss of its frozen realms. And the Dawn Court, caught between light and darkness, fights to regain its delicate balance.

Such is the tale of the courts of the Aelorin, a story of their majestic past and the challenges they face in the present. Their destinies interwoven with the very fabric of the realm of Liorin'ae, they stand as an example of the ebb and flow of time, and the enduring spirit of the fae.

Fae historians sure do wax poetic...But this is how most of the thick volume continues; waxing poetic on the loveliness of the courts and more details about how they worked and what their gifts were. How the seven courts of the Aelorin each held power in a different way and how their natural inhabitants each thrived on power that resembled the same. There is very little other than the mention of war and fracturing in regard to why the courts fell in the first place.

The "Everlasting Dance" proves far more useful in that regard. Still nothing to enlighten me on what existed before the courts, but much more on how the courts worked, or rather didn't in the end. Boringly detailed on fae dynasties, including my own, it also deals with the courtly intrigue, power struggles, and secrets that fueled or collapsed ambitions.

The Day Court, where I am now, was apparently once the seat of power and that's why the council meetings are still held here, I assume. Tradition and all. The real families of the Day Court "basking in the warmth of sunlight" commanded both respect and adoration and that's why we, they, became a target. I don't see Brandis ever being respected and adored...feared maybe.

The Shadow Court was always something of a mystery. In times of trouble, any historian knows that the things we don't understand often become misunderstood and I think that's the case here. The Shadow Court became known as a den for covert alliances and whispers of betrayals.

The Court of Bloom reminds me of the typical college campus; a realm of lively celebrations and tempestuous passions. Their festivals were well known for debauchery in the "most natural of senses." Whatever that means. I bet it's something Jadis understands all too well.

The nobles of the Court of Thaw exhibited the natural cycles of growth and renewal with their aspirations and desires. Which I'm not sure how to translate, if it does. Maybe I translated it wrong or there's some idioms that I simply don't understand in their literal wording.

The Dawn Court, or also Court of Dawn, always aligned themselves with Day and Shadow, dancing along the precipice and interplay of twilight and dawn. Loyalties were easily torn but their destinies always equally intertwined. It sounds an awful lot like typical sibling rivalries where you love them and hate them at the same time.

Eventually all the betrayals and intrigue, or I get the impression, the simple threat of betrayal, eroded away the foundation of this system and led to its downfall. Which, from my previous research is highly plausible. The threat of doom is often more damaging to a society than the disaster itself. Actual disasters tend to bring people together, threats of potential disaster push people to othering, conflict, and violence.

Acts of treachery and manipulation, fueled by personal ambitions and longstanding grudges, became like cracks in the foundation of the once unified courts. At the heart of the unraveling lay a web of complicit alliances and power struggles among the noble houses. Fae houses, driven by their thirst for influence and control, engaged in secret plots and covert machinations to undermine their rivals. They sought to weaken the standing of opposing courts, undermining their authority and sowing seeds of discord not only within their noble ranks, but with what they referred to as the under fae. I haven't tracked down exactly who that group of people are.

Among the fae, betrayal takes many forms. Ambitious courtiers use their charm and charisma to sway loyalties, pitting court against court, manipulating key figures, and spreading information that fuels particular and beneficial consequences. Marriage alliances, that were once seen as a means of strengthening ties, became tools for treachery too. Hidden agendas and ulterior motives poisoned the unity of the courts.

It's a complex and not completely understandable situation to follow. Intrigue thrived within and between the courts as these hidden alliances were forged and then shattered. Secrets were whispered in the darkened corners as the radiance of the sun began to fade, hidden agendas were quickly set into motion. Lies began, and from what Tressa has told me, that's a dangerous line to walk. But, half-truths or what I believe is referred to as minced words, became the norm rather than the outright truth. Minced words and half-truths were the new currency of power, as the nobles sought to gain advantages over their rivals, even at the cost of jeopardizing the very fabric of the fae realm.

It literally damaged nature and the balance of power. The disintegration of the court system was a slow and painful process, fueled by these seeds of an unbalanced way of life that had been sown over generations. The once glorious courts lost their luster, and the realm found itself fractured and vulnerable. The fae are so intrinsically linked with nature, their troubles caused ripples.

The walls of the Day Court, that once were home to golden sunlight now had deceit casting shadows that stretch and take hold. The Court of Bloom lost its radiant glow and is now marred with conspiracies and shattered loyalties that bring cold to the hearts of the people. The Court of Thaw no longer held the secret to eternal youth and bore witness to the decay of trust in a physical way. The darkness seeped into the very roots of the land. People started to age, slowly, but much more than history had ever known. The Court of Flame found itself ensnared and happiness disappeared, replaced by mistrust, desires for solitude, and depression.

Other courts suffered even more. The chill of the Court of Frost disappeared despite the cold currents of betrayal. The once-illuminating Dawn Court, lost the balance they delicately maintained between night and day, shifting the hours out of balance and disrupting the growing seasons across the entire kingdom.

It's disturbing actually and I can see why they're so hopeful that I will return to the court system and fix it, but I have no idea how. The only hope for the people came via a prophecy, one that no one knows the origins of. Here's where I get excited, for no reason. I sit on the edge of my seat as I turn the last page, waiting for my job to finally be revealed to me. The air catches in my throat, something lodged there keeping anything from passing.

> *The prophecy of the Deliverer, whispered in hushed tones among the Aelorin, speaks of an enigmatic figure destined to emerge from the shadows. Foretold in ancient verses and veiled in cryptic symbolism, the prophecy alludes to a time of great upheaval and transformation in the realm of Fyrala Liorin'ae.*
>
> *The words of the prophecy speak of a chosen one, a beacon of hope, whose arrival shall herald a new era. They hint at a convergence of forces, where the fate of the Aelorin hangs in the balance. It is said that this fated individual shall possess the power to bridge the realms, to bring harmony where discord reigns and restore equilibrium to the troubled lands.*

And the next page is blank.

"What the fuck?" I exclaim, I thought to myself.

"Elora?" Comes a male voice that I have been trying very hard to avoid.

Chapter Thirteen

"*Vaelinae thalna syloriniel vaelrin sylorin naelith.*"

Peace flows like a breeze where knots are undone

BRANDIS STANDS A FEW FEET away, a small book in one hand, both of which are lifted up in a defensive stance. The look on my face must be venomous since he instantly takes this position.

My heart races as I see him, and for a moment I'm not sure if I should be angry or glad. He's been avoiding me ever since the council meeting, and while part of me is secretly relieved that he hasn't confronted me with his thoughts, another part of me still resents him for it.

"Elora," he says again. "Is everything alright?"

His shoulders, once squared with that arrogant confidence, seem slouched, maybe burdened by the weight of his own mistakes? The lines etched in his face, usually firm and resolute, now appear softened, revealing some of his wariness that I'd never witnessed before, something that goes beyond physical exhaustion.

In his pale blue eyes, I glimpse a flicker of uncertainty, a hint of regret. The fire that I had seen burn fiercely within them is dimmed, replaced by something closer to a flickering and dying ember.

Gone was that commanding presence that demanded respect and obedience. Instead, there stood a male who, for a fleeting moment, allows himself to be stripped of titles and responsibilities that weigh on him. In this vulnerable state, I find it easier to perhaps empathize with him, foolish me, and the walls that I built to shield myself, preparing for when I saw him again, begin to crumble. A glimmer of the compassion I normally show others shines through. Though still cautious, I allow myself to hope that, perhaps, a brother still resides inside that usually hard facade.

"It just stops." I turn back to the offending book on the table in front of me. It still sits on top of my scattered sheets of paper covered in my scribbled translations. I gesture with my hands at the betrayal of this manuscript and the blank page in front of me.

He approaches the table with caution, his movements calculated, and I can feel his stare the entire time as he leans in to see what I'm reading. "Ahh, yes. The prophecy. There's not much else to write I'm afraid. No one knows exactly what the prophecy stated. You understand these texts? They're all in Fyrala Liorin'ae. I didn't think you spoke our language, anymore. Has it come back to you?"

"Uh, no. Tressa found me a lexicon. This has taken me forever because I'm translating as I go. I've been in here for over a week." The little tidbit on the prophecy wasn't lost on me and was shocking to say the least. I whip my face to him, and he jumps back in response. "What do you mean no one knows? How the hell did I become the 'Deliverer' then and get sent off to the human realm to raise myself?" I snap. "I had a target placed on my back over a few vague words that no one understands? I'm supposed to give over my life, my freedom for that?"

"I should rephrase," he says backing up into his defensive position again. "The one person that knew the prophecy and risked his life to get it to our parents is indeed dead. No one left alive knows the actual prophecy, to my knowledge."

"How convenient. How the hell am I supposed to know what to do then?" I ask this more of myself than my brother.

"If I can be frank?" He asks this and I give him a quick nod to encourage him to continue. "I would just be myself. If it's your destiny as our parents thought, then everything you do and decide will line up with what's needed."

"And yet, you still argued with my statement and stance at the council meeting. A little hypocritical don't you think?"

He steps closer, looking sheepish, and shifts his weight from foot to foot like a child who got caught stealing a cookie. "Elora," he says staring at his shoes, lifting a hand as if to reach out but stopping short. "I am sorry. I want to say sorry. Much as this is all a shock to you, it's hard for me as well. I was raised with the impression that everything was arranged, and you would return and immediately step into your role. I have a lot on my own plate and you coming back, as you did, disrupted everything. That's no excuse, but I am sorry for what happened before. This isn't easy for me either. It was wrong of me, and I knew it then. But I thought you didn't want to see me so...I stayed away. Until now, anyway, when you seemed upset. Which is why I said something at all...I let my own frustrations get the better of me. Please, forgive me?"

I regard him with a mix of surprise but also curiosity, my mouth is definitely hanging open in shock. Out of everything I expected from him, an apology wasn't even on the list. Especially one where he takes accountability. He didn't seem the type. All the questions I have been wondering about in the past days jostle their way to the forefront of my mind, and what spills out instead are the words, "Are you a bastard?"

His answer is instant; incredulous eyes staring back at me, lips open but no sound escaping. He shakes his head slowly, I thought as an answer, but then he closes his eyes, a slight nod of the head confirming the real answer, "Yes."

I can't believe what I'm hearing. His words are direct, so unguarded and raw—it's a side of him that I've never seen before, not that there has been much time to. I expect to have to read between the lines to decipher his meaning, but he is open and honest with me. This new honesty stirs up feelings inside me that I'm not sure how to handle.

"You seem shocked," he says when I don't respond and sit there with my mouth hanging open, the slow and steady breaths drying out the tip of my tongue.

"Not about the bastard part," I finally say. "But the part where you simply told me the truth...because fae can't lie."

"It's not that we can't lie, but the act of lying comes with a serious, often deadly magical consequence, but I can easily stretch the truth. I won't deny it or pretend otherwise with you, Elora. I am the bastard child of our mother, Lady of the Day Court. She was in love before she was betrothed to your father, the Lord of the Day Court. I was already on my way, so to speak, shortly before our parents were married. They still met and fell madly in love, despite her myanir, her...mate in another realm."

"Why?" I ask.

"Why, what? Why did our mother have a tryst?" he says, the confusion evident in the lines of his face.

"No, that all makes sense. Why tell me the truth?" I lean more comfortably into my chair, setting a relaxed elbow on the arm opposite where my brother stands.

"Oh...um...I...I desire to start over with you, myriel tharin, uh dear sister. My apologies but my mortal tongue is a little unused. We didn't get off on the right foot, I believe Jadis said this is a phrase from the human realm? I want to build a bridge between us, we're the only family we have left, if we can. We have both found ourselves in positions we never asked for, and I want to try and start over, if you'll let me."

"So, Jadis helped you with your apology?"

"A little, yes. Do you find that offensive?"

"No, not really. Just a surprise."

As the silence settles between us, he shifts the topic, gesturing with his hands to the tome on the table that I've already finished. "Poetry, isn't it? More than history, really."

A soft laugh actually escapes my chest, the tension easing between us. "Indeed, it is. Though I find beauty in the words, and the language, I crave something more substantial. I was hoping this one would give me that, but alas, I'm again disappointed and have wasted days translating almost nothing."

"Because of the only brief mention of the prophecy?" He settles in with this question, leaning a hip against the table. I tense, wanting to move further away, but resist.

"Yes and no, not really. While I would like to know why exactly everyone thinks I'm this Deliverer and what I'm supposed to do, I came here looking for information on what existed before the seven courts. I want to know what lies beyond the courts' time in history."

"A little poetic yourself, I see," he teases with a raised eyebrow. A moment later he moves to the adjacent shelves, scanning along with a single fingertip before plucking a worn volume from its place. Before handing it to me, he's kind enough to blow off the dust, the cloud settling in the beams of warm sunlight filtering in from the windows above. "Perhaps 'The Fading Veil' will offer some insight. It contains the most comprehensive account of that time, or what little remains of that information. There isn't much written, or perhaps, what was once there, has been intentionally obscured or destroyed," he adds with a shrug of the shoulders.

I accept the book with a mixture of anticipation and gratitude. It's a small step, this gesture of sharing knowledge, but it speaks volumes about his willingness to actually help me instead of control me. That feeling is only substantiated when he offers to sit with me and translate the passages while answering any of my questions. In that moment, I realize that perhaps, just perhaps, there is a chance for a new beginning between us. A flickering hope of understanding.

BRANDIS SPENT THE rest of the afternoon reading by my side as I absorb the little information housed in "The Fading Veil." There aren't many questions to ask him, but he stays, nonetheless. What questions I do ask, he doesn't have many answers to. It's not even something they learn growing up. No one really cares what existed before the seven courts.

Most of what the book reveals is ambiguous. The ancient fae lived in harmony with the natural elements that shaped their existence and blah, blah, blah. Very immature of me, but it is what it is. The book hints at a primordial realm, untouched by the intricate politics and divisions that would later define the seven courts.

This early realm was a time when the boundaries between the realms were more fluid and that might be an important fact, if Brandis or myself knew exactly what that meant. The supposition is that the fae could move between the realms with relative ease, whereas now, only a handful of fae had the gift to open a portal, or thalorin. Not to be confused with the caelorin, or portals between realms. No one can open new caelorin as far as Brandis knows. At least here, he doesn't know about over the wall, which is a subject that's intriguing but outside of my current purview. Thalorin are those like Margwin opened in the forest that led right to my room, a location within the realm. Margwin would be apparently known as a thalor'ai, i.e., someone that can open a portal. A unique gift, especially since she already has the gift of healing.

It did say that the fae of old lived in harmony with the land. Their magic was intertwined with the flora and fauna that flourished around them. Each people lived exactly where they were meant to. So, it makes sense that if people moved and the realm was diminishing, then so would their magic. The old era was one of profound connection with nature where the fae reveled in the 'wonders of the wilderness' and drew strength from the pulsing energies of the world. Even I can enjoy a good prose, but the nature of these texts, with all the poetic words, is really starting to get on my nerves. Brandis gets a good chuckle out of this.

Asshole.

As I turn the pages, the wording grows vaguer but still expresses a sense of melancholy. I wonder if it was written by someone of the future Court of Flame, but Brandis has no idea, however, he's impressed with my studies thus far anyway.

The tiny book hints at a cataclysmic event and the gradual emergence of discord within the fae realm. It alludes to ancient conflicts and rifts that shattered the unity and led to the subsequent establishment of the seven courts. However, the details are still vague, lost in time or perhaps conflict where they were intentionally obscured to maintain the status quo?

With a headache firmly pulsing behind my eyes, I bid Brandis a good evening and retire to my room to try and absorb everything I learned today, more about Brandis than anything in those books. I need to take a moment and plan my next afternoon of reading.

I CONTINUE MY research campaign despite the growing frustrations of the same information reworded in more flagrant prose or something absolutely terrible on the eyes. I've put in a lot of hard work and feel only slightly more prepared when Brandis invites, yes invites, me to attend another council meeting.

In the serene confines of my chambers, not room, as I have been informed they're called, Tressa and I continue our age old conversation of what I should wear. More like argument as the gentle rustle of fabric punctuates our words with her shuffling around through my choices for today and lays them on the bed. The hidden wardrobe looms before me, a thorn in my side.

After weeks here, I now know where the door is, hidden in the patterns of the wall. I open it, the soft creak filters through the air, unveiling a literal treasure trove of garments. The shelves are lined with neatly folded things, each chastising me about fae history and tradition.

The faint sunlight trickles through the nearby windows as it peeks around this side of the building, casting a warm glow on the rows of dresses and robes. The manor and surrounding town are called Rythianeth, literally meaning house of the sun. It fits, I suppose.

The closet smells of lavender and moss. An interesting mix but fitting I guess with how intrinsically the fae and nature are, or are supposed to be. The wardrobe seems to extend endlessly, offering an array of colors and textures that normally would capture the senses. I find it entirely overwhelming.

Silken gowns brush over my fingers with hues of emerald, sapphire, and amethyst. If I were to wax poetic like all the books I've been reading, I would describe them as ethereal, their presence reminiscent of moonlit dances and enchanted groves. Maybe I should spend a little less time in the library...

Delicate lace embellishments trace across the bodices, resembling detailed webs. Tressa tells me the lace is spun by an elite and elusive class of weavers who are only rivaled by the virtually extinct weavers of the formal Court of Frost.

On the opposite end, robes of crimson, golden yellows, and earthy greens hang with regal elegance. Embroidered with shimmering threads, they illustrate scenes of blooming flowers, swirling leaves, and suns, each garment capturing the essence of the former Day Court. I have yet to be asked to wear one of those, as they're reserved for public court appearances that don't happen anymore.

As Tressa joins me, I sift through the assortment, the touch of each fabric speaks volumes and I try to find one that sends the message I want to send to Brandis: peace. But, I still want to stick with my principles of comfort and human-raised. Some are as light as a whisper, graceful and delicate, not my personality at all. Others possess a weightiness that conveys more strength and regality.

"You know, milady," Tressa says, her voice soft with reflection as she grasps the edge of one of the weightier dresses, "the tradition of wearing dresses among the high aelorin, especially during formal occasions, has deep roots in our history that you seem so fascinated with. It symbolizes grace, femininity, and a connection to our ethereal nature. The flowing lines of a gown evoke a sense of elegance and nature, a reflection of the innate beauty of our people."

I do listen intently. I appreciate her insights into the culture here, but I can't help but focus on that single word again, ethereal. A word that can't and has never been used to describe me. I never considered myself ugly, only average. The trials and tribulations of my life shaped me literally into the woman I am today. The scars, both physical and emotional, litter my body with a raw authenticity, but of what? I'd carried and birthed a child, experienced the joys and pains of motherhood for a decade, and came out transformed by the passage of time for sure.

In the human world, the concept of ethereal beauty often carries different connotations. It seems to more represent an otherworldly allure, a delicate and untouched elegance that I feel no connection to whatsoever. My body was once referred to as voluptuous, a word that most use to be kinder than saying chubby in womanly places. These curves have worn down over time with trauma and the simple life I led that borderline self-neglect. I let the trials and sacrifices rule me and it showed. Some of the curves have returned in these last few weeks, but not enough to even try and refer to myself as ethereal.

"Where did you go just now?" Tressa asks this of me quietly, breaking through the thoughts passing quickly through my mind with her usual gentleness.

"Oh..." That's all I can say at first. I pause, wondering if I should share any of these personal things, these deep seated opinions that maybe tell too much about who I am and what I've become. In the end, Tressa is supposed to be my friend and perhaps it's time to let go a little and reach out. "You mention the aelorin being ethereal and it's mentioned hundreds of times in those history books I've been reading. That's the furthest thing from who and what I am, despite you insisting I'm high aelorin. I suppose I was stuck in a mental analysis of how far I am from ethereal." I end this with a swift gesture along my not ethereal body.

"Well, beyond the fact that you're a beautiful female and have nothing to worry about in that department, ethereal has nothing to do with your physical appearance. Ethereal simply means there's a connection to the natural world and the magical energies that flow through your veins. It's more of an inner glow. Our ethereal nature is a reflection of our deep bond with the world around us, it's our expression of our....divine inheritance, I suppose. The only connection with physical beauty is the inner radiance that emanates from the core of your being, and I see that even if you don't. It's a luminosity that transcends mere mortal understanding, so I can understand your confusion."

"And what does all that have to do with dresses?" I can't help being a little condescending. This all still seems so farfetched to me.

"It's fascinating to me, how our attire carries meaning. Clothing is so much more than mere fashion. The high aelorin dresses embody the very essence of our courts, showcasing the harmony between nature and fae magic, the connection that makes us ethereal."

While she starts off strong and confident, the light in her eyes fade as she speaks, her posture falling slightly as she leans more against the open door behind her. "Well, what it used to be anyway."

"I hate dresses."

"I know, you've said so, many times." She sighs. Tressa crosses her delicate arms over her chest. I think I catch the faint quiver of a toe trying to tap at the floor, too.

"But...Brandis has extended an olive branch, so I suppose I should do the same."

Her rapid snap in posture shows her excitement at my statement but her scrunched facial expression tells me she's suspicious. "What does a branch of olives have to do with wearing a dress or not?"

Sometimes I forget how different our upbringings are. Our conversations come so easily now, it's hard to remember that we are from different worlds, she and I. My idioms, while second nature to me, are as foreign to her as court etiquette is to me.

Taking a deep breath, I begin to convey the meaning in a way that she might understand. "In the human realm," I start, my voice gentle yet earnest, "we have a saying. When someone wants to make amends or show a gesture of peace and reconciliation, we say they are 'extending an olive branch.'"

Her eyes widen a little, a curious glimmer to them. "An olive branch? Why a branch of olives?"

"Yes, well it's historical and religious really. The Christian Bible tells a story about a great flood and a dove brings an olive branch to the man who saved all the animals of earth on a boat. The branch signaled that it was safe for them to disembark, that land was uncovered again. And then the ancient Romans and Greeks used olive branches to signal during battle, usually when they had been defeated, that they wanted peace."

"All the animals of the mortal realm fit on one boat? Mortals do not possess magic, what kind of magic is that? Who's magic?"

"That's not the main point," I laugh. "The point is that an olive branch became symbolic over time." It's hard searching for the right words to paint a more vivid picture in her mind. "In human tradition, an olive branch has become a symbol of peace. It is said that in ancient times, when conflicts arose between warring factions, a representative from one side would carry an olive branch as a sign of goodwill, a gesture to begin negotiations and find common ground. Oh! Almost like your knot magic."

Tressa nods, deep in thought. "So, extending an olive branch means offering peace and a chance for harmony? I think we need more branches of olives here." She cracks the joke and we both huff out a short laugh. It's funny, but at the same time, I know this land has been cut by war and conflict for quite some time.

I did smile, relieved that she grasps the concept rather quickly. "Exactly, Tressa. It means reaching out to someone, putting aside differences or past grievances, and offering a hand in friendship or reconciliation. It's a way of saying, "Let's start anew. Let's find a way to bridge our differences and come together.""

Her features soften, a glimmer of appreciation shines in her eyes. "That sounds like a beautiful tradition, Elora. I can see why it holds significance for you. Plus, olives are tasty."

"You're right, it is, I hadn't thought about it much. It's just something we say without thinking about the concept." A wistful smile tugs at my lips as I think about it. "And maybe, extending an olive branch to Brandis means I can open doors to a new chapter in our relationship, where understanding can maybe flourish a little more. I don't trust him yet, I can't. I won't put myself in that position again, but I need to at least try. To give him a chance."

Tressa nods. Her support is most welcome, evident in the way she gently squeezes my hand. "I believe it is worth a try. May this olive branch bear the fruits of reconciliation and unity."

She turns to shuffle through the wardrobe once more with haste, her words muffled. "Perhaps, in this case, we can find your branch of olives where you don't have to completely give up your convictions. A dress that captures your intent and the essence of high aelorin attire while still allowing for the practicality and freedom you cherish so much."

I can't help but shake my head and hope she's not looking for something with a literal branch of olives. We look together, exploring the myriad of options available. As we sift through the delicate fabrics and designs, Tressa's eyes land on a stunning riding dress, it's silhouette a perfect blend of elegance and practicality.

"Milady....uh, Elora, look at this one." She holds up the riding dress I'd already seen. "It possesses the flowing elegance of a standard high aelorin dress, but with a structure that allows for ease of movement. The trousers beneath resemble the full skirts of a gown creating a fusion of both styles." Her excitement is written all over her face. "Why did I not think of this before?"

The fabric is resplendent with a delicate pattern of intertwining vines and flowers, as always. The rich golden hues mirrored the vibrant colors associated with the former Day Court. "It's practically perfect." My voice is surprisingly filled with admiration...for a dress. "This is more me, while still showing my desire for change. It's a nice symbol of who I am and who I'm trying to become, or at least maybe willing to become."

She helps me slip into the dress as we've already wasted too much time if I'm going to make it to this meeting. I'm marveled at how it embraces my changing form, accentuating my figure while granting me the freedom to move. The soft fabric caresses my skin like the gentle touch of a lover.

With a final adjustment to the masses of lacing in the back, Tressa takes a step back, her eyes filled with a pride I haven't seen before. "You look absolutely radiant, milady. This dress is most definitely your branch of olives. It's harmony personified on you. If I may say, I think it also represents the strength inside you."

A gentle knock interrupts our moment, followed by Jadis' voice. "Lady Elora," he says, so formal. "If you're ready, I'm here to escort you to the council meeting once again."

I blow out a breath through pursed lips. This is the moment, my moment, the chance to prove myself and show who I am. A chance to bridge the gap between me and my only family. It's strange that I even want a relationship with him after last time.

Tressa lets Jadis into the room. As I step forward, Jadis' gaze takes a sweeping look at my flowing outfit, a genuine smile lighting up his features. "*Thael aelith naelithor ilthor caelar.*" He forgets himself and I have no idea what he says but it sounds pretty, and he follows it with a warm kiss to the knuckles of my right hand. Those pretty words, whatever they mean, and that small gesture shouldn't have started the warm tingles down to my toes, but it did and that is entirely unnerving. "You've chosen well today. I'm gathering you want to continue to please Brandis then? It's a nice compromise, if I may say so."

I nod. That's all I can manage without revealing what he's done to me. With Jadis by my side, we make for the council chambers. I catch several side glances from him, his gaze approving, not that I need nor want his approval, but it's certainly a boost to the self-esteem.

With every step, the riding dress embraces me like a second skin, proof of my own evolution. I am no longer the lost human girl thrust into a realm of mystery. I am prepared, I am knowledgeable, and I am Elora, the Deliverer and walking the path of my choosing.

Who am I kidding? I'm not ready to let a few mysterious words determine my future at all.

Chapter Fourteen

"Vaelithil lorynor, vyrith myrran thalna."

Frost whispers, but fire breaks the earth

GET TO SIT BESIDE Jadis again. This time, Brandis sits to my right. We are all seated closer to that subtle head of the table, a seat that Brandis has surprisingly left empty. He smiles at me when I enter this time, instead of putting on his best frown and sneer. That's progress on its own, because that was before he looked at what I am wearing. When I went to sit, it is Brandis that pulls out my chair instead of Jadis, catching him off guard as well.

"What happened in that library?" Jadis whispers into my ear and I shrug.

As the council meeting progresses, the air is thick with discussions on repetitive matters, ranging from minor conflicts between the neighboring courts to pressing trade agreements. The aelorin leaders sit around the oval table, more of them this time, each wearing their distinctive regalia and emanating an intimidating aura of authority. They easily make me feel well out of my league.

To my left, on Jadis' other side, sits Lord Aric, the dignified leader of the fallen Dawn Court, his golden red hair shimmers like the dawn he should be representing. His eyes hold a steady gaze, and his presence seeps warmth, surprisingly. I'm not sure what else I feel—vitality maybe. He speaks with a measured tone, his words carrying the weight of wisdom and experience, despite his youthful appearance. It's the eyes, I think. Within the eyes something is aged while the body is ageless.

Across from me, Lady Sylphine, the inscrutable ruler of the Shadow Court, who didn't appear at the last meeting (well, apparently hasn't appeared at any meeting previously) commands the attention with that ethereal beauty and her cascading midnight hair. I see that inner light Tressa mentioned earlier. Her eyes are deep and seem to conceal a multitude of secrets, and her voice is like a haunting melody, weaving through the air as she talks about the conflict plaguing her people.

Beside her sits Lord Caelan, the regal leader of the Court of Bloom, who exudes energy. His honey mane and blue eyes mirror the intensity of the summer sun, and his every gesture shows confidence and strength. With all of this, he's incredibly soft spoken. He looks vaguely familiar, and I can't place why. It's not because he spoke at the last meeting either. A whispered conversation with Jadis verifies that we have never met before, formally anyway. Caelan is most passionate about his court's affairs, particularly the fertility of the land and the lack of bountiful harvests that are needed to sustain his people.

Next to Lord Caelan sits Lady Eira, the serene ruler of the Court of Thaw. She is the spitting image of that renewal and growth I read about. Her emerald green attire mirrors that lush green growth of the season I know as spring, the season she should preside over. Her gentle voice carries a soothing quality. She speaks of the delicate balance between nature and civilizations that is obviously disrupted all over the realm. She wants harmony returned.

On the opposite side of the table, Lord Asher of the Court of Flame. The sad male is in deep contrast to his russet colored robes and his warm, chocolate brown hair. He actually personifies autumn. His penetrating gaze catches me and seems to hold a thousand tales and I take note. He talks of balance, rather than his own court, emphasizing the importance of regaining control of the realm and reinstating the equilibrium the courts provided. Light and dark need to work in tandem again.

Next to him is another new face: Lady Vetle, the formidable ruler of the Court of Frost. I would think you'd have to be formidable to rule over a realm that's always encased with ice and snow, or at least it was. Even her gaze is icy. Her pale complexion and piercing blue eyes mirror the frost-kissed place she governs, and her voice even feels chilly. She speaks of standing strong, together, in the face of adversity. Seems reasonable since her court faces the harshest of environments and thrives, or they used to anyway. That seems to be the theme of late, what used to be.

Last at the table today is my dear brother, Brandis, who I honestly haven't paid much attention to, physically anyway. The always broody leader of the Day Court, former. None of these leaders rule a formal court anymore, but a remnant of one. They do their best for the people and land that remain. That's what I'm told. Brandis' almost silver hair cascades down his back and his stormy eyes hold a complex mix of authority, with that new underlying vulnerability I first noticed in the library. I wonder if anyone else sees it? He commands the respect of his peers, but that can also be fear for all I know. His presence is a constant reminder of the unyielding strength he possesses but today it settles under a more reserved demeanor.

As the discussions weave throughout the chamber, Lord Asher makes mention of the under fae or lesser fae he calls them. Curiosity sparks within me and I apparently have lost all control of my tongue. It seems to be a permanent affliction. At least my manners remain intact because my hand excitedly shoots into the air before I can stop it. All eyes turn toward me.

"Forgive my interruption..." My voice is surprisingly steady under so many sets of unusual eyes that point to me. But points to me for maintaining professionalism and decorum. "But can someone enlighten me on the nature and role of the under fae? My studies have yielded very little information on their existence."

I'm answered with silence as these leaders exchange knowing glances. Lord Aric eventually leans forward, his reddish-hazel eyes fix on me narrowing slightly, the subtle tension hinting at both curiosity and restraint, like a predator unsure whether to pounce or retreat.

"The under fae," he finally speaks with an obvious air of contempt at their name, "are of no consequence and thus do not get pages in important books. They dwell in the shadows and fulfill menial tasks."

"So, they're treated as second rate citizens then?" My voice is laced with thinly veiled disdain. This is an antiquated position about any living being and it makes my skin crawl. My jaw hurts as my teeth grind together and I glare at him and his answer with my own intense reproof.

No one answers me.

Any answer that may have come is drowned out by deafening chaos as the far window is reduced to a shower of glass and splintered wood that rains across the floor. My heart freezes in my chest as I see the reason—cloaked figures hidden under terrifying masks, their sinister features only hinted at with the sliver visible around the eyes in the shifting darkness. Unlike any stray thugs I have ever encountered, these beings move with an unnatural grace, like dancers weaving through the room in perfect synchronized harmony. Their armor seems to sparkle and shimmer like moonlight on a lake's surface, sending chills racing down my spine as they get closer.

Their eyes are unpitying and icy, filled with a burning malice that seems directed at me as they make their way around the table. Every strike of their blades is exact, a deadly performance of martial artistry right out of a movie. Those with bows hum together, releasing arrows that would have caused certain death if I had been standing in their way. Fear flows through my veins like wildfire, I did not sign up for this, I didn't sign up for anything, and I feel every muscle in my body tense in anticipation, from my toes to my jaw.

Our attackers fill my vision, and a primal, gut-wrenching fear claws its way up, leaving me paralyzed. They're close enough that I can see the shimmers of their armor are actually intricate symbols that I feel in my bones, convey some hidden meaning. They move like a single entity, highly trained, and guided by an unseen force, striking fear into every heart. Nope, just mine. It's clear this isn't a random attack—these are soldiers under orders.

"Defend yourselves!" A male shouts nearby. I don't think that was necessary as all involved had already taken action, except me.

The air crackles with tension and magic as council members fight for their lives, each focused on their own survival. No one has noticed that they aren't the intended target yet. It's a fragmented battle, with individual acts of defense against a slowly encroaching threat.

Jadis, a fierce golden light sparking in his eyes, sidesteps an attacker's blow and kicks him in the stomach while he's off balance. It's the tiniest moment that I don't even notice until after it's over. I'm in way over my head.

"Stay behind me, Elora!" Jadis commands me and I don't care at all. His voice cuts through the air, sharp and firm, each word hitting like the crack of a whip. That same attacker now falling to the floor like a sack of bricks.

I stare. I'm subconsciously torn between embracing Jadis' words and his protection while battling with the understanding of what the hell is happening around me. The clanking of blades against one another fills the air with a cacophony of destruction and chaos. Brandis joins Jadis' side, providing me with another layer of defense, perhaps he has come to the same conclusion as I have.

They want me.

My heart races in my chest and up my throat as I watch the enemy move with lightning speed and precision. Each strike is calculated and designed to chip away at our defenses and instill terror in us. *How the hell do I know this?*

With a sharp breath, Jadis lunges forward, his sword a blur of motion. Steel flashes in the sunlight as he carves through the chaos, each strike swift and deliberate, his movements precise—calculated destruction. Each powerful stroke is perfectly timed and strikes with inhuman precision, which I guess is true. He deflects every attack with ease to form a wall of protection around my frozen self. His movements have the grace of a deadly animal, as if he were dancing in the most macabre ballet before the eyes of death himself. But still, more foes advance.

The air is heavy with the strength of my despair, an unshakable tension that seems to sap away my strength. The odor of fear fills the room, the scent of sweat and blood mingling into a sickening perfume. My eyes widen and dry in terror as I watch one after the other of our attackers' dark eyes fade until extinguished by Jadis and the council. Yet for each one that falls, their relentless assault only intensifies, new faces taking up arms against us, against me, undeterred by the losses they already sustained.

The battle rages on and I find myself caught in a whirlwind of fear and disbelief. The clash of weapons unknown to me, the shouts of combat, and the agonized cries fill the chamber, painting a grim tableau of brutality and survival. I catch a glimpse of Brandis and Jadis' faces, each taut, jaws clenched and brows furrowed, their eyes fixed with an unyielding focus, fighting with a fervor that defies that darkness that quickly creeps closer.

Jadis grabs my arm with his calloused hands and spins me around, pushing me towards the nearest exit. His face is ashen, his eyes full of worry. "Go, Elora! Find a safe place where you can hide until Brandis or I fetch ye." He shouts at me above the metallic slide of sword against sword, giving me one final shove before dashing back into the fray.

The door closes with a snap in my face. I hear the sound of footsteps approaching, pounding in rhythm with my racing heart and I sprint for my life. My chest burns with each ragged breath, my legs trembling as they pound the floor, every instinct screaming to keep moving toward the only place that can save me. My body screams in protest, muscles stretched to their limit, yet something raw and unrelenting pushes me forward, the instinct to survive drowning out the pain.

A guttural scream pierces the air as a vice-like grip wrenches me backward. I feel my attacker's fingers wrap around my plaited hair, weaving and tugging it like a noose to keep me under control. Hellish agony flares through my scalp, accompanied by dizzying fatigue that threatens to take me down. Yet, just as quickly, an electrical charge surges through my veins, steeling my nerves and readies me for battle.

I scream with every ounce of breath in my lungs and strain against the iron grip, my panic pushing me to break away from his hold. Every muscle quivers with rage as I unleash an onslaught of untrained blows, my fingers curled into rigid claws as they rain down on him. Every punch feels like a hammer pounding metal, yet still he holds fast. My hands throb with pain but I still refuse to give up, driving my fists into his body with all I have. If only I had listened to my instincts and taken those self-defense classes when I had the chance! But now it is too late; I can only hope that my last desperate attack will free me from his grip.

In a single moment of miraculous relief, I manage to break free. I don't question how as I stumble forward with wild, unsteady steps. I never felt the blade, but I can feel the warm blood trickling down my side. The pain only intensifies my fear, but I refuse to succumb to the paralyzing grip of fear again, never again.

Tapping into a deep reserve of strength I didn't know existed, I sprint away with every fiber of my being. My lungs explode in protest as I gasp for air, each inhalation seeming to scorch my throat. The sound of my attackers footsteps behind me is like a siren, urging me to push further, faster. I use my fear to drive me on.

Sheer panic has me aiming for a large pot. The soles of my boots scrape desperately against the ground as I propel myself deeper into the shadows. Then I hit the ground with a sickening thud that sends tremors through my entire body. My breathing is now hindered by pain as I wriggle myself into the small shadow beside the pot, praying fervently to anyone who will listen that its leafy foliage and dark cloak of shadows is enough to hide me.

The footsteps are a relentless dirge playing at my own funeral and they get closer and closer. I feel my heart thumping against my ribs as if trying to escape my chest. With each step the fear coils stronger within me, a nauseating dread that threatens to overwhelm me and leave me paralyzed in its wake. As my body starts to shake, I wait helplessly for what seems like an eternity.

The menacing steps, that clack against the stone tile like a hammer on metal, ring through the air as black boots encroach on my sliver of darkness. His gaze sears into my soul, piercing me with a fury I've never seen before as our eyes lock. Every second feels like an eternity as a malevolent force spills from his eyes, a power that can consume the world around us.

As I cower in fear, overwhelmed by the entire terrifying situation, the innocuous plant beside me surges into motion. Its tendrils lash out with a startling ferocity, ensnaring my assailant in a crushing grip that is impossible to escape. All at once, the attacker's screams cut off as he's pulled into the maw of the carnivorous beast, vanishing deep within its depths in a single frantic breath.

I had fallen over in the chaos and now step completely out of my little shelter, feeling mixed, confused. Relief sits on the surface, washing over me, but I'm also filled with an immense feeling of awe. The devastation in the chamber I left behind is something I can't unsee; corpses of those now gone forever flashing in my thoughts. Life suddenly seems so much more fragile, something I never thought possible after losing a child.

My body trembles with fear and adrenaline, the rapid thumping of my heart echoes in my ears as it slowly starts to calm. Sweat trickles down my brow, mingling with dirt and grime that now smudges my skin. Every muscle is tense and ready to spring into action or flee at a moments notice. My breath is shallow, my chest barely moving in an effort to slow my racing pulse or prevent the pain, I don't know.

Dust and debris float on the air, my thoughts cannot keep up with the storm of feelings raging inside me. Shock and disbelief struggle to find a footing against an even greater growing anger that seems intent on consuming me whole. How can there be such cruelty? All my naive dreams, my hopes, about this place are being ripped apart, reminding me that, most especially here, violence reigns supreme.

I will never forget the sight of my attackers' eyes growing dull and lifeless. In those moments, I feel the cost of taking a life, no matter how necessary it is, no matter that my hand wasn't directly involved. While my thoughts are full of hatred for what they have done, my heart yearns for peace and understanding—the ideals that I strive to embody in my daily life. I'm left with a terrible inner turmoil as I grapple with the reality of violence, death, and war.

As I stand here, my mind whirring with a thousand worries, I feel a gentle pressure on my back. I spin around to find Jadis. His right hand still holds a blade stained with blood, but his left wraps reassuringly around my shoulders. His eyes clouded with worry, a reflection of the fear that is knotting up inside me. Without a word, I throw myself into his arms, feeling his strong chest against mine and allowing the warmth radiating from him to course through my body. I need him, someone...no him.

My breaths come hard and fast again with the effort of attempting to ground myself. The chaotic screams still echo through the air, and I can feel the energy of all the emotions racing through my veins. Jadis holds me tight, his blade dropping to the hard floor with a clang of metal on rock.

"We need to get you to safety, Elora." His voice holds steady, each word clipped and deliberate, though the faintest tremor betrays the worry he can't quite hide. "Come on, let us make our way to your chambers, you'll be safer there."

The words pierce through the haze of my thoughts, reminding me of the whole situation I find myself in. He bends down for his sword. I nod, trusting him, as we start to navigate through the corridors. My heart still races with each step, the weight of it all becoming too much.

As we get closer to my chamber door, Jadis' grip along my back tightens ever so slightly, offering silent reassurance. I'm not sure if it is entirely for me alone. I turn my face upward and his eyes meet mine, searching back and forth over my face and then moving down the rest of my body. They rest hard on the blood soaked fabric at my side, widening with alarm.

My lips curve up into a faint smile, masking the discomfort that pulses through my body. "It's nothing to worry about, Jadis." My attempt at playing down my condition is overturned by the strain in my voice. I don't want him to fret over me; there are more pressing matters at hand.

He nods and presses his hand to the latch of the door, peering inside through a small crack first. He motions for me to come inside, but remain near the door. While I do as he asks, it wasn't because he tells me to, I simply have no drive or desire to move.

Jadis walks the room, and my world seems to sway, a wave of dizziness washes over me. The pain in my side intensifies, demanding to be acknowledged. It's only then that I really comprehend what I just put my body through, the toll it had endured, the limits it has reached. My feeble attempt to downplay the severity of it all crumbles beneath the weight of my exhaustion.

Jadis' concerned gaze meets mine, his stormy, green eyes reflecting a whirlwind of emotions. The lines etched on his forehead and the furrow of his brow probably mirrors my own.

I watch as his jaw clenches and he shifts his weight, his body tensing ever so slightly. His eyes dart around the room anxiously, pupils dilated as he glances in each corner.

I didn't notice when his attention returns to me, searching for signs of distress that I'm sure are now written all over my face. "Elora," he says with urgency, "your wound is worse than you implied, isn't it?"

I open my mouth to respond, to wave off his concern, but the edges of my vision start to darken. Not again. Everything around me dims and I feel like I'm being pulled down into a deep abyss. My body slowly starts to give in, and I can feel exhaustion seeping into every inch of me, my adrenaline finally running out.

Chapter Fifteen

"Caelar lorynor, thael thalnor."

The stars whisper, but the step is yours

MY SENSES SLOWLY RETURN WITHIN the blackness, the echoes of voices reaching my ears, drawing me out of the hazy depths of unconsciousness. I listen intently as the sounds of a passionate, but angry conversation filter through the fog of my mind.

Brandis' voice flows through the room. Each word carries a sense of his usual authority but is laced with frustration and palpable concern. The timber of his voice rings with the weight of it all. I think he's speaking from somewhere near the window. I must be in my bed. Someone is pacing, the distant rustling of clothing punctuates the silence between words.

"We cannot afford to overlook the gravity of this situation." Brandis' tone carries a steady edge, his words firm but tinged with the weariness of someone who had explained this far too many times before. "Elora's safety must be our priority. We need to fortify our defenses, establish measures that will ensure her protection here, within these walls."

The crackling of the fire fills a pregnant pause before Jadis counters Brandis' argument. His words flow with conviction, every syllable enunciated with purpose. One you would expect when someone was repeating their words once again. "Brandis, I understand your concerns, as I share them with you, but hiding away will not quell the storm that now brews."

The distinct clinking of armor comes from the direction of the fireplace. "We must take the fight to them, to our enemies, her enemies, reveal their true intention. That is, if you will not let me move her around the land. To protect Elora, we need to stay one step ahead."

They continue to argue, and I grow restless, the energy returning to my muscles and screaming to be let out of their cage of unconsciousness. Jadis' words fly through my mind again, like a little bird in a flock all flitting about in too small a space, it's hard to keep a thought for long. I want to meet people and see the world. I want to learn more about this place hands on. I'm supposed to be a part of this place and I can't do that locked inside these walls. Reading books only goes so far. I want experiences. The idea of hiding away feels stifling and the thought of sitting here and waiting for the next assault gnaws at my insides.

My eyes lose their heaviness and the flickering candlelight casts long shadows over the males faces, emphasizing the gravity of the last few hours, or was it days now?

"How long have I been out?" The words stick in my throat as my dry tongue fails to work properly. Before I can make much of what I see around me, two males lean on either side of my bed, Jadis to the left and Brandis to the right, each grabbing at a hand. *Talk about stifling.*

Brandis catches my gaze first, weariness etched into the lines of his face. Concern dances behind his pale eyes as he reaches with his other hand, hesitating for a moment before placing it softly on my shoulder. "Two days, darling."

Darling? "Huh, and yet I don't feel rested at all, go figure." I shrug into my stack of pillows. "I heard part of your argument just now, as I was coming to. I appreciate your concerns for my safety, but I cannot stand to stay hidden away, just waiting for the next attack, because we know there will be another and another. I was going to ask anyway, I think. I want to be proactive, no more hiding in the library and reading books, despite how delightful that is. I want to explore this world first hand. I let fear control me once and it cost me everything."

Brandis' chest rises sharply, his unspoken words lingering in his throat as his wide eyes search mine in a silent plea. His hand, warm and surprisingly rough, gently tucks a strand of lose hair behind my ear. "Elora, I can't stand the thought of not being there for you, now that I have you back." He speaks in a whisper, but it still knocks me flying. *Did he get hit in the head? Does he have a concussion or something?* "We have to think carefully about what we're doing here."

I want to believe what he says, that losing me would be unbearable. I fight to ignore the idea that it has more to do with the power of that prophecy than any sentimental attachment he's suddenly developed for me over night...or rather two nights. No matter how hard I try, I can't help but wonder if his worry is due to us being family, blood, or the power I provide.

Jadis' leather jerkin creaks as he shifts closer on the bed, the metal leaves covering his shoulders and chest sliding softly against each other. He places his heavily calloused hand over Brandis', effectively making all three of us hold hands. "Elora will be much safer if she's always moving. Here, no matter how much you boost the defenses, she's a sitting duck." His expression flinches and he gives me what looks like a wink.

"What does water fowl have to do with Elora's safety?"

A snicker escapes my lips before I can subtly cover them.

"Sorry," Jadis says, "rather she will eventually be helpless because they will keep trying and will find a way to break through. We send her out, moving, never staying in one place more than three nights with a small contingent of our best and most trusted soldiers. They all dress in common clothes. In the meantime, I will track down the bastards that did this and find out who they work for and what their aim is. You made me captain of your guard for a reason, Brandis, let me do my job."

Brandis pinches the join of his nose and brow with a sigh, shifting heavier into his seated position next to me. "I can see the fire in your eyes, Elora. I don't really have a say in this matter, do I?" I open my mouth to answer, and he stops me with his hand. "I know I cannot dissuade you. Just promise me that you will exercise caution and never forget the value of your life, to all of us."

"I know how *valuable* my life is," I seethe, but he hushes me once again.

"Jadis, you will not pursue the enemy," this time putting a hand up to stop Jadis' protests that had only just reached his lips. "If Elora is to traipse about the countryside, you will be at her side at all times. And I mean all times, Jadis. She will not leave your sight for a moment, even if she needs to take a piss."

My mouth drops open, and I shake my head in disbelief at the casual language Brandis just whipped out. A smirk curls one side of my lips as I sarcastically remark, "Oh, really?"

He turns his attention back to me, "Promise that you will exercise caution and never underestimate the dangers in this realm. In other words, don't torment Jadis too much," he says, smirking.

"Yes, my Lord," Jadis says with so much formality it sounds like it's coming from a different person.

Excitement bubbles up in my chest. The males look at each other with a mix of worry and the tightness I interpret as challenge. They both seem to know the gravity of this decision, maybe more than I fully comprehend.

"Rest," Jadis commands in that formal tone. "We leave once Margwin deems you've recovered."

"Bossy."

Chapter Sixteen

"Sylrin thalna caelar aelithor valeinae vrithar."

No tree grows to the stars without the wind

FIND MYSELF IN FRONT of the mirror, wearing nothing but my soft, white undershirt, which lets me easily examine the small pink scar that now stretches across my stomach. It starts just below my left armpit, tracing a curved path across to my waist, about six inches in length. It's a lasting reminder of my first battle where I failed miserably.

I trail my fingers along the jagged line, slowly, letting my mind wander to all the emotions that stir beneath the surface. Pride at having bravely faced what I believed to have been formidable adversaries. Humiliation at being bested by 'novices' according to Jadis. Fear at what darkness may lurk just around the corner in this unknown world. Apprehension about the price I am paying for venturing into it. As I move my hand away, having reached the end, I feel the tension in my body more than before. Maybe my haste to leave is set to be my biggest mistake.

Lost in my thoughts, I feel a familiar presence hovering nearby. Tressa is bent over the bed, her hands working their way through a pile of freshly laundered clothes, folding each one neatly into a crisp square. Every few moments, I sense her eyes on me, drawing me out of my mind, turning my head to meet hers with an inquisitive look that usually goes unanswered.

This time she hesitates a moment. "You know, my father used to tell me that scars have a way of telling stories. They remind us of the battles we've fought and the strength we've then discovered within ourselves. They're really a reminder of our strengths rather than any weaknesses."

"Your father sounds like a wise man indeed. It's hard to think of them that way though."

"Male, remember, fae are male and female, humans are men and women. I mean, it's in the name hu-man." She tutts this at me, reminding me once again about our regularly repeated conversation on etiquette.

"Right. I am getting better about that though," I say sheepishly, and she laughs.

My fingers trail along the ridges of my skin, tracing over the raised lines and softer stretch marks that make up my own personal roadmap. I feel a slight wave of shame as I think about their origins but then remind myself of all I have managed to do despite them. With a deeply drawn breath I steady my voice and declare, "Perhaps I should embrace my scars as symbols of all the obstacles I've faced and survived. Like you said, a reminder of my strength, even if I don't always feel it." The words hold more conviction than I feel, but it's a start.

Tressa smiles, her eyes lingering on that new scar for a moment before she returns her attention to the task at hand. "We've come a long way, Elora, and this journey is just beginning, your journey. I can't help but feel excited for what lies ahead, and I think I'm a little jealous that I'm not going."

"No, you're not," I jest with her, the smirk pulling at the entire side of my face.

"No, you're right, I'm not." We laugh together.

As she moves around the room with practiced grace, the travel essentials are collecting on the bed. Her hands tremble, barely perceptible, but it's there. Her mouth then contorts into a small grimace. She's holding something back. There's now a palpable tension in the air that leaves me feeling uneasy.

She doesn't falter though, just keeps organizing my small pack on the bed with her carefully collected items. Her fingers move with such practiced purpose, I am in awe.

She packs a few changes of clothing, still neatly folded. Next, she adds a selection of herbs and potions, providing me with remedies for any common ailments we might encounter. Into an intricately embroidered pouch she slips soft fabric liners and...my eyes widen. Tucked amongst the absorbent fabric is a small vial of deep red liquid. One I know for a fact I won't be needing. No chance of babies in my future with or without it. Her thoughtfulness is endearing with or without the fae form of contraception.

Leave it to her to consider all the natural rhythms of life that will continue even in the midst of my adventure. It shows the growth of our friendship and the lengths she will go to make sure I'm comfortable, even when apart. I can't help but feel an intense gratitude for her and the way she looks out for me. My first friend in a long time. I can't help but feel...cared for. This is the right choice, this path, and I need to stop doubting my intuition.

"So," Tressa begins, hesitantly, "Jadis has decided Mik will accompany you too, then?" She stills her hands for a split second and a fleeting expression crosses her face, one that I can't quite decipher. It's almost like a mixture of longing with a side of melancholy.

"Yeah," I answer, "He figured since I knew him too that I'd be more comfortable with the combination of him and Jadis. It makes sense when you think about it. I'm less likely to get into trouble, because we both know I will, and I don't really know anyone else other than you and Brandis."

"Aye, that's true." Her voice is strangely subdued. "So, where do you think you and Jadis will travel first?"

We hadn't really discussed this together, but I'm sure Jadis already has our entire journey planned out, his strategic mind working overtime. "There are so many places to explore." The excitement of the prospect starts to bubble in my stomach again. "Maybe we could go to the lands of the Court of Thaw? I've been curious about all the tales of color and blossoming gardens.

Wouldn't we cross over a considerable stretch of Day Court lands to get there?"

"The widest part of it actually. Court of Thaw does sound enchanting, at least it used to, much like the Court of Bloom," she murmurs, her gaze briefly flickering toward the window as if searching for something beyond the castle walls. Well, manor, it's not really a castle. "The blooming flowers, the scent of fresh dew...It's supposed to be a place where dreams and desires bloom and are made whole."

I frown at her back. There's a delicate quiver in her voice and the softness in her eyes is puzzling. There is something unspoken in her words, a hidden layer of emotions that hints at more. I want to pry and dig deeper, to ask about the source of her wistfulness, but I hesitate. Tressa has always been guarded when it comes to her personal life, and I respect her too much to impose on her desire for privacy.

Instead, I decide to finish dressing. We opt for a practical but stylish ensemble that allows for ease of movement. The colors are muted earth tones that blend with the landscapes that we're supposed to travel through.

I chose a pair of fitted trousers made from a supple fabric that promises comfort even during long stretches of horseback riding. They hug my legs just right, providing the flexibility I need without sacrificing durability. They're a rich shade of forest green, the color of the lush forests I'd already seen when I arrived.

In compliment, Tressa chooses a loose fitting tunic in a soft shade of warm brown, its fabric stitched with a delicate pattern of embroidery along the neckline. The tunic drapes gracefully over my frame, providing that effortless elegance that suits the aelorin, apparently in all things. Graceful and elegant were never words used to describe me. The long sleeves can be rolled up for practicality, so that I can be comfortable regardless of the weather.

Because we could be riding into danger, Tressa pulled a sleeveless leather vest of a caramel color in contrast to the more earthy tones underneath. It provides a little bit of added warmth and some minor protection. I top it all off with a pair of boots of supple leather. Their rich chestnut color is polished to a subtle sheen. With these boots on my feet, I finally feel ready to attack the terrain outside these walls. They even add a little swagger to my steps.

Chapter Seventeen

"Fionis myrran thalna."

The first root breaks the earth.

THE SMALL VILLAGE OUTSIDE THE Day Court manor is nestled among hills and lush meadows. From the elevated steps of the grand house, past the surrounding walls, huts dapple the hills and meadows as far as my eyes can see. The farther away the land stretches, the fewer homes there were—just like in rural and urban settings back home. At least somethings don't change.

While this once could have been an amazing view, I can't help but feel a sense of weariness clinging in the air.

The presence of the fae (or aelorin but I'm not sure where that distinction lay quite yet) and the absence of humans is obvious. The very structures in front of me seem to grow from the earth itself. The dwellings are fashioned from natural materials like shimmering crystal-like substances, twisting vines, and living wood. They follow the curves and contours of the land, blending with the surrounding nature. Delicate carvings sprinkled the facades, showing scenes I study as we walk by with horses in hand. The scenes tell stories, myths and legends according to Jadis. It's tradition in the Day Court, the celebration of the knowledge this court was once known for.

The streets had obviously bustled with lively activity, but now seem hushed and subdued and I don't think it had anything to do with our presence. The homes and the carvings are weathered and worn up close. The paint is faded, and obvious patches and signs of fast repairs are scattered everywhere. Tangled vines cascade down the sides of buildings, leaving a new story of wear and tear.

As we walk, faces peer from shadowed doorways and alleys. Those I can make out bear the weight of their burdens. Lines are etched deep on their brows, their eyes reflecting pure exhaustion and despair. Their clothes, threadbare with patches, hint at a scarcity that touches them and not those I have already encountered in my time here. Despite it all, a spark of hope flickers in their weary eyes as we pass. That should inspire me, but only makes me hide myself further behind the chestnut beast at my side. All the while I can feel my determination slowly evaporating away. I have no idea what I'm doing and they're pinning their hopes on me.

The village square, which should be a bustling hub of activity in any village, seems little more than an average street. The market stalls that should have overflowed with goods are sparsely filled, their wares modest and meager. The smell of freshly baked bread that I had expected is replaced by cold, stale air of dirt and stone. My heart drops as I realize that the cheerful laughter and bustle I had imagined so many times before is missing. I wish desperately I had refused Jadis' insistence to leave the safety of our manor, but it's too late to turn back now.

Servants bustle through the village alongside what I can only describe as creatures. I assume their difference in appearance means these are the under fae that no one wishes to talk about. The high fae servants are met with a complex mix of emotions from the others. Some eye them with reverence and bitterness, while others cast down their gazes, their eyes clouded with resignation and inner silent defiance.

These interactions, of course, peak my interest. They signal underlying tensions that tell me so much about what went missing from the history books. The under fae keep their distance, careful not to attract unnecessary attention or invoke the ire of their counterparts. If I guessed, I'd say that probably wasn't hard to do, peak their ire. When they had to make an exchange, the body language and tone are laced with polite formality that thinly veils the much deeper undercurrents of a strained relationship.

The sudden silence is the only hint that someone approaches from behind. Then, the deep bows of everyone lining the street barely precedes Brandis' voice.

"Elora." He trots a few paces behind, his cheeks flush and his breathing is heavy as he tries to catch up. In his hands is a large rectangular package wrapped in a soft fabric; it looks almost velvet, yet its texture seems lighter than air as it moves. "This arrived for you this morning," he says, handing it to me.

"What is it?" I turn it around in my hands and flip it over, looking for some identifying feature.

"I don't know, but I thought you might want it before you left. Jadis, can you check it before she opens anything? There's no indication as to who sent it."

Jadis nods and lifts a hand over the wrappings, a feint buzzing warmth travels through it and into my fingers that still touch it. "Nothing there by way of magic." Jadis tells Brandis as that tingling fades as quickly as it came. "Seems safe enough. Perhaps there's a note inside?"

I untie the fabric carefully and a small notecard falls to the dirt road, the intricate dark script in a single line reading, *Vyn sylnael lir sylnor thael.* "I only recognize 'I' *vyn* at this point. What does it say? I don't want to dig out my lexicon."

It's Brandis who answers me first, "I think this might interest you." He translates with none of the degradation I expected. It's the perfect chance to remind me of how little I know and he chose not to.

Gold script weaves across the leather cover of a large tome *Thyranis Faerin: Sylorineth Caelarin Vaelrin Illyr.* Brandis translates without me having to ask, "The Under Fae Compendium: An Illustrated Guide to the

Realm Beneath...well in essence, the literal translation would be Beneath Fae and a Compendium and Illustrations of the Realm Below."

"Thanks for the help...and the lesson." I smirk and he returns it.

"This is an extraordinary gift. There's nothing like it, even in our collection." He reaches down and picks up that card. After flipping it over, he frowns. "It's odd they wouldn't sign their name to such a generous gift. There's no indication of who sent this."

Jadis takes the card himself, turning it to and fro like he'd see something that Brandis didn't. "It had to be someone on the council. They're the only ones who know she's interested in the under fae."

"Well, this will make for some light reading when we make camp," I say as I wrap it back up and stuff it haphazardly into the saddle bag. It has only a tiny amount of room left in it. "Thank you for bringing it to me."

He gives me a small, precise bow before turning away, his back to our party. But just as suddenly, he stops. A hesitation. Slowly, he turns back, his gaze sweeping over my face, searching—though for what, I can't say. His expression flickers, emotions shifting too fast for me to catch, but something in his eyes tightens.

Without warning, his hands grip my shoulders, firm but not forceful, and before I can react, I'm pulled into his arms. The warmth of him seeps through my clothes, the steady rise and fall of his chest pressing against mine. His breath ghosts against my ear as his voice drops to a hushed murmur.

"Be careful, Elora. Please, come back safely, once everything is said and done."

His grip lingers for a heartbeat longer before he finally releases me and walks away as quickly as it all began. I stand with my mouth agape watching my enigmatic brother walk back the way he came.

AS JADIS AND I pass into a more desolate region of the village, he pulls his steed to a stop behind him and eyes me skeptically. His green eyes narrow, "You've never ridden a horse before." It's hard to decipher if that's a question or statement.

The sun already hangs low in the sky as I stand next to the enormous steed that Jadis has selected for me, insisting he's as tame as a babe. I can feel my own eyes bug out of my head as I am dwarfed next to the warm chestnut gelding and take in the sheer size of this monster. I am the shortest member of this party and seem to have been given the tallest horse. They're all snickering behind their hands.

Jadis has a mischievous glint in his eyes and steps forward, a confident smile playing on his lips. "Now, Elora, riding a horse is an art in itself. You must be one with the beast, as graceful as the wind and as sturdy as the earth beneath your feet. Ready?"

"What the fuck is that supposed to mean?" I ask through the all out laughter breaking free behind us. Mik is struggling to stay on his own mount. I glare at Jadis from around my beast's shoulder, my head tucking neatly beneath the horses large cheeks. "The last time I got on a horse, I ended up in a rather undignified position on the ground, so you're going to have to do better than that, asshole."

He stands tall and proud, a deep rumble escaping his chest as he lets out a hearty chuckle of his own. His long hair is wild and untamed, his green eyes sparkling with his unfair amusement. He places an encouraging (obnoxious) hand on my shoulder, "Fear not, my dear Elora. I shall be your trusty guide on this equine adventure. Now, first things first, get on the bloody horse."

He grabs a handful of mane on his horse with one hand and a piece of the saddle with the other. In one, smooth motion he is on his horse, shifting his weight until he's comfortably seated in the stirrups. His horse snorts and shifts under him as he looks down on me with a challenging expression. He lifts an eyebrow, furthering his challenge, silently daring me to match him.

I grasp the leather reins and the saddle in one hand and stretch my foot forward, trying desperately to reach the shining stirrup. No matter how much I lean forward, I can only just barely get my toes in. The thought of hoisting myself up high enough to flip the other leg over seems like an impossible feat. Actually, it is impossible. As if sensing this, my dear horse snorts with laughter and decides to join in the fun. He dances away from me each time I put pressure on that foot, his mane flaring as he turns the both of us in circles, me hopping on one foot as we go.

Mik, the utmost gentleman, finally takes pity on me, interlocking his hands to create a step and with a shaky move, I thrust my boot into it and hoist myself up. The motion of the horse startles me; he has already begun to trot off before I have even managed to settle in. The stiff hair of his coat is still soft against my arms as I cling tightly to his neck, feeling the warmth of him against my chest. He smells of warm hay and animal.

"Elora, darling, that's what these are for," Jadis quips at me while holding his reins in his hands, jiggling them in my direction. I give him the best glare I can muster as I hug my new friend, sliding one hand down his smooth, warm neck to feel for the leather reins. When I finally gain the courage to sit up, Jadis continues his incredibly helpful lesson...

"Now, remember to sit tall and relaxed. The horse can sense your energy, so let your body move with its rhythm."

That's actually a little helpful. I give him a snide nod, not ready to surrender, my fingers gripping the reins tightly, leather digging into the flesh of my palms. I feel his muscles ripple beneath me and a surge of something runs through my veins. A gentle squeeze with my legs and he starts to move faster, then taking one step after another, coming up alongside Jadis' antsy mount.

"Ah, a natural rider, I see!" It's not a compliment, I can hear the mischief in his voice. "Now, let's work on your balance. Close yer eyes and imagine yourself as a graceful dancer, swaying in harmony with the horses movements."

I frown at him from my now higher vantage point, my gelding is skittish and dancing in place. "I have never been a dancer nor described as graceful you ungrateful prick," I say through gritted teeth, struggling to bring the reins down and keep the horse still. "For the love of God, stop with the nonsense."

"Relax. Faeryl there knows exactly what he's doing. I wouldn't put you on a horse that wasn't easy to ride. He can feel your fear, lass, and reacts to it."

I huff in frustration and urge Faeryl into a trot down the road. The wind picks up just enough to rustle the wispy pieces of hair around my temples as I concentrate on shifting in sync with his movements. Before long, the familiar rhythm clicks into place, and I exhale a sigh of relief.

Just as I'm getting the hang of our new arrangement, a squirrel-like creature darts across the path, causing him to jolt to the side. My grip on the reins and saddle falter and I teeter precariously to the far side.

"Steady, little naerinaelith," Jadis calls out, his voice is still filled with amusement, despite the speed at which he approaches and snatches the reins to calm my horse.

With a newfound determination, probably elicited by the teasing and snickering that surrounds me, I regain my balance. I can't help but laugh triumphantly, Jadis grinning alongside me.

"Yeah, I think that's as fast as I'm gonna go on this thing," I say, as soon as the laughter fades.

Jadis shakes his head, clucking his tongue. "That thing is a horse and his name is Faeryl."

"Yeah, yeah, I know." My mouth stretches ear-to-ear in a wide smile as my eyes, I'm sure twinkle with glee.

"And, since I don't intend on involving you in any high speed chases, I think you'll be fine."

I give him a pointed look, and my voice drops an octave, "What you intend and what actually happens can be two very different things." My words instantly temper the jovial mood.

"I don't plan on letting anything happen to you, Elora. I'll protect you as I promised." He looks me in the eye and speaks gravely, his hand stretching to warm my thigh. His voice is so full of conviction that I almost believe what he says.

"Jadis, you can't prevent everything, but I thank you for the sentiment anyway. So, where are we going today? I'm sure you have our journey planned out at least two weeks ahead?" I want a lighter subject.

Mik laughs again from somewhere not too far behind us. "There's another small village around half a days slow ride from here. I figured we'd camp there for the night and ease your backside into the idea of being in a saddle." He says with a grin again as I shift against the hard leather underneath me, asking myself why he thinks I need to stop after half a day.

I had no idea what I was looking forward to.

Chapter Eighteen

"*Caelar vaelrin vaelithil thalnor.*"

The stars shine, even after the frost

HE VILLAGE, IF YOU CAN call it that, I assume was once a lively place but now appears desolate and worn, like everything else in this forsaken realm. The lingering shadows of despair are the same that hover over the village at *Ilthorien Arthorin*, the Day Court capital. Jadis and Mik are determined to teach me the language and have been quizzing me the entire day. I was informed that it's not the "Day Court Manor", its formal name, for the house alone anyway, is the Radiant Citadel, or *Ilthorien Arthorin*. The house and surrounding gardens have a completely different name. Even with a fancy name that slips nicely along your tongue, you can feel the heavy weight of sorrow on the air there and here.

As our sunlight fades over the horizon and the ache in my backside and legs grows, I watch the villagers, clad in tattered garments, gather in small groups, huddled together for warmth as the loss of light cools the air. Their faces, too, are etched with those lines of worry and exhaustion, but their eyes don't hold any glimmer of hope here, it fades just like the light of day.

When I ask Jadis why, he says they believe that the absence of the court's influence has disrupted the delicate balance of nature. If the fae are as connected with nature as the books imply, then the consequences of this imbalance are quite obvious. He doesn't seem to agree with them, the only hint is in how he phrases his explanation, but I don't pry—this time. However, whatever the reason, the once predictable seasons have become erratic, causing unusual weather patterns and unpredictable crop growth. Fields that were once lush and abundant now yield only meager harvests and the villagers face a constant threat of hunger and scarcity.

I watch the people, the few that remain, gather around a distant fire, their faces lit by its flickering glow, casting shadows and only accentuating the deep lines of their faces. Jadis hops off his horse with an ease I know I'm going to be jealous of. I can't even manage to remove my boots from the stirrups, my body's so stiff.

He walks over and slips one of my boots from the nearest and grasps my waist, pulling me down from Faeryl's back. He moseys over to the other horses, continuing to cradle my waist, waiting for me to gain the ground again under my teetering legs. He says nothing, no jokes at all, even with my obvious discomfort. His thumbs trail little circles against my sides where he holds me, leaving a flush of heat in their wake. Right now, I don't care.

After a moment or two, I place my hands on his, "I think I'm good now. Thanks."

A curt nod from him and he releases me, and I'm left feeling strangely empty. I'm not ready to do anything more than stand at the moment, so I watch and listen. Mik and the others have already unpacked some food, wine, and ale, and sit by the fire, sharing with the villagers. Their conversations are animated and longing, even speaking the local language I can feel their emotions. With the presence of fine food, their spirits brighten and Jadis informs me their reminiscing about the old harvests and exciting festivals that were once celebrated in all the courts, before he says something to the group. He must have asked them to speak mortal tongue because they shift, almost mid-sentence into the language I can understand. I feel like the shift to my language brought on melancholy and mourning. They speak of the loss of bouncing dances, the joyous melodies, and the feasts that used to last for days at the high festivals.

I'm so absorbed in the conversation, I didn't realize Jadis had my hand in his until we're moving to take a seat with the others. The villagers seem eager to have someone to listen to their struggles and concerns. They speak in frustration and neither of us want to interrupt.

The seasons continue to slip away, and the villagers are gripped with a sense of uncertainty about the future. I don't blame them. Their connection to the natural world, which I gather was a form of symbiosis, has been severed, and now they struggle to adapt to every change that's thrown their way. The absence of the court's guidance only makes it worse. Then, throw in the lack of protection and they're left vulnerable.

"It's been tough, I tell ya," Eamon says, his voice weathered like the calloused, knobby hands resting on his knees. "The seasons ain't what they used to be. Our crops failin' and the weather all topsy-turvy. We barely scrape by. I lost my little girl nine moons past. She withered away to nothing." His wiry frame seems bowed by more than age, the edges of his auburn hair almost looked streaked with gray. The tears still well in his eyes at the mere mention of his loss and my own vision gets blurry at the edges.

His wife, Maeve, adds with a steady, but exhausted voice, "We've heard talk of prophecies and saviors, but what good are they if our bellies go empty? Our children need warmth, not stories." Her sun-kissed skin holds a puzzle of lines from years spent in the fields, and strands of silver do weave through her dark braid.

Jadis leans in to speak, but I still him with a hand on his arm. He gets the message and relaxes back at my side, quiet.

It isn't too much longer before I decide to break the silence myself, "Do you think there's a way to restore the balance? To bring back the harmony you lost?"

Apparently, that's a touchy subject because they all shift uncomfortably in their seats, eyes turning to one another in a silent conversation. Finally, the elder woman named Saoirse with her silvered hair and weathered face speaks up. "Child," she calls to me, her voice gentle and motherly, "We've seen the seasons falter and witnessed the imbalance that plagues our lands personally.

We feel it out here more than most. The key to restoring the harmony lies in reconnecting with the natural forces that sustain us."

"Well, how do we do that, though?" I lean into the conversation, my curiosity more than piqued.

A burly man, his hands rough and worn from tending the fields around us, nods in agreement with her. "Aye, we must honor the land and its rhythms, but it's more than that. We've forsaken the old ways for so long, we no longer remember them, focusing solely on the desires of the courts. It's time to heed the whispers of the forest, the songs of the rivers, and the dance of the wind."

Say what?

Maeve chimes in again, her expression one of conviction. "We need to find a way to settle the under fae, bridge the gap again. They fight for land that's not even their own anymore, not just their original homelands."

"So, do you think restoring the courts is the way to restore balance then?" I ask, maybe a little too gleefully as I peer at Jadis, pretty sure I know what their answer will be.

"Nay, child. What's fallen has fallen. The courts took too much power, the court's destroyed the balance. If your quest is to restore the balance then you need to seek the guidance of the ancient beings, the old ones, that witnessed the rise and fall of these false empires. The spirits of the land, the guardians of the forests, and the keepers of the forgotten wisdom. They hold the key to finding what's been lost," Saoirse says.

"Well, who are these ancients then, if that's who we should talk to for answers?" I finally feel like I'm getting somewhere. Even Jadis is showing obvious interest in where this conversation is going.

Don't know," is her frank and incredibly unhelpful answer. "Not sure what a mortal would accomplish anyway dear, though your interest is commendable. Yours are hidden away for a reason, these lands are too dangerous for your kind."

"Hidden away?" I'm immediately distracted from the topic at hand. "There are humans here?" I turn to Jadis, my confused expression should be apparent in my tight, narrowed eyes. He doesn't answer me, but Saoirse offers up the information with ease. I like her.

"Aye, those descended of the slaves hide in sparse villages scattered about. Those that survived the fall of the courts anyway. Some say they were saved by witches, those that follow the DuLoupthe and now focus solely on revenge and death.”

“That sounds ominous. Who are the Du-“ I try to ask but Jadis grasps my arm hard.

“We don't speak of them, for it calls them to you, little *naerinaelith*. It's not important right now, aye?”

I nod, wondering what would make even males as strong and formidable as Jadis, fear speaking a simple name. I understand that names have power here, I've been told that twice now, but to fear speaking it all begged more questions than he was willing to answer.

The conversation peeters out from there, returning to more mundane things. Maeve and Eamon speak ardently of their surviving children already tucked away in bed. A melancholy takes hold in my chest that, no matter how funny the story they tell, can not be broken. As the villagers leave, we gather our bedrolls, me hobbling over on stiff and sore legs to grab mine. The stretch over my head to untie it from Faeryl's back makes me wonder if I even need it.

Jadis pats a patch of grass next to him after I cave and deal with the pain. It's near the log we had just been sitting at and he wants me to take my place at his side. *So, this is how it's going to be then, huh?* I want to take that book out, but my eyelids grow too heavy.

Aye. His voice comes into my head free and clear. *You promised your brother, naerinaelith, that you'd stay at my side, remember?*

Get out of my head, Jadis.

Make me, Elora. He teases raising an eyebrow over that infuriating dimple.

Why do you keep calling me that, naerinaelith? What does it mean?

Force me out of your head and I'll tell ye.

I don't know how. I stomp my foot which of course draws Mik's attention to our silent conversation.

“Then I guess you're going to have to learn, little *naerinaelith*.” Jadis turns his back on me, laying peacefully on his bed roll.

As the moon hangs low in the night sky, casting a pale silver glow over the fields, I find myself drifting into a restless sleep, waking occasionally to the flitter of light along the tall grass that quickly disappears to nothing but a waking dream.

Chapter Nineteen

"That noris, cael thael sylorin."

Two paths, but only one step forward

"SO, THIS IS THE SILVER Springs?" I stand at the edge of a moss covered path between a thin copse of trees.

"Do you see any water yet?" Mik chides, passing to my right, brushing up against my arm through the narrow break in trees.

I trail after him, my legs working hard to keep up with his much longer strides. He seems unfazed by the uneven ground and roots that stretch across the path, while I stumble over exposed roots and rocks the whole time. "Well, when you said it was just a legend, I didn't know what to expect," I say, puffing out the words as we march forward.

"Actually, we said the business about the oracle was ancient tales and legends. The spring itself is real. The silver color is supposed to come from the rare and natural stone here."

I jump at Jadis' voice, his footsteps hidden by the soft moss under our feet. The air carries a faint scent of blooming flowers and that soothing sound of trickling water.

"Lass, I'm not sure I've met someone clumsier or more out of shape."

His comment elicits a strong glare from me, the muscles of my face twisting in a way I didn't think possible and a snicker from Mik.

The spring rests perfectly within the center of the copse of trees, emanating an unnatural glow that seems to permeate the entire grove. As the sunlight filters through, it dances on the water's surface, casting shimmering reflections in every direction. The waters of the spring flow with a crystalline clarity that holds the males' attention. Always on guard, they both stand close at my sides.

I balance at the edge of the spring, the morning sunlight dancing upon the surface in glittering brilliance, hiding an inner glow from beneath the surface. It beckons me, a tug, soft and delicate, in my stomach.

Jadis hovers close, his strong arms fixed on either side of me as I get closer. His breath is hot against my ear, sending a shiver through my body, "They say these springs have been blessed with olden magic."

Mik nods in agreement, a strand of his brown hair pulling from the knot he keeps it in at the base of his skull. His exceptional sense of hearing picking up even that faint whisper, his gaze still fixed on the glimmers of sunlight on the water's surface, searching. "They say these legends speak of their ability to reveal hidden truths and offer glimpses into the future. Too bad no one can agree on whether it was an oracle long gone or a magic in the water itself that has faded. It would certainly come in handy right now."

Magic or not, this place has a tranquility that is beyond special. "Maybe it wasn't magic at all," I say, lightly swaying my hand under the water's surface, watching the silver light ripple over my skin. "Maybe the calm and tranquility simply allow people to relax and wrap their minds fully around their problems. You know, like meditation."

"Perhaps," Jadis whispers politely.

"Thus explains a mortal," Mik scoffs.

"Did you just accuse me of mortalsplaining?" He doesn't get to answer.

A rustle of leaves catches all of our attention, both males swiftly placing a hand on the hilt of their blades, Jadis' knuckles grazing up my back as he still stands so close.

Ripples on the other side of the water intensify, slowly moving toward us. Jadis bends around me, placing his arm across my chest, moving me back a step, but I push it away. I feel only calm, despite the change in atmosphere. It could be my naïveté when it comes to all things magic, like a charmed snake, but I feel no threat in the air.

The water bulges at the surface, slowly manifesting a figure cloaked in silver. Their eyes, as deep and mysterious as the depths of the spring itself, seem timeless. I didn't know how else to describe them. They send shivers down my spine as Jadis settles his warm palm at the small of my back. Somehow, I know it's him, his hand, without even looking behind me.

Every movement of this being ahead of me is fluid and graceful, like they were made of the waters themselves. With each step across the glittering surface, ripples cascade in their wake, creating a mesmerizing dance of liquid silver.

A sense of reverence fills the air, and I can't help but feel the weight of their gaze on me. My breath hitches. It feels as if they can see into the depths of my soul and that is a terrifying concept. Flashes of memory cross through my mind. Memories I've tried to bury.

Their voices fill my ears. Not one, but many even though they manifest as one being. It isn't something coming from my ears, no, but an echo in my head, not quite like when Jadis speaks there, but similar. *The waters of the Silver Springs possess the power to reveal what is hidden and guide those who seek their path.*

My resulting gasp grabs the attention of both of my males as they whip their heads to me, "Elora?"

The oracle smiles, the gesture radiating a calm assurance, this time speaking to us all, but looking to me alone. "Within your hands, the threads of fate are woven, just like another to come. A choice awaits you, one that will shape the destiny of the realm. Seek truth, embrace your power, and the path to balance shall be revealed."

With that cryptic message they retreat gracefully back into the depths of the springs. "Wait!" They don't heed my call and melt into the water.

My companions remain still in abject silence, their brows rising high, eyes wide.

"Well, I guess all the legends and theories were right," I say, planting my backside solidly on the moss near my feet. "But, that wasn't really helpful at all."

The panic settles deep in my soul. Despite the truth in front of me, I feel no closer to finding a solution to my problem, only more problems.

Chapter Twenty

"Ithrin naelith sylor thalnor."

When uncut threads still pull

Y FEET STUMBLE UPON THE decayed cemetery, the broken gravestones like sentinels looming over me. The smell of stagnant soil is thick in the air, its sickly odor mixing with an eerie whisper rustling through the trees. An oppressive dread seems to fill every inch of this forsaken place, a sinister force pushing down on my spirit until I feel as though I can't breathe.

My steps falter as I balance on the threshold of this morbid landscape, my heart pounding in my chest. Fear creeps through me as I kneel before the small grave, encircled by wilted flowers and remnants of fading memories. My hands tremble as I reach out to touch the cold, silent earth; a chill surging through my fingertips like icy venom, ravaging my soul. I shiver uncontrollably as sorrow floods every corner of my being.

The ground quakes beneath me, as if the fabric of existence has been torn apart, spitting me out into a realm of death and shadows. The grave opens with a thunderous crash and from its depths emerges an eerie figure, illuminated by the faintest glimmer of light, shrouded in tattered garments with bruises on its neck. My heart races and lungs seize as I stumble back under the heavy weight of fear and shock.

My Emmie, my little girl, looks at me with an intensity that is beyond this world. Her cheeks are ghostly pale, her eyes wild and desperate with a silent plea for help. Her trembling voice rings through the air with a deep-seated longing and despair as she begs me to release her from this hellish nightmare.

"Mommy," she whispers, her voice a haunting echo that pierces the depths of my soul. "Save me, Mommy...Why didn't you stop him? Mommy—you knew what he was," she cries in anger, "You knew, and you knew what he would do. Why didn't you stop him, Mommy?"

The tears stream down her cheeks, dark lines against that otherworldly glow as the same stream down my face in hot lines. "Emmie...I'm so sorry, Emmie."

The guilt and sorrow envelop me, pressing down on my shoulders like a heavy burden that I can't seem to shake. The tingling sensation races through my veins, pounding with every beat of my heart, never letting me forget my biggest mistake. With each passing minute, grief floods my soul in an endless wave of misery and agony, making me feel as though I am drifting further away from the shore and into a sea of loss and emptiness.

Emmie's bony fingers brush my skin like knives, sending chills up my spine. My throat tightens, and the words of sorrow bubble out on their own accord. The crushing regret sinks deep into my chest like a boulder, pressing down with such intensity I think I might collapse. Every breath is filled with bitterness and misery as if all hope has been lost in but a moment.

I reach out to hold her, to mend the damage I've done, but my hands pass through her, as insubstantial as my efforts to save her.

Her pleas continue, echoing in the empty void where my heart used to be, scraped out as if someone had carved out my insides with a dull, rusty spoon. She fades back into the earth, swallowed by the abyss.

My screams echo off the walls of the inky black abyss, reverberating off into nothingness. Tears sting my eyes as terror and despair threaten to overwhelm me.

My eyes snap open in a sudden surge of terror, my heart pounding against the walls of my chest like a frightened, caged animal. The air feels thick and suffocating, pressing down on me like an invisible weight as piercing sweat runs down my face with each labored breath. I desperately clutch at the darkness for comfort, yet my mind still cowers from the terrifying depths of the nightmare refusing to be soothed. Finally, I feel a comforting warmth surround me, despite being pulled away by the claws of fear, the warmth calls to me.

Jadis' hand finds mine, and his fingertips trace patterns on my palm, a soothing rhythm that makes me feel like I can breathe again. He wraps his arms around me as though he is that last shelter in a storm. But instead of finding refuge, my heart pounds against my ribs with an intensity that threatens to shatter them. I struggle to take deep breaths and choke back another scream. I push him away, but he refuses to let go, his strength tangible even through my trembling frame.

"Elora, it's alright," Jadis whispers against my head, his voice laced with concern, his arms tightening around me despite my futile resistance. "You're safe now. It was just a dream."

But my heart, still trapped in the haunting, refuses to believe his words. My struggles continue, my body tense and unyielding, as I try to break free from the shackles of fear that hold me captive. I want to believe him, to hear him, but it's hard.

Jadis' voice softens, each word wrapping around me like a promise, his arm tightening as though to shield me from the past. He seems to know exactly what battle wages inside me, the scars that run deep and threaten to tear me apart. With unwavering patience, he whispers soothing words, his touch a lifeline pulling me to the present, holding the pieces together, because I can't.

Slowly, the tension inside begins to subside, my resistance melting away as the realization finally dawns that I'm not alone in this darkness anymore, not today. Jadis is a light and anchor. I surrender to his strong arms, my trembling body melding into his, seeking comfort in the sanctuary he's offering.

As I lay nestled against his warm chest, inhaling that scent of woods and leather, my racing heartbeat gradually steadies, finding a rhythm in sync with his. He becomes a balm to my shattered soul.

When the trembling ceases, he asks quietly, "Do you want to talk about it?"

"Not really," I sniffle into his chest.

"Sometimes it helps."

It's hard, opening up to someone. It's never helped me in the past. It's usually the exact opposite. But then again, I'm pretty sure that therapist was sleeping with my ex-husband and therefore not really on my side. I realized quickly she wasn't going to help me and stopped talking about anything important. Jadis might be a rake, but maybe, this time, it won't do any harm. However, this would be the first time I admit, out loud, my guilt over the death of my daughter.

I tell him everything about that night. About how I saw it happen in a dream, a dream that felt so real I raced to the airport to get home the moment I woke up. It was real.

Carter's story was that she fell from the tree in our yard onto the fence of the adjacent pasture. The fence caught her neck, snapping it, but I knew better. I knew he did it. I saw everything, but no one would believe me and why would they? I wasn't even there.

I tell him what she said, in my dream just now, how I should have stopped him and that's when he finally stops me to say something.

"Sometimes, the magic here can amplify the guilt and emotions we feel subconsciously. It can make them feel real. Don't let the guilt consume you. There's nothing you could have done, We're talking about Cartwell, Elora, and you were mortal, you still are to a certain degree. His magic is powerful, even in the mortal realm, and he likely would have just killed you too."

Something snaps inside me. Maybe it was all the emotional turmoil at the surface, but now, after all these weeks, it breaks the dam and it all comes out.

"Magic can't be real." The accompanying sob rips at my throat despite my protests, the sheer struggle to hold them back. I'd promised myself I wasn't going to waste anymore tears on my past and look at me now.

"I thought we'd moved past this notion," he says, holding his hands up, showing me his palms like I've seen him do with an agitated horse. "You've seen so much of it already. I don't see how we're still fighting the idea, Elora. I get it—"

"No." My voice comes out sharp and jagged, barely above a whisper, but it feels like a shout in the stillness of the camp. My hands shove against Jadis' chest, fingers curling into the soft fabric of his tunic before I push away. I sit up, boots scuffing harsh lines into the packed dirt as I scramble back, desperate to create distance.

"You don't get it, Jadis. You have no concept of my life. You. Don't. Get. It." My words break apart as another sob tears free, raw and unwelcome. Hot tears carve trails down my cheeks, the cool night air biting on my damp skin.

I stagger to my feet, heart pounding in my ears, the world tilting slightly as I sway. My breath comes in uneven gasps, chest tightening like a vice. I need air, I need space. I stumble toward the edge of the firelight, the shadows beyond beckoning like an escape.

"Then tell me," he pleads, his voice low but thick. I hear the shift of his boots against the ground as he takes a step forward, his presence impossibly close despite the distance I've tried to put between us. "Please. Make me understand."

"Magic isn't real," I try again only to glare at him when he inhales to speak. "It can't be real, after everything that happened to me, to us. I prayed to God over and over to make it stop, to save us from the unending torment, to help me find a way out. I prayed for justice and when he ignored my pleas, I begged everyone and everything that might listen, whoever was out there with the power to help me, to help us and...nothing."

I pause to breathe but the next inhale catches in the dripping from my nose as those treacherous tears continue to fall, the edge of my tunic now cold against my chest with moisture. I turn away, raising the back of my hand to swipe at all the moisture on my face.

"If magic existed, then someone could have stopped him, someone could have saved her and chose not to. If there's magic, she should be alive and here next to me, not dead and buried where I can't find her, where I can't kiss her goodnight, or tuck that little piece of hair behind her ear as she smiles at me. If magic is real, then I was found wanting. I wasn't good enough to receive help and she's gone because of me...just like he said.

If magic exists, then I am everything he says I am...unwanted, selfish, unhinged, an unlovable bitch and it's all my fault."

Jadis doesn't say anything as my knees buckle and my body trembles, the cold suddenly overwhelming. I feel his warm chest against my back as his arms settle around me again, squeezing me tighter, resting his chin and then his warmer, softer cheek, on the top of my head. He just holds me until the shaking stops again, until my legs find themselves again, until the tears dry up and my nose clears and I can breathe again.

The rise and fall of his chest against my back anchors me, a quiet, unspoken reassurance in the chaos. The tension in my shoulders slowly unravels and he turns me gently in his arms, his grip firm but not confining, like he knows I could shatter again if he holds me too tightly. The tension in my shoulders falls as his fingers trailing lightly along down my spine, light as the brush of a falling leaf, steady and unhurried.

"You know that's a bunch of horse shit, right?"

I snort, inwardly blaming the tears for the sound and wipe at my face again. "And what makes you come to that conclusion, pray tell? You've known me what, a month, two tops?"

"I've known you much longer than that and you know it." His arms tighten slightly around me, probably making sure I don't run away again. "But that's beside the point. You've been back in this realm, thrown into it, I might add, for over a moon cycle yourself and while most others would cower or fight for their old life back, you fight for others. Every. Single. Day."

His words are determined and might actually sink into me, or that's just the rise and fall of his chest against mine, the rumble of his voice sending vibrations deep inside, grounding me even as my mind continues to spin. One hand shifts, tracing slow, soothing lines along my arm.

"You've already taken on a cause for the people here that have no voice. Don't think I haven't seen it in your eyes." His voice is softer now as his breath brushes against my temple. "You've become their voice, and they love you for it."

I swallow hard, my throat tight and he keeps going, unwavering. "Even over the last few weeks, I've seen you fight the fear and the anger you feel and stand against anything you view to be wrong and unjust. And I know you're just getting started."

His hands slide to my shoulders, pushing me back to look at him, steadying me as my vision blurs again. "The people want to see you, not your brother. You." His words are weighted with certainty, one I don't feel, as his fingers brush a strand of hair from my face. "The people smile for you, and we haven't even left Day Court lands yet.

He pauses. His eyes search mine as if willing me to believe him. "I saw them give you gifts in the village square to honor you and what did you do?" His rough thumbs catch the fresh tears slipping down my cheeks, wiping them away with a tenderness that breaks something inside me.

"You gave it back to them, quietly, because you see they have so little, and you do it sneaky like, so they don't notice and get offended." His lips twitch, almost a smile, but the sadness lingers in his eyes.

He pauses only to brush a stray tear from my cheek with the back of his hand. "You aren't unwanted or selfish, you're selfless and caring, to a fault I might add." His hands settle on top of my shoulders, as his green gaze pierces through me, as if daring me to argue.

"You keep an even head in the hardest of circumstances...mostly." His lips do curve slightly this time, the faintest tease breaking through the seriousness. Then his expression shifts, darkening. "An ability that concerns me for other reasons, mainly how you learned to be like that."

I swallow, the air between us thick with unspoken truths, but before I can respond, his grip tightens ever so slightly. "Now, listen closely Elora Aurelius," he says, leaning in until his forehead brushes mine. "I will hunt down and kill anyone who ever spouts any nonsense about you being unlovable."

His voice drops, low and raw, each word carrying the weight of a vow, an oath, a binding one. "I may not be some poet with pretty words, but I promise you this, I fell under your spell the moment I laid eyes on you and will be your sword in this dark world until the end of my days."

The sheer intensity of his words steals the air from my lungs. He cups my face with an incredible gentleness, his rough palms warm against my cool skin. "Our Gods may not have heard your prayers," he murmurs, his voice breaking slightly. "They can't anymore, but I do."

His thumbs brush along my jaw as his bright eyes search mine, filled with a pain that mirrors my own. "I may be too late to save your little girl," he says, his voice barely a whisper now. "And that kills me, but I will keep you safe. As long as I draw breath, no one will ever touch you again."

I stare at him, eyebrows raised, the cold night air drying my wet eyes. His words may not have been poetic, but were pretty, nonetheless. Pretty words I've heard before. Many times. I have no reason to doubt Jadis, his conviction, but the doubt is still there. The doubt is always there. I huff a breath through pursed lips, shoulders slumping in defeat. The guilt I feel day in and day out slithering to the surface until the hushed words slip from my mouth before I can stop them.

"It's my fault. All of it. I made my bed, despite my doubts, and condemned my daughter to a life of psychological abuse and a violent death. All the signs were there, I saw them every day, I remember them every day since and every night in my dreams. I should have stopped him, she's right. I should have left and saved us, but I didn't because I lied to myself and buried those doubts deep inside. I ignored my feelings to spare him and…"

"You can't blame yourself, lass."

"I can't? And why not? What do you know of any of it?"

"I know that male plays with your mind, your soul, your emotions. I know that."

I can't help but snap again, I'm so raw. "How can you possibly know what he does?" I try to pull away again, but this time he doesn't let me.

"Because he did it to my sister before he disappeared and found you."

The revelation stuns me. We didn't talk much about his past, Carter and I. What he did reveal was always vague, I realized after the fact, only giving me enough information to placate me. "I'm sorry," I say. "Is she okay? Your sister?"

He jerks slightly, taken aback by my question maybe? His features do soften again in memory. "No," he says, "She wasn't as strong as you. She chose to cross the veil right before I volunteered to live in your realm. That's partly why I took the job."

"And the other reason?"

"Because my spies said he was there." The hatred glows fiercely behind those meadow green eyes with a flash of gold.

"I see." My energy is gone, and I slide down to the softer ground to lean against a prone log nearby. He joins me, just to the left, close enough to feel the warmth of his thigh along mine.

"You're looking at this the wrong way. Your life with him." The venom is obvious every time he refers to *him*. "Now, after you have the big picture, like the lid of a puzzle box. With that final picture, yeah, it's easy to see how those thousands of tiny pieces fit together and what they mean. But you weren't given the final picture, just tiny pieces and only a few at a time. Don't blame yourself for not seeing the big picture from those tiny pieces. Most of them mean nothing on their own. There's no way you could have seen it. When you had enough of the pieces to get suspicious, you tried to get out, but you were fighting forces you couldn't possibly comprehend. Don't ever blame yourself for his actions or choices."

I sit in silence, for a moment. His words ring true. I know that. "You make it sound so simple."

"It is that simple and I know you're fighting all the lies he filled your head with. I just ask that you try and see it for what it is. I'll help you fight the lies; just promise me you'll tell me about your battles so I can."

"Ok...I'll try. It won't be easy though, to share—"

"I know. You've been feeling alone for a long time and have been punished with your emotions."

"You might have to sit me down and tell me I'm being stupid..."

"I don't mind," he says, reaching his arm around and squeezing until I let my head fall to his cushioned, muscular shoulder. "You're not alone now, Elora. Never again. Between light and shadows, between hope and despair, there is a middle ground, meet me there."

I nod, his warm body thawing the emotional cage I'd woken up in. My eyelids grow heavy as I stare into the embers across the clearing until it eventually fades into blissful darkness.

Chapter Twenty One

"Vaelrin fionis naelithor aelish."

Even one seed can produce a flower

WAKE TO STICKY EYES as the night surrenders to the timid rays of dawn. Jadis still remains at my side, his comforting hand on my hip. I carefully slip from his grasp and walk out to nestle myself in the tall grass of the serene meadow that surrounds us.

A quick nod to Dagen, the dark-haired Viking of a male, standing watch and then let the lush grass caress my weary body.

The meadow stretches before me in the soft, growing light, a patchwork of colors and delicate fragrances. Gentle hills roll in the distance covered with a thick carpet of wildflowers that sway in the light breeze. The first light of day touches the horizon, bathing the meadow before me in golden hues.

The darkness under the surface rises in the tranquility and the warm, silent tears trail down my cheeks like the golden rays that slither across the grasses.

No, not slither—carried. They are being carried, dragged, the sudden realization bringing my hands to wipe at my cheeks and my knees to rest up under me. Delicate tendrils of mist, twirl in a soft pale glow, pulling the golds, pinks, and lavenders across the landscape. Wisps of pale light seem to dance and twirl in the early morning air. My eyes grow scratchy and dry, aching with the need to close, but I'm afraid to blink. The wisps flicker and shimmer like distant stars brought down to earth, their graceful movements captivating. I glance to Dagen, but he doesn't seem to notice as they dance past me, blending into the sky beyond.

I sit there, my lips and mouth joining the dryness of my eyes as they hang open. The excitement of what I have just witnessed, ends, my heart still weighs heavy in my chest and without the distraction of whatever that was, I return to my melancholy. At least it is there, instead of the hollowness that has plagued me for so long. The guilt still plagues me, and the oracles words taunt me. I couldn't save my own child from a monster and one decision on my part could save or destroy all of this.

The sun gradually emerges from its slumber, painting the sky with strokes of pink and orange. I bask, eyes closed, in the warm glow of the sun as they caress my swollen face. When I open them again, little creatures, so small I almost think them fireflies, flit and stretch on the flowers nearby. Their little wings lined with glowing filaments.

One lands on my nose, and I can see its wide, luminous eyes and wild hair flying in different directions. As I look at it, it's face splits into a wide grin, and I can't help but match it. The weight I've been holding lifts a little. Strange.

It laughs and others join in, dancing around my face and hands. The sound is infectious, bubbling up in my own chest until I'm laughing too, the noise stirring the camp from sleep.

Jadis and Mik are the first to reach my side. Jadis runs a hand through his sleep-mussed hair, blinking at me like he's still half-dreaming, while Mik stretches with a groggy groan.

"What are they?" Mik asks, his deep accent highly apparent in his sleepy voice as he squats at my side. Some flit to his face eliciting a cross-eyed stare that has me laughing hard enough my ribs ache.

"I have no idea," I squeeze out between giggles. Their infectious energy and carefree spirit seeps into my being, casting a soothing balm over all the wounds that plague my heart. It's as if the land itself can hear and feel my thoughts. Which is impossible, right?

ANOTHER DAY OF riding passes. I've managed to get better at riding. Enough, anyway, that I can study my lexicon as we go. I really need to learn the language and I'm making great progress. Jadis and Mik had a heated argument partway through the day and I was able to recognize many of the words.

Mik leans over his saddle, getting closer to Jadis, his voice hushed but harsh, "*Vael* tell her *thyrelith*, Jadis. *Vaeloth* fight it?"

Jadis doesn't lean any closer or hide his voice. I don't know if it's because he doesn't care if I hear it, or because he doesn't think I've learned enough of their language to understand. "*Valeloth* can never be. She's above *thyranis myrran*. Brandis would never approve *sylorin* and you know it."

Mik is obviously upset and raises his voice. "Above your *thyranis?* You're a shading *noror thyrenor,* High Lord of *Aetherwild.* You're the same, you and she."

Jadis is obviously angry now and the tone gets more heated. I had been tempted to ride up and ask what's wrong, but now I think it's best that I hang back here. Especially if I'm the "she" they're talking about.

"You *naeloth loryn*, Mik? *Nael* exists *Aetherwild. Thael* High Lord *naelrin. Thael ilnor* guard of the Day Court, and she *ilnor sylaelin. Naeloth sylorin*, will *naeloth sylorin*, and you will *vaelrin.*"

I have a feeling 'vaelrin' has something to do with let it go or be quiet because Mik kicks his horse and rides ahead with his shoulders almost to his ears.

AS NIGHT SETTLES over our next camp, Jadis and Mik have appeared to settle their argument from earlier and sit near the crackling fire, pouring over a map. Their silhouettes are cast in flickering shades of orange and gold, their faces illuminated by the warm glow of the fire. The scent of freshly cooked stew wafts through the air, mingling with the crisp fragrance of the surrounding meadow.

I sit beside them, as always, my gaze alternating between the large tome in my lap and the map they study. They're speaking in hushed tones in their language again, but I'm understanding most of it. The guards on watch circle leisurely about the perimeter, only a flicker in my peripheral vision.

"Did you figure out what that little sprite is, lass?" Mik asks, pulling my attention away from the map.

"What? Oh...um...I think so. I think it's a Sunspark Sprite from the description. It's one of those that doesn't have an illustration so I can't be sure. I mean, they're said to uplift spirits and that's kind of what I felt, plus they live in the lands of the Day Court, so it fits."

"Sunspark Sprite...hmm. Never heard of them before. Maybe that's why there's no illustration eh? No one's seen them for a time?"

"Maybe." I return to my pages, watching Jadis in my peripheral vision. He's kept distant today, especially after their argument.

He traces a finger along the winding path on the map, his brow furrows in contemplation. "You should draw them then." He doesn't even lift his eyes from the map as he speaks and then quickly shifts back into fae to Mik, "The shorter route through the woods would save on time, but it would also take use closer to Shadow Raider territory." He sounds concerned.

I tilt my head, curiously. "Why not go through the woods? Are the Shadow Raiders dangerous? Because a change of scenery might be nice." I speak my best Fyrala Liorin'ae and the shocked look on their faces makes all the effort over the last week to learn it worth every minute. It's disjointed, my accent is terrible, and I don't think I got all the words exactly right, but they catch my drift. It amazes even me with how fast I'm picking it up. It's almost like digging at old memories long forgotten.

Mik leans forward, a lock of his bright, curly hair draping down his forehead, his keen eyes reflecting the firelight. "The woods hold secrets and dangers we can't ignore. The Shadow Raiders are a formidable group of rogues, skilled in stealth and ambush tactics. Crossing their territory could lead us into a confrontation we'd rather avoid, especially with your riding skills, or lack there of." He finishes with a wink.

I grab a small pebble from the ground and throw it at him, nailing my target right in the cheek.

"Well, at least your aim is better than your riding," he roars with laughter, doubling over as he clutches his stomach.

I roll my eyes. scoffing. Somehow, these two have the unique talent of making me constantly act like a teenager. But despite myself, a small smile tugs at the corner of my mouth.

Jadis remains quiet, his expression placid and unfocused. I study the map, my eyes tracing the outline of the forest. The dense trees drawn there guide me in with a whisper of secrets that's both entrancing and terrifying. Their trunks are drawn like witches' fingers on brooms.

"Is there another way through, a safer route?"

Jadis nods, a small smile now playing on his lips. "There's a small path that skirts around the woods. It may take a bit longer, but it means safety and avoids unnecessary risks. Wouldn't want you to fall off your horse...again."

I give him my best 'are you serious' glare, but it doesn't phase him in the slightest, so I raise a more frank finger.

Mik chimes in again, before Jadis can respond to my gesture. "We are here to protect you, Elora, first and foremost. Your safety is our priority."

"I guess we'll avoid the woods then,"I say with a sigh.

Jadis must have noticed the sadness, "It's for the best, little *naerinaelith*. While most won't know who you are yet, we can't risk the raiders finding out or getting their hands on you. They don't just raid and steal. They blame the high fae 'oppressors' for all their misfortunes and rarely waste an opportunity to make them pay."

"Are you ever going to tell me what that nickname means?"

"Haven't you found it in your little book yet?" He asks with a tilted smirk. I shake my head. "It starts with 'n' if that helps."

I'm once again glaring as he turns his back to me.

Chapter Twenty Two

"Ithoryn vaelrin naeloth thalna vyrith."

Wisdom alone does not always prevent failure

THE SUN HAS JUST CROSSED its zenith, its light finally piercing through the morning fog, as I ride along the edge of the woods. The tall trees serve as a protective boundary as we travel. There's not much to look at other than nature or the backside of the horse in front of me, so I marvel a little at nature's beauty—the yellow and pink wildflowers that line the path, the soft moss carpeting the ground nearby, the gentle sound of birdsong floating through the air.

My horse walks along slowly, almost as if he can sense my awe, his slower speed gives me time to take in the serenity of the forest. We round a bend, and I see a larger clearing ahead. Sunlight bathes the meadow, new or old I can't tell anymore, in golden light, mixing well with the bright colors of the trees. The beauty of my surrounding stirs something in my soul, awaking a deep longing and a desire for adventure. Something I haven't felt in a long time.

The path follows the edge of the wood and then curves out into the meadow up ahead. I feel a sense of freedom I have never felt before and know that I'm only now truly alive. Everything seems within my grasp, and I feel a wild joy in my heart.

The peacefulness of the forest is ripped apart by the deafening sound of pounding hooves and splintering wood. Evil laughter reverberates through the trees as they emerge from amongst the trunks, their weapons clanging loudly against one another along with a sparkle of steel in the sunlight. The brutes have arrived, despite our caution.

The bandits, their faces masked by dark scarves, slip out of the shadows like vengeful spirits, but I suppose that's what they are. Their eyes are filled with that predatory gleam you'd expect, and they scan our group with a mix of greed and malice. Each one bears the mark of a life spent outside the boundaries of law and order—roughened and scarred hands, unkempt hair, and tattoos etched into their weathered skin. Not that I think tattoos are criminal, but the subject matter certainly fits the stereotype in this case.

As they close in, their weapons raised high, my heart speeds its pace, fear and adrenaline surging through my veins. Their voices, laced with arrogance and a twisted sense of power, fill the air with threats and jeers. They're having fun, playing with us.

"Shades," Jadis says under his breath.

"Why the stars are they outside the woods?" Mik says through his teeth, his horse bouncing on its toes to my right.

"Well, well, what do we have here? Lost little lambs straying from the flock," a first man says, his horse sidestepping in agitation.

I don't know what's wrong with me, but I laugh. I can't help it, the sound pushes through my lips like it's an entity all on its own. The words coming out of his mouth are so cliché I expect them in a B-rated movie. Jadis gives me one serious side-eye from his position slightly in front at my left. I try to rein it in.

"Looks like we stumbled upon a feast, boys," another speaks this time and I fight hard to swallow down the next snicker and fail miserably.

"Not helping, love," Jadis says from the side of his mouth.

"I'm sorry," I whisper back, now focusing on getting my horse to stop sidestepping around. "It's just so cliché." That statement earns me a slight upturn at the corner of his mouth.

The male at the center of the group scans our persons with intelligent eyes, "Purses, food, and maybe a few valuable aelorin heads to add to our collection."

That stops any bubbling laughter in its tracks. Jadis chooses that moment to draw his sword, while I decide to attempt some diplomacy. I didn't look aelorin, after all, so I choose mortal tongue to maintain my persona.

"We mean you no harm. We're simply passing through. Please, just let us pass and we can pay you for your trouble." I work hard to keep the nagging tremble from my voice.

"Well, ain't you a pretty thing," another to the left croaks out. "You'll fetch a pretty purse at the slave market in Obsidian."

"Like the lady said, we wish to pass in peace. Let us do so, and I'll let you live." Jadis counters with a growl, his hand tightening on the hilt of his sword, the muscles in his arms tensing under the thin fabric of his shirt.

"Peacefully? Ha! Hand over yer valuables and we might consider letting you leave with your lives," the first one speaks again, his blue eyes flashing against the dark scarf.

"We have nothing of great value to give you," I try halfheartedly, my horse getting more agitated as the tension thickens in the air.

The man at the center growls, letting his horse gain a little ground toward us. "Don't play dumb, girl, it's beneath you." His brown eyes are warmer than I expect them to be. "You're dressed in fine leathers and frost linen, you're worth a fortune by your clothes alone."

"Yeah, she could strip out of those fine, valuable things right here," another snickers out, which was a mistake because he's now firmly in Jadis' radar. Jadis jerks forward, placing himself between me and the one in the center, who I assume is their leader from the subtle changes in the other males as he moves forward.

"Oh, look at the noble princeling, traveling with a bunch of misfits," the bandit to the left chimes in once again, but his comments earn him a glare from their leader, in this moment united with Jadis. I, however, stare at Jadis.

"Princeling?" He ignores my question, which is probably best, but I file that away for later. He swings his sword instead.

They close in on us faster than I think possible. I tighten my grip on the reins, my knuckles turning white as Faeryl lurches in all directions. It's too late, he panics, instincts overpowering any of my feeble attempts to control him. Poor boy is definitely not a war horse.

With a sudden lunge, he rears, his powerful muscles tensing beneath my legs. I cling desperately to the saddle, my heart pounding harder than ever in my chest. In a frenzy of panic, he bolts forward charging into the depths of the woods at a thundering gallop.

I hold on with every ounce of strength I possess, twigs scraping along my cheeks and pulling at my hair. The bandits and my friends recede into the distance, their voices and the clashing of blades fading into the backdrop of my pounding heart, or are those Faeryl's hooves? The world around me transforms into a blur of greens and browns all muddied together, the wind whipping through my hair and stinging my eyes. Branches and leaves lash at my face, as we careen through the dense undergrowth.

In the midst of the chaos, a gnarled and twisted branch strikes my arm with a sharp snap. Pain shoots through me, but I refuse to let go. The ground beneath us grows more uneven with hidden roots and fallen debris.

As abruptly as it all began, the wild gallop comes to a jarring halt. Faeryl skids to a stop in a small clearing, his hooves sending up a spray of dirt and leaves. I'm flung from the saddle, my body crashing against the forest floor with a thud. The impact knocks the breath from my lungs, leaving me disoriented and shaking, gasping for air that won't come.

THE STILLNESS OF the woods is overwhelming, and I have to struggle for every breath. Faeryl grazes quietly nearby. Asshole. I'm alone, deep in the very heart of the wood I was told was extremely dangerous. Even my brave companions, my champions, would not dare go here. Fear and panic well up inside me; what am I doing here? How can I possibly defend myself against whatever creatures lurk in this darkened forest? I can't even stay on my horse.

Every attempt to inhale brings a sharp stab of pain in my side, and I begin to worry that I might be bleeding internally. Again, I feel so out of place here amongst the wild and foreign, so helpless and weak—why did I think I can make a difference?

I try to sit up, the process slow, a surge in pain that shoots through my body making me wince and grit my teeth, fighting nausea. It feels as though every muscle in my body protests to the slightest movement.

My limbs throb with a dull ache as I move them one by one, taking stock. Sharp twinges flare everywhere, catching my breath in my throat. A pounding headache at my temples pulses, its rhythm intensifying with every movement.

As I try to get to my feet, the world spins in that dizzying blur of green and brown again. I struggle to regain my balance, my senses reeling from the fall and who knows what else. I'm back on the ground and it feels unforgiving, the jagged rocks and twisted roots digging into my flesh, leaving their mark as reminders of my second rough landing.

I reach out to touch my bruised and grazed skin, wincing at the tenderness that greets my fingertips. Since I can't seem to get up, I focus on gathering my breath and trying to steady my trembling limbs.

A rustling of leaves draws my attention fast. My head turns slowly toward the source of the sound. I'm alone. I'm unarmed, but my heart still remains steady in my chest even as the dappled sunlight reveals a flicker of movement, a small creature in the shadows at the base of an ancient tree.

It's dainty form shimmers with an iridescent glow, as if the very essence of moonlight has taken a shape. Maybe I started hallucinating? A massive concussion?

Wings of gossamer flutter with a grace and purpose I don't even think my addled mind can create. The sprite's luminous eyes hold a hint of mischief that's unnerving. Maybe this tiny being is privy to the secrets of the forest itself, or maybe my inner stupidity. But who am I to say that it isn't?

It dresses itself in the vivid hues of our surroundings—leaves and petals woven together to form a quirky garment that dances in the gentle breeze.

"Um, hello," I croak out a rather unpleasant sound. I'm suddenly embarrassed by my own ineptitude. My face grows hot when it giggles in response. The tiny tinkling sound unmistakable even if strange.

The little sprite's slender fingers, barely bigger than a toothpick, reach out for me and I draw back. I slide back away from something so small and fragile looking. Apparently, my mind knows something I don't. The feel of it, its presence vastly outweighs its diminutive size.

My back hits a tree at the edge of the clearing and with nowhere further to go, the sprite's small hand presses gently between my eyes. Her touch is warm and soft. I'm certain I'm a sight to see as I sit there bracing against the tree, covered in dirt, leaves, and twigs staring cross-eyed at some kind of forest sprite in complete and utter terror, even though I outweigh her by factors of ten, more even.

A sense of tranquility settles over me, the pounding in my temples ceases and some of the ache leaves my body, to the point where I slump against the rough trunk behind me.

The sprite's sweet voice trills in the air. It's language is almost melodious, nature's music, and I don't understand a damn thing she's saying, but she's smiling so it must be good, right?

The mischievous twinkle still lights her eyes, this little Forest Sprite, which I'm pretty sure she is, extends her hand in invitation. I huff out a breathy laugh but extend a single finger in response and somehow, she pulls me up to my feet.

"Thank you," I say, because what else do I say? I brush debris off my trousers, "I feel a lot better, thank you.

Do you think you can point me—"

"ELORA." A familiar and very welcome voice rings out.

"Jadis!" I call back in the general direction of his voice, turning my back to my new friend for a moment. "Those are my friends," I try to tell her as I turn back, but she's already gone.

Jadis is at my side in an instant, his warm, calloused hands cradling my face as though I might break, which isn't entirely wrong, at least not a moment ago. His thumbs brush lightly over my cheekbones, his eyes searching mine with a mix of fear and urgency. "Elora," he breathes, his voice low and unsteady, as if the word itself might anchor me.

Without hesitation, his hands move lower, skimming over my shoulders, arms, and sides with a deliberate, practiced care, checking for any sign of harm. Each touch is firm but still so tender, his presence steadying. The rough texture of his palms catch on the fabric, contrasting with the gentle way he moves, and I can't help but cling to the strength he radiates, the lifeline.

I muster a weak smile, grateful for their presence again, but someone is missing. I search around, looking for Triph, "Just a few bumps and bruises."

"Tell us the truth, lass, "Mik says, grabbing the scruff of the man at his feet. "This one was told that his future depended on the state you were found in when, and if we found you."

I glance at Jadis, and he simply lifts an eyebrow at me. "Really, I'm fine. Let him go." I nod at the prisoner Mik's manhandling. Mik's gaze shifts from the struggling captive to me, his brows furrowing in hesitation. "But Elora, he led the attack. Triph fell to the sword. Minimum they were going to rob you senseless, worst take our heads and sell you into slavery," he argues, his voice laced in renewed anger.

I didn't know Triph well, but it's still a blow. He was here because I needed protection, because I wanted to leave the protection of the manor. He's dead because I was bored, and I will never forget that. But isn't that enough, the loss of one life?

"Did he strike the killing blow?"

Mik shakes his head. I meet his blue eyes hopefully getting my point across, my need for compassion. "You all look no worse for wear, yes?" I ask the rest and get a series of nods in response. Jadis tries to take my hand in his and I turn to address Mik fully again. "I understand your anger, Mik. I feel it too, but toward the one who stole Triph's life. But if we resort to their tactics, we become no different than the oppressors they claim we all are in the first place," I reason, my voice surprisingly steady, resolute. "I want to bring...I don't know...balance, unity. I don't want or intend to continue these constant cycles of vengeance."

Jadis does grab my hand this time and he gives Mik a slight nod. Mik's gaze softens a little, the fire in his eyes diminishes slightly. With a sigh, he releases the male, severing the ties that bind him. The bandit, bewildered and incredulous, stares at me with a mixture of obvious surprise and I sense some begrudging gratitude.

"I have one question for you, sir," I state as he starts to massage his wrists. "Why did you leave the woods to attack us?"

"We were sent a message stating it would be well worth our time and that we should take no bargains as you were a dangerous lot."

"I see. And no indication as to who sent this message?"

He shakes his head.

"Okay, thank you."

"Who are you?" His brown eyes plead for an answer.

"This is Elora Aurelius, daughter of the Day Court," Jadis announces for the entire clearing and anyone listening nearby.

As the male stumbles to his feet, his eyes meet mine, filled with a glimmer of something. He nods, placing a fist to his chest in a bow and trots off back the way they came.

"All right then," I say once he disappears from view. "What's this about a princeling, Jadis?"

Chapter Twenty Three

"Vyrnor thalna, caelar sylorin."

The strong fall, but the stars remember

S THE SUN BEGINS ITS daily descent, casting that warm glow across the clearing, even this deep in the woods, Jadis decides we're staying here for the night instead of actually answering my question. It irked me until I realized he was more focused on Triph's rites of death.

Mik takes charge of gathering wood for a fire, his agile form moving swiftly through the surrounding trees, his footsteps barely making a sound on the forest floor. It's shocking how a male as large as him can move so quietly. His connection to nature is evident in his every move.

The clearing is quiet, save for the crackling of the fire. The trees loom around us like silent sentinels, their branches intertwining creating a sacred space when it's needed. The air seems thick with the scent of pine and the faint, bitter tang of smoke.

Jadis constructs a pyre in the center of the clearing, something he insists on doing alone. Twisted branches, scavenged from the forest floor, form its base, and soft moss cushions the body of Triph.

I didn't know him well—honestly, the least of all of my companions. But that doesn't make this any easier. His absence is still a hollow space among us, one that can't simply be filled with silence and duty. I stare at the pyre, at the way Jadis moves with quiet purpose, and realize I don't know how to feel. Grief, regret, relief it wasn't someone closer to me? It's all tangled together, impossible to unravel.

The wind shifts, rustling the trees, and I force myself to take a steady breath. Wildflowers—delicate blues, purples, and whites—are tucked among the wood, their petals trembling in the gentle breeze.

The five of us remaining stand in a loose circle, our shadows flickering in the firelight. No words are spoken, they feel too small, too fragile for this moment. Instead, one by one, they all step forward to lay tokens of memory onto the pyre. A carved pendant, a shard of stone, a sprig of herbs. I don't know what any of it means, but don't have the heart to ask.

When the last token is placed, Jadis sets the flame with only his hands. It catches quickly, the fire climbing the wood in greedy bursts. The orange glow warms and softens the sharp edges of grief, wrapping me in its warmth as sparks dance toward the star speckled sky.

The silence is heavy but not oppressive. It holds pain, loss, love. As the fire consumes his body, it feels as if the forest breathes with us, its whispers carried in the crackle of the flames.

We all stand, watching, waiting, until the last ember fades, the clearing dims. What little ash remains will be scattered across the clearing when we leave, marking it as a sacred place made hallowed by the memory of the one we've lost.

Jadis and I work in tandem to set up camp in companionable silence, our actions synchronized with days of practice behind us. His noble demeanor makes sense now and is something I never saw in my world. His face is soft in the light of the campfire revealing glimpses of vulnerability. Is this something he never intended on sharing with me? We secure our packs and blankets, arranging our belongings, he looks at me. The way he looks at me now makes my heart skip around like a stupid teenager, traitorous body. I can't help but wonder, once again, who the she was in the argument with Mik.

"You do realize that you just had us release Raynor Blackthorn, the infamous leader of the Shadow Raiders, yes?" He breaks the silence and settles down on his side of the blankets.

"Now I do," I say quickly and follow it with an indignant huff.

"Does that change your mind then?"

My answers come without any hesitation. "No. That was still the right thing to do."

"Well, it will probably come back around to bite us in the arse," he says laying back, stretching his arms behind his head and staring up into the canopy. The muscles of his arms strain at the seams of his shirt as it tries to stretch to accommodate them. *Look away now, Elora, this is not real. This is not going to happen. There's nothing there, you're imagining it all.*

"You know what? Nevermind. I should have kept him."

"Aye, lass?" Mik asks as he settles at the fire with us.

"Aye," I say, mocking him. "I would have kept him as a guest at my fire so I could ask him questions since he seems to know more about you than I do."

Mik snickers at this and Jadis grabs a small twig from the ground and tosses it at his friend. "I mean, she's nae wrong, Jadis."

Jadis sighs, but keeps to his study of the canopy above us.

"I'm captain of your brothers guard by choice. I wasn't born into servitude. Mik and I hail from a court long gone from this realm—Aetherwild."

I look across to Mik and he leans in, listening intently, watching my response, his eyes glimmering in the firelight. "Aetherwild? And you're the prince of Aetherwild?"

"Can't be a prince if your kingdom no longer exists, lass. That's why your brother gives me a seat on the council, even though I'm only his Captain of the Guard. Did you not wonder why I was there?"

I hadn't, honestly. I thought he was there to support me which now seems a little egotistical.

A solemn smile plays at Jadis' lips. "It was a thriving court once, known for its deep connection to the land and everything of the natural realm, hence being home to shifters. But as time passed and the realms changed, Aetherwild faded into obscurity, its existence is nearly forgotten today. Shifters are few and far between."

"Why do I think it was far more complicated than that?"

Jadis keeps quiet, so it's Mik that answers, probably tired of Jadis hiding everything. "You have to understand, Elora, most aelorin don't think shifters belong with them, but with the under fae and unseelie. They didn't think we deserved the power and authority that came with a formal court."

"Why? That seems presumptuous and downright ridiculous." I lean in toward Mik, since he's the one answering my questions. Jadis remains prone, staring into the canopy, but his eyes seem almost glazed over, lost.

"You'd have to ask them to answer that one. Never made sense to me either.

Jadis and I, we come from the remnants of that court. Jadis, the last of the royal line and my family a part of the upper nobility. Those that are left are tasked with safeguarding its knowledge, teachings, and the hope that one day, the balance and our home will be restored."

Mik stares me down intently as he speaks. Almost as if he's trying to push me to read something between the lines, to force me to comprehend his point. The crackling of the fire punctuates the silence that follows as I process his words.

"Is that why you both came to watch me? In the mortal world?"

A sigh escapes Jadis again. "Partly. I told you the other reason already. As Brandis and I got closer, he told me about you and the prophecy. We, Mik and I, saw in you the potential to restore the balance, despite the council's intentions for you. We saw the potential for renewed harmony that Aetherwild once stood for. We believe that, together, we can face the challenges and actually make a difference. The prophecy finally gave us some hope for our people, the few that remain."

"And now that you've met me? Now that you know me, what do you believe?" I ask, bracing myself for their epic disappointment.

Mik answers, his voice a gentle rumble. "We have witnessed your strength, Elora, your unwavering spirit. And in you, we found the beacon of hope that we have been searching for."

His face shimmers through the blur of tears I refuse to let fall. His answer isn't what I expected—a sharp ache settles in my chest anyway.

"No pressure," I mutter under my breath.

He laughs, but the sound feels distant, as if I'm hearing it from underwater.

"Get some rest, lass. You've had a rough day, relax, read your book, draw some of the things you've seen."

Chapter Twenty Four

"Lorys loriel naeloth thyrenil."

The past cannot be undone, only accepted

WHEN WE RISE IN THE morning it's decided, together for once, that we'll continue through the woods. We've already encountered the biggest threat they were worried about and lost someone, how much worse can it get?

Mik thinks I should see the Radiant Grove and since the Shadow Raiders shouldn't be an issue, Jadis didn't see anything wrong with that plan. Besides, trying to avoid the woods didn't keep me from the harm they were hoping to avoid anyway.

I'm beginning to notice the difference in the air as we approach these special and sacred places. It's something that settles gently in my gut, a feeling like intuition. Or, that could be the remnants of the fall I neglected to inform my friends about yesterday, but I'm not about to tell them that now.

As we travel deeper into the woods, the ambiance shifts, and a sense of wonder falls over me, for lack of a better term. Shafts of sunlight finally permeate the canopy overhead, casting dappled patterns of light and shadow over the forest floor.

I keep searching the undergrowth, my gaze flitting between trees, hoping for another glimpse of those creatures. I really think it may have been a Forest Sprite that healed me, but there isn't even a glimmer of movement now. Other than the Sunspark Sprites, I've been the only one to see things, and a nagging thought creeps into my mind—what if I'm just imagining it? What if the pressure of everything is finally breaking me?

A warbling birdsong filters through the rustling leaves, breaking the uneasy silence. It's a welcome distraction from my restless thoughts, and the damp scent of leaf rot rising up from below.

The path the horses trod leads us right to the entrance to the grove, a place where the heart of the forest dwells. Stepping inside the boundaries feels like slipping through a veil, as if the world has shifted around me once again. It isn't as disorienting as last time, but time seems to slow, along with my heart, matching the thrum of the earth beneath our feet.

Tall slender trees stretch toward the heavens and much like the Silver Springs, we dismount and our foot steps are cushioned by a carpet of lush moss. There's even those humming and singing mushrooms I encountered in my first moments in this realm.

Wildflowers dot the ground amongst the mounds of green, their petals unfurling in a kaleidoscope of colors. Delicate bluebells sway gently in the breeze, their fragrance wafting through the air, while clusters of golden daisies add a touch of warmth.

"What do you think?" Jadis surprises me, sneaking up alongside me.

I'm taken aback by the natural beauty before me. Everywhere I look, there are luminescent flowers—their petals glowing with some kind of supernatural power. Moonlit whites, gentle lavenders, and pale pinks all seem to be alight even in broad daylight, yet somehow their grace clashes with the harshness of reality.

"They say it's a place where the veil between worlds thins, where the energies of the fae and something...other, meet," he adds when I don't answer him. "Of course, my first thoughts of this place, more recently, came to mind in a certain alley as I informed you that I didn't even need both hands to ruin you."

I whip my head so hard in his direction my neck shrieks in pain. Jadis hasn't teased me like that for some time.

"You're disgusting," I mutter, though the warmth in my voice betrays me. "But this place is beautiful."

I turn away to hide the smile that curls at my lips.

"Aye, that's why you made me think of it."

Amidst the foliage, creatures make their presence known. Butterflies with wings as iridescent as stained glass flutter from flower to flower, their soft movements akin to a ballet. Songbirds perch on branches, their melodies filling the air with a chorus of sweet harmonies.

I trip over a mound of moss right into Jadis' warm chest. A sly spark dances in his eyes as he lifts his hand, wiggling his pinky with infuriating amusement.

Without hesitation, I smack his chest with my palm, ignoring the quiet huff of laughter that escapes him.

Once my feet steady, he holds my gaze, warmth traveling from his grip down through my body. Now, my heart races and my tongue slides out to wet my lips. Jadis' hand moves up my arm, grazing over my cheek as he tucks an errant piece of hair behind my ear.

"Careful love, whispers are rampant that there are mystical beings residing here in these woods. Keep your wits about you."

My jaw slacks and I have to shake my sense back into place before I nod, and he slowly releases his grip. His gaze flicks to my lips as I wet them again. I force myself to pull my stare from Jadis and move around the grove, willing my heart to settle back down. I remind myself that it's not real, what I'm feeling. No one, no one real, looks that way at me. I'm not worthy. It's not real and I'm only going to get hurt thinking it is, hoping it is.

Squirrels scamper along tree branches, their fluffy tails trailing behind them. It's nice to see all these familiar beings for a change.

As I travel deeper into the grove, a mist begins to weave its way through the trees. It curls and twists, dancing around my ankles and then higher and thicker.

The mist swirls thick and impenetrable, swallowing everything around me. I spin in place, my breath quick and shallow, straining to catch a flicker of shadow or the faintest hint of movement. Nothing. Only the oppressive gray pressing in, wrapping me in silence.

Panic claws at my chest, a familiar feeling as I stumble forward, arms outstretched, hoping to brush against a familiar form. My heart pounds louder than my footsteps on the damp earth, a relentless drumbeat echoing in my ears. This is the second time in 24 hours I've lost them. The thought gnaws at the edges of my mind. It doesn't bode well for the future.

The luminescent petals blink even amongst the mist, the butterflies inner light shines brightly so I follow the nearest one along the edge, hoping to find someone. Jadis was just here, he can't be that far away.

The minutes tick by. "Jadis?"

I spot him at the edge of the trees. His figure is only a shadow against the shifting mist but one I'd recognize anywhere. His back is to me, shoulders unnaturally still. I rush to his side, my boots crunching softly against the forest floor, and only then do I notice the translucent figure standing before him.

She's barely more than a hint of light and shadow, her presence sending a ripple through the air. His gaze is locked on hers, unblinking, his eyes glassy and distant, as though she's drawn him into a world I cannot see.

When my own eyes meet hers, and icy shiver claws its way down my spine, leaving my breath shallow and my limbs heavy, rooted to the spot.

Her eyes are pools of shimmering mists, purples, blues, and indigos. Her pale skin fragile looking. Her long hair floats about her head, blending with the shadows she hides in.

Mik steps up cautiously, his hand resting on the hilt of his blade. "Banshee."

"What? As in cries out to foretell your death, Banshee?"

Mik nods and goes to draw his blade.

"Let him go, please." I beg of the woman. I don't dare touch her. I'm not even sure what Mik thinks he's going to do with a blade against something made of mist.

She doesn't even blink or acknowledge that I said a word. I look to Mik for answers only to shout out some nonsense when another figure appears behind him.

Her voice carries a haunting melody as she places a small, frail hand on Mik's shoulder, stopping him, his rigid stance softens, the tension in his muscles unraveling as if drawn away with her simple touch.

"Fear not, for my sister only comes bearing solace."

Her voice is surprisingly soothing for a banshee. I had imagined something more like nails on a chalkboard.

"She felt his presence when he entered the forest and only wishes to unburden him from the guilt he feels for the souls he loves across the veil."

"His sister," I say, the tension in my own shoulders easing at her words. Only now do I notice that Jadis, too, has shifted into a calmer stance.

I watch as the other sister gently touches his shoulder. The tight creases of his face soften, the weight of unseen burdens lifting from his expression.

Mik's shoulders fall as he watches his friend carefully. "He told you then?"

I nod. The second banshee turns her attention to me, her gaze piercing and pained. "Your pain is palpable," she says with an unexpected softness that shoots straight to my heart. "I wish we could offer you the same solace as he."

Could being the operative word. Jadis' guilt is unfounded and could be relieved with some truth. I know my truth, my guilt, and it's real. They can't take that from me.

"Why can't you?" I ask anyway, my vision blurring.

"Your Emmie did not cross the veil. Lyraeth," she says, gesturing to her sister, "escorted his loved ones across the veil, but your Emmie hasn't crossed. I cannot bring you the same peace."

"Why didn't she cross the veil? Is it because she died in the mortal realm?" I grasp her surprisingly corporeal arm without thinking.

"Mortal realm or fae, it matters not. She simply did not cross. I do not know why. Her fate remains shrouded, hidden."

Heat burns the back of my eyes, my sorrow and yearning tearing away at me again. Her words stir up that same anguish; that Emmie still has not found peace. Even as I wish for release, I feel a part of me that's unwilling to accept it.

Jadis takes a heaving breath, as I cry quietly into Mik's chest not understanding how I got here.

The mist begins to dissipate, releasing its hold, as I catch tidbits of Mik's voice—low and steady, explaining what happened. Before I can fully process the words, Jadis pulls me from his arms into his own, the smell of pine and leather engulfing my senses, wrapping around me like a personal shield.

Chapter Twenty Five

"*Loryniel ryvith ilyshar vyrith naeloth.*"

A quick mind is sharper than any blade.

UR PATH WINDS DEEPER INTO the woods. For three days, we meander at a leisurely pace, not encountering even a whisper of something otherworldly. I get tired of my view in the back. You can only stare at a horse's rear end for so long before losing patience. But the alternative isn't much better. If I move up, Jadis will take it as an invitation to cheer me up, and I don't have the energy to pretend I want that.

"Stop fighting it, brother," I hear Mik state to Jadis again, recognizing the words from the earlier argument.

"What are we fighting?" I ask, sidling up beside Mik's horse.

"Ah, she speaks!" Mik slams his hand against his chest in mock shock. When I don't laugh and simply raise an eyebrow, he lets it go. "Ah, nothing important, lass, just the stubbornness of a fool."

"Jadis? Stubborn? Never."

Surprisingly, they both laugh. Jadis can't let it be though, breaking the nice revelry. "We're approaching the swamp, lass. Nothing good comes from the swamps. Stay close."

"Of course, I couldn't possibly go a few days without being in mortal peril."

His half smile reveals one of his infuriating dimples as he leans forward to see me on the other side of Mik.

"Ack, in all seriousness, lass, the path gets narrow and its more than the terrain that's dangerous, " Mik intercedes.

Great. I'm not sure I made the statement aloud, but Mik slowly slides to the rear and Jadis gently tugs my reins to pull me closer. Close enough for his thigh to regularly touch my own. It's downright torture.

I grit my teeth, trying to focus on anything else, and that's when I notice it—the air has changed. Heavy, damp, and clinging to my skin. The sharp, pungent scent of wet decay reaches me before the landscape does, the overwhelming stench seeping into my clothes and filling my lungs. The mossy forest floor gives way to sharp spears of grass jutting from the waterlogged ground, mud sucking at the hooves of our horses.

"I'm assuming you didn't bring me here on purpose?" I whisper across the tiny space.

"No. We have to cross the swamps to enter the lands of the Court of Thaw."

Faeryl stumbles beneath me, lurching forward. Jadis grabs the reins first and then the back of my jerkin to steady me and keep me in the saddle.

My breath comes too fast, my pulse hammering in my ears. I try to regain control, but Faeryl's unease ripples through me like warning bells.

"He senses your fear and anxiety," Jadis says, his voice firm but even. "That's what gets him all agitated. Calm yourself and he will calm."

I swallow hard, tightening my grip as I force a slow, measured breath.

"Steady, Elora, there's qui—"

Faeryl lurches again and I wonder, first, why Jadis gave me this bloody horse, and second, why the hell I didn't just go back through the doorway to my home and my realm. Despite the stabbing, it's far less dangerous!

Faeryl's hooves sink into the thick, muddy ground. As he stumbles about, leaving the path and pulling us from Jadis' reach, his front legs sink deep into a patch of sand with such speed it's impossible for me to maintain my own balance.

"El," Jadis cries as I fly forward, thankfully clearing the quicksand that captures my horse but plunging me instead into the murky waters.

God damn stupid horse.

My lungs ache as I struggle against the weeds, trying to figure out which way is up. The murky depths leave everything to my imagination as the forest canopy surrounding us lets in very little light. My eyes see nothing but grey and green water mixed with the shadows of decaying plants.

A faint light appears a short distance off, and I latch onto it. Reaching the surface, I gasp for air and freeze. The light shines from the sinister yellow eyes of a large serpent like some mutant horror film version of the already terrifying angler fish. It's sinewy body covered in slimy, mottled scales while its forked tongue darts in and out of its mouth, tasting the air for its prey. Tasting the air for me.

Settling on a slow retreat, I find my feet some purchase on the muddy bottom, but for every minuscule movement I make, the snake slides that much closer. I'd seen water snakes before and could guess that I have no chance of outrunning one in this realm.

My eyes dart around me, looking for anything to use as a weapon, settling on a large branch to my right.

I launch my body, lunging for the branch, waiting for the snake to strike. The branch crumbles under my fingers, falling to dust. My chest tightens, a surge of fear twisting in my stomach and stealing the air from my lungs as I turn to face the snake, I'm certain should have struck by now.

It barely moved and it smiled. It legit smiles, toying with me as I realize I have nothing to protect myself with.

Something warm and wet sprays my face just before a slimy, scaled head smacks my cheek. I wipe at my face; green so dark it looks black smears my fingers and the sinewy body sinks into the murky waters in front of me.

I turn to the nearby shore expecting to see Jadis brandishing his sword, but no. Their forms are small and nimble, with skin as black as the deepest night sky. Their bodies no taller than a foot or so, blending seamlessly in the shadows of the surrounding swamp. Some hide so perfectly it's only the blinking of their gleaming green eyes that hints at their presence.

"Grimscale serpent," the closest utters, his slender limbs shift around a large spear that drips the same green substance that I'd wiped from my face. Blood, serpent blood. As he shifts, elaborate patterns shimmer on his skin, fractals etched into the night. "Nasty, vile, and venomous creatures. You should keep your distance...Deliverer."

I think I might be sick.

He holds out a hand for me, I think as introduction until his tiny frame pulls me from the water. *What is with all these small, down right diminutive beings having superhuman strength?*

I land hard on the soft ground right in the middle of it all. Looking closer now it clicks and my heart skips. "Shadowmire Imps," I whisper to myself as Jadis and the others crash through the nearby brush.

"Elora, come away now," he yells, sword ready in hand as the closest imps help me to a seated position.

"Calm yourself, princeling," the first imp says, turning to Jadis grinning widely, displaying his rows of shiny, sharp teeth and a glint in his eyes. "Not all of us have been corrupted by magic. I'm sure we can come to an agreement."

"An agreement?" I ask, attempting to wring water from my shirt dripping under my leather jerkin. "What for?"

Surprisingly, Jadis answers first. "They saved your life, lass, you owe them a debt, usually taken in blood."

"Ah, but I've no taste for blood, yet. I'm sure there's some other way to settle this, knowledge perhaps...information?...a game? Entertain us? We haven't had visitors for quite a time."

"For good reason," Mik mutters, earning him an elbow to the stomach from Jadis.

The others stand behind, leaning on one foot and then the other. I wrack my mind as they speak, thinking about what the book said about these mischievous creatures. But then again, a lot of the creatures of my book are labeled as mischievous.

"Riddles!" My voice is sharp against the silence. Three heads swivel in my direction, their eyes widening at the sudden noise. Jadis' brow furrows and he shakes his head slightly, mouth turning down into a frown of warning.

"Elora..."

I pull myself to my feet and face him, my hand lightly resting on his chest. I can feel his heart racing, my normally stoic protector. "No need to worry," I say with confidence, a grin tugging at the corners of my mouth.

"How about we have some fun? A contest of riddles, for your entertainment. What do you say? You like riddles, yes?" I say turning my head to the imp.

"Indeed," he muses, "and what will the stakes be, my dear?"

"I need information and you're guardians of knowledge," I propose, my voice steady because I read about these folks and I know what I'm doing. "I answer your riddles correctly and you give me the name of someone who can help me find the truth."

"Alright," he says, his fellows whispering in the shadows, the intensity of their glowing eyes increasing in the excitement. I hope it's excitement and not the thought of lunch.

"If you miss my riddles, then you also tell me where I can find them."

The corners of his lips twitch and he nods. "And if I guess them right, I get to ask you for one truth."

The crowd murmurs around us, some of them emerging from the shadows, getting closer. "And if you get my riddles wrong, Deliverer?"

"Elora, stop," Jadis demands, grabbing my wrist and pulling me away.

"Jadis, trust me, please. I can do this. Piece of cake." I twist from his grasp, but he follows my hand, pulling it right back to his chest, his palm pressed over my wrist. I understand why he's hesitant, my track record in this realm has been less than glowing. "I'm asking you for some trust. I trust you with my life for some crazy reason, so I'm asking you to return the favor." This is something I'm good at, something that doesn't require magic. Knowledge can be more powerful than magic in my book.

His thumbs trace lazy circles, distracting circles on the back of my hand while he holds my pleading gaze and nods. He won't release my hand as I turn away.

"If I guess wrong, then I remain here to pay my debt as you see fit."

"Jadis," shouts Mik, but he is stayed as Dagen clamps a hand on his shoulder.

"Mik, she's asked for a little trust, and we need to give it," comes Dagen's infrequent but deep rumble.

I smile at him as Mik rips at his hair and turns away.

Every breath seems to halt, even the water ceases to move as my challenge hangs in the air. A wry smile curls across the imps spectral face. "Speak your first riddle, Deliverer," he challenges, his large eyes gleaming with an insatiable hunger. My stomach drops.

"No, I insist, you first, since I issued the challenge. It's only proper."

He raises an eyebrow, carving deep furrows into his dark forehead. The air is saturated with pressure, thick and heavy like a fog that threatens to suffocate me, my confidence waning. I can feel my heart beating fast in sync with the drum of silence in the swamp.

> "In murky depths where darkness reigns,
> Creatures dwell with scale that bear stains.
> Slithering shadows, lurking unseen,
> Their presence elusive, like a fleeting dream.
> With stealth they move, in waters they reside,
> Hiding in shadows, their true forms they hide.
> A name, a hint, to uncover their guise,
> Reveal the beings with gleaming, scaled eyes."

"So, it's a creature. Are you giving me my prize in the answer itself?"

"Clever girl. This should be quite entertaining, indeed."

The drum of the quiet is broken by Mik's foot tapping, the whole swamp echoing with each slap of his boot. He clenches and unclenches his fists, the tension radiating from him like a taut bowstring. Jadis stands still beside him, his arms crossed tightly over his chest, the flicker of a muscle in his jaw betraying his worry. The two other men exchange nervous glances, Fallon chewing on his thumbnail while Dagen fingers the hilt of his dagger like it's a lifeline.

"Now, I find one fault in your riddle though, as I would consider Lurkscales cave dwellers rather than water creatures."

The imp gives a sharp clap and grins, "Well met. Now your turn."

Mik lets out a loud whoop at the same time, throwing his hands into the air and spinning in place, his grin wide enough to split his face. I can't help but smile myself. Jadis exhales sharply, his shoulders slumping as relief floods his features, and a small smile tugs at the corners of his lips. Fallon slaps Dagen on the back with a bark of laughter.

"Fine." I smile to myself, my excitement building. This is going to be fun—he has no way of knowing what I have in mind. Outsmarting him is going to take more than just a few riddles, it's going to require all my cunning and wits.

"I live without breath.

I see without eyes.

I have no mouth,

But words I can speak."

His fingers rise to his chin as I finish, murmurs floating in the shadows behind him. I know he has it when his pointed, needle teeth gleam behind a grin. "That was a good one. An echo. Now a truth from you."

"And what do you want to know?"

"Do you love Cartwell?"

His question is a punch to the gut. How can he know my deepest fears with such accuracy? I'm mortal, I can die. Is taking that chance worth not answering this question? But what would be the point of that? Do I love Carter? Did I ever love Carter? That question has been haunting me for years, but I still can't find the answer.

"It's a simple enough question, Deliverer. Do you love him?" He asks again, tilting his head, his pointed ears twitching at the motion as his green eyes glint with a flash of silver like the gleam of cat eyes that catch a light in the dark.

"No," I spit out in haste, but it feels right.

"Lies," he seethes. He strengthens his grip on the spear in his hands, the meager light glinting off the sharp edge of the long blade at its tip.

Jadis makes to take a step forward, but I stop him.

"Not a lie," I say quietly. My gaze falls away to what distance I can see. "The man I married, I loved him deeply."

"See, lies. You married Cartwell, you fool. We all know this."

"No, still not a lie. Yes, I married Cart...well, but I didn't love *him*..."

His head tilts again, his eyes still flashing with anger but there's a softer edge.

"The man I married, the man I fell in love with, was a character he played. The man I loved was a figment of my imagination, a lie. So, no, I do not, nor have I ever loved Cartwell. I loved a lie. I still do."

The imp's head bobs up and down, his skin wrinkling as he squints his eyes thoughtfully. He exhales before turning his palm upward in an understanding gesture, a faint smile playing at the corner of his lips.

"In shadows deep, where darkness thrives,

They dwell among the ancient lives.

Rooted in gloom, they silently sway,

Mysterious guardians of the night's day."

Ancient lives...ancient lives...that could be anything in the realm of immortal beings. My fingers come up to tap my lips, the rhythm matching the frantic patterns of my thoughts. I begin to pace, the damp, spongy ground of the swamp squelching softly beneath my boots. Whispering to myself, I weave the riddle around as if saying the words aloud might force them into place.

Jadis shifts behind me, his protective instincts pulling him forward despite the warnings. He steps closer, only to stop short as the tip of a spearhead levels at his throat.

"No cheating, princeling. She must answer alone," the imp growls, his grin suddenly sharp and unsettling, the antithesis of his kind and mannerly nature thus far.

Jadis raises his hands, his expression darkening as he steps back, his boots grinding against the gnarled roots beneath him. Mik mutters a curse under his breath, crossing his arms and glaring at the imp like he might set him on fire with sheer will. Who knows, maybe he can. I still don't know the full extent of the power my friends possess.

I barely register any of these goings on though. My focus narrows as I circle the riddle again and again, whispers tumbling from my lips. "Roots...gloom..." My steps falter, and I freeze in place, my breath catching. "Guardians..." The pieces lock together in my mind, and the realization slams into me like a burst of lightning.

"Gloomroot Dryads!"

The words bounce of the gnarled trees around us and the imps pause, their wide eyes glinting in the dim light. A collective murmur ripples through them, the sound as strange and unsettling as the swamp itself. Behind me, I hear Fallon's low laugh of relief, Dagen clapping Jadis on the shoulder. Mik lets out another whoop, startling one of the imp guards into dropping its spear.

My imp challenger is surprisingly pleased. "A difficult one. Not many remember those people anymore. I'm impressed. Your turn, Deliverer."

"It's Elora, please."

"Elora, then, try your best."

I draw a deep breath, my mind racing to conjure a riddle worthy of his obvious cunning. Funny how the mind refuses to function now, when so much is on the line but refuses to stop functioning when you're trying to sleep. As the words escape my lips, the tension in the air grows again.

> "I have cities, but no houses,
>
> Forests but no trees,
>
> And rivers but no water."

I can't help the grin that crosses my face as the Imp begins to pace as I just had.

"Imagination. You've got a good one if you think that's a riddle."

I clap my hands together and yelp in delight, my smile so wide that it nearly splits my face. I start hopping from foot to foot as I shout excitedly, "Map. A map."

The imp grunts and waves a hand with spindly fingers tipped with sharp claws in the air. "Fine, here's your prize.

> In the depths unseen, where shadows entwine,
>
> Amidst the trees, my secrets align.
>
> Silent whispers beneath the moons glow,
>
> A realm of darkness where secrets flow.
>
> The dryads you seek will be found there."

"Seriously? My prize is another riddle?"

"I have given you the answer you seek. You never said I couldn't make you work for it." The sneer that stretches across his face reveals more bloody, infuriating dimples.

I grunt and stomp my foot like a petulant child. "Fine, lesson learned. Be more specific when dealing with imps. Your turn, *Imp*."

"Nyx. As you have shared your name, I find I should give you mine."

"Pleasure to meet you, Nyx." He scoffs a laugh at my pleasantries.

> "In the halls where stone meet masterful touch,
> Artisans skilled, creating beauty as such.
> Their hands carve wonders, shaping with care,
> Crafting sculptures beyond compare.
> Deep in the earth, where secrets abide,
> Their talents revealed, where shadows reside.
> Whisper the name of these skilled architects,
> Who sculpt the stones with their affects."

Another smile fills my face, I had read about these people only last night. "Stone Carvers."

"No hesitation. Perhaps I'm making my riddles too easy."

"Not in the least.

> In darkness I thrive elusive and sly,
> I follow your steps, as you pass me by.
> I dance on the ground, but have no true form,
> A companion to light in every storm."

"Too easy, Elora. You need to try harder than that to trick me with shadows."

"Shit," I mutter and both Jadis and Mik sigh behind me in unison. Mik is quickly growing exasperated as he slumps onto the nearest log that will hold his weight, raking his hands through his already disheveled hair.

Nyx sneers again, the mischievous glint in his eyes making my stomach flip. Considering how personal his last truth was, I barely take a breath waiting for his next question.

"What are your feelings toward our princeling here?" As if he already knows the answer, he raises a brow and crosses his arms around his spear, leaning in closer.

My cheeks burn hot. I don't dare look at the male in question, there's no way I will survive that. What are my feelings? I feel safe with him, protected. He promised me as much and that's all there is. The tingles don't mean anything, just lust after a decade long dry spell. Still, I want something deeper and that surprises me. Can I ever trust him enough to put my heart in his hands?

"I don't know."

"Oh, please, princess. You know that's not an acceptable answer." Nyx claims.

"Stop," Jadis demands. "This is too much, you're asking for more than she can give. Pick a different question."

"Afraid of the answer, princeling? Elora agreed to these terms. She will answer the question fully."

Nyx's question hangs in the air, and I feel a surge of emotions swirling inside. "At first," I start with a soft laugh, "I thought him an arrogant, egomaniac, who thought himself God's gift to women."

Mik's deep, booming laughter echoes off the cypress trees and stirs up the lurking reptiles. Chirps and croaks from frogs and crickets create a lively cacophony of sound, "You're not wrong." I can feel the warmth of Jadis' body behind me, his chest rising and falling with each hearty chuckle.

Nyx finishes his own laughter with a deep inhale, "And now, Elora?"

"Jadis...he's been here by my side, unwavering and supportive, even in the darkest of moments. When trouble comes for me, despite those opinions, it's him I hope for. I don't know why really."

I feel a connection to him that makes me feel safe and secure, but how am I to know what that means? I trust him with things I haven't told anyone else, and that should mean something, but does that trust go beyond companionship?

He promised he would protect me until the end, but is this feeling of assurance worth more than the words we share? I want to know the truth, but I'm afraid of what I might find out.

My breath hitches a little as I contemplate the rest of my response. I can't help but feel a tug of excitement in my chest, and yet I know that it could be caused by fear or the fact that danger is lurking just out of reach. It doesn't necessarily mean anything more—simply an instinctive reaction to stress and uncertainty. Plus, there's the other woman Mik argues with him about.

The warmth that spreads through me when I think of him is nice, but I know I must remain steadfast and protect my heart. He holds me close during moments of pain, and his eyes seem to light up when he looks at me, but I can't help but feel hesitant to assign a label to any of it.

I understand the role he's chosen for himself—my protector—but it's only that. Nothing more. At other times he keeps his distance. It's easy to get lost in his embrace, but if I do, I know I'll be putting myself at risk all over again.

"I trust Jadis. I trust him with my fears, my hopes, my past. With him I find sanctuary. He protects me, even from myself, without judgment." Jadis squeezes my shoulder and I feel that comforting heat leave and can't help but feel my answer doesn't live up to expectations.

Nyx almost looks sad, but nods. "Fine then.

> In realms unseen, where darkness unfolds,
> Their threads of shadows, secrets they hold.
> With nimble fingers, they spin and entwine,
> Crafting illusions, a web so fine."

A shiver traces its fingers up my spine as I suss out the answer. I most definitely don't want to encounter these creatures, but it appears I need to. "Shadow Weavers."

"Very good," Nyx whispers in return and I start to understand there is far more to this game than meets the eye. It's time for me to reveal my secret and end it before he gets another truth that just might send me too deep inside. This Nyx knows much more than he should.

> "I have keys but no locks,
> I have space but no room,
> You can enter,
> But can't go outside."

As Nyx paces in front of me, I know Jadis has cleverly figured out my play when his hand wraps around my upper arm, waiting to pull me away.

Time passes slowly—five minutes, fifteen, I don't know but it feels like hours before Nyx turns to me defeated.

"Well, Elora, you have accomplished a feat that no other has managed. I am at a loss. Perhaps though, it is just a bad riddle," he says, narrowing his eyes.

"So, you give up?"

"Indeed."

"A keyboard," I say. His eyes remain narrowed at me and Jadis puts more pressure on my arm, slowly tugging me backward. "A keyboard for a computer from the mortal realm."

"The mortal realm?"

"I grew up there," I say, as I shrug, fighting Jadis, but only a little.

"I think that counts as cheating, Elora," Nyx says inching forward.

"I think that's simply me learning how to play the game your way, actually."

We stare at each other in interminable silence. Suddenly, Nyx bends over, placing his slender hands on his knees and lets out a whooping gawfaw.

My own laugh comes out much softer and hesitant and Jadis releases his grip on my arm, but his fingers remain in place.

"Playing my game indeed," Nyx says between harsh breaths. "Come, we'll lead you out of the swamp. The safest route changes almost daily now."

NYX AND HIS people do lead us to the border with ease. We walk our horses and have pleasant conversation on the way. It takes most of the day to reach the edge of the forest, but Nyx says it's safe to camp. His people will watch from the cover of the trees.

On the way, he gave me a simple list of potentially helpful beings after he revealed he knew about my book the whole time. Some, he knew where I can find them, others, I'll have to find on my own.

He's surprisingly pleasant company. He explains that his people got a bad reputation because a few of the past leaders, from another line, were easily corrupted by power, a concept I'm all too familiar with.

"Elora," he says, taking my hand in his small one as we reach the edge of the wood. "Don't fight it so hard. Your mind can cloud things if you let it take complete control."

"Fight what?"

He sighs and squeezes my hand. "You'll see eventually. You are meant to do great things, Elora, if you so choose, and will be richly rewarded, with happiness and love. The choice is yours."

"You're the second person that's mentioned I have to make a choice. What choice?"

"If I told you that, then it wouldn't be your choice. Stay near Jadis, he will protect you, no matter what happens. Trust that it will all work out, even when it seems hopeless, never give up hope."

Not helpful, again.

Chapter Twenty Six

"*Nororin lorynin thalvith.*"

Fighting over ashes

TWO UNENDING WEEKS IN THE saddle and I'm finally to the point where I can walk on my own at the end of the day. Jadis, Mik, and I make small talk throughout the day, meandering through the field that connects the Day Court and the nearby Court of Thaw, but something has fundamentally changed between us. Ever since the swamp, three days of distance and generic conversation are starting to take their toll, the metaphorical distance between us growing. I had who they think told the raiders to leave the woods when they weren't known to before. Who told them where we would be and when? My questions were met with silence, so I pushed harder. My enemies are growing in number and somehow knew exactly where we'd be even though very few people knew our intentions. Brandis' court has a mole. I don't even know what I'm supposed to be doing as this 'Deliverer' or even if I want to do it and they seem hell bent on stopping me either way.

As we draw nearer to the Court of Thaw, the air has been getting warmer and warmer during the day. A strange juxtaposition when one would think the Day Court would be warmer and Mik tells me it is strange and unusual.

Tiring of it, I dismount and walk beside Faeryl, running my fingers through the tall meadow grasses. The scent of freshly brewed tea, flowery and tart wafts through the air as the sun descends to the horizon behind me. My daydreams appear to be reaching new heights, imagining scents with the sights and sounds. That is until soft mutterings of conversation reach my ears.

A deep, rumbling voice weaves alongside a soft, airy one, their words threading through the stillness--something about battle and futility. I take another cautious step, and the sharp crack of a twig under my feet shatters the quiet.

The conversation cuts off mid thought. My stomach clenches.

I clear my throat, awkward and exposed, and manage to choke out a hesitant, *"Hello?"*--because maybe, just maybe, I can convince them I wasn't eavesdropping.

Silence presses in, thick and suffocating. Only now do I realize how far I have strayed from the group. My heart sinks as I imagine them thinking what an idiot I am to wonder off alone...again.

What was I thinking?

Heat crawls up my neck, shame mixing with something darker. They'll think I'm a fool—again. That I'm reckless, incapable, a liability. And maybe they're right. Maybe I am. I can't comprehend how stupid I've become.

Or maybe...it's worse than that. Maybe, deep down, I still don't care what happens to me.

But that doesn't seem right either.

"Elora," that deep voice calls to me. "Come, join our fire, you are most welcome."

The fact that he knows my name is disconcerting, to say the least, and I find myself frantically searching for any sign of Jadis or Mik. I'd welcome Mik too. Honestly, I'd welcome Mik a bit more than Jadis considering my foolishness.

The fire crackles, and he speaks in dulcet tones that soothe like a melody played with a cello, those rich, deep notes that settle deep into your soul. "Do not fret. Prince Jadis approaches as well. We mean you no harm, Deliverer."

I'm really, truly getting tired of a title that means nothing to me. The weight of it presses against my chest, but I push it aside and step forward with hesitant footsteps.

The grass beneath my boots is flattened, trampled by previous feet. I'm assuming the feet of whoever is speaking to me. The wind shifts a little, carrying the scent of warm grass and lingering smoke, and something richer, like the dark spice of tea.

The large humanoid being crouches by a fire, a kettle on the stone before him. His slender form is draped in shimmering green scales, reflecting the flickering flames in the dying light. His back is draped in delicate, translucent wings, silver filaments dancing along the edges.

On his shoulder, no bigger than a hummingbird, flits about a ball of warm light, the other soft, breezy voice emanating from it. It flits in my direction and as the light approaches, I can make out sparkling eyes and a charming smile. He continues to speak in a wispy language that I can't comprehend.

"I'm sorry, I don't under—"

"He's inviting you to come sit and tea with us," the other rumbles, grinning widely, showing off his remarkable straight and brilliantly white teeth. He is stunning.

As the little light being gets closer, I cautiously extend a hand and I see Jadis crest the ridge in my peripheral. The little fairy descends gently, landing in my outstretched palm. His touch is as delicate as a whisper.

"Solanar!" Jadis extends a hand as he joins the group in the clearing. "It's good to see you, friend. I take it they're at it again if you've returned here?"

"Aren't they always," Solanar says, grasping Jadis' forearm firmly. "Come, you're just in time for tea."

"Lumis, you still hanging about this old coot?" Jadis asks, poking at the tiny being in my palm. He wisps out a response that makes Jadis laugh.

"You understand him?" I ask from the side of my mouth, trying to be surreptitious, as Jadis places a hand at the small of my back. His touch, as always, send shivers of warmth up my spine, and he guides me closer. That's the most physical contact we've had in days, and I can't stop the sigh from escaping my lips, treacherous body.

"You'll find it easier to understand the languages when you've completed the change." He leans into my ear to whisper, "Should you choose to."

I stare at Jadis' friend as he bends over the kettle. "Wait..." I whisper to Jadis, "He's a sentinel, isn't he? Solanar?"

"Aye, a moonshadow. Why?"

"You're friends with a Moonshadow Sentinel?" I lean in closer, my shock snapping from my mouth in a loud whipser.

"Aye," he answers as if it's nothing. As if being on friendly terms with the very beings that maintain the balance between night and day and harness the moon is nothing to write home about.

As we sit near the fire, Lumis flits back to Solanar's shoulder while he gracefully passes a small mug to me, the heat permeating the ceramic and seeping into my stiff hands. Solanar's eyes sparkle with the reflection of the night sky, the incredible depth sucking me in.

"I have heard your words, your hopes, and your questions, Elora," he hums, blowing gently over his own steaming cup.

"You and everyone else it seems," I say which starts a warm, deep laugh in his chest. "Do you have any words of wisdom for me that aren't incredibly vague and slightly condescending? And don't tell me I have a choice to make, I've heard that twice already and it's most definitely not helpful and that was incredibly rude, I'm sorry."

He laughs outright and it seems to shake the ground beneath me. "Oh, your candor is refreshing. A fine pair you two must be." He pats Jadis on the shoulder with a pale, luminous hand.

"You have many choices to make, my child, and tests to pass, one very soon again, some you'll have to complete alone, but you're doing well so far.

I understand vague is frustrating, but many will be attracted to your presence, good and bad, and those who dabble in the work of the fates know how dangerous it is to reveal too much."

"Dangerous?" I follow my question with a tentative sip of tea. The first sip is warm, the floral notes unfolding slowly before a hint of herbs lingers on my tongue. There's a delicate sweetness to it—unexpected, unfamiliar. Heat spreads through me, sinking into my limbs, curling around my toes like a slow-burning ember.

Lumis is perched on Solanar's shoulder with a tiny, leaf-shaped cup, fluttering his wings absentmindedly, creating faint ripples on the surface of the tea in Solanar's cup.

"Indeed. Too much can rip the fabric and change everything. We're too close now to risk it."

The fire crackles softly, sending lazy spirals of smoke into the cool night air.

"Too close to what?" Jadis asks for me.

"A new beginning."

That's all he would say. His words hang in the air, final and unyielding, like a door slammed shut. It was the literal end of the conversation, but I still have so many questions, need so many answers.

Jadis, already knows me so well and steps in to spare me from further fumbling. Or maybe he simply wants to steer the conversation in a new direction. Either way, his smooth pivot saves me. "So," he says, his tone light but deliberate, "the tensions between the Spritelings and Fire Dancers seem to be growing again."

"The Gods have always been at the heart of this conflict," Solanar states, easing back into a more comfortable position. "But, yes. I thought we had ended this and suddenly, now, they're at it again." His long fingers toy with the edge of his cup, and the firelight casts shifting patterns across his sharp features.

"We have found other forces at work recently, perhaps they are involved. But yes, the Gods, or rather, their misguided interpretations," Jadis interjects. He cocks his head, his eyes locking on mine for a moment. His lips curl into a half smile, not mocking but inviting, as though he's testing if I'll follow his line of thought.

"The Spritelings and the Fire Dancers have been battling each other for centuries. A long standing, deeply seated rivalry. Mostly over territory and resources, now, but it all started over controlling the energy of a sacred grove. Both sides believe they have a Gods given right to it."

"They each revere different deities, embodying opposing aspects of the natural world," Solanar explains. "They believe their Gods deserve loyalty and supremacy."

"Like I said, misguided," Jadis finishes.

I settle into Jadis' side, my shoulder crawling back down away from my ears as I sip at the gentle tea in my hands. "Aren't the Gods all powerful beings that wish to be revered? How is that belief misguided? Aren't most religions based on reverence and sacrifice in hopes of receiving a blessing? In this case, power." Our conversations have never steered this direction, other than Jadis mentioning their Gods wouldn't have heard my prayers.

Solanar takes the chance to answer, his voice almost as soothing as the tea, the deep baritone thrumming in my chest. "Our Gods were powerful beings."

"Were?"

"They rest in eternal sleep, now, after the realm changed," Jadis' voice hums in my ear.

"We fae acknowledge the existence of the Gods, obviously," Solanar says, "We even hold reverence for them, that's not the issue. Our connection to the divine is more inherent and intrinsic. Rather than seeking constant guidance, as the mortals do, or even intervention, we draw strength and inspiration from the magic that flows through our very beings."

I ponder these words, trying to fit them into my own research. In this realm, magic is an integral part of their existence. The aelorin, and maybe even the under fae, view themselves as manifestations of the mystical forces of nature. So, they are supposed to view their abilities and powers as innate connections to the divine. Any interactions with the Gods would have been abstract or symbolic.

"So, your faith is more centered around the understanding that you are conduits of divine energy then?"

"Aye, so that m—" Jadis starts, but Solanar cuts him off with a raised hand, his eyes fixed on me. He watches the gears in my mind turning, his lips curling into a knowing grin, as though he can actually watch the pieces falling into place before I do.

"Your actions and choices are intertwined in the natural balance. No prayers or guidance, no intervention but your own agency through the innate magic you possess as a guide. Your connection with the land is supposed to be your guide."

"Indeed," Solanar says, his voice smooth as he lifts his cup to his full lips. The firelight reflects in his star filled eyes, giving even more of an otherworldly gleam as he drinks deeply.

I glance as Jadis, whose brows knit slightly, though he nods in agreement. The flickering flames throw shadows across his face, softening his sharp features as he leans in to listen.

"The conflict then, over a sacred grove would be futile."

Solanar sets his cup down gently, the ceramic clinking softly against the stone in front of him. "Precisely," he says, a satisfied glint in his eye. "But why?"

"Because the magic of the sacred grove was given to it through an innate connection with the Gods. If the Spritelings and the Fire Dancers don't already have that connection, no matter how long or how hard they fight, they can't create something they have to be born with."

Solanar claps sharply, leaning back far enough that his feet temporarily leave the ground, eyes twinkling. "She's a sharp one, isn't she!"

Jadis smiles, "Like I said, misguided."

We settle in beside Solanar's fire and I mull over what they told me. The information tosses about in my head, like a ball in a pinball machine, for a good part of the night. It seems insanely silly to fight over something, killing and maiming each other, with no chance at victory or at least achieving your end game.

I APPROACH JADIS in the morning, catching him off guard as the words burst from me, sharp and unrelenting, before I can even consider the usual pleasantries. "So, they're killing each other for nothing? And you do what? Sit here and just call them misguided?"

He turns slowly, his expression hardening, the warmth I'd come to expect nowhere to be found. "What do ye propose we do, Elora?" He asks, his tone flat but dangerous as he returns to tending his horse. "They've been fighting over this for centuries."

My hands curl into fists at my sides, trembling with the force of my conviction—or perhaps with fear that he might be right. "We...we...we challenge their perspectives," I snap, my voice rising. "We remind them that there's another way to live, without violence and hatred. Get them to see reason."

He spins then, his face twisted in a mask of rage that sends a chill down my spine. The cords in his neck stand out like stretched wires, his jaw tightening so hard I wonder if he might snap. When he speaks, his voice is razor-sharp, every word cutting through the air, slicing me. "And how do ye plan on doing that, hmm? Ye have some brilliant idea that no one else has thought of in three centuries?"

The weight of his unexpected anger slams into me, and for a moment, I falter. My chest tightens, but I refuse to back down. I glare at him over my horse, every nerve in my body taut with defiance.

A snicker breaks the tension, Mik's quiet amusement spilling from the shadows where he leans lazily against a tree. It's like flint to a spark—Jadis and I whip our heads toward him in unison, matching glares silencing him instantly.

"Watch me," I snarl, swinging myself up into the saddle with more force than grace. The leather creaks under my grip as I grab the reins, my knuckles white. My pulse thrums in my ears as I stare Jadis down, daring him to stop me. He takes a step forward, his lips parting as if to say something, but I don't wait. I nudge Faeryl, the sound of hooves on packed earth echoing all around.

IT ISN'T HARD to find them. The scene before me unfolds like a waking nightmare—a cacophony of chaos and violence. Flames dance and crackle in the air, painting streaks of orange and red against a darkened, smokey sky. The acrid smell of burning grass and charred flesh stabs at my nostrils, mingling with the sharp, metallic scent of blood.

The ground trembles beneath us, despite the small size of those involved. Their fierce expressions fueled by rage and hate. They move with startling speed, each blow landing with a force that belies their size. The sound of their war cries cuts through the crackling flames, shrill and unrelenting, leaving the air heavy.

I stand frozen for a moment, the heat of the fire licking at my skin as the scene sears itself into my memory. There's something primal here, something ancient and unyielding that no words could ever fully capture.

As I urge Faeryl forward, his hooves pound against the earth, the vibration traveling through my body. Fear clenches at my heart, but I can't just stand by while violence consumes them, while lives are needlessly lost.

My eyes dart from one side to the other, taking in the warriors locked in combat. Spritelings and Fire Dancers clash with spells and weapons, magic mixing in a dazzling display of power. I'm most definitely in over my head. The air crackles with energy, sparks lighting up the darkness like fleeting stars. The hairs on my arms rising beneath my shirt sleeves, brushing against the soft fabric.

I feel the surge of adrenaline course through my veins as I maneuver through the chaos, my heart pounding in my chest. A stray spell grazes my arm, leaving searing pain in its wake, but I push forward. I made this decision; I'm sticking to it.

Voices blend together, a cacophony of threats, shouts, and battle cries. I strain to make my voice heard above the clamor, begging and pleading for them to listen, to see reason, but my words seem to be swallowed, carried away by the wind.

I ride toward the edge of the battle, searching for an opening, a chance to make them hear me. The ground grows uneven beneath us as we approach the outskirts, the terrain changing from grassy fields to more uneven mires. With a jolt, Faeryl stumbles.

"Shit, not again," I yell, but damn it, I maintain my seat. Sparks fly from every direction straight at Faeryl's chest and he screams in pain and rears. I'm not as lucky this time. I fly from his back, landing hard on the muddy ground with a squelch.

Pain shoots through my body, an all too familiar pain, as I struggle to regain my footing. My muscles protest after my sudden impact. I force myself to my feet, feeling the sting of minor injuries and the growing weight of impending exhaustion.

"Faeryl," I yell, as he bolts in the direction we had just come from.

I look around. A short distance away, two figures lay, soaked in their own blood, the crimson seeping into the ground beneath them. Their chests heave desperately for air as they writhe in pain, their faces contorted with anguish and terror, frantic, young eyes begging for mercy. The horror of the scene is almost too much to bear. What did I do?

I crouch down beside them, my hands shaking as I hold their battered bodies close. Blood soaks into their garments, and their breaths come out in ragged gasps, the grip of death tight on their fragile souls. Tears trail down my cheeks, cool against my hot skin as I stare sorrowfully at their faces.

War and death are not for me.

"This is senseless," I cry to no one. "I'm so sorry."

A rumbling growl of rage reverberates through the air as a small, cold, steel blade presses against my throat. I can feel every drop of sweat trickle down my spine as I'm met with a blistering accusation of "What did ye do?", each syllable oozing malice like venom from a snake.

"Elora," Jadis roars in the distance as I still, barely breathing as that only pushes the blade harder against my skin.

The slap of steel sounds, and I'm pushed aside. Mik's wolf floods into the space beside me, snarling with teeth like white daggers against his night black muzzle. No sooner have they been summoned; the males close in—their angry faces demanding my retribution.

"I'll ask one more time, woman, what did ye do to my son? His voice booms like thunder, and his red eyes are pools of boiling rage. Still, I can see the grief that flows from them like rivers, tearing away at my soul as his words cut through me.

The only thing that draws his gaze way from me is the approach of a Spriteling, their leader perhaps from the look of her. Her tiny frame flitting in swiftly, the dust trailing behind her shimmering with an almost violent intensity.

"I did nothing but try to bring comfort to the dying! This is your fault," I scream, my throat hoarse from the force of it as salty tears slip onto my tongue.

"Your son lay here dying, alone, because of your reckless ambition for power, power you would already possess if you could ever have it and you damn well know it. You cut their lives short, their dreams shattered by the very people who are supposed to protect them." I shudder in pain as I intake air into my ragged body.

"Don't you even see what this foolishness is doing?" My voice cracks, raw with desperation, as I lean in closer to the fray. "Can't you see the cost? The grove won't give you anything more—neither of you. The Gods won't bless you with more power than you already have."

I gesture my cradled hands toward the battlefield, the flames casting grotesque shadows over the carnage, grassy meadow all but gone. "Is your hunger for power worth this? Worth your sons? Your daughters?" My voice rises, trembling with both fury and grief. "Look around you. Count all the lives lost as a consequence of your insatiable thirst."

The Spriteling's eyes blaze with fury as tears brim at their corners, her petal wings drooping behind her, "Sometimes the few must be sacrificed to save the many. We are suffering and dying in droves. Our beloved land is evaporating before our very eyes."

"*Your* people are starving?" The Fire Dancer leader roars across the divide I sit in, his face twists in anger, his eyes burning like hot coals, his flaming hair wild and tangled. He thrusts an accusing finger toward me and his kin in my palm, his lip curling in disgust. "My people can barely stand—their bellies forever aching. We have no children born with the spark of life. What few babies are born are weak, their flames barely a flicker before they're snuffed out."

The clash of steel interrupts his tirade as the two leaders collide, their blades meeting in a storm of sparks and ringing steel. Around them, the cries of the dying hang heavy in the air. The Fire Dancer soldier in my hands lets out a ragged gasp, blood bubbling from his lips as his body collapses like a puppet with its strings cut. His life leaks away, crimson pooling beneath him like water into a cracked canoe.

"Don't you see?" I lift my hands gently toward them, desperate to get their attention. "You state yourself that no children are born and yet you're wasting the lives of those you already have. You suffer the same fates. Are your children strong, do you have babies born?" I ask of the Spriteling lady, my voice carrying through the air with something I've never heard from myself before.

Her reply is venomous, her voice slicing through the air like her blade. "What children?" She spits, her wings quivering with barely restrained fury. "Unlike these bastards, not one child has been born to us in decades." The spittle flies from her mouth, spraying the Fire Dancer lord straight in the face.

Shaking with rage, I shout the words that feel like fire in my throat. Tears spill down my cheeks, and I feel desperation as life slips away in my hands. I look at them, pleading with wide eyes for some kind of answer to this nightmare. "And how in the hell will possessing a sacred grove change any of this, you idiots," I cry, sensing a life fade further in my palms, my tears falling on their bloody faces. "You can't take that power for yourself. Your Gods gave you everything you need already. You're supposed to protect your children with every fiber of your being. How does grasping at nothing help them? How does it save them from this?" I ask, lifting their children to their faces, shaking my hands. "Their blood, all this blood, is on your hands."

"You know nothing, fae whore. He said it was possible, that this was the only way" The Fire Dancer seethes, sparks flying in his wake.

I glance at my four companions—my friends. Their faces are etched with exhaustion, resolve, and something deeper: trust. The weight of it all presses against my chest like an iron band, threatening to crush me. This is my doing. I put us here. And now, I have to find a way to make it right.

I square my shoulders, forcing the trembling in my hands to still. The stares of my opponents burn into me, but I refuse to flinch. Instead, I lift my chin, meeting their glares head-on.

"I'm Elora Aurelius," I say, my voice calm but unyielding, ringing out over the tense silence. "The Deliverer. That's what I know."

The words hang in the air, the first time I've uttered them myself, but still heavy with certainty. I am the Deliverer. Around me, the fire crackles faintly, and for a moment, even the forest seems to hold its breath.

"You all know how important balance is for this realm, correct?"

Surprisingly, they both share angry, tense nods.

"You've lost sight of this," I say, my voice trembling, the weight of the truth pressing hard on my soul, but it is the truth. "Everyone has. The balance is what holds this realm together, and instead of working to restore it, you've fought harder—century after century—to tip the scales further in a futile search for more power."

Jadis stands rigid at my side, his arms crossed tightly over his chest. His jaw clenches with each word, the muscle there twitching as if holding back his own outburst. Beside him, Mik shifts uneasily, back in his fae form, his boots scuffing the ground as he glances between the others. For once, he says nothing, his smirk absent as he watches me intently, the dagger in his hand held still, a rarity in itself.

I take a shaky breath, my chest heaving as tears collect on my lower lid. My voice cracks, raw with anguish, as I continue. "Power should never come at the cost of innocent lives. Never at the cost of your family."

Fallon stands at the edge of the group, his breath leaving him in a sharp exhale. His fingers tighten around the hilt of his sword, his knuckles stark against his skin, as though holding his tongue takes as much effort as holding steel.

Beside him, Dagen shifts closer, his brows drawn tight with unease. His hand finds Fallon's shoulder—not to restrain, I think, but steadier, a silent warning or maybe a quiet, softer resistance.

My words falter, a sob breaking free as I pull my arms in tighter, trying to hold the grief in, while not harming the bodies in my hands any further than they already are. "It should never come at the cost of our children."

Around me, the air feels charged, the tension crackling like an invisible storm as my words settle. The Fire Dancer lord paces a few steps away, flames licking at the ends of his wild hair, his fists clenched as though the truth of my words strike deeper than he'd like to admit. Across from him, the Spriteling female's wings quiver, her glare faltering for the briefest of moments before she straightens, spitting her defiance at the male in front of her.

I don't let her speak any more vitriol.

"Our children should not have had to endure such suffering," I seethe, my voice like a whip that lashes the air in my bitter anguish. Tears pool in the corners of my eyes and run like tiny rivers down my face. I do realize that I'm projecting my own loss on them, but right now I don't care. It's one thing to have your child taken from you because of someone else, but to cause it yourself is something I cannot understand.

"Their lives are precious, and yet you toss them aside like simple pawns in a game. I would give anything to get mine back and you throw yours away. For nothing."

I can't see. My vision ripples, distorting the world around me.

I'm drowning.

The weight of past and present grief pulling me under. My breaths come fast and shallow, each one scraping against my chest. I try to surface, but the pain is too much—it's all too much.

My lips part, but no words come. The silence burns in my throat, a dam holding back the flood I can't bear to release.

Jadis steps closer, his presence steady and grounding as always, but when his hand touches my shoulder, I flinch. A shudder wracks my body as I shake him off, unable to bear the comfort—or the pity—I know he means to offer.

The Spriteling lady is the first to break, collapsing on my leg with her hand desperately grasping at her son's still face. "My Gods! I am lost. What have I done?"

Her pleading gaze pierces mine with agony, "Please, understand, we're desperate. More power could free us from our suffering. That's what we were told. That there's a chance. We are so desperate that we're grasping for a glimmer of hope, though you describe it as a criminal act...your people stealing our land..."

I feel my chest tighten as the fury in her voice shifts and I wonder if I've gone too far this time. I can feel my own men behind me, tense and ready for the worst, but I dig in my heels. Part of me feels as if my words have been too sharp, too pointed, and that I deserve to be ushered right back to Brandis and thrown away, locked in my chambers. A punishment for putting my nose where it doesn't belong.

I nod, maintaining my empathy with her over the loss of a child, and I don't think what she said is untrue. I have an aching feeling that the Aelorin have caused many of these hardships in their own quest for power, a power that has nothing to do with magic.

"Power can corrupt, but unity can heal. When we see our shared pain, our shared struggles, that's where we find the strength to overcome, to build bridges, to make change."

My words pound the air, smothering the screams of battle and crushing all sound into a brittle stillness. Everywhere is silent, save for the sour memories of the males that had been taken by war laying in my hands. The faces of starvation twist their features into grotesque masks of pain, making this battlefield crueler than any that I have ever read about.

"Sharing our pain won't bring my son back," The Fire Dancer cries out from my other side, his small fingers digging into my flesh through the soft leather like twigs when you push into a bush.

"No, it won't bring my daughter back, either, otherwise she'd be here next to me now. But we can make the effort to honor their lives by not letting their deaths be meaningless."

His piercing eyes fix on mine, searching for an answer to his unspoken questions. He then shoots a hateful glare at the lady before the muscles of his face contort and his voice rises back to a growl. I tense waiting for the violence to return, but his next words surprise me, "Our petty differences have consumed us, blinding us to the cries of the innocent." His hand flies out toward me as he exclaims in a demanding tone, "We must forget our differences and forge an alliance against our real foes!"

"Uh, perhaps you should help your people gain strength first," I stutter out. This was not going as I planned, not that I had a plan, but starting another war, against the Aelorin would be slaughter.

My jaw drops as the petite Spriteling bows her head and offers a hand. Her voice grows soft but determined as she says, "It won't be easy, but I am willing to lay down arms, temporarily, and try. Perhaps we need a third party to mediate arguments, Flame Thrower?"

They look to me, but I don't have the time to think much less answer as Solanar speaks suddenly from the shade of a nearby tree. "Elora has other duties to attend to. I would be happy to aid you in your new endeavor." He smiles at me, the pride gleaming.

Okay, maybe I did do something right for once.

"The Deliverer," the whispers start close by and then further afield. The two leaders grasp the other's hand. The moment they touch, sparks of light burst out and fall to my tears still glistening on the bodies still in my hands. The light spreads over them like a falling blanket.

Gentle warmth flows back into their bodies, like water filling a sponge. Life returns slowly to their fragile forms, breath returning slower than the rest to their motionless lungs. The wounds that marred the surface of their skin begin to mend and they flit from my still hands.

"What the hell?" My head snaps up as the expletive bursts from my lips. I stare in disbelief at what lay before me. My hands lift slowly, almost involuntarily, to hover in front of my face. They're trembling—no, shaking violently—as if my body refuses to process what my mind is struggling to accept.

"The Gods have blessed this peace," shouts the Spriteling and the whole field cheers.

I glance at Jadis, expecting to find joy on his face too, but instead he glares back with a deep resentment that burns through me. I can feel the heat rising to my cheeks as I realize how angry he is, still. Even though I had just achieved a great victory and should be celebrating, his anger hits me like a ton of bricks. He walks away, his heavy footsteps thundering around us as one of the, once dead, young sprites timidly returns to me.

"Lyraeth wanted me to tell ye, well done," he says and then flits off to his people.

The Banshee.

Chapter Twenty Seven

"Ithrin sylraen thalnarae, lyrien naelsylor."

Once the barriers break, the heart is free.

THE FIRELIGHT SEEMS TO ACCENTUATE the swirling emotions in Jadis as he returns, his long strides still hinting at anger. A plume of dust follows him as he marches back into our camp. The orange light from the flames makes his figure appear almost surreal.

His penetrating stare sends shivers up my spine. His emotions seem to go back and forth between anger and then softer concern, a battle continuing inside.

My heart races with fear while I fight back the tears that have crept to the surface. They well up in my eyes as I will myself not to let them fall. His anger hurts me, deeply. Not that I should let it, but he's become important to me, his opinion important, no matter how hard I've fought that connection.

Mik materializes at my side just as Jadis closes in, his steps deliberate, his presence crackling like a coming storm. The air between them tightens, thick with unspoken fury. I expect his glare to land on me, but instead, his gaze locks onto Mik, sharp, brimming with something raw and territorial like two opposing, even feral packs of animals.

"You do not need to protect her from me," he snarls, his voice a low, guttural rasp that sends shivers down my spine. The sound isn't entirely human.

His eyes flicker gold--gold like Mik's.

"Are ye sure, Jadis? Yer time alone does not seem to have quelled the beast."

Jadis growls again, the sound rougher, deeper—not like his usual growls, but something more primal, edged with a vibration I don't recognize or understand.

Mik must sense it too because he immediately steps away, retreating without a word. The heat of his presence vanishes, replaced by a cool loneliness that prickles against my skin like the ghost of a touch that never quite lands.

Then, Jadis turns to me.

"Elora, what were you thinking?" His voice cuts through the air, sharp with his unchecked anger, but there's something else beneath it, something raw and tangled.

I swallow hard, but he doesn't pause.

"You risked your life without a second thought, in more ways than one, galloping off on a horse...into battle." His breath is uneven, his words a mix of fury and something dangerously close to fear. A fear that means he cares too much. "It was reckless, dangerous. You could have been killed!"

As he speaks, his hands move in memory, pulling a silver tin from his bag. The metallic scrape of the lid opening sets my nerves on edge. He's chastising me like a child, but the weight of his words hit hard against my chest, heavy enough that I find myself wishing for the ground to open up and take me whole.

The pain in my arm pulses, a constant reminder of the risks I had, indeed, taken. The adrenaline crash earlier already has me analyzing my stupidity. Not that I would admit that to him.

I try to meet his gaze, my voice defiant, "I understand your concern, but I had to take that risk. The loss of life was senseless, and someone needed to stop it."

He scoops the greenish salve from the tin, the thick ointment clinging to his fingers before he spreads it over my raw, singed skin. A sharp sting bites at first contact, but almost instantly, the fire fades, leaving only a ghost of warmth behind. His touch is careful but rigid, his fingers tracing the edges of the burn as if checking the extent, as if he still can't believe it, or is wishing it away.

"You should have waited for the rest of us," he retorts, his voice taking on a thicker, deeper tone. "Should have shared your intentions."

My pulse jumps, anger coiling tight in my stomach.

"You were arguing with me. You didn't even think I could do it." The words spill from my lips, bitter as spoiled wine, my breath becoming sharper. I bring my face close to his, close enough that the heat between us feels tangible, our breath mingling in the small space left, our noses almost touching.

"You were wrong by the way."

His chest rises and falls too fast, too hard. A muscle jumps in his jaw, the raised vessel at his temple pulsing.

His face is flushed, fury tightening his features, but his eyes—his eyes are locked into mine with more than just anger.

"I was right behind ye, ready to assist." His voice is taut, his accent thickening under the weight of emotion. "There was no need to rush headlong into danger. He had a bloody sword at yer throat, Elora."

The campfire crackles, mirroring the tension between us. I keep locked eyes with him, my own emotions in a whirlwind. "Sometimes risks need to be taken in order to succeed," I argue, my voice only slightly quivering, revealing a hint of the vulnerability I feel. "I will not let fear control me, Jadis. Never again. Do you understand that? I let fear dictate my every move before and she died! Fear will not rule my actions ever again."

The intensity hangs too heavy in the air, the flames casting flickering shadows on our faces. I reach out, my hand gently caressing his cheek, feeling the tension in his muscles gradually ebb away.

Then, in a moment that defies all logic and reasoning, Jadis' anger transforms. His warm, soft lips crash on mine. A ferocious, burning kiss that releases all the intense emotions that his words cannot express. I feel an electric current run through me as his passion engulfs my entire being, overwhelms my senses.

For a brief, exhilarating moment, the world around us ceases to exist. The pain in my body, the disagreement, all fade into insignificance as our lips move together. His tongue traces the seam of my lips, demanding entrance and I don't fight it. The kiss is full of longing and fire, sending sparks throughout my body.

As quickly as it started, it ends. Jadis pulls away, his breath ragged, his eyes searching mine for answers.

"Fear helps keep you alive, Elora."

He turns, stiff, and storms off into the night, leaving me standing there, wide-eyed, mouth agape and my heart pounding in my chest for completely different reasons.

Mik settles back at the fire on the other side muttering under his breath, "About damn time."

Chapter Twenty Eight

"*Zythal naelvith, nororin lorynin.*"

What is forgotten or ignored will be fought over again.

THE MORNING LIGHT CASTS THAT familiar glow over our surroundings, painting the world in hues of gold and amber, a welcome change from the dull, grey rain of the past few days. Despite the beauty of the morning, a heavy cloud lingers over me still.

Jadis continues to keep his distance after that life altering kiss. The memory of his warm, soft lips on mine still hovers, drawing heat to my body despite my still wet clothes. But also igniting a cascade of conflicting emotions. He refuses to talk about it, nothing but "It was a mistake" and "It won't happen again."

I can no longer deny the chemistry between us. Well, I can, but that would be a futile waste of breath. There has always been a magnetic pull between us, one that defies all reason.

In that moment, though, the world faded away, leaving only the intensity of our connection, but now? Jadis wants nothing to do with me. His avoidance and distant demeanor leave me questioning everything I thought I felt.

Now, I wonder if that passion I felt was some fleeting moment that meant nothing. I'm some used goods that are useless to a Prince. Or, was I just a pawn for his own agenda and that's a line he simply won't cross. Maybe he was trying to prove a point? That my decision making skills were non-existent.

I can't deny the allure of his presence, the way his touch ignites a spark deep within me, simply because of how much I now miss it.

"Elora, yer drenched, love, why didn't ye change into some dry clothes?" Mik breaks into my thoughts, his brow furrowed as I trudge through the latest patch of mud.

A storm had ravaged the landscape overnight, leaving behind its mark of destruction. The once majestic trees along the edge of the woods, now stand bent and broken, their branches reaching out in silent anguish. In my frustrated state, I can't help but draw parallels between the damaged forest and the fractures in my own heart.

Mik must read it on my face as we both glance to Jadis up ahead, pulling a large branch from the path.

"Ach, lass, don't fret. He'll turn around," he says.

"I don't understand what his problem is," I say, my voice tight. I kick at a loose stone, sending it skittering across the muddy path. The impact vibrates up my boot, sharp and unsatisfying. Mud splatters up in its wake, the only response I get in the heavy silence.

The tense atmosphere between Jadis and me is palpable. It's like an invisible wall was erected, separating our once inseparable selves. My heart very much yearns for his presence, apparently Mik and his warm eyes feel it too. I want reassurance that nothing has changed, but it has. Every attempt I make to bridge the gap feels useless, met with a cold shoulder or curt, overly polite responses.

"Duty," Mik says.

"Huh?"

"His sense of duty, his and yers. No sense wanting something ye can't have."

"I don't understand your meaning, Mik. What are you getting at?"

Mik sighs and moves a little closer to maintain our private conversation. "It's obvious, to all of us, he wants ye lass. I don't blame him." He runs a rough hand through his wavy hair, pausing his words, "but yer brother would never approve."

"First off, I could give a rat's ass about what Brandis thinks about my life. But why wouldn't he approve? I thought they're friends?"

"They are, practically brothers, but shifters are still considered scum amongst the aelorin, lower than low, remember? It would be considered disgraceful and considering what Brandis and the council want ye to accomplish, would prevent ye both from fulfilling yer duties."

"Horse shit. Wait, shifter? Jadis isn't aelorin? You're not?" I stop my horse behind me and turn to Mik fully concentrating on where this conversation is going.

Mik pinches the edge of his nose between his eyes. "Aye, lass, ye've seen me shift, have ye forgotten me already?"

"Of course not," I scoff at him, resuming a more leisurely pace, determined to give Jadis the space he is adamantly demanding. "But Jadis can do that too?"

"Aye, didn't he tell ye?" I shake my head and he says, "Pity. But what did ye think the mark on his arm meant?"

"That you both have a fondness for big dogs?" I say, the tone in my voice rising in pitch. "I don't know, Mik. I guess I never thought that deeply about it, you know, getting stabbed and shot at."

"Does it bother ye? That he can shift?" He kicks at an errant pebble and watches it bounce off into the taller grasses.

"No. I mean, other than the shock aspect. It didn't bother me that you can either. I don't care about those things. Plus, the more we travel, the more determined I am that reinstating the court system is the wrong path. I'm not going to let Brandis and those stuck up regents dictate any aspect of my life, especially who I spend my time with."

He smiles at me, a knowing but kind smile. "Aye, lass. I expected as much, but you'll have a harder time convincing mister goody two shoes of the same. He's dutiful to a fault."

"I'll never back down from a challenge," I whisper to myself. Maybe that will manifest the courage.

The conversation amongst us all veers to the storms aftermath, and the damage it has wrought. Mik and the others express concern over the treacherous conditions with the wind howling again. I can't help but wonder if I'm being escorted back to the Day Court now, Jadis having grown tired of me. While they all urge caution, my eyes fix on the young looking being that has crossed into the path ahead and what I catch consumes my thoughts entirely.

At a wider clearing in the path, a young looking fellow with green-grey skin and tousled, dirty hair, walks straight toward the branches on a leaning tree. His attention appears to be focused on what looks like a chunk of stone in his palm. My instincts scream out as loud as the howling wind that sways the trunk whose roots barely remain in the ground.

The reins slip from my fingers, forgotten, as I race forward. The world blurs around me, every nerve focused on the swaying tree ahead. As I pass, Jadis' fingers graze my bicep, a fleeting, desperate attempt to stop me. His voice follows—a faint, strained "Stars, Elora!"—but there's no time to heed it.

The tree groans, its massive trunk swaying precariously, each creak and snap ringing like thunder. I shout, waving my arms like a mad woman, my voice cracking. "Move! Look up!" But the youngling doesn't react, oblivious to the danger.

Panic floods my chest, my heart pounding so hard it drowns out everything else. The final crack sounds through the air, and I know—it's too late.

A surge of adrenaline propels me forward. My legs burn, the ground a blur beneath me, as I throw myself toward him. My arms lock around his small torso, the force of the motion jerking a startled cry from him.

Then, impact. A larger body slams into my back with crushing force, driving the breath from my lungs. The world tilts as we hit the ground, the youngling pinned beneath me.

The sharp, splintering crash of the falling tree roars behind us, sending tremors through the ground and an excruciating pain through my arm and side. Leaves, branches, and debris surround the three of us as yelling, both familiar and not, fills the air.

The youngling quivers beneath me, his words muffled by my body as Jadis lifts himself off my back.

The small, sturdy body beneath me starts to squirm. His wild untamed hair is full of dry leaves as he stares at me with curious grey eyes. His features, despite his small size, are a blend of rugged strength and a more youthful vulnerability. His cheeks are bespeckled with dirt and the image sends a pin straight through my chest, memories flooding me.

"I'm fine, Da," he calls out over his shoulder, and I release him. More of his kind approach with expressions a mix of shock, gratitude, and relief.

They approach me slowly, their steps deliberate, almost too measured. I count seven faces, each one guarded but strangely in sync, like leaves swaying together in an unseen current. The boy runs to a female's arms, and they tighten around him while the male next to her places a hand on his head.

"By the ancient stones," the male says as he turns to Jadis and me, still standing in the leafy branches of the fallen tree. "Rurik went missing in the wee hours before dawn, the curious sot. We saw what you did and are forever in your debt." He thrusts out a hand and I return it as he grasps my forearm fiercely.

I sway on my feet, spots flickering in my vision, darkness encroaching on the edges. As the male pulls my arm closer it brings the sight of a wicked, gnarled branch, still in my bicep, oozing blood.

"By the Gods, Elora," Jadis whispers. All the voices around me come across soft and muted. "Why?" He snarls at me as he grabs my arm surveying the damage and then moves to my aching side. Ripping off his belt, he wraps it tightly around my upper arm and I flinch. Pain radiates through me as he once again chastises my actions. "Why would you risk yourself like that? I would have made it on my own."

The anger numbs the pain a little. "Do you really want me to answer that?" I ask, my voice barely there. I raise my heavy brow at him, a task that almost feels impossible, taking way more effort than it should. I'm losing too much blood.

His eyes widen as he lowers his shoulders. I find a warm arm under my thighs and another at my shoulders as our new friends offer the skills of their healer.

Jadis lifts me with ease, holding me tightly to his chest, a place I have very recently longed for under different circumstances, ones where he was not fulfilling his duty. No matter. I bask in the warmth of his body as mine grows cold, his heartbeat echoing in my ear.

I almost think I feel the warmth of his full lips on my forehead before there's nothing.

SOUNDS RETURN TO me first, a soft, melodic tune of wind chimes, a gentle hum of whispers, a rustle of loose fabric shifting at my side. I lay on a small but soft bed, I think anyway. It's far more comfortable than anything I've slept on for weeks. The fabric under my fingers has a pleasant nap to it, not the rough texture of my bedroll.

A soft glow emanates from the lanterns that float at the ceiling, a warmer light filtering in through the nearby windows.

The walls surrounding me are furnished with jars of herbs, vials of potions, and various tools I don't recognize. The home of the healer they spoke of, perhaps?

The air carries the soothing scent of herbs and tea. Lavender and chamomile blend with the earthy aroma of moss and damp wood.

Jadis sits anxiously at my side, his eyes drawn, rimmed red, and dark patches stain underneath. His body static and tight, quickly shifts as he finds me staring at him. His grip on my hand tightens, a warmth in his touch that I miss so much. I have to hold my breath to stop the tears from welling in my eyes in relief.

The older male, the boy's father I assume, stands nearby softly speaking to another female with weathered features and long, silvered hair.

"You're awake," Jadis says, drawing my attention back to him. "You had us all worried."

I don't know what comes over me, but my hackles rise up at the sound of his voice. "You going to yell at me for that too?"

"I—"

"Nalona is an excellent healer, rivals the best in the land," the male from earlier says, stopping our argument. Up close, his skin holds a rougher, weathered look and his broad shoulders are draped in a worn, animal fur cloak that hangs to his knees. Long, wiry hair, the color an earthy brown, cascades down his back mingling with a thick beard that conceals all but his bottom lip. Despite his brusque appearance, his bright, emerald green eyes are kind.

"Nothing but the best for the woman who saved my Rurik. I am in your debt, Elora Aurelius," he says, placing a fist on his chest. "Thorgar Stoneheart, chief of the Thunderaxe Clan, well, what's left of us," he says, offering his hand.

I reach out to take it with my injured arm and realize there's no pain. How? No bandage covers my arm and as I run my other hand over the skin of my bicep, I only feel the soft change where new skin has formed. I look to Jadis, and he only gives me a wide-eyed nod—okay, not normal.

"I told ya, she's the best," he winks, pulling me in close, with a hand over my shoulder. "You possess a rare and noble heart, Elora. Your actions speak volumes as to yer character."

My strength starts to return and maybe some semblance of sanity, the conversation now turns to the recent events in the swamp and the escalating tensions between the Spritelings and the Fire Dancers. More importantly, the constant mention of someone else, the still unknown entity, encouraging more violence. Jadis has apparently filled the troll clan in on most of it while I was out. They have no information of their own as to this unknown entity but agree that it doesn't bode well. Any sparse descriptions that can be given are all different.

The two leaders exchange stories and concerns as I sip at a sweet tea Nalona gives me. Apparently, there has been a darkness spreading, from the sounds of things, along the path behind us. Thorgar has also heard of growing activities around the Obsidian Palace and apparently that's bad. There are bandits and other nefarious groups leaving their normal hunting grounds looking for something.

As concerning as that all is, my eyes grow heavy. With a promise to help me find the people of my riddles, they all leave to let me rest.

Chapter Twenty Nine

"Thyrelis ilyrian, ithorynen lorynor."

The past teaches, the wise listen.

ADIS AND MIK DECIDE THAT the extreme injuries I sustained warrant a longer stay than the four days I'd been unconscious. This is decided under the pretense that I need to heal, even though I feel better than fine. I think they actually need some time to recover mentally and emotionally.

I'm not complaining. I want to stay with the trolls. These people are kind and funny and I feel a comfort here I haven't felt for a long time Maybe even long before coming to this realm.

Jadis hovers by my side constantly. In fact, the only moment I can't see him is as Rurik drags me by the arm with my book tucked under his. His scrawny but muscular frame leads me through the winding paths of the village. The air here is thick with the scent of damp earth and the sounds of lively chatter. The trolls move about the small village with a sense of purpose, hopping out of our way as I apologize, their sturdy forms and colorful garments a striking contrast against the mostly stone landscape.

Following Rurik's aggressive guidance, I find myself in the heart of the village, centered on the Shaman's cave. The village itself is nestled within the rugged hills. Their hearty huts are carved and built right into the hillside almost like the hobbits from my favorite Tolkien novels, just with more stone than wood.

Paths meander here and there, winding between the dwellings and leading to the communal areas. Lush vegetation sprouts between the crevices adding bursts of color, almost mimicking the trolls themselves, or perhaps it's the other way around.

Even though Thorgar mentioned their numbers dwindling, everywhere I look, trolls of various sizes and ages putter about, though Rurik appears to be the youngest. Some are engaged in animated conversations, their laughter and boisterous voices carrying easily through the air.

The entrance to the Shaman's cave is decorated with detailed symbols. As we step inside, said Shaman is bent over the central fire, her muscular figure covered in weathered stone like skin that seems to be common, with the green-grey color.

The cave itself is heavily decorated, the walls painted with colorful hues that tell the stories of natural wonders, and maybe some of their history. One scene, a group of trolls, some with obvious injuries, mourn a heavily adorned and well armed female. She lay next to a large cauldron, surrounded by blue light. On the other side the same female warrior stands with her people again. Or, maybe I'm reading this wrong and it's like some Arabic languages and read right to left. Before I can try and make sense of the story, Rurik yanks my arm, yet again, dragging me over to the fire.

The Shaman, Thora, now sits on a woven rug near the same fire, her eyes sparkling. Rurik and I take places opposite her.

"Welcome, young ones," she says, "Thorgar mentioned you are on a quest for answers in the old ways. Yes, Elora?"

I nod, clutching my book in my lap. "Yes. I was gifted this book from...well I honestly don't know who gave it to me. It's a compendium of sorts about the people the Aelorin call the under fae. Some things its says seem a little farfetched to me and perhaps outdated. Thorgar thought you might be able to decipher it?"

Her eyes crinkle in a small smile as she beckons me to her side with a weathered hand. "Let's see what this says, hmm? The old stories, legends, still hold a kernel of truth, hidden within layers of myth and symbolism."

"Agreed. I'm afraid I don't know enough about this realm to tease out those kernels of truth."

Thora leans closer as I open the old pages, the leather binding creaking in protest. Her tattooed fingers trace the lines of text, her touch gentle and respectful.

"These speak of creatures tied to the elements, guardians of ancient knowledge," she says pointing to those I'd marked after my time with Nyx. "But there's also those mentioned here," she says pointing to another section, "The Forest Whisperer, The River Serpent, the Starbound Phoenix…Each of these existed at one point, hunted for their knowledge. Each holds their own unique power and may offer you what you seek, if you can find them. That will be the hardest task."

Rurik leans in closer, his grey eyes fill with firelight and curiosity, "But how do we find them, Auntie? How do we know what's real and what's legend?"

"Well, that's why we're here, yes?" She laughs, "And what is this we, Rurik, are ya planning on cutting yer strings early and joining young Elora here on her dangerous quest, hmm? Does my brother know of yer intentions?"

"Aww, Auntie Thora, don't snitch. Ya know I can fight and protect meself."

She glances at the pale pink scar on my bicep and raises an eyebrow. Rurik only answers with a small dismissive noise from his nose. How very teenage of him…

Thora nods thoughtfully, her eyes now searching mine. "The creatures of old, they exist in the realm between what we perceive as real and what lies hidden. To encounter them, you must attune yerself to the natural world, the eb and flow of magical energies. Seek out places of power, where the boundaries between realms are thin. Listen to the whispers of the wind, the rustle of leaves, and the murmurs of rivers. The magic will guide you easily enough."

"One problem, I have no magic. Still human." I say as my shoulders slump at yet another impossible hurdle.

Thora's eyes soften even more, the firelight reflecting in their depths like embers smoldering low. The air in the cave is thick with the scent of dried herbs and damp stone, the walls closing in around us like silent witnesses to whatever ancient forces linger here.

"Ya are the Deliverer, Elora," she says, her voice steady, confident, but also laced with something reverent. "The magic that courses through your veins has returned, in part. It connects ya to the ancient forces that shape our world. How else did ya think ya turned back time for those two sprites, eh?"

A shiver races down my spine. I blink at her, puzzled, her statement settles uneasily in my chest because I don't know what exactly happened with those sprites. The flickering lanterns along the walls cast shadows that dance, making the cave feel both sacred and secretive all at once.

Thora chuckles, the sound low and knowing. "Eh, we'll nurture yer magic another day. Maybe tomorrow." She turns toward a rough-hewn table, her fingers trailing over her own worn leather tome. "Today, let's go through yer book and seek out the truth in its pages."

TONIGHT, WE GATHER around a crackling fire, its golden flames licking at the dark sky, casting shadows that dance on the grass and stone. The smoke curls upward, carrying the faint scent of burning pine and herbs. Thora planned something special—an offering in honor of my arrival.

Jadis sits close on my right, pressing his thigh against mine, sending a faint shiver through me. The warmth of his body settles in my core. I have to work hard on keeping my breaths steady. I focus instead on Thora as she rises, her face aglow in the firelight, streaks of yellow paint catching the shifting glow.

"Long ago," she begins, her voice rich with emotion, "in a time when the lands were untouched by darkness, our troll clan thrived in the arms of our ancestral homeland."

The rhythmic crackle of the flames syncs with her words, pulling me in. Her voice carries a weight of pride and longing that stirs something deep inside. I lean forward, the shadows of the fire stretching and shifting as she continues.

"The valleys were lush with flourishing flora, the rivers teemed with life, and the air was filled with the melodious sounds of nature," she says, her eyes sparkling as though she can still see it.

As she speaks, the swirling smoke from the fire between us begins to shift, forming faint shapes—a valley here, a river there. My breath catches as the tendrils seem to come alive, weaving through the night to illustrate her words. Jadis notices my reaction, his hand brushing against mine. A quiet squeeze steadies me as I gasp softly.

"I don't have to imagine it," I whisper. Before me, rolling hills and verdant forests take shape in the glowing air above the fire. It's beautiful and heartbreaking—a distant dream, forever out of reach.

"We are a powerful and peaceful clan, living in harmony with the land and its creatures," she continues, her voice filled with pride, but I sense sorrow there too. "We had a deep connection to the natural world and our ancient knowledge was passed down through generations, a sacred thread that bound us together."

She speaks deeply of their roles as caretakers, protectors, and guardians of the land, their sole duty to maintain the delicate balance that allowed life to flourish.

"But as with all things, change came. Darkness crept into our world, spreading its tendrils of discord and corruption," her voice dips, her tone turning completely somber. "Forces of chaos and greed sought to disrupt the harmony we cherished, and our clan found itself facing a great threat."

The fire snaps loudly, and I flinch. Across from me, Fallon's brow furrows, his hand gripping tightly at his belt where his sword normally sits, as if he's ready to fight the shadows themselves. Mik leans back, his face unreadable, but his foot taps against the ground with restless energy, like he knows how this story turns out.

I lean in more, somehow, drums beating in the distance, my heart pounding to the same beat.

Thora's voice softens, and her gaze sweeps over us. "In the face of adversity, our clan stood united—brothers and sisters joined hand in hand, fortified by the knowledge that our love for each other and our homeland were unshakable.

But despite our tenacity, we were forced to abandon our ancestral lands, leaving behind the sacred place we held dear."

Thora's voice swells with fervor, her words weaving through the air like a song carried on the wind. She leans closer, the flickering firelight casting patterns across her weathered face as she speaks of the cauldron, its power.

The flames leap higher, crackling in time with her tale, but the heat isn't what makes the hair stand on my arms. The story itself lingers heavy in the very air around us, ready to pounce. Smoke drifts higher, carrying the scent of burning sage and resin, mingling with the crisp night air.

Somewhere beyond our circle, I hear a distant owl hoot, or something like it, its low, haunting call settling over the gathering like an omen. The ground beneath me is still cool and solid, a sharp contrast to the pulsing energy everywhere else.

"Our legends speak of Galdor, the mighty warrior and fierce leader who valiantly fell in battle," her eyes gleam across the darting flames. "In her final moments, as her life-force waned, the divine gift of Ceridwen bestowed on her a second chance."

Images flash before me as if conjured from my own mind: a bloodied warrior rising from death, her wounds closing, her eyes blazing with unearthly power. Thora's voice carries strong in the stillness. "Resurrected by the cauldron's magic, Galdor returned to our clan as an embodiment of hope and courage. With her newfound vitality, she led our people through countless trials, becoming a beacon of inspiration and symbol of strength in times of adversity.

Throughout the generations, the lineage of Galdor has guided our clan, their leadership marked by the strength and wisdom bestowed on them. It is a sacred duty, a sacred bond between our family and the Cauldron of Ceridwen."

As her tale unfolds, my mind summons images of the cauldron, a vessel brimming with energy. I can almost hear the sounds of battles fought and victories gained, the pulse of life coursing through its very essence.

"Our spirits were tested as we wandered, seeking a new haven," Thora's voice trembles, thick with an old sorrow. The night air is still, holding on to her words as if even the wind dares not interrupt.

Embers rise brightly like fleeting memories, their glow brief. "But in our hearts, the flames of hope never wavered." The conviction in her tone is unshakeable, yet I can feel the spirits of her ancestors, their ancestors, struggling to press against its edges.

Her eyes fall to mine, searching, reflecting more than just firelight. "We carried our traditions, our knowledge, and our homes with us."

She speaks of the hardships they faced, the challenges they overcame, and the unyielding spirit that sustained them.

"And now, here we stand, in this humble village nestled in the hills," her eyes trained on the flickering fire, a glimmer of pride shining from them. "We may have been driven from our ancestral lands, but we have never forgotten who we are, where we came from, and the bonds that unite us."

As her words charge within me, I feel a deep sense of admiration for the trolls and their enduring spirit. Their journey mirrors my own in some ways, a search for identity, purpose, and a place to call home and they'd managed it so much better than I ever have.

"We share this story with ya, Elora, not just to recount our past, but to forge a new future," Thora's gaze lingers on mine, her eyes filled with hope, "Ya carry the blood of your ancestor, the legacy of a family, intertwined with ours."

"I don't understand."

Her expression darkens as she describes how the forces of chaos and turmoil threatened to consume the realm, unleashing a torrent of destructive power that put the trolls and Aelorin in peril. In their desperation to safeguard their own kind, my ancestors made a pact as the future entities of the Day Court seeking a means to restore the balance.

"In a fateful exchange, our ancestors agreed to entrust the sacred Cauldron of Ceridwen to your family, bearers of aelorin blood," she explains with palpable regret. "They believed that the cauldron magic, combined with the wisdom and strength of the Aelorin, would be the key to restoring equilibrium."

However, the alliance proved to be a double-edged sword. As the years passed, the Aelorin grew consumed by their own desires for power and dominance. Greed twisted their hearts, leading them astray from their sacred duty, to protect the realm.

"Driven by their insatiable hunger for power, your ancestors turned their backs on their promises. They hoarded the cauldron's magic, using it for their own gain, and abandoned their duty to the balance.

As the trolls fought to reclaim their rightful place, the cauldron slipped further from our grasp."

Thora's voice grows softer as she walks away, her shoulders heavy with the weight of her words. "But in our hearts, we never forgot its significance, the promise it held for a united realm."

MY HEART IS heavy with the pain of the truths I've been told. The fire still glows warm in front of me, yet it suddenly feels much colder without Thora's presence. I can feel every emotion in the air, tension thickening and my inner turmoil growing with each passing second. I can sense an impending storm on the horizon, one that will break out sooner or later.

"If I said ye had a beautiful body, would ye hold it against me?" Jadis' warm breath caresses my cheek. I haven't heard this tone from him in a while.

"Excuse me?"

He kisses my cheek, a quick peck that still sends heat flowing everywhere, especially places I don't want to think about right now. "Ye seemed stuck in your head again. I learned pretty quick how to break ye out of that when we first met."

"What? That's why you make all of those crass comments?"

He shrugs. "Now that you know me better, I'd think you'd understand that I have better...what's the term? Game? Than that."

"Couldn't prove it thus far," I say, lifting an eyebrow. The others appear to have snuck off in the meantime, leaving only the two of us at the dying fire.

He wraps an arm around my shoulders, resting his head on mine. "Aye, lass, I've been a right prick of late and I'm sorry."

A contented sound escaped my lips, and I snuggle in closer to the body beside me. My skin soaks up the warmth radiating from him, and a soft breeze moves through our hair as we enjoy the comfort of the night.

"Did you know?" I ask after a few minutes.

"About the cauldron?" He asks, his breath hot on my forehead. I nod silently and look up into his eyes. "No," he says, firmly. "I had no idea it was in your family's possession."

I sit in silence, my throat closing up as I process the conflicting feelings that course through me. I swallow, my voice barely above a whisper, "My family betrayed them." A veil of shame falls over me.

"No, lass. Your ancestors maybe, but this happened before even your parents were born."

"But my parents didn't fix it either. They still reaped the benefits of the betrayal. Who's to say that what they accomplished, the heights to which the Day Court rose, would have happened if they'd returned it?

Where do you think it is? Does Brandis know?"

Jadis' hands run through his long, dark hair and the wispy tips brush my neck. I shiver, both from the softness of his locks unraveling against my skin and his words, "I don't know if your brother knows of the cauldron, but more than likely it's in the ether, the in-between. It's a place where the Aelorin keep important objects that they want magical access to, things they want to maintain a connection to."

"How do I get it out of the ether? Do we need to go back to the manor?"

"We're heading there anyway, the reports I'm getting are concerning in regard to your safety, but no, not necessarily." His breath is still hot against my cheek compared to the cool night air, and I feel the muscles of his back tense as he says it. In a softer voice, he goes on. "Anyone of your bloodline can access the ether of your family if properly trained."

"So, magic required," I say, dejected.

"Aye. And I don't think Brandis will find it at all important to placate a small clan of trolls at the moment. Not from the sounds of things."

"Thora offered to teach me how to use what magic I have right now. Do you think that will be enough for me to access the ether?"

Jadis thinks for a moment, drawing slow circles on my thigh with a thumb. My eyelids droop. "I mean, you harnessed the power of the cauldron across the ether for those sprites, I think, so it might work if that's what you wanted."

"It is."

Jadis reaches out for my hand, linking our fingers together, "Elora, I will stand by your side, whatever you decide. No matter how much you trigger the beast inside me."

His touch and words ignite a warmth inside me, a spark that burns brighter than ever before and that terrifies me.

Chapter Thirty

"Loryniel lythin ilythor ryvithor, ithrin vyralis loryniel naelvithis ilyrian."

A child's mind learns faster, as a troubled mind blinds itself to learning.

APPROACH THORA THE NEXT morning with reservations. After learning what my family had done to them, I wonder, first, why they're so keen to help me and then, question their motives. What is Thora's goal, her end game by sharing that story with me last night? I question her intentions thoroughly. I'm not unfamiliar with manipulation tactics and have a hard time believing she is simply sharing knowledge. But, then again, I also know that I am suspect of people's intentions when I shouldn't be.

I meander my way to her home, my thoughts focused on all the possibilities, but they all end the same way. I return the cauldron. No matter what her intentions are, innocent or otherwise, I will always choose to return the cauldron. It's not mine to keep.

So lost in the circles of thought, that's exactly what I blurt out as I enter her home. She shoots up from her desk with a squeal and I flinch, smacking my palm to my forehead.

"Sorry, I should have started with a simpler, Hi."

"No, it's fine. You simply surprised me." She takes a deep breath of composure and draws closer to me. There are bags under her eyes as if she drained herself and has yet to recover. I feel her warm hand on the edge of my shoulder. "You do know that wasn't my intent, yes? I did not share these things with ya to make ya feel guilty. It was yer ancestors, distant ones, behavior not yers and ya owe us nothing. On the contrary, we owe ya."

Her declaration is kind, but my doubt still lingers. I think, really, that's a me problem. "I want to believe that. You've given me no reason not to—"

"But yer past still haunts ya. I know. One day, the smoke will fade, and it will all become clear again." Her kind eyes glisten in the dim light and I can only give a weak smile in return. I wish I had her confidence for my future.

"The one problem with the whole thing is Jadis and I are pretty sure they tucked it in the ether. I should be able to access it, but I don't know how. I sure as hell am not asking Brandis to do it."

"I take it the reunion with yer family did not go the best?" She meanders back to her work table as our conversations starts a more normal flow.

"No, not really. Brandis is all that's left." She lifts a brow at this statement, and I'm not sure why. "He has a bit of a temper and that has made forming a relationship...tenuous."

She laughs. "Ah, but yer lessons in diplomacy appear to have gone very well.

It's no matter. As it seems ya've already tapped into the cauldron's magic, what ya have should be enough for ya to navigate the ether."

She agrees to help me harness this dormant magic and has the patience of a saint. In the quiet solitude of her hut, bathed in the soft glow of flickering candles, I sit across from her, my impatience and disappointment simmering more with each passing hour.

"Close yer eyes, Elora," Thora's voice fills in the large space. "Breathe in deeply and release that tension ya carry."

I try, I really do, but my mind is restless, a whirlwind of self-doubt and frustration. As I attempt to calm the racing thoughts that plague me, impatience gnaws at my core. Why couldn't I tap into my magic on purpose? Isn't it supposed to be innate? Why is it so elusive, slipping through my fingers like grains of sand?

"Relax," Thora's voice does help to soothe, her words a balm for my restless spirit and mind. "Let go of any expectations." Ha, easier said than done. "Visualize a flickering ember within ya. See it, feel it, it's a spark waiting to ignite."

But my impatience is a persistent companion urging me to hurry. It's not wrong. Jadis is already discussing when we'll move on from here. He believes it's dangerous to stay in one place for too long. Even more so now than before. Considering the reports we got upon arriving here, he's not wrong. I think less about me and more about not wanting to put these wonderful people in danger. I push hard, trying to force this connection that seems just out of reach. Each failed attempt only fuels my own doubts, whispering cruelly that, perhaps, I'm not meant for magic. That I lack the innate ability that everyone around me possesses so effortlessly. A failure. A word that whispers and slithers in my mind.

Thora continues to guide me, her words gentle and steady. She knows I'm fighting, everyone does. I haven't figured out how to keep anyone out of my mind yet. My impatience refuses to yield, drowning out her wisdom with its insistent demands for progress.

In the flickering candlelight, I struggle to silence the critical voices in my head, to drown out the doubts that threaten to consume me, or rather continue to consume me, louder and louder the more I push. Relaxing is apparently out of the question. My frustrations only mount, a storm raging inside.

Thora senses all of this, I can see it in her calm and understanding gaze. "Magic cannot be forced, Elora," she says, softly, her words piercing through the thickening fog of my mind. "It is a dance between intention and surrender, a delicate balance that takes time to master. I think that's enough for today."

"No, I can't stop. Jadis wants to leave, to protect me."

"Magic is not a destination, Elora, it's a journey of self-discovery, of embracing yer unique connection to the world around ya. Release the need for immediate answers and trust in the unfolding inside ya. Perhaps there's a way to convince him to stay a little longer?"

Trust, yeah no, that's not something that comes easily, not anymore.

"I understand he's very protective of ya," she adds.

"That's the understatement of the century."

We both laugh at this, some of the tension leaving my shoulders.

"Perhaps ya should suggest some lessons in self-defense?"

That's not a bad idea. Obviously, magic isn't going to help me anytime soon, so learning to protect myself in their absence is a great idea and it just might be enough to delay them a little longer.

Chapter Thirty One

"Ithorylin lyris thaerin vyris myrrathil."

Kindred spirits bloom in the unlikeliest soil.

T TOOK A LITTLE CONVINCING on my part to get Jadis to agree, but agree he did. The sharp rays of the afternoon sun filter through the dense canopy, the dappled patterns of light dancing on the forest floor. I stand at the center of a makeshift training ground, my body glistening with sweat. My muscles quiver with exhaustion from the relentless drills I've been put through the past few days.

Jadis and Mik are opposite me, their expressions focused yet playful, ready to put my new, old skills to the test. The sounds of chirping birds and rustling leaves under Rurik's feet provide a soothing backdrop to today's training session.

Jadis, with a mischievous grin in his eyes, twirls a dagger in his hand, his voice carrying a playful tone. "Come now, El, show us what you've learned. Don't hold back."

I fill my lungs deeply as I feel the weight of the blade in my hand. My muscles ache and my mind fills with doubt. I've been struggling with my magic lessons in the morning, and the exhausting and unending thrashings in the afternoon from Jadis and Mik are starting to wear me down.

But I can't give up; I won't. I square my shoulders, determination written across my face. I tighten my grip on the hilt of my blade, the blisters and new callouses on my palms serving as a reminder of these countless hours of training.

Jadis lunges forward, his movements swift and practiced. I sidestep, narrowly avoiding it at least. I retaliate with a swift parry, but he counters easily, our blades clashing.

Mik circles around us, his watchful eyes offering occasional words of encouragement and guidance. "Use yer agility, he's still a big oaf. Trust yer instincts, they're good. Find yer opening."

I actually enjoy this more than I thought I would. I catch on pretty quickly, and Jadis wonders if it's a subconscious memory of lessons from my childhood, before I was bound and sent away.

Every fiber of my being is engaged; my senses heightened as I focus on each movement. I duck, weave, and dodge, my body responding with an instinctive grace. The exhaustion is gnawing at my muscles, but I push through. It goes beyond needing to fight no matter how tired I am under real life circumstances and into a deep need to prove myself.

Jadis, always the provocateur, can't resist injecting a dose of banter into our exchange. "Remember, Elora, a well-placed strike can bring even the mightiest opponent to their knees. Or, in yer case, maybe on their back," he teases, a sly grin tugging at his lips.

I groan. "Careful, Jadis, or I might show you how effective a low blow can be."

Our banter continues, interwoven with the rhythmic clash of steel. Sweat trickles down my brow, mixing with the dirt and leaving streaks on my flushed cheeks. I can feel the grit when I wipe at my face. Yet, in these moments, a strange sense of exhilaration courses through my veins.

With each strike, each dodge, I feel a growing confidence surging. The hours of training, the bruises, and sore muscles, are all proof of what I can accomplish, of my success. I'm no longer some helpless human girl.

Jadis reaches out to wipe a streak of dirt from my cheek. "You've come a long way in such a short time. I'm proud of you, for what it's worth."

"Thanks. That means a lot, actually." I breathe out, my chest swelling just a smidge. "You two can have the lake first today. I need a moment."

"Alright, lass, but not too long, aye?"

AS THE SUN dips closer to the horizon, it casts long shadows across the small wood. I can hear the hustle and bustle of the village, preparing the square for the Harvest of Bountiful Spirits, a fertility and thankfulness celebration. There's so much joy, even with their inability to bear children. Rurik, at fourteen, is the last having been born, and even that was a miracle. The festival means we're leaving tomorrow, probably at first light, knowing Jadis. I understand his reasoning, but I feel a growing sense of loss at the thought.

Lost in thought, I wander deeper into the wood, scanning around for anything interesting. A faint flicker of light catches my eye, and I follow the gentle glow.

Nestled in another small clearing, amidst the fading twilight, lies a solitary figure, an Emberkin from the look of it. It's flame reduced to a mere flicker. The tiny being shimmers with a slight glow, its frail form struggling to maintain a quickly dwindling energy. Her flames are no longer dancing along the edges of her limbs, her hair dull grey at the roots fading to even duller yellows and reds instead of the vibrant blues, golds, and auburns they should be.

My heart swells. Without hesitation, I kneel beside her, my hand outstretched with a soft touch. The Emberkin stirs, her dim flame growing ever so slightly.

I scoop up the tiny female, cradling her against my chest, insulating her in any heat I can find. I don't know if it will help, but I have to try.

I'm at a loss for words, saying whatever comes to mind. "Hang on, little one. I'll find you a fire. Just hang on a little longer."

The Emberkin's tiny wings flutter weakly; her soft sounds exhausted. My eyes dart around me, then focus on the dim lights from the village ahead. Time is slipping away, and I need a fire, now.

Clutching her small frame firmly against my chest, I kick up a storm of dirt and leaves as I race forward. My feet pound the ground with such force that the earth seems to quake underneath me for once. Every nerve in my body screams for me to stop, but I push through the pain and exhaustion, propelled by sheer willpower alone. The faint flicker of distant flames dance before us like a beacon, urging us forward through the tangled underbrush. There is no time to waste—a life hangs in the balance.

As I burst into the village, the commotion draws the attention of the trolls. They pause in their tasks, their eyes widening in surprise at the sight of me, which I'm sure is a little terrifying. I probably look mad as a hatter.

The festival fire burns already in the center of the square, and I race over, flinging my charge into the hot blaze.

The trolls close in, their larger forms casting shadows across the firelit ground as I stare at the limp body, still and fragile at the base of the flames. The heavy scent of charred wood and the damp earth clinging to me surrounds us, mingling with the acrid smoke.

My breath is trapped somewhere between fear, hope, and an aching pause before the unknown. My eyes shimmer as I hold my breath, hoping against another failure, hoping I got here in time. I can't lose someone else; I don't even know her name.

Her wings tremble, delicate as brittle leaves in an autumn wind. The fire's glow washes over her, painting her frail form in molten gold and ember red. Heat radiates outward, prickling my skin, wrapping around her like a living thing. For a moment, her light dims, and there's a loud intake of breath all around me—then, suddenly, it surges.

The limp, greying wings ignite in brilliant flames of orange and yellow, each pulse of fire sending a cascade of glowing embers into the night. The sharp scent of magic crackles in the air as the trolls erupt into cheers, the sound vibrating my bones and reverberating through the night.

Thorgar appears at my side, his presence a steady weight in the chaos. "Ya have a rare gift, young one. Yer compassion will change this realm."

Nearby, Thora stands with Mik, his hair still dripping from his bath in the lake, dark strands clinging to his face. Water trails down his temple, glistening in the firelight as he stiffens at her words. "Deliverer of hope, kindness, compassion...Deliverer of life," she whispers.

Mik whips his head to her, "Is that what the prophecy means by Deliverer?"

"In part, I believe." She catches my eye, her expression unreadable. "The rest has yet to reveal itself."

THE LITTLE EMBERKIN rests peacefully in the fire as anticipation fills the air. I learned that her name is Pyra, which makes me giggle and then apologize profusely. Unsurprisingly for a fire-based sprite, she has a bit of a temper.

The village comes alive with more color, more sounds, and enticing aromas. Elaborate decorations cover the huts and wooden stalls, woven with wildflowers and shimmering ribbons that flutter in the gentle breeze. Lanterns and torches are lit, casting a warm and inviting glow across the festivities. The smell of savory dishes and sweet treats waft from the cooking pits, teasing the senses and causing my mouth to water.

Trolls, their faces painted with swirling designs, dash around with boundless energy, chasing after one another in a playful game. Their laughter echoes through the village, infusing the air with an undeniable sense of joy and merriment.

Music flows from a central gathering area where a lively band plays traditional tunes, the melodies weaving their way into the heart. It beckons everyone to dance, and my still sweaty person is quickly dragged along.

We twirl and spin, smiles splitting faces, breaths coming fast. The dancing becomes a whirlwind of colorful attire, twirling skirts and stomping feet, the very ground pulsing with energy.

Jadis grins and laughs as he too is caught up in the storm, the others pressing me into his arms only to be spun away again.

As the song ends, I spin myself quietly in the direction of the lake, eager to wash away the day's sweat.

Before I can strip away my shirt and trousers, a commotion of raised voices sounds behind me, two voices I recognize.

"What's the problem, Pyra?" She jumps at my voice with a squeak and spray of sparks.

"This big oaf is trying to peek in on your private moment to bathe. He took offense at me telling him to turn around and go back where he came from." She leans over towards me, the back of her hand covering her next words. "Us girls have to stick together. I got your back."

I'm not about to spoil her fun by telling her his shifter senses can still hear her words. My cheeks burn from smiling so much, and I feel a lightness in my chest that has been absent for years. It's like I've been granted a do-over, and this time, I'm determined to make it work.

"While I appreciate it, this big oaf is allowed, Pyra." Jadis raises a brow at my continuing to use the name while Pyra's mouth forms an 'o' at my declaration.

She lets him by, making sure to warn him to be nice with a glare and then shooting me an exaggerated wink. He does his best not to smile, the corners of his full lips barely twitching.

Moss lines the edges of the lake and is refreshingly cool and soft against my bare feet. Jadis makes no noise as he follows me, but I feel him, the warmth of him, as the air suddenly becomes much harder to suck into my lungs.

"Everything alright?" He asks.

"Yes, perfectly fine. I just wanted to finally wash away all the stinky, sticky sweat."

He edges in closer, the pale moonlight reflecting in the green of his eyes, the tips of his fingers catching a tendril of hair along my face. "Ye smell fine."

The moon is full, and the birds still flit about despite the late hour. "I find that hard to believe."

He moves closer and my pulse pounds in my ears, his rough stubble caressing my skin. "Your aroma is overwhelming, a maddening mix of dewy sweat and jasmine petals. Every time I'm near ye, the intoxicating scent only intensifies until I can barely keep myself from succumbing to it.

"Really?"

I find myself breathless, my heart racing as I feel the warmth radiating from him. An intoxicating aroma of his own, leather, pine, and the sweet citrus of his soap fills the air around us, making my legs wobble.

"Aye, Elora. And, the way yer face lit up like a thousand stars as you spun and twirled left me weak in the knees. I've never seen anything so breathtaking, so beautiful."

"Then your life has been very sheltered," I breathe, the words trembling out of me as his lips skim along the line of my jaw. My skin catches fire beneath each ghosting touch, every nerve pulled taut. It's too much. Not enough. I melt against him, chasing the heat of his mouth as if it holds my next breath.

"Tell me to stop, Elora," he murmurs, his voice low and ragged at my temple. "Tell me this is wrong, burning for ye like this. Make me step away."

My breaths come in ragged heaves as I turn to stare into his darkened eyes, trying to ignore the smolder that threatens to consume all my inhibitions.

"What if I don't want you to?" I whisper. "What if I'm done lying?"

His gaze holds mine, and my heart flutters as heat floods my veins, pressure building inside me.

The last of the distance evaporates. His mouth captures mine, firm and searing. One hand finds the laces of my shirt, tugging with shaking urgency. I shudder as the cool night air brushed over newly exposed skin, made sharper by the heat of his palms.

He lowers me gently to the moss. It's damp and soft beneath me, the scent of earth and green things curling up around us. The wind slips through my hair, tugging strands across my cheeks. His warmth presses down from above, consuming me.

His firm, warm hands grasp my hips as tendrils of his own silken hair tickle my thighs, sending tingling sensations up my spine. I gasp when his hips find the curve of my hip, a whisper of heat that sends spirals straight through me.

"Jadis," I gasp, my vision blurring as the dizzying sensation of a freefall takes hold.

He rises above me again, gaze molten. Our mouths collide, rougher now. I claw at the ties of his shirt, desperate to feel him—only him. The fabric yields, and he peels it away, revealing skin like sunlit stone, warm and golden. My hands find him, fingers splaying over the hard lines of his chest.

He tangles a hand in my hair, drawing my head back until I arch beneath him. His mouth descends—hot and unrelenting—on my breast. I moan, legs curling around him, a heel pressing into the firm curve of his backside. He growls, low and primal, the sound vibrating through my core.

The air thickens. Time stops. His hips press to mine and everything narrows to that burning point of contact. I am unraveling, threads pulled loose one by one under the worship of his touch.

He fills the empty space inside me—not just with his body, but with something deeper. A tether. A promise. A surrender.

My hands slide along his spine, feeling the tremble in his muscles. His hair spills through my fingers like liquid silk, and when his hand drifts lower, fire sparks under my skin.

I fall—shattered and whole all at once—his name a broken cry on my lips.

He follows with a gasp, collapsing beside me, breathless. The moss cradles us both as he pulls me across his chest, his fingers brushing lazy paths up and down my spine. Our breaths begin to sync. Slowly, the stars return to the sky.

As Jadis and I snuggle together by the lake, I sense it, finally, deep inside, that spark and I focus on it. As it grows, I conjure the image of the cauldron, picturing it in my mind's eye until we both hear a soft plunk in the water next to us.

Jadis sits up alarmed until his eyes focus on what now lay there. "Well, if I knew that showing ye the skills of my pinky finger would help ye find yer magic, I would have had ye on yer back a while ago."

I smack his chest playfully while a great grin stretches my face. His laughter bounces off the entire valley.

I feel like I'm finally home.

Chapter Thirty Two

"Vaelithen sylvaen naelithor caelar naelithir."

Grief remains still after the stars fade.

PYRA DECIDES TO STAY BY my side as we leave the troll village at midday. Jadis had intended to leave at first light, as I suspected, but the return of the cauldron escalated the festivities well into the early morning hours.

I hated leaving. I know we need to, but it feels wrong nonetheless. While Jadis fears for my safety, I fear what my presence would bring on these wonderful people. For good reason.

We set out just after midday, the sun filtered through a thin veil of clouds, casting everything in a strange silver glow. The village behind us still smells faintly of cooked rootcakes and woodsmoke, of laughter echoing against stone walls and moss-covered roofs. Pyra flits beside me, her small form trailing a faint, pulsing glow—a heartbeat of fire.

We move in silence for the first hour, the camaraderie of our departure slipping into something more uncertain. The forest is too quiet. The birds that had chattered all morning have gone mute, and the trees seem taller now, their trunks pressed too close, as if listening.

Even Faeryl senses it. His ears twitch at every shift of wind, and I catch him tossing his head more than once, huffing like he's swallowed a storm. The air feels heavier with every step. My knuckles are white on the reins. The laughter from the night before echoes in my memory, out of place here—too loud, too bright for this shadowed path.

Jadis rides ahead, his posture rigid, eyes scanning the underbrush. Mik is unusually quiet, his fingers twitching restlessly at his side. The moment comes without warning.

Pyra stiffens midair—her body going rigid as a shard of ice—and then she zips upward in a streak of flame. My heart leaps to my throat just as Faeryl rears, nostrils flaring.

The forest explodes.

Shadows burst from the undergrowth—figures clad in rough leathers and gleaming mail, blades already swinging. A horn bellows from somewhere behind us, low and ragged like a beast's roar. Faeryl screams and bucks. I lose my grip on the reins and slam hard into the saddle horn, the jolt sending a stab of pain through my ribs.

"Ambush!" Jadis shouts. His blade is already drawn, glinting silver in a shaft of pale light, and his horse pivots beneath him as if anticipating the next move.

I don't have time to think. Pyra's scream splits the air as she lets loose a jet of fire, the stream arcing through the trees. The scent of burning flesh strikes me a second later—putrid and metallic. These warriors don't flinch. They come in waves, snarling, silent, or grinning, eyes full of madness.

Mik is a blur beside me—his blades flashing, carving clean arcs through armor and throat. Blood mists the air. The clash of steel-on-steel rings in my ears, and it's all I can do to raise my own sword as a brute charges me.

The first impact nearly knocks me flat. I stagger backward, boots slipping in soft loam now slick with blood. I strike on instinct, blade meeting flesh. The scream curdles in my throat as he collapses.

The air crackles with energy as the whirling tempest of a battle surges around me. Pyra's flames rain down on our enemies, her powerful fire scorching their hides and searing their skin. Fear and adrenaline race through my veins as I fight by the side of my friends, my family, it doesn't control me. My blade cuts a swathe of destruction in its wake. The guttural growls of rage, the ringing of steel upon steel, and bellowing shouts of defiance fill the air, a deafening roar that thunders through the small clearing.

Jadis is at my side a moment later. "Stay with me," he barks, voice harsh with panic. A sword comes for him and he deflects it with the elegance of a dancer—but there's fury in his movements, fire behind every blow. The emerald of his eyes has darkened.

The enemy fights as if they're possessed, slashing and jabbing with unrestrained savagery. Crimson blood spills from gaping wounds, stains the ground in an eerie painting of death. Agonized screams of pain are drowned out by the relentless roar of blades slapping and sliding.

Dagen fights with terrifying efficiency, hurling enemies aside like straw dolls. Beside him, Fallon parries blow after blow, blood streaking his brow.

But we're outnumbered.

"More coming in from the north!" someone screams.

Then I see him.

Cartwell.

He emerges from the smoke like a vision from a nightmare—taller than I remember, broader. His hair is longer, tied back with a strip of bloodstained cloth. A deep scar cleaves the left side of his face in two, but his eyes... gods, those grey eyes are still dead.

The sight of him paralyzes me for a heartbeat too long.

A blade whistles past my cheek and I jerk back just in time. Pyra shrieks in warning, unleashing a second torrent of fire that drives our attackers back—momentarily.

"Stay close!" Jadis shouts again. His voice breaks through the din like an anchor.

We press together, fighting in tandem. Every movement is instinctual now—slash, duck, block, lunge. Sweat stings my eyes. My arms burn with the strain. Blood pools in my boots and I'm not sure if it's mine or not.

Mik, his daggers glinting, whirls through the chaos with a dancer's grace, his blades flashing like bolts of lightning. Jadis, his face a mask of controlled fury, parries and strikes with precise elegance. With every swing, every dodge, every strike, we fight as one, but it's not enough. Cartwell's numbers are greater, their bloodlust nauseating.

Then I hear it.

A wet, gurgling sound.

Dagen.

He crumples to the ground, hands clutching his throat as blood fountains between his fingers. My scream rips through the chaos, primal and raw. The world narrows to a pinpoint, and I can't breathe. I can't move.

Time slows.

And in that stillness, Cartwell strikes.

The scream is my undoing. As the battle reaches its climax, I catch a glimpse in my peripheral of Jadis in a fierce duel with Cartwell. His blade clashing hard against the wicked curves of his opponent. I look away at that moment, complete faith in Jadis' skills. That's when I scream at Dagen's fall.

I barely hear the sound of my own scream—just a ragged, broken noise swallowed by the clang of steel and the shriek of fire. But Cartwell hears it. He watches me as Jadis turns his back to defend my flank, his mouth twisted into that same monstrous grin I remember from the battlefield ruins of my past.

He sees his moment.

Jadis doesn't.

Cartwell moves faster than any man his size should. His blade, jagged and blackened at the edges, cleaves down in a perfect arc, whistling through the air. I watch it descend as if in slow motion—an obsidian crescent descending toward Jadis' exposed back.

"No!" The word rips itself from my chest, but it's too late.

The impact lands with a bone-cracking, soul-shattering thud.

A shockwave rolls out from the point of contact—the air shimmering, dust and ash rising as if the world itself flinched. Jadis stumbles forward, legs folding. His sword slips from his hand with a quiet clatter, completely at odds with the carnage around us.

Then he falls.

Not like a warrior.

Like a tree struck by lightning.

His body crashes to the earth, his cloak fanning around him like torn wings, the moss beneath him stained dark in an instant. His hand twitches once, reaching for a weapon that's no longer there, then goes still.

Silence descends in my head, drowning out the world.

The copper tang of blood invades my nose, so thick I can taste it at the back of my throat. My knees hit the ground hard. My palm finds the dirt, smeared warm and sticky, and my breath hitches in my chest as I crawl to him, choking on a scream I can't release.

"Jadis?" My voice is paper-thin, a whisper lost in the roar of the fight. I shake him once, then again, harder. His eyes flutter. A sliver of green shines through the blood and soot, dull and glazed.

"Stay with me," I beg. My voice cracks. "Stay with me, dammit—"

His lips part, but no sound emerges.

A tremble runs through his limbs, and then—nothing.

No rise of chest. No flicker of breath. His beautiful emerald eyes, once so full of life, now dulled, their warm green glow fading to nothing.

Just stillness.

My whole body floods with cold, as if someone dumped ice water into my veins. I scream his name, a raw, wretched thing that rips itself from my throat and echoes across the clearing, silencing even Pyra's fire. My fingers dig into his coat, into his blood, into the hollow spot where his warmth is fading too quickly.

Behind me, Cartwell laughs.

The sound punches through my ribs like a hammer.

Tirae myanith, ael vyrin, comes his voice flowing gently, quietly fading through my mind.

A scream of anguish pierces my ears and I realize it comes from my throat, making my bones shake. The sound one of pure anguish, a wordless expression of pain and sorrow, of torment, that threatens to never end.

I can't move.

Everything around me keeps shifting—people running, flames screaming, steel clashing—but I can't move. Jadis lies still beneath me, the heat of the battle pressing against my skin, and yet he feels cold. Too cold. His blood seeps into the moss and coats my hands, sticky and thick like sap, like it belongs in a nightmare, not here.

Not in this clearing.

Not in this life.

My chest tightens until I can't breathe. It's like drowning in smoke, only the fire is inside me. I press my hands to his chest, over his heart, begging it to beat again. Begging something—magic, fate, the stars—to fix this. The flames of Pyra's wrath crackles somewhere nearby, and yet I feel frozen, split down the middle by something sharp and invisible.

The world feels too bright. Too loud. Too much.

Everything slams into me all at once—the stench of blood and scorched leather, the rough earth biting into my knees, the burning sting in my throat from screaming. My mind fractures into fragments. Jadis laughing beside a campfire. Jadis glaring across a council chamber. Jadis whispering my name like it mattered more than fate.

I can't lose him.

Not like this.

I scream again. A broken, jagged sound that tears from the depths of me, raw and brutal. It shudders through the clearing and draws every eye, but I don't care. Let them look. Let them see what he meant to me.

Let the whole damn world know.

And then—something shifts.

Cartwell's laugh cuts through the chaos, vile and sharp, like a wolf gnawing on bone. I barely hear it over the pounding of my heart and the shattering inside my chest. But it finds me. Finds the weak place and worms its way in.

Mik roars—wordless, defiant—and launches himself at the nearest soldier. His blades gleam, catching the firelight as they whip in blinding arcs. For a moment, I believe he might hold them off. He fights like something ancient, primal, each movement driven by fury and desperation. Sparks fly as steel clashes with steel. A blade sings past his ear, close enough to shear a lock of hair.

I try to cry out, to warn him, but my voice is shredded from screaming Jadis' name.

Three of them come at him at once—hulking warriors, eyes wild with bloodlust. Mik parries the first, sidesteps the second, and buries one dagger deep into a gut. But he's slowing. His shoulders heave with effort. His left leg buckles slightly.

The third finds his opening.

I watch it happen in terrible silence.

A jagged blade plunges into Mik's side. He stumbles. Another slams a mace across his back. He goes down hard, his head hitting the moss with a sickening thud. His hands twitch once—fingers grasping at empty air—then still.

"No," I rasp, scrambling to rise, my limbs numb with cold and grief.

That's when I feel it.

A hand—massive, iron-strong—clamps down on my arm. Cartwell.

His grip bruises instantly, wrenching me to my feet like I weigh nothing. The jagged armor on his chest scrapes my skin as he yanks me close. His breath is hot against my cheek, foul with blood and smoke.

"Lovely little firebrand," he growls, voice thick with mockery. "I think we've danced long enough."

I thrash in his grasp, twisting, kicking, clawing. My nails rake his jaw. He laughs. Actually laughs.

I'm crumbling. Inside and out.

This is what failure feels like. Not the quiet disappointment of loss—but the violent, soul-tearing realization that everything I love is being torn away from me, and I am powerless to stop it.

All I can do is watch it all burn.

Cartwell's arm locks around my middle like a vise. I buck and writhe, trying to shift, to flame, to do *anything*—but the magic's not coming. I'm empty. My body screams with exhaustion, my limbs trembling from too many wounds and too much grief.

He swings me up like a ragdoll, tossing me across the front of his saddle. The hard leather digs into my ribs. My cheek slams into the curve of his arm. I kick wildly, but the world spins as he digs in his heels.

The horse surges forward.

I twist, craning my neck back, searching for any sign of Mik. Of Rurik. Of *anyone*.

But all I see is smoke and blood and the broken silhouette of Jadis, unmoving beneath the falling sun.

And then—there, just at the tree line—eyes.

Rurik.

His pale gaze locks with mine, agonized, frantic. He's crouched low, concealed in shadow, but I can see the shimmer of unshed tears and the tremble of barely-contained rage. His lips move, forming a soundless plea.

Run.

I want to scream at him to. I want to beg him to stay hidden. But my voice is gone.

Cartwell spurs the horse again, and the world jolts around me as we vanish into the trees.

Chapter Thirty Three

"Caelaril ael ilithar myrrathil."

A single light can stir the world.

Rurik

A S I STUMBLE BACK INTO my village, my heart feels as heavy as a boulder. I hurry along the familiar paths, so much darker now, greyer, my feet flying from memory. Auntie Thora's hut is thick with the scent of herbs, wrapping around me like a comforting hug.

"Auntie Thora," I call out, my voice shaking with need. "Please, we need the cauldron. Jadis...he's gone."

"Hold yerself, Rurik. Explain the fear I see in yer eyes. Because we all know our friends left this day."

I explain to her, in great detail, what I'd seen befall my friends and her eyes fill with sorrow. "Fetch yer father. Now!"

My Da, Thorgar, gathers the warriors of our clan. Men and women alike stand side by side, a united front against the ever encroaching darkness.

Nalona, the healer, joins the sad gathering. Her gentle face brings a glimmer of hope, even though I'm afraid her skills are too little, too late.

As I bring all closer to the site of the battle, a chilling breeze sweeps across the land, carrying with it the strife and despair I feel in my soul. The once lush meadow has become a haunted place, full of destruction, scarred by the remnants. The air is heavy with the terrible scent of smoke, mingling with the horrid scent of blood and death.

Broken weapons lay about the trampled earth. Even the sky seems to reflect our souls with brooding grey clouds, swirling about. It seems as though the Gods themselves mourn the fallen too. The wind whispers a mournful tune, carrying the lost souls and shattered dreams, or at least that's what Auntie murmurs to herself.

Bodies lay scattered like fallen leaves in the wake of a storm. The clash of swords and cries of battle have been replaced with complete stillness. The scene is haunting. Auntie says it's as if frozen in time, suspended between the ghosts of violence and the looming presence of impending doom. Great evil had been here, and we must face it. She's always had a way with words.

Mik fights at Dagen's throat to hold his blood inside, praying aloud for time and healing. His face a mask of determination and anguish.

Nalona wastes no time and rushes to his side with a compassionate touch, murmuring soft words. She insists Dagen will be fine. His natural healing is already doing a fine job, she'll just help it along.

"Oh, thank the Gods. Stars above, how did ye know to come?" Mik falls to the ground, the muscles in his legs failing, sitting hard on his backside.

Da answers with a comforting touch to the wolf's back. "My son is quite enamored with you lot. Fortunate for ye, he snuck away and then came begging for help."

"Lad, I'm grateful and furious at the same time," he says, staring me down and a quivering shakes my spine. Mik glances to Jadis' prone form, Fallon kneeling at his side, "Some are beyond yer help." Tears gather in his eyes.

Thora leaves the body of Jadis, her tears falling freely.

"He took Elora and I can't..." Mik's hand grasps at Da. "I can't even think on what he'll do to her. We must get her back; we can't waste any time here."

"Rest and breathe, Mik. There are things that must happen first. Cartwell's proclivity for lies not only poisons his soul and magic, but his actions. He can twist and break the fabric of the fates. Take souls before their time. Lucky for us, Elora provided a tool to fix the threads of the fates. Rurik," she calls to me. "It was yer pure heart that called for the cauldron today. Bring it forward as ye will now wield its power."

"What?" Mik asks.

"Did ye not listen to my story at all?"

Chapter Thirty Four

> *"Nororin vyrithor ithrin lyrien naelithir."*

Fighting is heavy when the heart has faded.

Elora

RIDE IN FRONT OF Cartwell, trapped between his strong arms as they hold the reins. His presence looms behind me like a suffocating shadow. I know he speaks, the feel of his tainted breath upon my cheeks. Yet, his words are lost to me. The whirlwind of my own thoughts, or lack thereof, drowning them out.

Guilt, like a relentless beast, gnaws at my soul, its fangs sinking deep into the shreds that remain of my heart. I blame myself—for the deaths of my friends, for the loss of Jadis, who was much more than my protector. I know that now. I took so long to admit it and now it's all ripped away. The chill of love lost can't be erased, not even by the warm presence of Pyra, hidden inside my leathers. Every failure, every misstep, replays in my mind like a haunting melody of the life I just threw away, tormenting me with its bitter refrain.

I hoped for change; I hoped for happiness and started to believe that maybe, just maybe I could have it. I was wrong, so very wrong.

If only I had not insisted on staying longer with the trolls, maybe then we could have, would have remained hidden. If only I hadn't screamed, distracting Jadis in that critical moment. If I had just controlled my damn emotions, maybe he would still be by my side, his loving embrace a shining light in the darkness. If only I had been a better fighter, if I had mastered my magic, then maybe I could have protected them, shielded them from the harm my existence rains down on everyone.

The weight of the guilt threatens to consume me, to swallow me whole in its unforgiving grasp. I feel the suffocating tentacles of self-doubt wrapping around my mind, whispering insidious lies that I am to blame for all the tragedies that have befallen them. Were they lies? No. I am as I always have been: a bane and a burden to everyone around me.

As the wind whips through my hair and tears mingle with the dust on my cheeks, I feel the ghost of that touch, that warmth.

Remember, Elora, a well-placed strike can bring even the mightiest opponent to their knees, he whispers through my mind. *Don't give in*, he cries, or rather my broken mind conjures his voice. *Stay strong for me*. The abyss tries to take me again but this time the darkness isn't all consuming, there are stars and light and I know I'm not alone. I've never truly been alone. *The world deserves your light, Elora. It needs your light, it's better for it. Don't give in to the darkness.*

I am not afraid. "No," I say so softly I second guess the movement of my own lips.

"What?" Cartwell seethes against my ear.

"No..." I say, again, louder. "Never again." I lean enough to rip out the blade Jadis had tucked in my boot and twist, burying it into Cartwell's side.

I don't know if it was the twist or the shock to Cartwell, but I fall off the horse.

I gasp for air, my heart pounding in my chest once again, as I struggle to drag my battered body away from the sounds of an approaching figure. The pain radiates through every fiber of my being, each fall, as I trip and struggle, magnified by the harshness of the unforgiving ground. Tears mix with dirt on my cheeks, leaving a sharp grit I try to wipe away.

Looking up at the night sky, I yearn for some flicker of hope, a glimmer of salvation to rescue me from this nightmare. But the stars offer no advice, no solace, their distant light a cruel reminder that I'm on my own. The ground beneath me feels treacherous, as if it conspires with Cartwell to ensure my capture. Who knows, maybe it does.

I stumble again and roll to my side so as not to crush Pyra under my body. She tries to come out; to show herself and I beg her to stay hidden, just in case. Flipping to my back, I freeze. His wicked sneer twists his face into a grotesque mask of evil, a chilling display of his true nature, the sharp planes of his angular face adding to the intensity. I tremble, knowing that he revels in my fear, delighting in my helplessness. The realization dawns on me with a sickening weight—I have underestimated not only the depth of his depravity but how hard he is to kill. He slowly pulls the blade from his side without the slightest flinch, the exposed flesh knitting back together with ease.

With each step he takes, the sound of his boots crunching against grit and debris echoes loudly in my ears, louder than my ragged breathing. My heart drums wildly, an erratic rhythm that threatens to drown out every thought. I scramble backwards, fingers clawing at the jagged earth—sharp stones tearing into my palms, the sting immediate and hot. The scent of sweat, blood, and dirt clogs my nose. My legs slip in the loose soil as I search blindly for escape, the panic rising like bile in my throat.

Then, a grip like iron. Hard hands seize me from behind and wrench me upright, my cry muffled by the gasp that catches in my throat.

Cartwell draws closer, his malevolent grin widening. I fear this isn't going to end in my favor. He drags the blade up the leathers at my torso, resting the tip just beneath my right eye, the pressure pulling my lower lid down. "I don't recommend trying that again." He adds the slightest pressure to the blade, and I feel the warm drip before the sting of pain as he drags it down my cheek, slowly, increasing the pressure until a scream is wrangled from my throat. "It won't end well for you," he says, as I watch a red line start to drip down his right cheek.

THE BARREN LANDSCAPE stretches before me, a desolate expanse that seems devoid of life and hope. A fitting place for this monster to rule. The very essence of decay permeates the air, the land itself having withered and died under the weight of Cartwell. The fields were obviously once fertile and the forests once full of life, but they had transformed into twisted, gnarled remnants of their former selves, or that's what I imagine anyway. It makes me feel slightly better about my situation.

My face stings. The cut isn't deep and likely won't scar too much, but I have the sinking feeling that's only because a similar cut appeared on his face. That surprised him. His ire turned elsewhere for the remainder of the hard ride.

The sky above us is cloaked in a heavy shroud of darkness, almost a perpetual twilight that prevents most things from growing. The steely hues of gray and violet mingle together, creating an unsettling atmosphere that sends shivers down my spine. The ground beneath us is cracked and parched, drained of life.

Trees that mourn their old life stand as twisted sentinels, their branches contorted in pain. Leaves, that I can picture once verdant and lush, now cling to the skeletal branches, blackened and lifeless. The very essence of nature has been tainted by Cartwell's presence and I wonder if removing him from the picture would even do any good. I wonder if it's too late.

As we get closer to the looming keep, I assume it's his infamous Obsidian Palace. It's imposing silhouette dominates the horizon, a surprising feat considering it's nestled in the foothills of the Obsidian Peaks. The cold, black walls seem to absorb what little light remains here, casting deep shadows that dance with an eerie, haunted energy. Maybe my own sorrow influences the scene, but I can't see how one would see anything else. Cartwell is a sinister being and his magic has poisoned the land around him.

The corrupted land serves as a chilling reminder of his twisted reign, and I cannot fathom how I didn't see this side of him before. How could I not see the evil lingering under his handsome face? Was I that blind? How could he have hidden it so well when it seeps out of every hair, every pore?

The dark beauty of the walls of obsidian rising before us even stands in stark contrast to the life-sucking energy that pulses behind me. The towering walls, crafted from solid, glistening stone, loom against the backdrop of the dimly lit sky. The fortress exudes an aura of grief or mirrors it. I can't tell anymore.

Sharp angular edges and jagged spires reach skyward, casting unsettling silhouettes. The obsidian material gives the fortress an otherworldly sheen as it absorbs the scant light that dares to touch its dark beauty. It's the perfect representation of the foreboding I feel in my soul.

The entrance to the keep is flanked by heavy, ornate doors with runic carvings. The designs etched upon the glassy surface aren't dark like the rest of the land, they're happy and upbeat, images of mythical creatures like many of the other places I've visited.

The closer we get to the keep, the more a stillness settles on the air, broken only by faint whispers. Shadows dance along the walls, their movements like ghostly fingers playing the darkness like a harp. The air grows colder, sending a different chill down my spine.

The ominous feel ends with the doors. Inside, the walls are covered with complex tapestries and ornate sconces that give off an air of elegance and grandeur I wasn't expecting. Soft candlelight dances across the polished stone floors, casting an unexpected warm glow that belies what I believe the true nature of this place was. Before him.

The halls seems remarkably inviting, drawing me deeper into the heart of the castle with only the occasional thump to my back by Ravengar, who I learned is Cartwell's captain of the guard and far less personable than Jadis. God, Jadis...

The air is perfumed with a subtle hint of incense, mingling with the scent of aged wood and polish. The halls bustle with people of all types and sizes. The sound of my feet is even quieted by rich carpets and the halls and sitting rooms dotted with upholstered furniture. I don't know why, but I'd imagined Cartwell sitting on stone chairs as hard as his heart.

The unexpected comforts are only countered by the portraits hanging on the walls, their eyes watching me with an unsettling intensity, following my every move.

"Velasco," Cartwell shouts just ahead of me, stopping a new male in his tracks, his silver hair flowing freely from his back in his haste. The rich fabric of his robe hints at an elevated status, but so do his unusual eyes—liquid mercury.

"We have something to discuss." Cartwell traces the line on his face and then glares in my direction.

I think I see panic in this Velasco's eyes, but the moment is so fleeting, I might have imagined it. "Yes, sire." His quiet response with the downturned eyes belays what I sense all around me—fear.

"Ravengar, see my wife to her quarters. I will deal with her later."

"Not your wife," I seethe, but he doesn't deign to hear me as he wraps his long fingers around Velasco's arm and drags him into a nearby room.

"You are who he says you are and the sooner you accept that, the better your time here will be," Ravengar tells me, his voice remarkably calm despite the spark in his golden eyes. Shifter eyes.

"Not going to happen." The subtle lift to my chin is all the gumption I can gather at the moment. My body aches in so many ways, but I'm not going down easily, not again, never again. I won't sully the sacrifices made on my behalf in that way.

"Not my problem if you choose to suffer."

He grasps my arm in a similar fashion to Cartwell and drags me down an adjacent hallway. I expect to be dragged through multiple hallways and corridors, guided through a maze of lines so I won't be able to map my escape, but after only one left turn he stops outside an ornately carved door.

"Your room, Princess." He opens the doors, that have no obvious locks, and gestures for me to enter.

"What, no locks? Let me guess, magical fields that will only allow certain people to enter or leave?"

"No. No locks, no magic." He sneers at me, not a malevolent sneer, but one you might give a foolish child. "You try to leave, and you'll end up disappointed. The land out there can't be survived for long. You need a horse to pass the dead fields fast enough. The horses, they're guarded and guarded well. So, if you want to die, go ahead and try to leave. You'll be marching back with your tail between your legs within the hour."

"You underestimate my capabilities." I pull the door between the two of us, but his hand stops it before I can get it to latch.

"No, I apparently overestimated your intelligence if you're even considering it."

I feel my shoulders fall a little. "What kind of person would I be if I didn't at least try?" I mutter more to myself than anyone else.

"I'll give you that, Princess. I'll give you that," he says for only me to hear and my eyes shoot wide, a spark alighting in my chest.

RAVENGAR LEAVES ME to myself after his quiet declaration. Me and my own thoughts alone get to decide what those quiet words might have meant, if anything.

My room isn't uninviting, dark and mysterious as it is. The walls, painted a deep shade of blue, still seem to absorb the light. Black and purple draperies and furniture all add an air of mystery.

Unlike the lack of outside light would suggest, this room is built for sunlight. One entire wall is windows that bathe the room in subdued, diffused light. Each pane of glass sporting a delicate opalescent sheen, mirrored by paneling over the bed and on the larger pieces of furniture. The interplay of light and shadow create a mesmerizing dance, as rainbow shimmers play on the walls and floor.

Against the dark backdrop, the opalescent touches are more pronounced, celebrating the light in a land where no light shines. They make the plush velvet drapes that surround the bed and windows darker, like waterfalls made of shadows.

Lost in the dichotomy of my new surroundings, I almost miss the knock at the door. An unexpected show of respect in this strange place.

'Come in," I say, staring out my windows over the dreary land I had just traveled.

A small female enters the room at my words, a subtle touch of familiarity that quickly fades. She moves with a gentle grace, her steps light. Her deep violet eyes take me for a moment, glimmers of compassion hidden in their depths as she takes in my face, tracing my damaged cheek. Her gentle smile seems genuine, but I have been taken by a kind face before.

She comes closer in a measured pace, her hands clasping a small jar with a familiar green salve. She carefully inspects the cut, her touch gentle and deliberate. I find that sense of familiarity again in her touch.

"The salve will help prevent any scarring, my lady. Although, the cut isn't very deep anyway. It's a special formula that I prepare myself. Works wonders."

I can't help but respond with a tinge of skepticism, despite her apparent kindness. "And why would Cartwell care about scars on my face? He put it there, with intention. Is he suddenly concerned about my appearance?"

"Full honesty, Ravengar suggested he fetch me for you. Cartwell reluctantly agreed. I am Lavinia, by the way." She doesn't bother to offer her hand, seeming to understand that I wouldn't take it. Her gaze softens, her wide eyes meeting mine with a mixture of empathy and sadness. "It's not solely concern, my lady. Cartwell knows an unmarred face carries more influence with the people. It would be untoward for his wife to be marked so. He wants to present you as a symbol of beauty and power, someone they will rally behind. He made it clear that your face is the only skin that matters in this case. It can be seen, always."

I scoff at the notion, the bitterness seeping into my voice. "So, I'm a pawn, as always, in his twisted games. A puppet to be controlled and paraded around."

"And bred, I'm afraid."

"What?" The single word escapes in a breathless squeak, betraying my shock.

"I've said too much, my lady." Her eyes shift to the door waiting, watching. When nothing happens, she turns her face to my own again, her features tinged with regret. "I understand your anger, my lady. But, sometimes, surviving this world means playing the game, even if it's against our will. Please believe me when I say that I'm here to help you, in whatever way I can." Her words are barely perceptible. "Come," she says, much louder this time. "Cartwell is not a patient male and has demanded your presence in his study."

Chapter Thirty Five

"*Vaelys vylaror shalorin vyrithor.*"

The smile hides sharper teeth.

S LAVINIA GUIDES ME THROUGH the shadowed corridors, a knot of unease tightens in my stomach. The heavy wooden door of Cartwell's study looms ahead, also carved with the ornate pictures that seem to writhe in the dim candlelight. Lavinia pauses, her hand resting on the door handle, and I take a deep breath to steady myself.

"Prepare yourself, my lady. Cartwell awaits inside. Bank your emotions, use your head not your heart." Lavinia steadies her hand on the door, waiting for me.

I nod, bracing myself for the encounter. She pushes open the door, and we step inside together. The room is suffused with an air of dark authority, shelves filled with ancient tomes and artifacts, and paintings depicting appropriate scenes of power and domination litter the walls. A large desk dominates the center of the room, where Cartwell sits, his eyes gleaming, while Velasco stands at his side, eyes downcast but a smug grin etched across his face. A female stands to the side, watching us with curiosity and uncertainty.

Cartwell's voice drips with his calculated charm, "Ah, Elora, my dear wife. I trust you're beginning to understand the gravity of your situation. Now that you've had time to use your brain."

"There is no marriage, here, Cartwell. We got divorced. You have no claim over me anymore. Especially here."

"That's where you're woefully wrong, dear wife." He sneers, gesturing with two fingers to Velasco.

A wave of heat rushes through me, a mix of anger and desperation fueling my defiance. I refuse to accept his claims of ownership over me, but doubt creeps in as Velasco produces a scroll, its surface covered with tiny runes and symbols, with a flowery script from top to bottom.

I scan the parchment, and my eyes widen in recognition as I see my own signature at the bottom; a signature I have no memory of providing.

"That...that...no, I never signed this. I've never seen this before."

The room seems to close in and tilt around me, as if the weight of betrayal and manipulation is an actual, physical entity. I can feel them, not just on my shoulders, but across the back of my neck, pushing their way into my head.

"You did, my lady, as you signed your marriage license in the mortal world. The two documents were linked. It was clever but difficult magic to make it happen, required to be signed in blood and all." Velasco's eyes light up as he describes the nature of the piece of paper and how they slipped it in unnoticed. He points to the drop of brownish-red color near my name and memory flares. Carter had given me a paper cut in his excitement that day. I'd thought it an accident, but now I was obviously delusional.

As I rub the finger in memory, Cartwell grins, his lips carving into his cheeks.

"If this document is linked to the marriage license, then any agreement made should have dissolved when that marriage was dissolved." I say, the quiver in my voice not matching the strength of my words.

"You are adorable in your naïveté sometimes. That's not how this works. Our mortal marriage was meaningless and has no effect on this contract. You are, in fact, still bound to me. I own you and your body. You will provide me with what I want, willingly or not, or suffer the consequences. Anyone who tries to aid you in breaking this contract, dies." His words fall like lead in my stomach. "Anyone tries to keep you from me," he says, leaning over his desk to place his face in mine, "dies."

Jadis. His features shimmer behind the hot tears collecting in my eyes.

"That's, that's not all it says—" Velasco says, his demeanor not matching his physical presence at all.

Cartwell waves a hand at him mid sentence. "Serephine here has been assigned as your lady companion. Velasco has happily given the company of his wife to you. She will fill you in on the rules of our agreement as we have more important issues at hand. You will be appropriately attired and present at dinner in an hour." He looks to Serephine, who nods gracefully at him, and he leaves with Velasco winking to his wife as he, too, passes by.

MY DREAMS OF freedom burst in an instant like a bubble, leaving me with nothing but a suffocating sense of betrayal. A searing rage wells up inside me as my heart sinks into the depths of despair and sorrow. I can feel the cold fingers of fear wrapping around me tightly, squeezing until I think I can't take it anymore.

Serephine moves gracefully ahead of me, her beauty captivating, even in our gloomy surroundings, our footsteps almost echoing in the stillness. Her silver hair cascades down her back like a waterfall and her eyes carry a depth that seems to hold secrets as she glances over her shoulder, watching the tears trace slowly down my cheeks. She presses her full lips together each time.

How could I have been so foolish? The realization that I'm bound to him in ways I can't comprehend sends a heavy chill down my spine. The thought of him touching me again, feeling my skin, makes me want to vomit.

My only hope comes with trusting that this enigmatic female in front of me is truthful and doesn't try to lead me down another deceitful path.

Cartwell is smart, but nowhere near perfect. She holds the key to unraveling the intricacies of the contract, to finding the loophole or hidden clause that could grant me my freedom. But I have to keep my guard up, to be wary of any ulterior motives.

Stepping into my room, Serephine makes her way over to the large wardrobe, but instead of reaching inside for whatever suitable attire Cartwell demanded, she grasps a small opal leaf on the door and turns it. I feel, more than see the wave of magic that permeates the room.

"What did you just do?" I ask.

She raises a single finger to her lips and waits. With a small smile she says, "Can you hear me?"

"Of course I can hear you, I'm standing right here." My hands fly to my hips as I glare at this incredulous female.

"Not you, my lady...perfect. Now that's done, we can speak freely. To answer your initial question, it's a privacy glamour. Now, what is spoken in this room will be private. We can't leave it on all the time. We'll have to choose our moments wisely, but my husband will make sure Cartwell is distracted for at least an hour."

"What? I don't...why?" I plop my very tired behind in a soft chair, slipping my head into my palms.

This time she does open the wardrobe, removing a few gowns for perusal. I don't really care what she puts me in, at this point, it doesn't matter. "We need to talk freely about all the details of this contract you entered."

"Unwillingly," I snap at her.

"Be that as it may, there are certain provisions that Velasco added, unbeknownst to Cartwell, that may come in handy. You need to know all the minute details so you can navigate this properly."

"Why should I trust anything you're saying right now? Just because you're saying no one can hear us, even if that's true, you could be trying to lull me into a false sense of security. You serve him, willingly. What kind of person does that?"

She sighs and slowly settles into the adjacent chair, leaving the dress choosing behind. "We are all bound to him, Elora, much like you. Despite what you think, most of us wouldn't be here if we had somewhere else to go. Even bound to him, our lives are better than they would have been in the alternative. You'll find everyone here to be a mix of outcasts, cast-offs, those with dark pasts that are either seeking refuge, redemption, or more power. We survive, and some of us intend to help you survive." *Survive* was accentuated, her eyebrows raising slightly as if she means another word but can't say it. "There's no harm in talking with me. Mince your words, do whatever makes you feel more comfortable and use the information I give you how you see fit. That's all."

I have nothing else to do, no one else to turn to, but I can't depend on these people. I'm alone, weak and alone, but I have a decent head on my shoulders and can figure this out. She's right, what I need is the information and if I doubt what she says, I suppose I can verify the information by demanding to see the damned contract again.

I nod.

"Good," Serephine begins, her voice smooth, clipped, and down to business. She folds her hands neatly in her lap, the silver strands of her hair gleaming in the dim light.

I stiffen, my fingers curling into fists at my side. The weight of her stare makes me want to shrink back, but I refuse to break eye contact.

"First," she continues, her tone cool, almost clinical, "you are magically bound to Cartwell, it's more than a marriage in the mortal world." She pauses, her violet eyes narrowing ever so slightly. "He owns you."

The words land like a slap and I can feel the heat rising in my chest— anger, indignation, or maybe something closer to fear.

"You have limited freedoms while in his presence," Serephine adds, her lips curving into a faint, unreadable smile, as if she already knew how I'd react.

My jaw tightens. The room feels smaller suddenly, the air thicker, as though its conspiring against me too.

I lean forward slightly, the chair creaking under the movement. "Like a slave?" My voice quivers, but not in fear alone, there's a fire there, I feel it smoldering.

Serephine's expression doesn't falter. If anything, her serene composure sharpens, her violent eyes glinting like polished stones. She tilts her head, a gesture that's as measured as her words.

"In laymen's terms, yes." I grip the edge of the table now, my knuckles turning white.

"He owns your body and has made it clear he intends to use it. That was made clear right from the beginning," Serephine adds, her voice smooth and crisp, each word incredibly deliberate as if carved from glass. She sits impossibly straight, the delicate fabric of her robes unmoving despite the draft that curls around us. Next to her, I must look like a country bumpkin; a rumpled traveler dragged in from the woods. Oh wait, that's exactly what I am.

"And it elicited the first provisions that Velasco entered."

My jaw clenches making it difficult to speak as the room becomes so small I think I'm suffocating. "We had a child, he killed her. I don't see why he wants more." The weight of this situation pushes down hard on my shoulders, and I find myself fidgeting with the edge of my sleeve, unable to still restless hands. I glance around the room, scanning the elegant decorations on the walls, seeking a distraction.

"That's beside the point. He has his reasons that he doesn't share with the rest of us. All he relayed again today is that he plans on you birthing his heirs." She's obviously frustrated and I think I might vomit. Her graceful fingers rest delicately on the armrest of her chair now, exuding an aura of calm authority.

Her gaze locks on mine, her eyes soften with a depth of understanding that both intrigues and unsettles me. I take a moment to observe her, trying to figure out the secrets that she hides beneath this exceptionally composed exterior.

"Velasco added verbiage in regard to your physical safety. He couldn't negate harming you entirely," her tone is so even it's irritating, "that would have been too obvious once discovered." She pauses, her gaze briefly flickering over me, measuring my reaction.

The memory of my attempt at escape is fresh and flashes through my mind—the pain. My hand inadvertently touches the cut on my cheek.

"As you witnessed on your journey here," she says, her voice dropping slightly, "any harm Cartwell does to your body, intentionally, is mirrored on his own."

"Intentionally...ha," I say, my words seeming to charge the air between us. "Cartwell is a master manipulator he can make any word or action seem 'unintentional'.

She raises an incredulous set of eyebrows at me, tilting her head slightly downward. "This is magic, Elora," she says, obviously bored with my ineptitude, "It knows the difference between real innocence and feigned innocence."

"Wait," I blurt out gripping the table, the realization hitting me hard like a slap to the back of the head. "That surprised him. I could see it in his eyes. Didn't he know that was in the contract?"

My hands fall from the table, hovering in midair as if grasping for answers that aren't there. The memory of Cartwell's startled expression flashes through my mind. It was there, the brief flicker of shock in his gaze. It didn't fit—it shouldn't have fit. It's his damn contract.

"He didn't know. Males of his status don't often read the contracts. He probably assumes that his people fear him enough, rightly so, to follow his every dictate. Velasco is clever, thank the Stars, or he wouldn't have been standing in that study with us after Cartwell interrogated him about the cut."

"How was he not punished, dead even?" I ask, the words spilling out before I can stop them. My pulse quickens as I lean forward, the questions racing in my mind. "I assume Cartwell then demanded to see the contract? Were there... other things he had to explain?"

"Yes," she replies, her posture softening slightly as she leans back in her chair. "Like I said, my husband is clever, the tiny details were easily explained by the type of magic that had to occur."

Her voice is still calm and deliberate, but there's a trace of pride in her tone. I don't blame her, especially if her husband is as formidable as he looks. She folds her hands neatly in her lap again, the movements unhurried.

"Not only did the magic have to cross realms, but manipulation is not something that comes natural to it. Velasco simply wrote them off as requirements to trick the magic into binding you unknowingly."

Her lips curve into a faint smile, though it doesn't quite reach her eyes.

"Clever indeed," I stand, my lips thinning as a spark of defiance surges through me. My hands ball into fists against my sides and I feel a wave of restless energy pass through me, urging me to break something, anything.

She lay her hand lightly on my fist. "Please bear with me, my lady, there is more you must know. Don't shut me out just yet."

She proceeds to tell me that he cannot physically harm me without doing so to himself, in the hopes that would regulate his temper. Not very encouraging. Velasco wrote the section about people helping me very carefully. Words had to be spoken aloud about the intent to keep me from Cartwell for the death magic to be triggered. Intent without words cannot be punished. He placed nothing in the contract about me keeping myself from Cartwell. If I can get away, I am in no danger from the magic. Any help I receive only triggers the magic if it's given solely to keep me from Cartwell. The best part: if he tries to kill me, with his own hands or magic, even accidentally, the contract becomes null and void, but that goes both ways. Whoever takes that step will suffer the vengeance of the magic.

"What you're saying is, I need to piss him off enough that he tries to kill me and then hope and pray he doesn't succeed? This doesn't sound very promising." Unable to contain my restlessness any longer, I start pacing back and forth across the room. The sound of my steps echo against the walls, punctuating the silence that lingers. I need the moment, the physical manifestation of my reeling mind, to keep myself grounded.

"And in the meantime, I have to what? Hope that he waits long enough to force himself on me that I find a way out of here first?"

"There are other ways to control the situation." Serephine's eyes follow my restless movements, her gaze unwavering. How can she be so calm? Oh, wait, it's not her life and her body being used this way. The way she's looking at me is so measured and it hits me. The tone of this entire conversation was carefully planned. She wasn't exchanging mere words, I needed to read between the lines, because of the contract. She wasn't stiff but sending me subtle hints in body language and expressions the whole time.

Pausing my pacing, I turn to face her, locking eyes with her again. There is a silent understanding that passes between us, unspoken words that bridge the gap. Her fingers subtly tap against the armrest, a silent display of unease. It's a small gesture, easily overlooked, but it speaks volumes about the complexity of her role within this twisted web of deceit.

"I suppose I should get dressed *appropriately* and make my appearance at dinner then?"

"Of course, my lady," she smiles, getting up to twist that opal leaf back in place and the games begin. This isn't only about lies and truth, it's about mincing words and actions to trick magic.

Chapter Thirty Six

"Vylaror thyrelithil ithrin, elvinar thaelin; vylaror thyrelithil sylvaen, elvinar vynael."

Hide the truth once, your shame; hide it again, mine.

T DINNER, I FIND MYSELF seated beside Serephine, my heart pounding, the unease knotting in my chest. I am immediately jealous of this effortless poise she's perfected. The aroma of the feast swirls around me—rich spices, roasted meats, and something sweet I can't quite place, all mingling in the warm air. My stomach twists, not from hunger but from the strange dichotomy before me. The sumptuous dishes, meticulously arranged on gilded plates, seem at odds with the barren wasteland outside.

I glance down at my plate, its contents so inviting they feel like a mockery of the desolation just beyond these walls. How do they conjure this kind of abundance in a place where nothing should grow? My gaze flicks to Serephine, her violet eyes cool and unreadable, as though daring me to ask the question aloud.

Even though my stomach now begs me to break, I grit my teeth and push through the temptation. I want to prove to Cartwell that I am strong enough to make my own choices. I am determined to defy him at every turn.

Cartwell's cold and calculating gaze pierces through me like an arrow. His chair creaks as he sits up straight, his lips curl into a sneer of contempt. "What is the matter, my dear? You haven't touched your food." His words are more of an accusation than a concern, leaving me frozen in fear beneath the intensity of his stare. Fear I'm all too used to and that I will resist.

I lock eyes with him, my voice steady, every ounce of defiance I can muster coming out. "I will not be cowed to accept something against my will."

A cruel smile dances on his lips and is then erased, the gesture for me alone to see, to taunt me. "No one is forcing you to eat with us. You always were in a position to lose a little weight. I doubt a few missed meals will hurt you. You have some to spare."

The heat rushes to my face with the insult, and I feel the white-hot rage flood into my veins. I clench my fists in my lap and take a deep breath. Stay silent. Do not react. Don't let him know he got you. Stay silent.

"So stubborn. But remember, my dear, your choices will soon be limited. Once you bear my child, you won't have the luxury of skipping meals."

"I already bore you a child and you killed her, why demand another?"

"That was a terrible accident," he says, his voice smooth but edged with something that makes my stomach churn. His grey eyes, cold and calculating, flicker to mine before returning to his plate, where he casually slices into a piece of roast meat. "I'm hurt that you keep making me out to be a villain. I was always so good to both of you."

The clink of utensils fills the silence as the others at the table focus intently on their food, their gazes fixed downward, avoiding the charged air.

"I don't deserve these lies.," he continues around a mouthful, his tone thick with what I know is mock offense. He dabs at the corner of his mouth with a pristine napkin, his scar tugging slightly as his lips curl into a faint, humorless smile.

"Hopefully our next child will be more," he adds, his voice softening into something almost reverent, though his words make bile rise in my throat. "To honor her.

My hands clench under the table, nails digging into my palms as I struggle to keep my expression neutral.

"I had hoped your binding wouldn't affect your offspring, but I was wrong." He's so casual with this entire conversation about our dead daughter, like he's discussing the weather. "She was human, mortal." His knife scrapes across the plate, the sound grating.

The fire crackles loudly, the pop only escalating the tension around the table. Serephine's eyes flick to mine for the briefest of moments, her expression unreadable, before she returns to her meal.

"The others will be more, now that you're home."

My eyes widen and burn, his face undulating behind the angry tears that well in them. "You still deny it?"

"Of course I do. Why would I admit to something so heinous? That would be lying," he says, leaning back in his chair with a self-satisfied air.

I slam my hands onto the table, and rise, my voice trembling with raw emotion. "I will never be a prisoner to your desires. My body is my own, and I won't allow you to control it or dictate my actions."

Cartwell's hollow laugh drums in my ears as he rises from his chair. His height and presence alone are enough to send a ripple of fear through me, but I hold my ground as he slowly circles the table, coming to stand directly in front of me after yanking my chair around. He leans down, his cold eyes trapping me in a web of intimidation and menace.

He sighs. "Why can't you just behave, hmm? You constantly force my hand, Elora."

"Fuck you," I practically yell in his face, the anger exploding from my very soul.

"Do not raise your voice to me, Elora, or have you forgotten how the fuck to maintain propriety?" His words are daggers being thrust into me with unbridled force. I struggle to keep myself composed as he continues to chastise me.

The room falls into another uncomfortable silence, the tension thickening with every passing second. The gazes of those around the table bore into me, a mixture of shock and curiosity. But I pay them no mind. All my focus needs to stay on Cartwell.

He smirks at my defiance before straightening upright and addressing the others about my sudden silence. "So, she does remember."

He turns back to me, his eyes narrow in warning, "Always such a quick learner, biddable. I do love that about you."

My heart races and my fists clench tightly at my sides as Cartwell moves back to his seat next to me, at the head of the table. Adrenaline surges through my veins and I have to reel it in and take a deep breath before straightening my chair. Though every part of me wants to flee this place and never look back, I stay put. Running will do nothing but make things worse for myself in the long run.

Cartwell's expression shifts from amusement to anger within seconds. "You forget your place, Elora. I am your husband, and you will do well to remember that. Why do you insist on making me so angry?"

I meet his gaze with unyielding determination. "Your marriage is built on deceit and manipulation. It's not a marriage. I refuse to acknowledge it as anything other than it really is. I refuse to accept you as anything other than my captor."

His hand snaps across my face with lightning speed, I only feel the sharp pain in its wake. As my own palm moves to hold the stinging and most likely bruising skin, he too brings a hand to his own face. His nose wrinkles in disgust.

"Ravengar, call Magnus. I believe my wife needs a lesson in respect. You've forced my hand, dear. You make me do the most terrible things to you."

Velasco's apologetic gaze meets mine from across the table, but I don't really understand its meaning. A slap to my face to remind Cartwell not to try to harm me doesn't seem like much of a price to pay. That is until I see who enters the hall.

Magnus towers over the crowd, his mere presence unleashing a wave of terror and dread. His hulking silhouette is clad in rigid leather armor that clings precariously to engorged muscles. His incredible stature, coupled with his vicious glare and baleful aura, command absolute attention, leaving those around him paralyzed with fear, me included.

"Magnus," Cartwell seethes, he moves his hand and the purple bruise on his cheek stands out starkly against his pale skin. "I believe my wife needs a lesson in proper behavior."

There is no hesitation on Magnus' part, my dress ripping at the seams as he yanks me from my chair and back hands me again, right across the temple. The world churns around me from my new position on the floor. His broad shoulders seem chiseled from stone, and his arms, thick with sinew, bear the marks of countless battles fought and won. Each step he takes thrums with a low, ominous rumble, like the distant growl of an apex predator. The jagged scar that mars his rugged face only heightening his intimidating appearance.

"Oh, and Magnus, that punishment aside, make sure the rest don't show. We must keep up appearances."

Magnus' eyes, devoid of all emotion and humanity, shine with a predatory intensity that can make the bravest person cower in fear. As our eyes meet, I feel his merciless stare pierce through my soul, revealing a malevolent darkness that lurks deep inside him. It's like he's daring me to challenge him, too.

The hairs on the back on my neck stand up and my insides liquify as I struggle to maintain eye contact with this creature who seems more animal than male. Even in the dim light of the room, I can see the fire burning in his eyes that promises nothing but pain. He enjoys this, relishes it. He promises pain and suffering for anyone who dares cross him. And he makes good on this promise, over and over again.

My pain is unbearable, my lungs burning with every shallow breath I take. My legs feel like lead and refuse to move, yet he won't let me stay on the floor. With superhuman strength, he lifts me up with one hand, not letting go even as I gasp in agony. His presence is a heavy weight against my skin as I stand on unsteady feet, waiting for his next blow.

It isn't Cartwell that intervenes, he got bored about a dozen hits ago, it's Ravengar. "My lord, with all due respect, I believe Magnus has done a fine job. I beg permission to remove your difficult wife to her rooms to contemplate her decisions and behavior."

Cartwell sneers and flicks his wrist, dismissing us like pesky flies. In a swift motion, Ravengar scoops me up, his powerful arms cradling me as if I'm weightless. We immediately rush out of Cartwell's presence, leaving behind the stench of sulfur and danger.

MY VISION BLURS as my body is jolted with every step he takes. I feel my ribs crunching against his rugged leather jacket. His muscular arms are straining to keep me stable. The air is thick with tension as I grit out through clenched teeth, "Put. Me. Down."

"Calm yourself. When I said I thought you stupid, I didn't realize the depths of it. Are you mad?"

"Enough, Ravengar, the halls have ears." Serephine, I now realize, walks quietly alongside us and she whispers this harshly to us both.

"Aren't you going to stay with your husband and calm your lord?" I say, not looking at her. I no longer care to control my anger one bit. I don't have the energy.

"I am assigned to you, my lady. You think Velasco escaped punishment entirely for his writing of that contract? We are separated until further notice." The sadness in her eyes slices me like a blade.

"I will not taunt you further with remarks like Ravengar, but Elora, one word of advice, refusing to eat only hurts you and steals your energy. I admire your fortitude, but when he tires of your games, and he will, he will force the food down your throat, whether by having me hand feed you or placing it there by magic. I do not recommend the latter. Having a full meal appear in your belly instantly is quite painful."

"Speaking from experience?"

She doesn't answer, simply opening the doors to my chambers where Ravengar places me with a surprising gentleness on the bed, his gold eyes intense even in the low light.

With a steadying hand on my shoulder, he speaks softly, "You're smarter than this and I know it. Jadis would never have sacrificed himself otherwise."

His words are another punch to the gut, worse than anything Magnus could have inflicted. My breath catches in my throat, and for a moment, the world tilts. I wrench my shoulder away from his steadying hand, my body trembling as the pain surges fresh and raw, like a wound torn open all over again.

Don't," I rasp, my voice breaking. My chest tightens, and the air feels too thick, too suffocating. "Don't you dare say his name like that. Like he—" My voice cracks, and I choke on the rest of it, the memory of his face in those final moments crashing down on me. *Tirae myanith, ael vyrin.*

Tears burn in my eyes, blurring Ravengar's face into an unrecognizable smear. I ball my fists, nails digging into my palms, anything to make it stop.

"You know Jad—"

He slams a hand over my mouth, hushing me. "I will take my leave, Serephine. I suggest putting your charge to bed. Lavinia should see to her in the morning. Cartwell wants her prepared and she'll be in a world of pain."

Chapter Thirty Seven

"Thiralin inar lyrien vyrith lorys."

A name in your heart is a blade in your hand.

LYING ON MY BED, I feel the faint light of dawn seeping through the wall of windows, each ray of hope stabbing into me like a million needles. I'm surrounded by a relentless ache that seems to radiate from every inch of my body—as if I'm burning from the inside out. It's an undeniable reminder of Cartwell's cruelty and the loophole he so slyly took advantage of by having someone else do the beating. My ribs creak with each shallow breath, tender to the slightest touch. Bruises lurk beneath my skin everywhere but where they can not be seen, exactly as instructed. I haven't slept a wink.

Lavinia, with her calming presence, returns to tend to my injuries just as Ravengar suggested. Her gentle touch brings both relief and a tiny spark of gratitude. As Lavinia begins to speak, a loud crash sounds in the hall. She turns her head toward the door, her eyes widening slightly.

"Did you hear that?" I ask, foolishly.

Lavinia pauses, her brow furrows, and listens intently. The sound of hurried steps echo through the corridor, followed by muffled voices. She exchanges a quick glance with me before setting down her tray of salves and bandages and moves to the door.

"Stay there," she says firmly. "I'll go see what's happening."

Heart wrenching moments pass as I listen for more, needing more information to explain any commotion in this place I don't trust, in a place where I feel not even a tiny inkling of safety.

"Just a clumsy servant dropping a tray. All is well." Lavinia gives a soft smile and begins her meticulous work, applying salves with gentle strokes. The coolness of the ointment soothes the rawness of my bruises offering a fleeting respite from the pain.

She sets a pot of tea to steep. "Cartwell wishes you to be prepared. He wants you fertile so as not to delay things any further. This tea will make sure of that."

My eyes snap to the pot of tea as if it's a coiled viper. My fingers curl tightly into the fabric of the blankets, knuckles white, as I try to push away, try to put distance between myself and the steaming liquid.

A surge of panic prickles at my skin, and my gaze darts to Lavinia, searching for any hint of malice or deception. My throat's gone too dry, my tongue heavy, but I swallow hard, forcing myself to stay composed.

My hands twitch at my sides, torn between the instinct to push the pot crashing to the floor and the fear of drawing attention to my defiance.

"Don't even think that I—he never did listen to the word 'no'."

Calm yourself, child. What I speak and what I do will be two very different things today. Do you understand? Squeeze my hand if you understand.

She grasps my hand as if to comfort me in my pain and I squeeze as instructed. Her words don't come to my ears, it's mind speak. No one got the chance to teach me to block them. Because I'm a weak and helpless human who can't do anything without someone else's help.

Do not belittle yourself, child. Accepting help, trusting others, does not make us weak, it makes us formidable.

Now, you and I will mind speak as I work, do not acknowledge that I'm speaking unless it's with my actual mouth, yes?

I'm not drinking any tea. I'm not doing anything to help him, I tell her myself, showing I can respond at least.

Good, she says flatly in my mind. *I'd question your sanity if you did. This tea will be drunk, though. It won't prepare your womb for a child, dear, just the opposite actually. It will make it uninhabitable.*

I move a little to look at her with wide eyes, but she stops me with a pinch to my side, neatly avoiding my bruised flesh. She keeps moving her hands down my body, over my stomach and lower. She shifts her seat slightly and her elbow catches the steeped cup of tea, spilling the contents over the tray. "Oh, look at my clumsy self. Give me a moment and I'll get it steeping again."

You did that on purpose. Why? I ask, trying very hard not to raise an eyebrow at her.

She answers while pinching herbs from her various jars and adding them to a new cup. *Because I have decided to not make your womb uninhabitable, unless you want to vacate the child that already resides there?*

What? I ask and she turns me to my side, hiding my face from the door as the tears collect and start to fall.

You had a lover, then? She asks, trailing her palm lightly over my back as if I were sick to my stomach. A legitimate ruse considering the beating.

I force a single word out and it feels like it physically drags my chin to the ground. *Yes.* Even though we're only communicating through thought, I can't mask the pain behind that three letter word.

Will he come for you?

I collapse back onto the bed, its softness wrapping around me like a comforting embrace. This room is my only refuge and that isn't saying much. I have nowhere to hide from the pain that keeps closing in on my chest.

Why are you helping me, I ask, my eyes frantically searching hers for an answer, for recognition. I need to believe in someone, to trust in the kindness of a stranger. But all I see in her eyes is a silent promise, a little understanding, that this time the world might be different.

I know the marks of my sister's magic. She answers me, touching the skin of my chest and upper abdomen and the tiny pucker of a scar on my shoulder. *Margwin does fine work, especially with a human, well mostly human. Her magic was always much stronger than my own.*

If Margwin is your sister, then why are you here, serving him?

My past is full of bad decisions, youthful foolishness. I betrayed your parents to their enemies because I thought I loved someone and he loved me back. I was wrong, and this is my consequence. Everyone here is bound to him for one reason or another, no one escapes it. Even this life is significantly better than the alternative for most of us. It doesn't mean we serve him willingly or blindly as I think you're beginning to see.

My eyes wander toward the window, the outside world obscured, partially, by the heavy curtains and the weight of my predicament. My hand flutters to my lower belly, to the life she says sleeps inside.

He's dead, I answer, finally, the tears trailing down my temples and into my hair. *He won't be coming for me.*

What does Tirae myanith, ael vyrin mean? Those were his last words, and I don't have my lexicon. What did he say, please?

She strokes the hair along my forehead, holding one of my hands in hers. *Two hearts, one breath. He cared for you dearly. It's a phrase we say to describe a great love; a love so close that two people feel as one.*

I had nothing to say to that. The tears fall in earnest, no space between each one.

If he's not coming, then you're just going to have to buck up and do it yourself, she says sternly. *There are plenty of people readying to get you what you might need for your life here, belongings that will prove quite helpful wherever you might find yourself. Whatever you might need as you venture out on your own two feet in this new land.*

"Here dear, drink up, you'll feel better," she says aloud, helping me sit up with one hand, the cup of fragrant tea in the other. *Oh, stop fretting, you look ridiculous. It's tea, with a little boost to your womb to protect the child after your beating. Ah, ah, no more tears, the babe is fine, strong, and healthy. Yes, I can tell even this early.* She answers all of my questions before I can even ask them. My concern is apparently written all over my face. I heard once in the mortal world someone say that they can shut their mouth all they want but their face has subtitles and I feel that hard lately.

"All of it, child, every last drop so as to please your lord and master."

I admittedly grinned a little at her word choices. Lavinia is apparently an expert at mincing words and I'm growing to enjoy it, since it is in my favor.

Now, we won't have much time if you want to save that brother of yours. Word is he is preparing for war and if he comes after you, you already know what will happen to him. You're strong and my work will make you stronger. I think you'll be right as rain in no time to go climb some walls and take a walk in the fields before us.

Ravengar said the fields are much nicer from horseback, I say, learning the way of things and wording. It's hard lying here and pretending we're not talking at all.

Aye, but sometimes it's better to not tempt fate with company as finicky as horses, the stableman is right nasty about people taking his horses. You'll find other ways to enjoy your walk.

Our quiet and secret conversation continued with her mincing words to tell me of the plans to the best of her ability and how I need to prepare. I'm on my own, but not without a little help to get me on my way. I just have to survive the next few days without getting another beating and that may be the hardest task yet. I have to placate the bastard, play nice, walk on eggshells...again.

MY BRUISES HEALED, I act the submissive wife, watching my words, banking my emotions like late night embers. I'm shocking even myself at my control. I'm also shocked that I have to thank that damn therapist because she actually taught me something useful about emotions. Cartwell uses my emotions against me. If I don't give him any fuel, there's not much he can do.

I have no choice but to eat now that I know Jadis' child grows inside me. I will not harm the child in that way. This child is my hope, my driving force, a piece of him that I will hold on to for dear life.

Serephine draws me a bath after every visit from Cartwell to my chambers. Sometimes she moves a chair to the windows after and she brushes out my hair, growing long enough to tickle at my waist. It grows faster in this realm. As she works through my hair, she tells me of the land and its pitfalls, but she also shares about how it used to be, when poison hadn't seeped into its very being. She shows me the small village, far off in the distance, that is home to little boats that cross the river. She points out the ancient forest barely visible on the horizon, that holds secrets and hiding places for anyone, bandits and all.

The thing is, nothing that Serephine and Lavinia tell me requires a great amount of trust on my part. Information on things I can see with my own eyes, other than the child Lavinia claims to be in my belly. This is soon enough proven when I don't bleed, then the morning sickness comes. None of what they are doing requires me to go against my intuition and blindly trust people who also claim to be bound to pure evil. But, I am beginning to trust them. They're proving their position through small actions every day.

Our preparations are taking longer than expected and that worries me. I thought I'd be gone well before the morning sickness started. The fields of death are vast and crossing them without being seen and caught seems an impossible task.

Pyra stays tucked away, only coming out to visit when the privacy glamour is activated. I agree with Serephine, that we don't want anyone to discover her presence. I know my trust in Serephine and Lavinia has grown when I feel safe revealing my friend to them. Most of the time the poor sprite hides in a lamp in the bathroom, a room only Serephine and I enter.

Slowly, food that will last, water skeins, clothing, and even small blades start to appear in the various drawers and cupboards in my chambers. I have no idea where they come from, but they appear here and there.

I'm about to take a sip of my daily tea when Cartwell bursts through the door, his eyes wild and nostrils flaring. He nearly knocks me over in his rush and I watch him from the corner of my eyes as he grabs Serephine by the shoulders and flings her into the wall, out of his way.

His words cut through the silence like the sharpest knife. "You're still bound!" As he shouts at me, his breath hot on my face, tiny droplets of spit fly and land on my cheek.

I wipe at my face, flicking my hand in disgust. "Yes. I thought you could tell, you know, human features and all."

"You performed magic. You were seen on the spriteling battlefield."

Tell him the truth, Elora. It will do no harm, whereas lying will harm you. Lavinia's voice floats in from wherever she is hiding.

"I started the change when I came to this realm, after you tried to have me killed. Brandis' healer thought it best to stop it as it was making me ill. With everything else I was dealing with, including healing, and the precarious nature of my presence here, she thought it best to not have me bedridden with headaches or worse."

"What has been the point of all this," he asks, gesturing his hand, flipping it between the two of us, "if you're still human?"

"Beats me. You own me, remember, not the other way around. I don't get to make the decisions, husband."

He lifts his hand, the stiffness of anger in his fingertips, but stops himself mid-air. "Lavinia will fix this, now. You will change and you will do so with grace. Do you understand me."

It's a statement rather than a question, but I find myself unable to resist using his own skills against him. "Of course, sire. I relish the thought. My family was always more powerful than yours anyway. I'm sure the people will love to see me at my full potential, others at my side hiding in my shadow. I found many in my time here that love me, practically worshipped me even as a human. Imagine the attention I will garner as a true aelorin. Imagine the attention any child of mine will gather before them, too."

Serephine coughs lightly into her hand, still seated in a mess on the floor, hiding a grin that curls her lips.

Ack, you learn quick, child, well done. Now it's my turn to spin words. Lavinia praises in my head as Cartwell turns heel and leaves without another word, his shoulders climbing up into his ears and I fall back into my chair, my knees buckling under my weight.

How come he can't see and hear my thoughts? I ask Lavinia, suddenly aware that none of this could work if he could access my mind as easily as the others.

He lost that ability long ago.

LAVINIA DOES WORK her magical words, something to the effect of one, the binding of my true self shouldn't affect our offspring now that I'm in my true realm, and two, it had started already so some magic is flowing, and three, she saw little aid in his endeavors if I was bedridden with headaches and fevers. It would be like "rutting the dead" she said were her exact words.

I find her company amusing and uplifting. She minces words, yes, but in a way I find hilarious, often having to hide my grins in a shoulder or behind a yawn. If I ever return to the Day Court lands, I think I will work on paving the path for her return, even if it's only to keep me and Tressa company.

I manage to avoid earning any new beatings, Cartwell often busy with whatever dark plans are in the works. If what they say is true, he should be preparing for war, although that news of Brandis was some time ago. If I weren't with child, I often think about playing spy and discovering what he is up to, for the bettering of the realm and all. I even ask for Velasco's council on one occasion, granting him reason to enter my chambers while I sneak off into my bathroom, leaving him and Serephine in peace. I'm in a constant state of flux between despising my circumstances but finding companionship perhaps even friends.

My peace, what peace I had found, ended at a fateful dinner, my last.

Chapter Thirty Eight

"Vaelys ilyraen naeloth silvarin aelithil."

Even fortune cannot block life forever.

DINNER PROGRESSES AS IT ALWAYS does with trays and platters of delectable foods, more than enough to feed those seated here, too much, I think, and I wonder how many are forced to go hungry to make this happen. I fill my plate, as always, with enough to satisfy me. I'm not a glutton and it keeps his eyes turned somewhere else. I try to maintain the established air of composure, even as his gaze seems to pin me to my seat. Every move I make is calculated, every word chosen with caution. But I can feel the weight of him, hanging heavy above me, like a brewing storm on the horizon. It's taking every last ounce of control to hide my unease.

I engage in polite conversation, answering questions of those around me with practiced diplomacy. Maintain the status quo. But tonight is different. I can't shake the tingling in my spine. I feel that every move is being scrutinized closer than before, that Cartwell is searching for signs of deception, that we have been found out.

I wrack my brain for any way we could have screwed up, any way that we went too far and someone nefarious caught on. There are plenty of those types about, but I can't think of the tiniest thing, which is why, I think we must have screwed up.

His gaze bores into me, I shift uncomfortably in my seat, the weight of his suspicion settling in the air. He leans forward, his voice dripping with thinly veiled accusation.

"Elora, dear, I can't help but notice your lack of appetite," he remarks, his tone deceptively casual. "Is there a reason why you've chosen to not partake in the fine delicacies before you?"

I hold his gaze, my eyes narrowing, only slightly, as I answer." Perhaps your efforts have proven fruitful."

His eyes widen in surprise, and I dash them in an instant. "No, they haven't. I simply eat enough to fill me, Cartwell. No sense in overindulging. I assure you, it's nothing to be concerned about."

A sly smile plays at the corners of his lips as he leans back, studying me with an intensity that sends shivers through me, my mind catches up and I figure out my mistake. "You know, my dear, a lady of your stature and status should always maintain a certain level of grace and elegance. Perhaps, you're right, a bit of restraint in the culinary realm wouldn't hurt."

The room falls silent for the first time in ages, the tension palpable, no doubt that everyone waits to see what I do, what I say. My grip on the silverware tightens, knuckles bright, as I fight to maintain the little composure I have left. He knows what buttons to push, and he pushes hard. He nods to someone off in the shadows and next thing I know, my plate is removed from the table.

Cartwell is relentless. He continues his assault, voice dripping with contempt. "You wouldn't want to lose that delicate figure of yours, would you? Obviously, grief and loss have been good for you in this way. A woman's value lies in her ability to maintain her allure, after all."

I square my shoulders, my voice still trembling a little against my will. "My worth is not defined by your shallow ideals, I'm afraid. I do not intend to be a mere object of desire, Cartwell. I was not birthed simply to please someone with my appearance."

Serephine's hand finds mine slowly under the table, a comforting and calming gesture that pleads caution. Her touch grounds me, reminding me that I am not alone and only need to buy a little more time. 'Stick to the plan' it says.

I allow my shoulders to fall and the hard grip on my now useless utensils loosens. As I breathe slowly in, 1, 2, 3, 4, 5 and out, 2, 3, 4, 5, I realize the right path was not to cater to his whims and stay calm. That was too suspicious.

"Velasco." Cartwell snaps his fingers, but maintains his gaze, drilling into my skull as if he's trying to force himself into my mind.

"Yes, sire," Velasco answers from behind him.

"Summon Luckayi."

"Luckayi, sire?" Velasco's voice actually quivers, and I find that mirrored in my own body. For him to show weakness in front of Cartwell speaks more than any words.

"Are you deaf? Do I need to find someone else more suited to advise me? Yes, Luckayi. My dear wife is hiding something, and I want to know what it is."

This time it's Ravengar who intercedes and that surprises me even more. The surly guard hasn't been seen or heard for weeks. "Sire, there are better ways to get that information. You know that Luckayi's gifts come with a steep price. She could addle what mind Elora has left."

"I don't need her to have a mind, Ravengar, remember your place. Has everyone decided to stand against me!" My words from my chambers are coming back to haunt me, and him, but I can't help but take a little glee in that. A single bead of sweat trickles from his hairline and slides down his temple, its salty trail blaring an alarm to anyone who can see. Though his hands shake, Cartwell refuses to back down.

Velasco doesn't deign to answer again but instead shuffles away from the hall with such alarming speed that his robes billow out behind him as if he's a demon fleeing from the gates of hell. As he disappears into the halls, I squeeze Serephine's hand so hard that my fingernails cut into her skin like razors.

Sweat pours down my spine, soaking through my bodice and basting me in its salty brine.

When the hall doors open again, I think I might wet myself or worse. A million horrific scenarios race through my head as I brace myself for the worst. But then Lavinia steps into the hall, and I have to take extra care to control my expression, so he doesn't see the immense relief. Stick to the plan, maintain the facade. For the baby—for Jadis.

A knot of anxiety clenches in my gut as Lavinia storms across the room toward Cartwell. Her usually composed demeanor has been replaced with a frenzied sense of urgency, and her voice carries through the chamber with a sharp edge of concern. Relief floods me like a bolt of lightning at the sight of her, but it's quickly overtaken by a sense of foreboding. What could have happened to cause such a drastic change in her? Are we too late? Is Brandis already here? I set my jaw, whatever it is, I'm going to find out, we're all going to find out.

"My lord, my lady," she says, turning to me as well, sparking a snarl from Cartwell. There's a wink, a barely perceptible movement in her one eye, but I'm sure I see it. "Forgive the intrusion. There is an outbreak of some kind of illness, it's spread throughout the keep. Many of the guards have already been incapacitated being crammed in those barracks together."

Cartwell's face darkens, his grey eyes narrowing as he demands an explanation. He leans forward, his fingers in a death grip on the arms of his mighty chair. "Illness? How did this happen? Are we all at risk?"

Lavinia nods, her eyes darting between Cartwell and myself. "It seems that almost no one is fit to guard the walls at the moment. I assure you, my lord, it should pass in an hour or two from my estimations. But, until then, we are indeed vulnerable.

He whips his face to me, his black hair tumbling from the ties holding it behind his head. "It seems your friends have delayed our discussions...temporarily. This is a foolish plan on their part, but I expect nothing less. Serephine, remove Elora to her quarters and lock the door."

Chapter Thirty Nine

"Vaelys vyril vylrin ilythor zakir."

Even dim embers can learn how to blaze.

SEREPHINE'S DEPARTURE IS LIKE A thunderclap in the silence of my chambers. Anxiousness and anticipation surges through me, paralyzing me with fear, and I know that I have to break out of this prison, mind and body. The once familiar hallways now seem eerie and ghostly, amplifying the pressure I feel to find my friends before it's too late. Every second that passes feels like an eternity as I muster the courage to take the leap.

My blood boils as I lunge for the door, only to find it secured by an unforgiving and unseen lock. She betrayed me. I pound on it, rattling the hinges, desperately pulling and pushing as if my life depends on it. Because it does. But no matter how hard I try, it doesn't budge—a cruel reminder of the hope she's taken from me in my single moment of need.

My back slides down the traitorous doors as my hands smear down my tired, tight face. I survey the room, searching for something I can use to pry it open. My eyes fall on an empty pack sitting neatly on the bed, accompanied by a soft bedroll tied with precision at the base. The realization hits me hard. It isn't my old friends, my family who arranged this escape, it's my newfound allies. They orchestrated the whole thing. There was a wink!

Pyra flits from the bathroom just as I realize it all, stating the same, her timing impeccable and I tell her so, my voice dripping with sarcasm. Together we race around the rooms, quickly gathering all the gifts stashed here and there, careful not to leave anything behind. Pyra is a blessing, my little spy, knowing when and where my allies hid everything.

At the window, a coil of knotted rope lay waiting in the chair. I place the pack beside it, feeling beyond scared as I focus on what I'm about to do, dear God help me. I think their assumption as to my capabilities are much too high as I peak down the side of the keep. My hands tremble and sweat as I reach for the window latch, my heart racing.

The door flies open with a thunderous crash, making the walls vibrate and the foundations shudder. I gasp in shock as Ravengar looms before me like a dark storm, his body heaving with unsteady breaths, an ancient looking blade glinting menacingly in his hand.

"Ravengar, you startled me."

"I came to make sure you haven't been afflicted yet." His gaze shifts toward Pyra, but he keeps silent at her presence. He takes another step closer, his blade still held in a defensive stance. And why, pray tell, does checking on my health require a blade?

My heart continues to thump loudly in my chest as I eye the bag concealed by the chair back. Only a few more feet and he'll discover it. He advances, carefully like a hunter nears its prey. Anticipation hangs thick in the air, leaving me petrified.

His eyes dart to the bag and rope in the chair, and when they meet mine, my blood freezes. His gaze holds such intensity that I lose my breath for a moment and my eyes widen, muscles tensing. Every fiber of my being screams out to run as far away from him as possible.

But I can't move.

The longer he stares at me, the more paralyzed I become, unable to look away.

He closes the distance, his steps measured and deliberate, his face contorts into a sickening grin, his white teeth brilliant against his dark skin.

I know, right then, that I am most definitely screwed.

He flips the blade in his hand, offering me the hilt. I stare, mind in a fog, mouth agape. Before I register the action, my hand grips the offered hilt, slowly. I run my fingers down the cold metal, its weight feels solid and balanced in my hand. I can almost sense a vibration, something dormant inside. The hilt is exquisitely crafted, covered in intricate etchings of intertwining wild branches and enameled leaves. The metal gleams, its surface reflecting the faint light that filters through the window behind me.

"I don't understand," I say, noticing the faint markings down the insanely sharp blade the length of my forearm, ancient runes.

"This blade, belongs to my people, the Aetherwild." I gasp, both at the shocking revelation and the sudden stabbing pain in my chest. "It was gifted to me by my Prince as a token of his thanks for saving his life once. Now, I offer it to you, may it protect you while you're alone." His expression opens as he speaks, his brow moving almost too much for what he is saying, overemphasizing certain words.

I try hard to keep my voice steady as I thank him, hiding the deep emotions. My heart flutters in my chest, and I can feel the meaning behind his gift even though he hasn't said it out loud. He watches me silently, letting the significance of the moment hang in the air. This blade belonged to Jadis. He knows.

"Thank you, Ravengar. I'm honored, truly, but I'm not worthy of such a gift. I can't accept this."

"You are worthy, my lady, in every way. The blade is meant for you now," his gaze darts to my stomach, "to protect you as you face the darkness alone."

With a nod and a fist to his chest, Ravengar takes his leave, before I can protest again, leaving me alone with my mouth hanging open, with the weight of his gift and the gravity of the words left unspoken. I hold the blade in my trembling hands, feeling the cold metal against my skin as the tears fall lazily down my cheek. I am alone, but not really, there are allies that believe in me.

Who believe I can do this and are willing to risk everything to see me free to try.

I PEER DOWN from that window ledge, again, my heart a thunderstorm in my chest, my hands shake in fear. The drop doesn't seem too far, but the prospect of descending is as daunting as it ever was. Pyra flits about my face, her gentle warmth a small reassurance in the face of my frozen apprehension.

"You can do this, Elora," I whisper to myself, trying to summon the courage that has fueled me thus far. "Just focus on one step at a time. You've faced worse."

Pyra chirps softly, as if echoing my personal pep talk, but then asks, "Does talking to yourself actually work?" She flits around me, her small wings brushing against my chest like a warm touch.

"All right, Pyra," I glare, but my voice finds some gumption. "Let's do this before we run out of time. You guide me, distract me, whatever."

I cling to the wall, my palms slick with sweat and I'd only gone about fifteen feet. My heart races in my chest, each step down feeling larger than the last. I don't know what is more slick, the obsidian beneath my feet or the state of my hands.

"Careful, Elora," Pyra chimes, her voice says she's concerned. We both understand we only have so much time to make this happen and I'm not making quick work of it. "Keep your grip steady. You're doing great."

I nod, my voice gone, too afraid to make noise, "I...I'm trying. But it's so high, and my hands... they're so sweaty. Who was I fooling thinking I could do this? I can't even manage the first step of this plan which is only get down the wall."

Pyra flies a little closer, her small form providing a surprising amount of reassurance. "Just take it one step at a time. Focus on the wall, find the nooks and crannies for support. You've got this."

Her words helped, reminding me to focus on the immediate task, not the big picture. With every cautious movement, I seek out the rough surfaces on the wall, finding small ledges and crevices that provide a small sense of stability.

"Pyra," I call out. "Keep distracting me, keep me focused on anything but the height. Tell me a story, or...sing me a song, anything to keep my mind off the sudden stop way down there."

Pyra's wings create a small breeze that brushes against my cheek. "Fine," she says, her voice turning melodic, "Let me tell you about the time I discovered a hidden glade in the forest..."

Her voice carries me away from the precipice, transporting me to a world of magic and wonder. I listen intently, letting her story weave through my mind, replacing the gnawing fear with a sense of curiosity, running my imagination. Pyra's stories become my lifeline, anchoring me in a realm of fantasy as I walk slowly down the side of a bloody tower.

But even with Pyra's distraction there are moments when my grip falters, when my heart skips a beat. Panic threatens to consume me again as I slip, barely catching myself on one of the knots. Yet each time, I'm able to gather my wits, Pyra's voice and the gentle touch of her wings bringing me back from the brink.

"Don't worry, Elora," she says, her voice so small.

"I think we're well beyond the don't worry line, don't you?"

"Put your feet down," she says louder and laughs in my face.

I'm at the bottom! A wave of relief washes over me so intense that I drop to my knees. "Were any of those stories true?" I ask through quick breaths.

"Nope." She giggles.

"Hello, Princess," greets a male voice from behind.

Chapter Forty

"Thyrenaril, elrynen thalior thalin vaelith thylenil sylriniel."

Sometimes, judging people is like chasing mist between the trees.

FUCK," THE CURSE SLIPS FROM my lips that are far too tired to hold anything back.

The blood in my veins feels electric, thrumming as he steps out of the nearby wall. Right out of the wall.

He has startlingly blue eyes and a mischievous smile that plays on his lips. He bows slightly and says, "I don't know what that means, but I'm sorry if I scared you, Princess. Wasn't there something about you needing to stay in your room?" His voice is like silk, wrapping around me like a warm embrace.

A pulse of panic surges through me, my breaths quick and shallow as I scan my surroundings for something—anything—that might save me from him. The shadows seem to close in, vast and unyielding, offering no refuge.

The darkness stretches endlessly before me, empty, swallowing any hope I might have had.

"No matter, none of my business, I say. Who am I to talk about sneaking out?"

He bends with a dramatic flourish into a sweeping bow. "Zephyr, thief, rogue, and admitted rake." His jet black hair hangs in unruly waves around his handsome face, framing those intense blue eyes with a twinkle of trouble. His lips curl up in a roguish little smirk, which no doubt aids him in his rakish tendencies. He is dressed to impress with sleek, form fitting clothes, pockets everywhere like some kind of modern day Robin Hood, and small rings dangling at the tips of his pointed ears.

The frenzied activity of my heart begins to calm as I look up and down his hard, lean body. Curiosity piqued. I squint and try to peer around him, wondering what is on the other side of that deep voice and those broad shoulders.

Zephyr's eyes glint with barely contained excitement, clearly reading the confusion on my face. "Ah, you noticed, did you?" He says, a grin spreading like wildfire. "Quite impressive, isn't it?"

He steps closer to the wall, his hand trailing lightly along the stone as though caressing a lover. "This wall conceals a secret passage, carefully crafted to satisfy the restless spirit of a thief contained in a keep. But..." he pauses, his grin widening as if savoring the moment. "Finding the entrance? Now that's the real trick. A pursuit only for those with a discerning eye and an insatiable thirst for adventure." It's like he's daring me to rise to the occasion.

He then makes an elaborate gesture with his hands and steps aside, revealing an opening large enough for two people to fit through side by side. I'm tempted to jump right in, but before I can take a step, Zephyr speaks up again, and says in a low whisper, "If you value your life, Princess, you will not take one more step towards this darkness."

I pause and look into his bright eyes trying to decipher what secrets lay hidden inside this mysterious male. He gives a warning but there's still something inviting about him that makes me want to know more.

He must sense my questions, my interest, because he quickly adds, "Not all is as it seems here, Princess. If you choose to trespass here, then at least hear my advice first—No place can be entered without permission taken from its master...even the walls have ears after all!"

He makes absolutely no sense, but maybe that's the point, maybe it's only the last bit that was needed in the first place and he's hiding his warning in a bunch of nonsense? There's something about him though, something captivating. He has a certain air of audacity and confidence that's intoxicating. He seems untouchable, no matter what danger he puts himself in. His words fill the air around me with mystery and I want to know more about who he is. Was this his magic? Is he invading my mind?

Now, I notice a glint in his eye—a subtle look of defiance—as if he knows something I don't understand. Here he stands, a thief, in the grasp of Cartwell's stronghold, and yet there isn't an ounce of fear visible on his face. Why? Why doesn't he fear what everyone else does?

I can't help but wonder what got him here in the first place. Was it merely a bold choice or has he been forced into this situation? I'm far too enthralled to ask but curiosity burns inside me like wildfire, waiting for answers I'll never get.

He steps closer and peers cautiously around the corner as if searching for something or someone. There's tension in the air, as if we're caught in a storm—suspended between two worlds, one full of freedom and one filled with oppression and danger. I shift uneasily. Yet, watching him, my heart stirs with admiration at his courage and boldness, unexpected qualities I'm finding in many of those trapped within Cartwell's walls.

I don't bask in the wonder that is Zephyr for long. Before I wake up, he's grasping my hand in his, placing a gentle but far too long kiss to my knuckles. "I bid you goodbye, for now, Princess. Don't pine after me for too long. Until we meet again," he says, winking, and then walks away, whistling a soft tune.

He vanishes into the darkness just as quickly as he had appeared, leaving me alone with my thoughts slowly swirling and searching for answers I can't provide.

Taking his words for their intended meaning is foolish. Considering everything that happened over the past few weeks, I must assume he's one of my new allies, a new friend. I have no other choice. The walls have ears means pass through silently and watch your words when near.

Chapter Forty One

"Vyralis ilithor elvanir vyrithae rilynor."

Fear can be the fuel that drives toward greatness.

T DIDN'T TAKE LONG TO hear the creaking of the gates opening and the pounding of horses' hooves as we race across the dead fields. Dry, cracked ground explodes around their hooves leaving a distant cloud as the only sign of their whereabouts. There is little shelter to be found much less any cover.

I stumble through the empty fields with Pyra, a heavy dose of hopelessness settling into my bones. The land seems to writhe in agony all around us, its desolation sucking all the life from me with every step I take. Remnants of forgotten farmsteads loom like ghosts, their ruins standing as grim reminders of everything lost. The air feels thick, heavy with grief, as if the sorrow of this place clings to my skin, refusing to let go.

The pounding hoofbeats of the riders carry across the desolate fields. We dart from one ruin to the next, pressing ourselves against crumbling walls and shattered beams for what little cover they provide. Every scrap of debris becomes a lifeline, every shadow a fragile shield.

The chase feels endless, the relentless rhythm of the horses' strides pounding in time with the frantic beat of my thoughts. My breath burns in my lungs, my legs scream in protest, but we don't dare stop. Every step feels like borrowed time, every moment an inch closer to being caught.

Finally, the sound of their thunderous strides fades into silence and we make it through another small victory. We collapse behind a jagged wall, hearts racing, as the tension eases just enough to breathe.

Pyra elbows me with a grin, her triumph infectious for a fleeting moment. But as her eyes drift over the horizon, the smile falters, giving way to grim reality. The weight of it all presses down like an iron shroud.

The task ahead looms impossibly large—Cartwell's contract, his control, the endless search for true safety. My stomach churns at the thought, and I force myself to look away. I can't see the way forward. Not yet.

But, we must move forward. I push against the rough stones and take another step but stumble to the ground, my body heavy with exhaustion. My eyes drift through the darkened night, desperate for a sign of hope or I'd settle for some solace.

Frustration boils over, and I smash my fist against the ground. The sound that follows stops me cold—not the dull thud of packed earth, but something hollow, solid.

I find a spark of energy somewhere. I drag myself to my knees, clawing at the brittle, dead vegetation. My fingers find resistance—a thick rope handle weathered by time. My hands tremble as I grasp the frayed fibers, slick with sweat and dirt.

The rope groans in protest as I pull. With one final heave, the resistance gives way, and an old wooden door creaks open, revealing a hidden space beneath us.

Pyra flits closer, her face is pale and drawn, her voice edged with fear as she asks, "What is it?"

"I'm guessing an old root cellar," I say, brushing dirt off my hands. "It'll be dark, but probably dry and well hidden. We can rest and start fresh in a few hours, preferably after nightfall."

"I'm not going down there," she snaps, crossing her tiny arms over her chest, her wings twitching in irritation. "I don't do underground."

"Pyra, come on." I sigh, pinching the bridge of my nose. "We need rest. I can make you a little fire down there, okay? I can't risk that up here—we'll be seen. If I can climb down that damn castle wall, you can spend a few hours underground. Can't you?" I arch an eyebrow, meeting her defiant glare.

She huffs, her whole body radiating indignation. With a dramatic stomp—more air than ground— she dives headfirst into the hole, her inner light flaring as she disappears.

The faint glow of her magic shows a small, rickety ladder leading down. "See?" Her voice echoes faintly. "Just a creepy hole in the ground. What could possibly go wrong?"

I pause only long enough to close the door behind me, the faint creak much louder in the enclosed space. I have to force myself to stand still in the darkness and let my eyes adjust. I'm not claustrophobic, but it has been a while since I've been in such a tight space.

The air is cool and damp, carrying the faint scent of earth and decay, yet there's a hint of something familiar—like the smokey tang of campfires on crisp nights from when I was a little girl. I inhale deeply, settling into the memory, even as the walls seem to press closer.

Pyra's light shimmers faintly ahead, casting soft, flickering shadows that dance along the dirt walls. Her tiny sword almost brushes against me at one point, the faint metallic gleam drawing my focus. It's a welcome distraction, laughing a little at her.

"Wait," Pyra says, shooting back up straight and alert. "You made a mess finding that door. Anyone who walks by will see the disturbed ground and find us in an instant."

"Shit. I didn't think of that." I wrack my brain on how to fix this, only someone staying outside and not resting would be able to cover our tracks and that's not an option.

"Perhaps I can help," a male voice says from a still dark corner.

Pyra lets out a shrill shriek as a shower of sparks erupt from her tiny mouth and into the corner of the room. The little being resembles a large gecko. Around the size of a small or toy dog, with light brown scales that blend almost perfectly with the dirt floor. We hear a muffled yelp from our new roommate as he jumps back in surprise.

"What's a sand sifter doing out here?" I ask him, letting my unease slip into my voice.

"Many people have been displaced lately, it's not unusual to find others where they don't belong. I could ask the same of you, dear lady."

"Valid answer, I suppose," I say, too tired to make more of a fuss. Even if he does tell someone where we are, it's no different than the predicament we already find ourselves in.

"You suppose," he says with a huff. "Would you like my help covering your tracks or not?"

Pyra takes a step forward, towering over him from her position in the air. She crosses her arms and the muscles of her small biceps bulge beneath the fabric of her bright shirt. "And how exactly can you do something we can't?"

"It's not that only I can do it, you could as well, little Emberkin." He grins like calling her little is an insult. Considering how she braces her spine again, maybe it is. His thick tail swishes back and forth behind him, stirring up a little dust and creating tiny mounds of earth on either side of him. "There's an air vent in the back that takes us to the surface, but I think it will be easier for me to wiggle around and cover the door than your little hands can accomplish in the same amount of time. I get the impression that time is of the essence."

"Indeed," Pyra says, with a grunt.

He scurries to the back, Pyra's light following him to the square entrance that sits a foot, maybe two above the floor. "It was designed to allow for a small fire as people hid inside. If you intend on lighting a fire for the Emberkin," he says, looking at me with his amber eyes, "I do kindly request that you wait until after I've returned so I don't fall to my death?"

"Uh, yes..of course," I stutter out. My poor mind is not coping well with all the new stimulation.

We huddle close to the wooden door, ears straining for any hint of movement beyond. The air around us is still heavy and stale despite our opening the door once already. We hear soft scuffling of feet and a whirring noise as if something is moving hastily.

A fine layer of dust trickles through the cracks in the door, swirling and glittering motes in the bright light from Pyra's inner flames. Each glowing mote floats through the cellar air like ash from an unseen fire, and I find myself holding my breath, afraid even the smallest exhale will make too much sound.

Once he returns, as promised, I light a small fire, just big enough for Pyra. Bits of brittle crate wood snap as I feed them in, the scent of dry rot curling into the air. The flame hisses low, barely audible under the sounds of our shifting breaths. I don't want any heavy smoke filtering out the vent to give us away, so small it stays.

I try to rest, curling into a corner where the wall presses cold against my spine, but the air clings to my skin with a clammy dampness, and sleep refuses to come.

"My mother used to tell us stories when we couldn't sleep at night," Solis, our new companion says, his voice a soft rasp. He tilts his small head, the firelight glinting off his eyes as that creepy third lid slides halfway closed. "Do you think that would help you settle your mind and get some rest?"

"What makes you think I need to settle my mind?" I ask, narrowing my eyes. My hand tightens around my knees, still not entirely sure I can trust the reptile who's sitting comfortably across from me.

Solis blinks slowly this time, his forked tongue flicking out briefly as if tasting the tension in the air. "Aelorin aren't the only beings that can access the mind," he says, his tone matter-of-fact, without malice. "And yours is practically screaming right now. If the door doesn't give you away, your raging thoughts just might."

"Right," I say scrubbing my hand over my face. "That's very nice of you to offer, but you don't have to. We disturbed your hiding place after all. You don't owe me anything."

He blinks again, his gaze steady and unreadable, it's unsettling. The faint flicker of his tail brushes against the ground, but he doesn't argue. He settles lower, his lithe body folding neatly into the shadows. "Nonsense, I love telling stories. Helps me too. Sit back and close your eyes.

Long ago, in the vast desert dunes, there lived a tiny seed named Zephyr..."

I snort, completely unladylike, but it just slips out.

"And what, pray tell, is funny already?" He asks, incredulous.

"Oh, nothing. I'm sorry. It's just...I met a Zephyr today, not a seed of course, but a rakish thief, so it's funny that your story...that the seed has the same name...sorry, please continue."

"Perhaps it is the same Zephyr and I speak in idiom?" He says, arching a spiked brow.

"Zephyr dreams of blossoming into a beautiful flower, but he is surrounded by arid sand and scorching heat. Day after day, he longs for a drop of water to quench his thirst and nourish his fragile existence.

One day, a curious sand sifter comes across Zephyr and listens to his heartfelt desires. The sand sifter, known for his ability to uncover hidden treasures, promises to help the little seed. With gentle movements, he sifts through the sand, revealing a hidden oasis beneath the surface."

Having a friend helps me escape the weight of my worries. As Solis speaks, I can't help but compare his tale to the Zephyr I met hours ago and wonder if the two are, in fact, connected. Perhaps this was some strange dream, and I will wake up with a headache like when I ate too much cheese. I can make it fit in my imagination, though not without noting there's something peculiar about the idea.

As Solis continues his tale, his voice fills the air, painting a vivid picture in my mind. I listen intently, finding solace in the rhythm of his voice. A strange thought and comfort coming from something so reptilian.

"As Zephyr's roots reached the fresh water source, he feels a surge of life coursing through him. With each passing day, he grows stronger and more resilient. Zephyr's leaves unfurl, displaying vibrant hues of pink and gold, reflecting the breathtaking colors of the desert sunset.

Word of Zephyr's extraordinary beauty and strength spread throughout the desert, captivating the hearts of all who hear the tale. Travelers came from far and wide, just to catch a glimpse of the wondrous flower that blooms in the harshest of environments..."

I listen to Zephyr's story and a wisp of hope unfurls within me, like a gentle breeze had just swept through the room. He speaks of determination and strength, digging deep to find what you need the most. It's a beacon of light amidst my dark thoughts.

Chapter Forty Two

"Vyrith thyranor thalnarae, lyrien sylrithae vaelys."

A blade ends breath, the heart holds it still.

"ELORA...ELORA," SOLIS' VOICE CUTS HARSHLY into my dreams of sunset flowers and plants with black hair and gold rings in their leaves. "Elora," he snaps.

'What?," I breathe, wiping the sleep from my eyes.

"Night fell a few hours ago. While they search the other side of the dead fields, it's only a matter of time before they turn their eyes in this direction. If we are to escape, we need to be in the village at the river before dawn."

"Shit. Yes. Pyra! Wait...we?"

Solis shrugs his low shoulders. "I could use a little excitement in my life. It'll give me more stories to tell. Maybe I'll write a book when it's all over."

"No. I told you how dangerous it is helping me. That's not excitement, that's acting a fool, Solis."

"Then I am a fool, dear Elora, for I have already made up my mind." He walks over and kicks dirt on Pyra's little fire as she wakes, sending the sprite into a fit of sparks and embers. "Besides, I don't think the magic of the contract is going to worry about under fae like us."

Solis leads the way, having made this trek many times before. It's comforting having a guide instead of working off only the vague knowledge the others were able to give me in secret.

The air is oppressive, choking us alongside the weight of our fear. Every rustle of leaves or snap of a twig sets our hearts racing and our fingers clutching tightly around weapons that are now slick with sweat. Our senses are on high alert, every movement deliberate as we inch forward, desperate to evade detection and reach the next shelter before the first light of dawn exposes us. We don't speak out of fear of who might be listening. The sound of our breaths fills the night like a chorus of panicked gasps anyway.

We arrive at the humble barn that Solis recommends for the 'night', nestled at the edge of the village. Its weathered wooden walls almost tell secret tales of countless nights spent shielding those in need, like us. Or perhaps that's just hopeful thinking spawned by the delirium of constant fear.

We slip inside, finding refuge in the comforting scent of fresh hay and the soft rustling of animals as they wake for the day.

The darkness wraps around us in the sheltered corner, like a protective cloak as we settle in. Our weary bodies seek respite. Our eyes all grow heavy, but someone must keep watch. Someone must be awake at all times. There are too many people about. Danger still lurks on the streets outside.

We crouch amongst the bales of hay like cornered animals, our eyes darting at every sound that breaks the stillness. My breaths come in short pants as I take my turn keeping watch the possibility of danger lurking in the shadows is too real to ignore. The faint glow of the rising sun filters through the cracks in the decrepit barn, only serving to cast an eerie pall over our situation. Excitement indeed. Each passing moment feels like a lifetime until night falls again and we can move on. Night can't come fast enough, even with how tired I am.

I munch on the jerky that had been wrapped in a drawer in my wardrobe while Pyra chooses some pieces of dried fruit. Solis declines, insisting he'd find some choice vermin later.

All our movements are slow and deliberate to avoid any unnecessary noises as the village awakens around us.

I bite into the meat, determined to savor it in spite of the tense atmosphere. Outside I hear the measured steps of advancing soldiers and a chorus of voices as villagers are interrogated for answers they, fortunately or unfortunately, don't have. The fear is palpable, washing over me like a wave of stifling heat as my conscience thrashes with guilt for putting this village in harm's way.

Solis creeps forward with a stealthy grace, his small frame casting a long shadow against the murky dawn. His destination is clear—the silent, decrepit cattle stall, seeking nourishment among the shadows.

Pyra and I freeze. The rusty barn door creaks open. I can feel her tense beneath my palm, so I place a finger to my lips and beg for silence.

A figure steps into one of the beams of bright sunlight, a silhouette of evil intent, with cruelty seeping from his every pore. As he stands there, dust motes cascade around him in a dizzying dance. My heart races as I take him in. His face is hard and twisted in wickedness, and the raven with outstretched wings, the symbol of Cartwell, is etched like a brand into the chest of his boiled leather jerkin.

He stands motionless, but his eyes lock onto mine like a predator trapping its prey. His pupils dilate and I swear I can feel the toxic delight radiating from him.

Wild energy courses through my body as the animalistic instinct to survive kicks in. I had been trained for this moment. Jadis and Mik had primed me for it. Grabbing the blade Ravengar gave me, a formidable short sword for my much smaller frame, I rush to meet him head-on. The clash of metal takes over the small barn as our weapons meet again and again. Out of desperation, I lunge at him with a mighty roar tearing from my throat, only for us both to hit the ground with a thud. My eyes wide with terror, I know deep in my soul that it's either victory or death ending this fight.

Time slows again as our battle resumes, my actions guided only by primal instinct to protect myself and those I love. The blade vibrates and hums in my hands as if calling for blood. Every muscle in my body tenses until I find my moment, my opening, and sink my blade into his chest, just under his arm, with all the force I can muster.

His blood coats my hand before I can pull my blade away, hot and thick. He falls to his knees, a gurgle the only sound erupting from his throat.

As the adrenaline subsides, I kneel beside my fallen assailant and weep. Hysterical sobs catch in my throat. It's too much. It's all too much.

"Elora," my friends both speak in unison, the sweet sounds sneaking through the fog. Pyra's small hands try to grasp my face. "Elora, we must flee now. We cannot wait until dark. They will look for him."

I tremble uncontrollably as I scramble to my feet, the urgency of the situation pressing down on me. Reassembling my wits and gathering my pack, I fly out the back door and run towards the boat moored nearby that we intended to take at nightfall. My chest feels like it holds a caged bird trying desperately to escape, and I throw my bag onto the boat and jump in.

No one notices the lone woman, in the lone boat, not at the edge of the village. It doesn't take me long to navigate us to the other side, even if we meander downstream a bit.

When we reach the opposite shore, I don't hesitate. I haul the boat onto the bank and sprint into the forest, the crunch of twigs and leaves under my boots yelling into the still air. Time becomes meaningless as my legs drive me forward, unrelenting, through the tangled undergrowth. Branches whip at my arms and face, but I hardly feel them, my focus narrowed to the desperate need to keep moving.

Eventually, exhaustion overtakes me. My steps falter, and I stumble into a small clearing, my legs trembling beneath me. My boots scuff against the uneven ground, dragging with every sluggish step.

The harrowing events of the day crash over me like a tidal wave, their weight unbearable. The memories sear into my mind, an unbearable fury that leaves me breathless and trembling.

The line between life and death had been blurred with my own hand, and I can't help but question the cost of survival in a world tainted with so much darkness. Why is life so fragile? Why is it so easy to dim the light in someone's eyes? I continue to question the fragility of life and the depths I need to fall to, to protect my own life, and I find myself wanting. The image of the soldier's face lingers in my mind, his eyes fixed, frozen in a mix of shock and defeat. What did he do? Did he have a family? Did I just take someone's father? What if they starve because of me? What choices did he make to lead him down a path that intertwined with Cartwell? What if I just killed an ally in a moment of pure, unadulterated fear?

Tears stream down my face, hot and unyielding, as my trembling hands clutch my belly, shielding the fragile life within. My breaths come in shallow gasps, each one snagging on the raw ache in my chest. A wave of shame crashes over me, tightening my throat and twisting my stomach.

What kind of mother will I be if I can take a life so easily? The thought stabs through me, sharp and unforgiving, as if it's not just my child I'm holding, but the weight of every choice I've made. My fingers press into my skin, desperate to anchor myself against the storm raging in my heart.

"Child, please do not berate yourself so."

The voice comes from the surrounding darkness, deep and weathers, like the steady pulse of an old, familiar melody. It carries a quiet strength, a warmth that wraps around the clearing and seems to seep into my chest, dulling the sharp edges of my guilt.

"Survival— life— sometimes requires us to do dark things, but that doesn't make us dark."

"I tore out his life with my own hands," I scream into the cool air, my friends cringing in shock as my anguished cry bounces off the trees. My mind refuses to accept what I have done, my heart broken from the violence I have taken part in. I feel a wave of guilt and shame rip through me like a hurricane.

"I know, lass, and I'm sorry for it. The troubles you've encountered are great, and I'm afraid they're not over yet." The voice trails in on the breeze as she steps from the shadows of the trees.

I wrench my blade back into my shaking hands as she appears suddenly, ready to fight for my life again, but my heart stills. The point of the blade falls to the forest floor, and the stiffness lifts from my shoulders. The hilt slips from my fingers until it thumps on the ground.

The mysterious crone steps from the shade, her movements far more fluid than one would expect from a woman in her condition. Her aged form is draped in tattered robes, with patches stitched over holes that blend with the colors that surround us.

As she gets closer, her face becomes clearer, etched with countless lines and wrinkles, with eyes that are dull with years of experience and stories to tell. Her silver hair is tied into a neat braid, settling down her curved back to tickle just beneath her waistline.

The tears that had been streaming down my face moments ago are replaced with a sudden calm, the shuddering sobs softening to a few hiccups and muffled sniffles as I try to clear my nose.

The woman makes a tutting sound with her teeth as she takes me in. "Come, lass, let's get you warm and that leg looked at."

"What?" I ask, dumfounded, still staring like a small child meeting a giant. Her presence feels far greater than her physical size. I can't explain it.

"Your leg is bleeding, dear. Being that you're human, that can turn in the blink of an eye. Let's get it clean and mended." She offers me her hand, the fingers knobby and slightly bent, the skin loose around the bones.

I look down, and there it is, across my thigh. I have a six-inch gash oozing blood as my pulse slows. I didn't notice it until I saw it; didn't feel it. Once I see it, the icy jolt of pain hits me like a cement truck. "I didn't...I hadn't noticed," I say through clenched teeth as I take her hand. Why I take her hand so willingly is beyond comprehension right now.

"Ah, that happens when one is overcome. Don't trouble yourself."

As she pulls me to her, with a strength I didn't expect, I look to Solis and Pyra for encouragement. They're no help, standing and floating off to the side with their mouths agape, staring at the old female. I have no time to think on that reaction as she starts moving in the direction she came from, dragging my tired and bewildered feet behind her. I stumble down, only for a moment, to grab my blade as we walk.

Chapter Forty Three

"*Lorynin lorynielis loth aelthil lyrien.*"

Even passing calm can shelter the heart.

WE TURN A CORNER, AND a cottage, right out of a fairy tale, barely visible through the foggy mist, springs into view. The irony of that thought does not escape me. The trees around it are so thick that if I hadn't been standing right where I am, I would have sworn it's an optical illusion.

The humble little place of wattle and daub with a thatched roof, weathered in time, has a few whimsical windows that let out a warm glow from within. The windows are covered with hexagonal planes of glass, which have been held in place by small wooden pegs. Those have since rotted, so the windows sag like tired mouths. To one side of the building is a small garden planted in rows of corn, cabbage, and other greens. As we pass through the small gate, I close my eyes and inhale the humid air. It's wet, but sweet, like a fresh rain cloud.

The front door opens with a wave of her hand, and I step in hesitantly. My mind has finally started really questioning why I'm trusting her so easily.

An odd warmth washes over me, soft and inviting, melting away my trepidation before I can question it. The air is thick with the earthy scent of incense and herbs, curling around me like a lullaby. The unease that gripped me moments ago fades into nothingness, leaving behind an unexpected sense of ease.

I follow her inside, curiosity flickering at the edges of my thoughts. There's something unsettling about how quickly my fear dissipates, yet I don't fight it. Exhaustion, physical, mental, and emotional, weighs heavily, and I surrender to the calm. Whatever happens, I'll face it when the time comes.

The rich aroma of herbs and wildflowers permeates my senses, mingling with the faint crackle of the central hearth. It reminds me of Nalona's hut— safe. The flickering light of candles dances along the walls as if alive, casting playful shadows that dart around those sent out from the central hearth.

She moves with deliberate slowness, settling herself into a creaky wooden chair by the hearth. The flames illuminate her face, lined with wisdom and an age I've never seen in a fae. With a quiet gesture, she beckons me forward.

The crone leans forward, placing a small wooden cup in front of me. Its sweet, malty aroma mingles with the earthy scents of the cottage, creating a soothing blend that makes my head swim.

"Drink, my child, let the ale ease your mind," the crone says with a kind smile.

I lift the wooden cup and take a tentative sip. The warmth of the liquid slips down my aching throat and settles nicely in my belly, the alcohol indeed soothing my nerves in my empty stomach.

Pyra flutters nervously near my shoulder, her light dimmer than usual. "Are you sure about this?" she whispers, her tiny wings brushing against my ear. It still amazes me how she can do that without burning me. Her distrust is palpable, though she doesn't seem to have the energy for her usual fiery defiance.

Solis sits quietly at my feet, his amber eyes fixed on the crone with unblinking intensity. His tail flicks against the floor in slow, measured movements, like he's trying to decide whether she's friend or foe.

"Who are you?" I ask, setting the cup down, my voice a little steadier than I feel.

"You may call me Wen, for now. I think that's enough." She gives me a cryptic answer, much like every other soul I've met in any woods thus far. Solis lets out a soft, low hiss—neither threatening nor entirely at ease. Pyra crosses her tiny arms, her light flaring slightly as she mutters, "I don't like this one bit."

There's a remarkably companionable silence as we sit. The ale settles into my mind, releasing my tongue. "I never wanted to harm anyone," I start, a tremble returning to my voice. "But I had no choice. He came at us with a blade. He intended...I don't know what he intended exactly, but something told me to defend not chit chat."

Wen nods. "Sometimes life forces us into circumstances we wish to avoid. The burden of taking a life is a heavy one, my dear. Dark deeds do not make a dark person. But know this: you defended yourself and survived. Your actions were necessary, and that does not make you any less compassionate or unworthy of peace."

Pyra hovers at my shoulder, her wings beating faster than usual, the golden light they emit pulsing unevenly. My hands are still stained with blood, and her small face twists in a rare moment of vulnerability. "She shouldn't have had to," Pyra mutters, her voice low but sharp. "This world keeps demanding too much.

Solis' amber eyes flick to my bloodied hands, then to Wen's face, his tail swishing. "Survival always leaves a mark," he says, his tone measured but laced with an edge of knowing. "The question is whether you carry it...or let it carry you."

My hands resting limply around the small cup tremble slightly, and I tighten my grip, trying to still them. Guilt tugs at my heart, the weight of it almost too much again. "I wish there was another way," I whisper. "I wish I didn't have to be so...violent."

Wen places a comforting hand on my shoulder. "There are times when violence is an unfortunate reality in this world, plagued by darkness, and it does not define who you are. Do you think Jadis to be dark because he takes lives, or Mik?"

Pyra flutters midair, her wings hesitating for a beat before resuming their motion. "Wait—how do you know about them?" She demands, her fire flaring brighter as she hovers protectively closer to me. "We didn't tell you anything."

Solis straightens from where he crouches, his slitted amber eyes narrowing at Wen. His tail flicks once, sharply, against the stone floor. "She's right. Elora has barely spoken of what happened to us. So how..." His voice trails off, suspicion lacing his tone.

Wen's expression doesn't falter, her wise gaze steady as it shifts between them, but I hardly notice. The mention of it...those names...it's all I can hear. Her words hit me like a slap to the face, and I barely notice her calm demeanor. The names—Jadis, Mik—they echo in my mind, drowning out everything else. A wave of grief surges over me, raw and unrelenting, dragging me back to every moment we shared, every part of my loss.

I'm taken aback by her compassion and care, yet that only makes my guilt all the more intense. Part of me wants to embrace her kindness, but another part of me rejects it out of shame.

"Your heart holds compassion and a desire for peace, and that is what matters most. Remember that, my child."

I swallow hard, my throat tight as I struggle to process her words. They feel like both an offering and a challenge, and I'm not sure I'm strong enough to accept either.

WEN MOVES AROUND her cottage sharing little stories about passing travelers and the animals she's seen outside, hoping for treats and warmth. A familiar healing salve covers the now stitched gash on my leg, and she tucks me into bed like a mother would and tells me to rest. We'll talk more in the morning.

Sleep came with a vengeance, first with meadow green eyes fading to lifeless orbs under my blade and then a dreamless sleep, full of the emptiness that plagues my soul with their absence.

Chapter Forty-Four

"Caelari ithoryn fion syloren thai fionae nor."

The stars know the path before our feet touch it.

THE MORNING SUN FILTERS THROUGH the windows, casting a bright glow over the small, cozy kitchen where we sit together for breakfast. Wen even sets places for Solis and Pyra with bustling insects and other vermin on one plate, and fruit on the other. The scent of fresh bread and warm herbs wafts through the air, adding to the sense of almost overwhelming comfort this cottage provides. I sip at an herbal tea, wondering how long Wen has already been up, when my eyes lock on her and I feel the overwhelming need to express the concerns that have plagued me since I woke.

Wen's face says she already knows what's been floating around in my mind. "I appreciate your kindness," I say, a deep longing in my voice, "but you don't understand the extent of Cartwell's power. He has men positioned everywhere, and if he finds out I'm here, there'll be consequences. Harsh ones." Fear pulses through my veins as I finish my statement.

Wen just smiles with a completely calm demeanor I can never hope to possess, waving off my concerns as if they are little flies. "Oh, don't you worry about that, my dear. I've lived in these lands for centuries, and I know how to keep a low profile. Cartwell's influence only extends as far as you allow it. You're safe here with me. Rest and breathe. You've earned it."

My brow furrows, pinching in tightly as I struggle to believe that I can ever truly be safe while his shadow looms over me, with what I know now.

"But the contract...he has power over me as long as he claims we're still bound. It's a magical contract. Anyone who keeps me from him dies. I've already lost one person I l...cared about. I won't lose anyone else. Even if I have to stay alone for the rest of my natural life."

She chuckles. She actually laughs. My spine shoots straight at the slight until I detect the twinkle of mischief in her eyes. "Magical agreements can be undone, my dear. There are ways around them if you're clever enough. Besides, he can't claim you if you hide yourself away. Just because I provide you a hiding place and know the tricks that will keep you from his prying eyes, doesn't mean I'm keeping you from him."

We keep chatting, I explain the rest of the contract, as I understand it, and she proudly declares Velasco a genius. I find myself slowly opening up to Wen, her grandmotherly ways making it almost impossible to stop pouring out my soul to her.

We discuss the prophecy that seems to cast a dark cloud over my life. "I despise the prophecy," I say with great frustration. "It's nothing but words on parchment, somewhere that no one can find, yet it has caused so much pain and suffering. My parents and who else had to die? If it weren't for this wretched prophecy, I wouldn't have a target on my back and Jadis...Jadis and Mik would still be alive. It took everything from me. A family, a life, a daughter..."

"And yet, you would have had none of those things without it," she says, stilling me. She's right. Without the prophecy, I never would have been sent to the mortal realm. Without the prophecy, I never would have met Carter—I never would have had Emmaline. Without the prophecy, Jadis and Mik would have had no reason to protect me, to get close to me. Jadis and I may never have...

"Words can indeed have a powerful impact, truly. But remember, it is not the prophecy itself that holds power—it is the choices we make in response to it. Fate may have its plans, but we have the ability to shape our own destinies, despite the challenges that lie ahead.

The words that name you the Deliverer, as they like to call you, were only part of what the great tree bestowed upon the listener. The rest? Lost to time."

"The great tree?" I ask, wide-eyed with curiosity and a bit of dread. Beads of sweat collect on my forehead as every muscle in my body tenses with anticipation. I'm desperate to learn who has caused me so much strife, even if some good things came of it.

"Yes, the tree from which all life spawned into this realm. Including myself."

She turns the conversation, giving me no more. Over our breakfast, Wen and I grow closer, forming a bond that I didn't think was possible in such a short time. In the sanctuary of her cottage, I find a respite from the chaos and danger that surround me. Here, I find a place where I can truly be myself without fear of judgment or harm, and I didn't realize how badly I need this until it's here.

As morning turns to afternoon, our conversations go on, sharing stories of my time in the mortal world, growing up in the foster system, Carter, and of course, my Emmie.

"How did she die?" she asks, the glimmer of tears unshed collecting in her eyes.

"Carter...or I guess, Cartwell. At that point he wasn't my Carter anymore. I had gone to a conference, so I wasn't home, but I dreamt it, I swear." My whole body tenses as I continue the story that always brings pity and disbelief raining down on me.

"Hush, calm yourself. Dreams aren't always just dreams," she says, running her long fingers along my knee.

"He told the authorities that she fell from a tree branch onto the fence in the pasture at the back of the property." I stare off through the window, the woods shimmering into memories of flashing lights and the fog of tears.

"In my dream, she screamed for me. She didn't fall. She screamed for me as she ran toward that tree. She climbed it for solace and escape. She said she could think there, and she felt safe, but I thought it was just youth and hormones. I never made anything of it until the dream. He caught up to her with a speed that made absolutely no sense to me. I wrote it off as a dream because what he did...it didn't seem possible. She fought him, hit him, kicked him, scratched at him, but he was too strong. He reached out his hands and he—"

"It's alright. You don't need to say it, my dear." Wen says quietly as I let the tears fall, but it's different this time, somehow.

"I...while I thought it was simply a dream, deep down, I was terrified. I couldn't put a finger on why. But, I had an urgent need to get home that I couldn't shake. I canceled my talk and got on the first flight home. The police were there when I arrived, and my heart turned to ash in my chest. He played the grieving father so well, but I couldn't shake that dream. When I saw her..I just knew it wasn't a dream. Somehow it wasn't a dream and he did it, he murdered our daughter."

"She's a warrior, taken before her time."

"A warrior? She was a child," I say, sniffling.

"Peace, my child. One does not have to be grown to fight. She fought for her life, she is a warrior through and through. It doesn't matter that you think you should have been there to fight for her. She made the choice to fight for herself. Just as Jadis made the choice to fight for you. He brought those ashes back to life, eh? Tended to them until your heart flamed once again?"

"Only to have it turn to ash once more," I whisper, looking away to the table we sit at. "Why are we talking about these things?"

"Because you're here to heal. To heal and gain strength so that you can do what must be done, should you choose that path. Now, since you're done with these thoughts...for now, I'll show you where to find fishing tools and other things you'll need while I'm gone."

"Gone? You're leaving?" My head spins around at her words, the panic stretching my face, which had grown tight with my tears.

"Aye, my child, there are things I must attend to. I won't be long, and the forest will protect you from prying eyes and provide you with everything you need. Everything that's not already here. While there's dried meat in the pantry, it gets old on the tongue after a while. There's a nice lake to the south, full to the brim with fresh fish for the taking. The garden is out back, and you can gather amongst the trees, too."

"But—"

"Ah," she says, putting a hand up to silence me. "No buts. You are perfectly capable of managing on your own. You don't *need* anyone. Besides, you need time to think on what's next for you, and I'll only distract you."

As we share another cup of herbal tea, I can't help but feel that, in this unexpected friendship, I have found a guiding light in the darkness, and now she's leaving me.

Chapter Forty-Five

"Vaelirae ilvathae ithor naeloth naelsylor."

The quiet speaks where thunder cannot.

THE EVENING SUN PAINTS THE sky with hues of orange and pink as we sit outside Wen's cottage, Solis, Pyra, and I. A soft breeze rustles the leaves in the nearby garden and lifts tendrils of my loose hair.

"Wen's been gone for days," I say, venting my frustrations. "Nothing has happened, including me figuring out what I'm going to do next. I'm tired of being cooped up in my own thoughts. Maybe we should go explore? See what lurks beyond the gardens and cottage?"

Pyra chimes in, her tiny body, with its fully flaming wings, glows brighter in the dim light. "It could be dangerous out there, El. We have no idea what lives in these woods."

Solis nods and snaps his jaws over a fly that flits in his face. "She's right. While it may be tempting to explore, maybe we remain cautious. Cartwell's reach is great, as you say, and he could be watching."

"Wen insisted we're safe here, in the woods. She even mentioned a lake. I'm tired of dried meat, and we aren't going to have fresh fruit here forever, Pyra." I sigh, feeling torn between the desire for freedom and the need to stay safe. "I can't hide forever."

"Sounds like you just made a decision about your next steps," Solis says.

Small orbs of warm light begin to flicker around the trees, swaying gently like fireflies caught in a slow waltz. They pulse faintly, as though breathing, their golden glow softening the shadows at the edge of the clearing.

"What are those?" I ask, unable to tear my eyes away. The orbs move with a sentience that means something more, something important.

Pyra flutters near my head, her wings creating a faint hum. "Soul wisps," she whispers, her awe apparent.

"Soul wisps?"

"They're said to be the souls of warriors taken before their time," Solis answers, his amber eyes reflecting the orbs' glow. His voice carries its usual calm wisdom, but there's a note of reverence in it. "They wander the realm, waiting for fate to grant them passage across the veil."

A chill prickles the back of my neck. "That's...sad. They're stuck here, punished because they died before the fates deemed it was their time?"

Solis inclines his head slightly. "Indeed. Soul wisps are tethered between the mortal and immortal worlds, caught in the liminal space where neither peace nor purpose can reach them." He pauses, his gaze following the orbs as they drift closer. "But there is hope. Legends say some find guardians to guide them to their rest. Others bring messages, whispers from the departed, left behind until their unfinished story is told. Or, they come across something or someone that can restore them."

Silence falls over us as we watch the wisps swirl and weave through the clearing. Their presence is both beautiful and haunting, a bittersweet reminder of lives interrupted. I can't help but wonder what stories they carry, what battles they left unfinished.

I take a hesitant step forward, my voice low. "They call them ghosts in my world. Souls with unfinished business, tied to the realm of the living."

Solis nods slowly, his tail completely still for once. "Similar, yet different. Here, they are said to bring more than unfinished business—they bring warnings, wisdom, even hope, if we know how to listen."

I shiver at his words, my arms wrapping around myself instinctively. The wisps drift closer, their golden light intensifying, and for a moment, I think I hear something—a faint voice, pleading. I hold my breath, straining to catch the words, but they slip away like smoke in the wind.

One wisp pauses between us, its glow warm and steady in the encroaching darkness. It hovers there, its light pulsing like a heartbeat, and a strange sense of calm washes over me.

"We should return to the cottage," Solis suggests, his voice cutting gently through the stillness. "The night grows dark."

I nod, but my gaze lingers on the wisp. "We'll stay with Wen a while longer," I say, my voice soft but resolute. "There's a reason we were brought here. I'll see it through—but I won't hide forever. We'll fish in the morning."

As we make our way back, the wisps dance with more energy, their light guiding us through the darkness. In the quiet of the night, surrounded by my friends, I feel a fragile peace begin to bloom. For now, it is enough.

PYRA AND I walk cautiously along a small animal trail, our senses on alert for any signs of danger. The morning sun has just begun to peak through the canopy of trees, making the shadows dance on the ground. The damp dirt beneath my feet feels somehow refreshing, and the smell of the wild is both invigorating and nerve-wracking. My life has become an unending dichotomy.

As we draw closer to the lake, we hear the distant call of a wild bird, followed by a rustling in the bushes ahead. Pyra stops abruptly and gestures for me to do the same. We remain perfectly still as we listen for any further movement. A large wildcat jumps from the shadows, its deep yellow eyes fixed on us.

We stand our ground, neither of us daring to move an inch. The wildcat seems to be sizing us up in the same manner before it slowly backs away, vanishing into the darkness it came from. Pyra exhales deeply and shoots me a smile of relief. As we start moving again, we're more aware now of the presence of wild creatures in the forest.

The lake comes into view. The beauty of the scene takes my breath away. The sun has fully risen now, illuminating the glass-like surface and setting the sky ablaze with a multitude of colors.

We have made it—we stand on the edges of one of the most wild and beautiful places on earth. Are we still on earth? This thought drops a rock into the pit of my stomach. It's accompanied by the instant urge to ask Jadis for answers. I wonder when that urge will finally wear out and give me some peace. I don't want to forget him—never—I just don't want to be reminded of him at every turn, bringing up the pain day in and day out. But, for a moment, the world is perfect, and we are just two small adventurers lost in its magnificence.

The lake is stunning. Nestled on one side by these ethereal woods, the water shimmers with unexpected clarity reflecting the ever-changing hues of the sky and surrounding foliage.

The surface is riddled with dainty lily pads bearing bright yellow petals. The shoreline is lined with reeds and willow trees that hang their long, slender branches into the pristine waters. It's peaceful.

A warm wind blows and caresses our faces. The currents of air carry a hint of cooling mist, a refreshing touch on our skin. It hangs in the meadow with tendrils of colored light that caress Pyra's flames. She does not like the mist much and hides behind my thick braid to protect her embers.

"You could have stayed at the cottage with Solis, watching for intruders," I say, mocking her.

"I could have, but someone has to make sure you don't do anything foolish, or clumsy," she gives back, matching my blow deftly with her own.

I settle into a little knoll that's free of reeds and trees and attempt to cast a line with a fat worm. I thought I managed a bite instantly, but when I pull the line, only weeds remain.

This continues for quite some time as the sun makes its way across the broad blue sky. Instead of catching a fish, the line is followed by a large ripple. A lady materializes from the depths of the lake, her hair flowing like liquid silver. Her eyes are light blue-green and full of splendor, like a spring meadow coming to life after a heavy rainstorm. At first, her gaze is seething, demanding who I am and what do I think I'm doing. Her words followed suit.

My answers tumble out of my mouth in a jumbled mess. Anxiety pricks at the back of my neck—had Wen sent me on a mission to get thrown off the edge of a cliff? This lady's expression gives away nothing, not even a hint that she would consider what I have to say.

"We mean you nor your lake any harm. I promise," I stammer. "We were told we could come here to fish. That's all."

She arches an eyebrow and tilts her head to the side, eyeing me. Her large, round hips are squared off as her hands perch on them like two angry birds looking for a fight. "Told by whom, pray tell?" She says, her voice dripping with mock innocence.

"Wen?" I say. "Please forgive us for intruding. We'll leave if you want us to. It's just Wen told me I could fish here and get some fresh meat while she's away."

"You speak strangely," she says, tilting her head the other direction. I can only shrug in answer. I honestly don't know what to say to that.

"Well, you're not going to catch anything going at it like that, and if you catch my hair with that damn hook one more time..."

My eyes fly wide in shock. "I'm so sorry! I didn't know!"

She huffs like I'm an exhausting child, which I suppose, to most of the beings in this realm, I am but a child. "Well, here, fine, let me show you. Good grief, she told you to call her Wen?"

I nod, not knowing what else to say to this female as she takes the line right out of my hands and quickly educates me on how it's done.

"She hasn't had anyone call her that for centuries," she laughs.

She starts up a pleasant conversation, which takes me aback at first, but I settle in. The rigidity of her stance eases, and a hint of curiosity appears in her eyes. She motions to the riverbank, where she expertly casts the line into the water and instructs me on how to pull it in. Then she turns to Pyra and points to a patch of deadwood by the nearby stream. "Gather some branches for the fire. We'll have lunch together."

"I haven't had company other than Wen for some time. We'll chat, and you can fill me in on what's happening in the realm." She says as she pulls in the third fish in a matter of minutes.

We sit on the shore, together, our feet in the cool water and a pile of freshly caught fish between us. She cooks them to a perfection I never could have managed, over an open flame, seasoning them with leaves and herbs she foraged along the shoreline.

As we eat, Pyra and I tell her our story and what's happening outside of the forest. We talk about the darkness that threatens everything and Cartwell's treachery. But then, as happens, our conversation shifts to more personal matters. I tell her of my love for Jadis and our unborn child, my hand instinctively resting on my still flat stomach. We laugh and cry together as we share our deepest hopes and fears. She wasn't kidding about not getting to talk often, and she needs to talk. She confides in me about her loneliness and how staying near the lake keeps her safe from the darkness, but venturing too far away puts her life at risk.

MORE DAYS PASS without Wen, and I find myself drawn to the lake and Lorelei, the lady of the lake, my new friend. She became a confidante, someone I can share my deepest fears and hopes with. She makes me think with her intelligent questions. Together we begin to piece together a plan, mayhap a foolish one, to break out of this damn contract.

As we talk life-altering matters, a cacophony of sounds booms through the forest, bringing us out of our comfortable trance. A branch cracks beneath an unknown foot, and our words are swallowed by the oppressive silence that follows. Fear quickly takes its place over any conversation, and neither of us dare to move.

My fingers curl around the hilt of my weapon, never far from my side. I spin in an instant, ready to face whatever terror lurks in the darkness. Adrenaline surges through me as Zephyr steps from the tree line with an impish glint in his eyes and a sly smile playing on his lips.

"Greetings, Princess." His deep, musical voice can't quite mask the amusement that's sparkling in his bright blue eyes as he gestures to my sword with one hand, a large bouquet of flowers in the other. The corner of the curl to his lips growing larger with each passing second. "I kindly request you sheath that blade before you hurt yourself."

I give him the most incredulous look I can manage as I sheath the Aetherwild blade at my side.

"I bring news, my beautiful lady," he says, his expression shifting to one of caution and discomfort. His mouth twitches with tension as he continues, "Your brother has successfully raised an army. He's determined to see you safe from Cartwell's clutches."

"No. He can't," I cry out.

He shakes his head and sighs, a shrug lifting and dropping his shoulders. "I know that. You know that, but obviously, he doesn't know that...my little dove." He raises an eyebrow along with the corners of his mouth in a sarcastic smile.

"So, tell him. Like you're here talking to me, go to the Day Court and tell him that Cartwell doesn't have me. He doesn't have to do this."

The male shakes his head and sighs. His free hand is in his pocket, and he stares at the ground. "Unfortunately, that can't happen. I'd be a fool to attempt it—not only would I be thrown into the dungeons for crossing the Day Court lands, but even if I got close enough there are two problems. First," he says, slowly raising his index finger from around the stems of the flowers, "I don't have much of a reputation to vouch for me. Thief, rogue, outlaw...not much trust there. And second," he says, lifting a second finger, "Most of us are bound not to help Cartwell's enemies. The only reason I can speak with you is because you're also bound to him and therefore one of us."

"Fucking magic," I yell, scattering flocks of birds from the trees and Lorelei giggles at my side. "So, what you're saying is I'm running out of time. If I don't do something, my foolish brother will confront Cartwell and the magic will kill him for trying to keep me away."

"In a nutshell...yes," he says, his eyes glued to the stone beneath his feet and his hand jams even deeper into his pocket. He shuffles his feet as if in an effort to shrink away from himself.

"How long do I have, Zephyr?"

"My network says he's calling all to arms now, and they shall arrive at the Day Court within the week. Then, they'll march to call on Cartwell on the Amber Fields. They aren't far from here if you come up with something...in time. Any ideas yet?"

"Not really, nothing solid," I say, dejected.

He grabs hold of my hands, and I feel the warmth and strength in his calloused palms. His eyes, blue and as deep as the forest lake, well with an emotion so strong that it seems to linger in the air between us. "If it's any consolation, my lady, I wish it were different. I wish you had more time, and I wish I could do more."

"Thank you, Zephyr. For everything. I know," my voice cracks. "I know what coming here could cost you. Thank you. Be careful and don't risk yourself anymore. I'll figure this out, one way or another and I'll set us all free."

His eyes widen at my declaration, his hands grasped together behind his back, leaving the flowers in mine, as he nods and turns away.

"And Zephyr," I call after him, "if we make it out of this, don't be a stranger. I'll break you out of the dungeon if you come visit." I say with a soft smile and a wink.

"You're family, Elora, one of us now. We'll do whatever it takes."

He quickly vanishes back into the woods, and my heart sinks to my stomach. Minutes feel like eons as I stand in fear. A single week. That's all I have left. It feels like the world has turned upside down again and all the air sucked out of my lungs.

The world feels unsteady, and I'm left gasping for air. Lorelei steps closer, her presence is usually a comfort but it's not enough to stave off the terror creeping up my spine.

"Breathe," she says, her hand finds mine before gently guiding me to the ground. She presses my head between my knees, her touch firm but comforting.

My breaths come in short, ragged bursts, the edges of my vision narrowing as panic tightens its grip. The air is sharp, almost biting, with every inhale.

With Brandis assembling an army, it doesn't matter how many he brings, he will die. I will lose the last of this newfound family I have left.

"He sends you more than the words he spoke aloud. Zephyr is a clever male."

"What?" I ask Lorelei as her words catch up with me.

"The flowers. He speaks with the language of flowers," she says.

I look at the large bouquet in my hands, full of a number of flowers, only just realizing how random they are.

"Flowers have a language?"

"Indeed," she says, touching each one with her fingers as she speaks, "yarrow means war is coming, as he said, and monkshood means the danger is nearby. Amaranth and anemone mean that hope is withering, and people grow fearful, but the madderwort pleads that you not be discouraged. With the milkweed, he's telling you there's still hope in misery. The asphodel means he, or they, will be faithful to you until death, and the false goat's beard means they will be waiting for you on the field of battle. The daffydowndilly ends the message letting you know they all hope for a new beginning."

"All that in a bunch of flowers," I comment flabbergasted.

"It's an ancient language not many know anymore. I'm surprised he bothered since you wouldn't know it."

The fiery orange sun drops lower in the sky, a glimmer of light in an otherwise darkening world. I feel the mounting sense of urgency as the pieces move into place for my inevitable confrontation with Cartwell. Time is running out, and failure is not an option. Literal lives depend on it.

Chapter Forty-Six

"Laralithi aelvyr thorin thala sylr."

New leaves still grow from broken branches.

WEN IS SOMEHOW MAGICALLY BACK at the cottage when I return, and she's already heard the news about Brandis and his army. She insists I sleep on it and try not to think of a plan now. "Start fresh in the morning," she says, and she's not wrong. A night of tears and dreams result in a more rational mind in the morning.

We huddle together in her dimly lit cottage. Wen and I carefully outline a plan, considering every angle and potential risk. The weight of the decision sits heavily. Wen knows the risks involved, and yet she stands beside me, offering her unwavering support. She also offers to return me to my true form—no more human Elora.

"Elora, understand this," she says, her voice gentle but firm. "This is your decision, no one else's. Not a prophecy, not your brother's, and not even mine. Only you make this choice, for you."

I take a deep breath. There's a heaviness, a responsibility to my unborn child, to protect them, keep them safe, and the thought of putting them at risk terrifies me. My hands instinctively move to my belly, cradling the life I desperately want to protect. I can't lose the only thing I have left of Jadis. I can't and I won't. I express this out loud.

"Do not fear for the child. The change won't touch your womb. It won't hurt the babe. On the contrary, it will only make both of you stronger, and he's quite strong already."

"He?"

"Aye, he. My old bones can sense these things, even this early on. Don't let the safety of your young one make you fret. He'll be fine." Wen places a reassuring hand on my shoulder, her expression filled with understanding. "Whatever you decide, I will stand by your side."

She says I have time to decide, but I know I don't. I have a week to make sure I'm ready, and the change will take a few days. I may need another day or two to recover. I have no time left to think on it, but as I do, I realize, I don't need time.

There's no question, no debate in my heart, "Let's do it. I'll complete the change." A weight lifts off my shoulders, and I can finally breathe again. This is the best chance I have to break free from Cartwell's clutches and protect my child.

"So, the illusions spell will cover the evidence of the change," Wen reiterates, her grizzled brow furrowed in concentration. "It won't be easy, Elora. It will take every ounce of your strength, but I have faith in you."

I nod, taking in a breath to steady my nerves. "I know. I'll do whatever it takes. We can't afford any mistakes. This has to be meticulous."

Wen continues, "Once I do my part, and the spell is in place, Cartwell will still think he's facing a human, but then you're on your own, girl. This is something you have to do by yourself. You need to stand against him yourself."

This entire plan centers on one, difficult, and potentially impossible task. "If he thinks he's facing a simple human and I make him angry enough, he'll strike. Facing an army, hopefully, he'll want to conserve his strength and only strike hard enough to kill a human, not an Aelorin. Hopefully, he'll want to save his magic for his stronger enemies. There's a lot of 'we hope' in this plan.

But what if he sees through the illusion?"

"That's where I come in," Pyra interjects, her wings fluttering fiercely. "I'll create distractions, fiery illusions, and blinding lights. I'll keep him off balance, so he won't have time to focus on you."

I look at Pyra, beyond grateful for her unwavering support and bravery. "Thank you," I say, my voice filled with emotion. "You're putting yourself at risk for me, and I will never forget it."

Pyra smiles, her eyes warm with affection, not just fire. "We're family, you and I. We'll stand by you, no matter what," she says, gripping Solis around the neck rather tightly.

I turn back to Wen, feeling so very full, the tears collecting along my lids. "And then what? The contract breaks and what happens to him?"

Wen's eyes gleam with that glimmer of mischief. "That's where I have a little trick up my sleeve," she says, cryptically. "I have something I think will do wonders for his disposition."

I arch an eyebrow, curious, intrigued. "What is it?"

She chuckles, her expression puzzling. "You'll see when the time is right. Trust me, it will all work out."

We finalize our complicated plan, and a sense of purpose settles on me. It's an uphill battle with so many pieces, so many unknowns and 'hopefully's' thrown in, but it's our plan.

As we settle in for the evening, Wen makes the potion that will restart my change, and I wonder why I waited so long to do it.

Then I'm reminded with excruciating detail.

Chapter Forty-Seven

"Ael nor ilith vyrith thalrin."

One step can shift the swords fate.

MY TRANSFORMATION DID, INDEED, TAKE days. I awoke, drenched in the sweat of a broken fever, feeling both exhausted and exhilarated. The colors around me seem brighter, the scents more intense, and even the breeze feels like a gentle caress against my skin. I'm newly alive to the world outside, craving its touches, and longing to experience every sensation I can.

I push up from my bed, and I'm met with broad beams of light shining through the window. They seem to fill me, not with warmth, but energy, vitality. My newfound vision sweeps across the room, taking in all the details I missed as a human. Furniture painted a lemon hue not tan, the walls are brighter, and the stone floor gleams with greens and blues. Everywhere I look, nature's touches bring life to the room: a vase of freshly cut roses that shine and glitter, an antique mirror reflecting the sun's light into the darker corners, and a bouquet of fading wildflowers still hanging on to their scent.

I feel a thrill of eternity, a sense of possibility, and a deep appreciation for the beauty all around me. I'm beyond ready to explore it, to seek its secrets, and discover its wonders. I am, at last, truly alive. For the first time, I feel like myself. I can't explain it. I am finally unequivocally me, no pretending. I am me.

Getting to this point has been a long and difficult journey, but as I step out into the world this morning, I am still grateful for the days it has taken me to get here and the people who made it possible.

My limbs ache, but it's a good ache—a reminder of the power that now courses through me, like after a good work out. But it doesn't last. While I slept, Wen received no more news on Brandis' progress. The only course of action is to pack provisions and rest at the edge of the wood, waiting for my moment to arrive.

So, here I am. I sit against the rough bark of a large oak tree at the edge of Wen's forest and the Amber Fields, about a day's hard walk from Wen's cottage. The ancient branches above me stretch high into the sky, sheltering me from the heat of the sun. The leaves above rustle softly, and I take a moment to bask in the peacefulness; perhaps the last I'll have for a while.

Pyra flits nearby, her wings humming as she darts between patches of sunlight filtering through the leaves. "You know," she begins, her tiny voice concerned, "sitting here doesn't feel like a great plan. Aren't you worried about being spotted?"

I open one eye and glance at her, the corner of my mouth twitching into a faint smile. "Wen said it's safe as long as we keep within the tree line. Besides, even I need a moment to breathe."

Pyra huffs, crossing her arms as she perches herself on a nearby branch. "Breathing is fine, but you're an awfully big target for someone lurking out there."

As I meditate, I hear the familiar sound of someone approaching, the faint crunch of footsteps. Pyra takes to the air, her golden light brightening as she circles above me.

"Did you hear that?" she whispers.

I spin around on my hands and knees, scanning the empty grassland beyond the trees. The blades of green sway in the breeze, dancing like a turbulent ocean, but no one is there.

Frantically, I turn my eyes to the dense foliage, as Pyra hovers at my side, her glow pulsing in alarm. "There—look!" She exclaims, pointing deeper in the shadows.

Lorelei's figure materializes. Her deep aqua eyes are large with fear and her silver hair cascades down her back like liquid metal.

Pyra darts closer to my shoulder, her wings creating a soft hum of tension. "That's never a good look," she murmurs, glancing between me and Lorelei.

"What are you doing here?" I ask, pulling her into my arms, her lithe frame fitting perfectly against mine.

"I had to come," she says, breathlessly. "I couldn't stay away once Wen told me you moved on and completed the change. You're stunning by the way," she adds with a coy wink.

My eyes shoot wide. No this can't be happening. "You can see? You're not supposed to see. There's supposed to be an illusion."

"Illusion spells don't work on ancients, silly. How are you feeling?" She says like I should have known that.

"Um...different," I answer, my voice soft, still adjusting to this newfound form. "But it's a good kind of different. Like I've finally found myself. But that's not the point, what are you doing here...out of your lake? It's dangerous, more so now than ever before."

Lorelei's eyes sparkle with both relief and admiration, which is a lot coming from an ancient. "I knew you would. You were always meant for greatness, El. I brought you something, something important. I'll be fine." She waves her hand in the air dismissing my concerns, while the other dips into a satchel at her waist made from woven reeds. Her fingers fumble slightly. She's more concerned than she's letting on.

When she pulls her hand out, she holds a delicate necklace, and my breath catches. A stunning blue gem, like the clearest water of her pristine lake, is set into silver filigree with intricate leaves and branches. The central stone seems to glow from within. White branches of an ancient tree stretch out from its center, each individual branch carved in great detail, as if yearning for the heavens and the stars themselves.

"It's a talisman that has been in the care of my family for quite some time. It will protect you...somehow...I'm not sure exactly—that's all I can really say,' she finishes, sheepishly.

I take the necklace in my hands, feeling the smoothness of the gem against my skin. It's exquisite, and I can't help but be touched by her gesture. "It's beautiful," I say, my voice awestruck. "But Lorelei, I can't take this. It has to be precious to you."

"It is," she says, her eyes shining with unshed tears. "But you need it more than I do. We were told that, one day, I would meet someone who would need its protection. It's a gift from my heart to yours, and only works when given freely, with love."

Tears fill my eyes. I am so very tired of crying, but at least these tears are for happier times. She stretches the tiny chain over my head, lifting my braid to let it fall into place, dangling the stone right over my heart. I pull her close, savoring the warmth of her body against mine. "Thank you," I whisper, choking the words. "I will treasure it, and you, always. No matter what happens."

Lorelei pulls away, her eyes glistening. "Be safe, El. I'll be waiting for you at the lake when you return. And you will return, I demand it."

I nod, unable to find the words to express what I'm feeling. I lost so much and gained so much more. With one last squeeze of her hand, I watch as she disappears back into the forest, her presence a bittersweet reminder of what has yet to come.

I WAIT THERE, against my tree, for what feels like years, each passing day heavy with anticipation and nerves. The days slip by like the running waters of a river that I can almost hear but not see. They fade into the distance, and the weight of the impending battle hangs over me like storm clouds on an empty sky.

Pyra, however, has no patience for waiting. She flutters around me incessantly, her light darting in and out of my vision. "Are you always going to just sit like this?" she asks for the third time just today, her tone sharp with irritation. "Because I'm starting to think trees have more exciting lives than you do right now."

I sigh, keeping my eyes on the distant horizon. "You might be right," I say with a laugh. "We can't all flit around and poke at things to pass the time."

"Well, maybe you should try it," she shoots back, landing on a nearby branch with an exaggerated huff. "You'd be surprised how entertaining it can be to, I don't know, *do something*."

"I am doing something," I mutter, my voice low as I clench my hands into fists. "I'm preparing."

"Preparing?" Pyra mimics in a high pitched voice, "It looks a lot like *sitting* to me. Maybe you should try pacing; at least that way you'd look dramatic. Or talk to me. I've got stories. Lots of them."

Her restlessness grates against my fraying nerves, but I don't have the heart to snap at her. I let her chatter fill the empty silence, her voice a constant buzz of words as I try to ignore the storm growing louder in my mind.

THE ARMIES FORM their ranks on the field, and the sun casts its warm light over the landscape. The antithesis of everything happening on the field. I take a deep breath, steadying myself for what's to come. Each footstep is as heavy as a stone in my boot; each clink of armor fills my heart with dread. Still, I'm almost grateful that it's finally here, that the waiting is over. There's no doubt in my mind that Pyra is grateful.

The two armies face each other. I stand along the middle line, still hidden in the shadows of the trees to the west. The sight of Zephyr and Ravengar with Cartwell sends shivers down my spine, but I cling to the knowledge that I'm not alone, on either side. Velasco is seated atop a horse to Cartwell's right, exuding that air of cunning manipulation. Thank the stars he's on my side.

To my left, Brandis sits high on his horse, adorned in bright armor in the shape of broad leaves at his shoulders, the sun emblazoned in yellow metal on his chest. The image is both striking and reassuring, and for a brief moment, I think I can see them—Jadis, Mik, and Dagen, hiding in beams of blinding light to his right—standing with him, united in their mission to save me, even after death. The stars have granted me strength, and I take a step.

From my place in the shadows, I watch Velasco's movements closely. His horse snorts and shifts beneath him, but his posture is unyielding, his sharp eyes scanning the enemy ranks. I can't tell whether his confidence is real or merely an act meant to unsettle. Cartwell's jaw clenches, his fingers twitching at the reins of his steed.

The two leaders stand face-to-face, the silence on the field heavy with tension as their eyes lock. The air around them feels charged with electricity as they argue over their differing points of contention. I can't make out their exchange over the clink of armor and the restless shuffling of soldiers, thousands of them, but the energy between them is palpable.

Pyra wrings her hands in my shirt sleeve either in fear or anticipation.

A ripple moves through both armies, the tension snapping like a drawn bowstring. The soldiers seem to breathe as one, every warrior clutching their weapon tighter, waiting for the inevitable command.

From my hiding place, I tighten my grip on my own blade, my palms slick with sweat. Pyra flits nervously at my shoulder, her light flickering like a candle caught in a draft. "I don't like this, Elora," she mutters, her voice a rare whisper. "Too quiet. Too tense."

"Neither do I," I reply under my breath, the dread coiling tighter in my chest. "But we have to wait for the right moment. He must be distracted first, angry."

The first horn sounds, a long, mournful note that cuts through the still air like a blade. It's a signal—a call to action that reverberates through the field.

Cartwell raises his sword high, his soldiers responding with a roar that shakes the ground. Brandis counters, his own blade flashing in the sunlight as his army lets out a unified cry of defiance.

The ground trembles as both sides surge forward, the field erupting into chaos. My breath catches as I step out of the shadows, my legs carrying me through the last of the trees between me and the fray. The sound of metal clashing against metal rings out, accompanied by the cries of men and beasts alike.

Pyra darts ahead, her glow cutting through the haze of dust and sunlight. "Stick to the plan, El," she calls over her shoulder.

I nod, the weight of the stars behind me, and sprint forward. The battle has only just begun, and I'm going to end it.

Every step is like a hammer pounding into the ground. I step out fully onto the field of battle, the clashing of swords in tune with my racing heart. "Enough," I yell to no avail. I feel it then, a warm pool deep inside me, swirling and churning, ready to let loose.

"Enough," I scream and the swords slow as males and females on both sides search for the source. Cartwell pushes warriors this way and that, fire burning in his eyes.

"This ends here and now, Cartwell."

Cartwell tilts his head, wiping at the blood dripping into his eyes with the back of his hand. A cruel grin stretches across his face. "Oh, the brave little toaster finally shows her face," he sneers, his tone mocking. "I believe that's how it goes."

His words slam into me like a fist, stealing my breath. My hands tremble as I grip the hilt of my sword. I can feel that pool coming to a boil, with no understanding of what that means, only that the pressure is growing.

"You don't get to reference her favorite story," I spit, my voice trembling in fury, not fear. "In fact, you never get to hint at or speak of her ever again. You stole her from me."

He takes a slow step forward, his boots squelching in blood-soaked dirt as he steps over another body. "I stole nothing," he snaps, his tone sharp and cutting. "She was mine to do with as I please."

"She was your daughter not some toy you get bored with!" I shout, my voice cracking under the weight of my grief.

"She was in the way," he hisses, his eyes narrowing into slits.

"In the way of what?" I demand, my chest heaving as the words rip from me.

Cartwell's expression twists into something cold and calculating. "You carrying another child," he says, his voice dripping with disdain. "I needed a child with magic, not some useless, worthless human child. You got distracted by her."

Velasco and Ravengar approach, just out of reach. Velasco idly drums his fingers on the hilt of his blade, as if debating whether to intervene or keep watching. Ravengar shifts uneasily, his jaw clenched, his weapon at the ready but not yet raised.

Pyra hovers near my shoulder again, her wings a blur. "Elora," she whispers, her voice sharp, "stay focused. Don't let him—"

"Quiet," I snap, my voice low but firm. I don't take my eyes off Cartwell, unwilling to give him even a moment's advantage as others approach, getting within earshot.

He steps closer, slow and calculating, and I step back. His lips curl into a cruel smile as his eyes gleam, turning his head only far enough to see those approaching and how close. "Elora, my dear," he croons, his tone dripping with mockery, "you couldn't resist the temptation to see your beloved husband one last time? Or perhaps it's the last time seeing your beloved brother, I should say."

"Elora, come—" Brandis shouts, but I stay him with a hand.

"Beloved husband?" The words rip through me like a knife, every syllable slicing away at my soul until I'm reduced to nothing more than a hollow shell. My stomach twists painfully, but I suppress the feeling and keep my emotions hidden. Fearful of losing control, I choose each word carefully, purposefully, slowly, with my underlying agenda—anger him as much as possible.

There's one way to accomplish that with people like him: take away his power, take away his importance. "Husband? More like tyrant," I retort and both my friends behind him shoot wide eyes in my direction. My voice carries eerily across the field. "A man who manipulates and preys on others' vulnerabilities to feed his insatiable ego, just to feel like someone actually needs him."

His eyes narrow, and his grip on his sword tightens. "You've always had a way with words, my dear. But words won't help you now."

He looks me up and down with disdain as if I'm nothing more than an annoying bug buzzing around his head. "You always turn back into a simpering little fool, begging for my love and affection. Desperate and needy. Your clinginess almost did me in, you know, and all the whining. If your lineage didn't promise intense power, I don't think I ever could have suffered through rutting you."

"The stars could have blessed me with less then, so I didn't have to suffer you." My face twitches as I attempt to suppress a smirk. My pulse beats fiercely in my chest, and I can feel the thumping in my temples. "Are you finished? I've had recent conversations with trees that didn't bore me as much as you are right now."

His confident grin falters as he glances away, scanning the growing crowd for who heard and who didn't, making a list. He's obviously trying to hide his surprise at my bold statement. I've taken him off guard. Zephyr smiles widely behind his hand.

"I don't need words to save me. I have something far more powerful at my disposal—the truth. And the truth is, I was wrong." His raised eyebrow and cocky grin only feed my confidence further—I have him.

"You're not a male. You're nothing more than a scared little boy hiding behind magic and lies. A scared little boy who let a ten-year-old girl get under his skin. A scared little boy who had to trap a woman into a magically bound marriage to get laid. A scared little boy who had to trap a woman because he didn't want her to leave him. No one can leave him, because being alone is what you fear most."

The red of anger starts to spread from his neck like a wildfire, a glowing ember that rises as if consuming him until his face is alight with rage. "That little girl was nothing! An obstacle standing in your way and a hindrance to your own potential. She had no power, no worth, and no further use in this world. You needed to move on, you pathetic fool, to leave those useless emotions behind and focus on what matters: creating more children to carry on my legacy. But no! Instead of fulfilling your purpose, you closed yourself off to the world and pursued some dead-end shading career—a complete waste of..."

"For a little girl that poses no threat to you, you put a lot of effort into getting rid of her. You're so afraid of losing control, of being alone, that you'll do anything to maintain your grip over others. I've seen right through your armor, Cartwell. I see you. The real you. What you don't understand is that you've always been and always will be alone."

With those words, Cartwell moves right for me. My heart races, but I've struck the cord, and have to keep going.

The air around me becomes so thick with tension I can almost feel it squeezing the breath out of my lungs. Cartwell looms closer; I move a little further away. His eyes burn with rage, and his fists clench so tightly I can see the whites of his knuckles through the blood, but there's something even more sinister lurking deep in his gaze—the fear he forces into submission. I hold my head high, staring him down, knowing that if I show any hint of a weakness, he will use it against me. Failure is not an option.

The others are moving closer, with obvious concern, as he looms ever closer to me.

"You think you can defy me, Elora?" he hisses, his voice sharp with venom. "You're nothing without me. A weak, pathetic human girl who couldn't even protect her own daughter, her own friends, her lover."

My jaw tightens, and I grit my teeth, trying to maintain my composure. He knows what to say to hurt, just as I do now. "No, Cartwell, that's where you're so epically and terribly wrong. You are nothing without me. I have everything you can never have: friends, family, people who love me for me, no matter what."

Cartwell's sneer deepens. The metallic tang of blood and sweat fills my nose, mingling with the acrid smoke drifting across the field. His looming presence still sends a chill up my spine, but I don't let it show. I square my shoulders, forcing myself to meet his burning gaze.

Velasco shifts slightly, his expression still unreadable as his hand brushes the hilt of his sword. To my right, Pyra's glow flares, her light flickering erratically as she hovers closer, her tiny fists clenched on my behalf. Solis creeps up through the grass out of nowhere, crouching low to the ground, his amber eyes tracking Cartwell's every move like a predator waiting for the perfect moment to strike.

I am not alone. I have never been alone, and it's time for my light to shine.

"You're nothing without me. You're nothing without this body, this womb, without my lineage, without my prophecy, you are nothing. I was weak, I admit that, but not anymore. I've changed and you hate it. I stand up to you and you want an obedient whimpering sot at your feet. Well, guess what? You're going to have to look somewhere else. I am not alone. I am Elora Aurelius, I am the light and I will not dim.

I am more. I am worthy. I am my own."

He takes a menacing step closer, my powerful allies fanning out from the side, his piercing gaze locking onto mine. "You dare to challenge me? I control everything you hold dear, and you're nothing but a silly...fragile...human."

The cracks are forming. It's almost time. "I will always outshine you, every step of every day."

He throws his hands forward, and the air around him crackles with dark energy. His fury is unleashed as a powerful wave of magic crashes toward me. I swallow hard, bracing for the impact as it barrels closer.

It strikes me. There's a contrasting flash of brilliant white light. I fly backward, the force like a freight train. My ears ring with the impact, the sudden stop of the hard ground behind me knocking all breath from my lungs. They now fail to bring in anymore air, no matter how hard I try, gasping through a closed throat. I feel the ground beneath me, the soft grass of the Amber Fields, as if I'm being pulled away from it. My vision blurs, the edges turning to darkness, and Jadis' voice sings in my ears, summoning me toward him across the veil.

This is the end? It didn't work, entirely anyway, he hit me with too much power, I guess. The contract will still be broken, right? But I won't reap the benefits. My heart still races, and I struggle to focus, to fight against the pull. But the pain in my chest is unbearable. I feel myself slipping away.

Strikingly bright blue light glares from the center of my chest, a tree of white. The sensation in my chest intensifies, and I feel like I'm about to burst. I open my eyes and see the sky above me, a kaleidoscope of blue stretching out for miles. As the sun lingers on the horizon, it casts an ethereal glow across the Amber Fields. Jadis moves closer, his figure illuminated by the golden beams. He looks so real, as if he could reach out and touch me any second. My voice trembles, "You came for me...is this it then? Did I fail?"

He smiles, those infuriating dimples on his cheeks that I never thought I'd see again, and the ugly tears fall down my temples as I try to process the overwhelming feeling of seeing him again. Trying to contain myself only sets the fire burning brighter inside, until I can no longer breathe through the sobs rising in my throat. I collapse back in anguish, every ounce of energy leeching out of my body as all my emotions come pouring out, the dam is lifted.

He takes my hand, and I feel a shockwave of electricity at the contact. His grip is unyielding, crushing mine as if he'll never let me go. *Please don't let me go.*

His touch sends warmth radiating through my body, and I can't take my eyes from our joined hands. Then, with one powerful tug on my arm, he has me held firmly against his chest. My trembling hand reaches for his face, brushing over the roughness of his beard as I struggle to contain my...*everything*. His strong arms encase me in security and protection. His heart pounds like thunder beneath the palm of my hand...his heart pounds.

My knees buckle, and with a gasp, he lifts me, his arms pressing tightly around my waist. I bury my face into his neck, inhaling deeply the scent of him.

"How?" I whimper against his warm skin, my senses completely overwhelmed by that familiar scent of leather and pine. After what seems like an eternity without breathing this smell, it fills me to the brim with a boiling emotion that threatens to burst from me.

My feet rest gently down to the grassy plain. His hands hold my face as he presses hard, needy lips against mine, until I'm left gasping for breath.

We lean into each other until our foreheads touch; his hands still cradling my face. His eyes are full of questions, and I know he wants to talk about what happened.

A hand moves back, a finger lightly tracing the edge of my newly pointed ear, and he smiles ruefully at me. "We have more pressing matters to attend to, and then I intend to have ye in my bed for days."

I grin madly as sobs wrack my body, a wild and unstoppable laugh shakes my chest until I think it will tear open. Brandis looks at us with a hateful expression and then turns his sword to the defenseless Cartwell, a cruel smile tugging at the corners of his mouth.

An invading yellow light wraps around Cartwell like a vise, thin ropes of magic squeezing until he falls to his knees gasping for air. It seeps through his skin, courses through his veins like molten gold, scorching every cell in its path. He roars in agony as the light tears him apart from the inside out.

Velasco hops off his horse with a disgusted curl of his lips. Brandis raises his gleaming sword high, prepared to strike. Mik steps in and places a steadying hand on his arm, while Dagen stands firmly at his side. A real, flesh and blood hand. Stands! Mik and Dagen stand of their own free will.

"As much as I'd like to see him dead, too, Brandis, tis Elora's decision—his fate."

My allies, my friends, my family. Jadis, Mik, and Dagen take their places to my left with steely determination. Ravengar and Zephyr cautiously creep up on my right, their wary glares laden with mistrust. Pyra perches on my shoulder and Solis stands tall at my feet.

One by one, I acknowledge every last one of them with an outstretched hand and a small smile, calming the sea of uncomfortable animosity. Tears swell in my eyes as each figure comes into focus, like a rippling wave crashing over me. I would recognize them anywhere, even through the blur. They have etched themselves so deeply into my heart.

"Why isn't he dead already?" I ask, my voice coming out hoarse and dry.

Velasco answers me, not surprisingly, as I think he has something to do with it. "A little bird came and suggested an intriguing addendum to your marital contract, my lady."

Cartwell sneers even while he struggles to breathe through his obvious pain, his face contorts. "You cannot change a contract already bound by blood, you fool. The magic chose to spare me because it knows I was tricked."

"Wrong, again, Cartwell. My, my how right our lady was. You really are nothing without us, aren't you?" Velasco snaps, dropping any respectful tone or moniker. "Addendums are easy enough when you have the blood of both agreeing parties. Since the little birdie carried her majesty's blood for me, I simply attached said addendum to a missive you angrily sent to Brandis here after punching a wall."

He turns to me to explain further, a smile of glee splattered across his face, the light in his mercury eyes blinding. "His magic is now bound. Only you can give him permission to access it or command it."

"Wen," I whisper, eliciting an arched brow from Jadis, his arm now wrapped around my waist, pulling me closer.

I stare at Cartwell, now on his knees before me. The power I hold in my hands, a heady experience. The male before me, the cause of all my heartache and pain. His life is now in my hands, and I struggle to decide his fate. I pull away and bend down so only he can hear what I have to say next. "This womb you're so obsessed with was full before you ever got your hands on me again."

"He lives," I say to the crowd, loud enough for everyone to hear, my voice steady despite it all.

"Elora, please, you cannot be serious?" Brandis cries out, his face turning beet red. His chest heaves as though he's about to erupt again, a sight I do not wish to experience. His fists are clenched, and he looks ready to challenge me, but thankfully he refrains.

"He lives, locked in the dungeons that Zephyr kindly informed me we possess.

Oh, on that note, dear brother, I want it known that my new allies are not to be arrested and thrown in cells if they cross our borders to see me," I say firmly. He wouldn't argue right now, but I know there will be more battles between us over this later.

Jadis' arms encircle me tighter as he pulls me in closer, the heat of his body pressing against mine. His warm breath tickles my ear as he whispers, "Tell me...why?"

The sound of his silky voice sends shivers down my spine, and I struggle to keep my thoughts straight.

"I have a sinking feeling we'll need him again before the end," I mutter, quietly, feeling the weight of that thought settle deep within me.

Chapter Forty-Eight

"Vaelys nelaril thalanor thalnar rytha."

Even the longest night remembers the sun.

RESSA'S FACE LIT UP SO brightly when we arrived back in Brandis' campaign camp days ago. She wrestled me into a tight embrace, tears streaming down her cheeks as she let out a squeal of pure joy. I reciprocated the feeling, relieved that my first friend was safe at my side again. We stood there for what felt like a lifetime, before finally separating and heading inside the tent, where Jadis prepared me a warm bath. As we talked long into the night, I told Tressa every single thing that had happened since we'd been apart, our conversations spanning from the mundane to the profound, the sad, to the overwhelming joy.

We returned home. Home. I rode with Jadis the entire trip, unwilling to be parted from him. He made good on his word of keeping me in his bed for days. Brandis continued to glare and give evil looks whenever he saw us being openly affectionate, which is, truthfully, often.

Jadis now knows about our child and asks me how Brandis handled the news. I never could hold back my frustration with Brandis' backward ideals and I find it even more difficult to back down now.

"He doesn't approve at all, as Mik expected. And, I suspect, you, too." He nods, his cheek brushing against my head. "I told him I don't give a shit." This statement starts him in a fit of laughter, and I have to pause until he can catch his breath again.

"I don't give a shit what he wants. It's my life, and I choose to be with you. He can either accept it or butt out of my life. He seems to have accepted the former, but I have no doubt he will pressure me over this as much as he will about Cartwell's fate."

Jadis smiles and his eyes fill with tenderness as he pauses to lightly touch the small swell of my stomach. His fingertips are gentle against my skin, and his voice a whisper in the air, "I'm not going anywhere."

We share our theories. About how the first attack on the council was not Cartwell's doing, despite what he did in the human realm. The attack in the alley, the gun, was all a ruse to get me here, to scare everyone. He wanted me alive. The stabbing is another matter. They had to be part of this unknown enemy as well, one that wants me dead. We have an unknown enemy lurking in the shadows, which makes us both uneasy, especially with our new circumstances.

I tell him what Wen, or Ceridwen as Tressa believes her to be, the great mother, not centuries old, but millennia, said to me about the prophecy. That the great tree had given it, and there was more than what labeled me as the Deliverer.

He shared with me how the trolls, how Rurik, used the cauldron of Ceridwen to bring him back from the veil. How the cauldron can bring back warriors that were taken before their time. Apparently, Rurik also has a new friend after that particular event, a soul wisp, that has taken to following him everywhere, like a little puppy dog. An interesting turn of events that has his Auntie in a tizzy. It's never happened before.

"There's much to do," I say, looking into his eyes. "Our battle with Cartwell may be over, but it's only the beginning of the war. I have my list of beings to find and see, we have an enemy to track down and a prophecy to decipher. It's a long to-do list."

He nods, leaning down and pressing his lips to mine. "Yes, our and we, but it can wait for now. I'll be by your side every step of the way, or under it, or over it, or..."

I smack him playfully, and he rolls me into his arms, his lips pressing into mine, his tongue tickling at the seam, begging entrance as his hands slip down and over my hips.

"We were talking...this leads to no talking," I say softly as he trails warm, sweet kisses along my jaw and slowly down my neck.

"Mhmm," he mumbles against my skin, the vibrations skittering down my spine. "It leads to moaning," he says, continuing his ministrations along my collar bone.

"I like that I can remove your ability for coherent speech." His hot mouth now slides over the top of my breast and down the side and I can't help but squirm, a moan escaping my lips.

His mouth spreads into a grin against my skin. "Aye, only incoherent sounds. It means I'm doing my job."

A knock at the door sounds through the chamber. Jadis' warm breath releases in a sigh against my belly button. He plants a kiss on the growing bump beneath and gets up from the bed.

Tressa bursts through the door, and I whip the blanket over my naked body. "Did you—oops, sorry," she says as she tip toes back a few paces.

"What is it, Tressa, yer timing is epic lass?"

She looks down at her toes, a blush blooming on her cheeks. "Lots of olives! There are reports to Brandis of fae bearing children that haven't done so for decades, and it's not just here in the Day Court, it's all over the realm. The other council members are getting the same reports."

"This is good?" I ask, a little confused.

"Aye, the best news! And there's more," she says, the excitement bursting from her being. "The Dawn Court reported just now that the Dawn Sentinels have returned, they were sighted this morning bringing on the new day for the first time in centuries..."

"And?" I ask.

"And Brandis requests your presence in the council chambers," she says, and begs our leave.

The council. "It's different this time," I say.

"Aye? How? It's the same council as last time," he replies, his voice muffled in the fabric of his shirt as he pulls it over his head.

"This time I have you by my side," I answer confidently, stringing the laces of my gown together against my chest.

"You've always had me," he answers, taking my hand and placing a chaste kiss on my palm. He reaches and pulls the door, gesturing for me to lead on.

"Well, out of the frying pan," I say.

"And into the fire," he finishes for me, intertwining his fingers in mine.

The End...for now.

Acknowledgments

First, as always, I have to thank my kiddo, my little sea monkey. Not only does she deal with mommy being locked in her room for hours on end, she's my sounding board. It's a great time when your child falls in love with writing too! I wouldn't give up our mommy and me writing dates and all the times I pestered you for your opinion.

To my family—both blood and found—I could not do this without you. My parents have supported me any way they can. To my sister who is not only a sounding board about good storytelling but helps with the crazy dogs so I can get some work done! My brother for all of his long distance cheerleading.

To my former sister-in-law turned soul sister, Heidi, thank you for always cheering me on. It helped more than you can possibly understand.

To all my favorite authors and readers who inspire me every single day.

I need to thank my former self and my new self. So many times I wanted to give up because I didn't think anyone would want to read my stories. Here's to us finding ourself and our imagination for making all of the good and bad into something wonderful—something healing.

Thank you,
Arin

About the Author

I was the second child of four; ideally, I would have been a boy. They said I was a boy, and that would have been it for my parents, but alas, another girl. Actually, I was born with my cord loosely curled around my neck, and I was blue, not from being strangled by the ever-important highway of oxygen and nutrition from my mother's womb, but because of those bright, blinding white monstrosities attacking my poor eyes from above. I simply had the breath scared out of me. My father loves to tell the tale of the doctor who needed to return to medical school, as when he was asked whether I was a boy or girl, he responded, "I don't know." Stunned, I tell you. In truth, he simply had not had the time to look yet as well... I was blue. My silence only lasted for so long, as when they suctioned out my airways, my father was sure they could hear me throughout the whole hospital in rural South Dakota.

We did not stay in South Dakota for long. By the age of two, we came to New York, Buffalo area to be precise, and I have lived here for the entirety of my life so far. I have traveled much, but Buffalo is still home. My father is a minister and historian, and my mother studied biology and medical technology but works for a bank now. Hospital mergers would have prevented her from seeing her children growing up due to insane schedules. The three from South Dakota became four in New York as my youngest brother (of two) surprised my parents two years in.

Family trips always had some element of history mixed in, a fort along our route or living history museums. History and its importance were always a large part of our lives. As young adults, my youngest brother and I, and eventually our parents, got involved in living history education at a local fort and engrossed ourselves in the 18th century. We now spend most of our summer weekends traveling back in time, educating the local populations on life during the French and Indian War (Seven Years's War) and the American Revolution. For me, this wasn't enough. I needed more history. I pursued a degree in archaeology in college and eventually earned my doctorate. While I love the 18th century, and it is a passion of mine, the medieval period is my heart and soul. It is a fascinating and complicated moment in history, especially so in Ireland and Scotland, the place of my roots. This is what inspired my first book...

During graduate school I fell in love, got married, had a beautiful baby girl, discovered I married a lie, a fictitious character created and played to woo me into a false sense of security, survived an abusive relationship, freed myself and my daughter from that physical, mental, and emotional prison, and earned my doctorate as a single mother living with my parents as an adult. But here is where it gets interesting.

Remember there at the top of the page... I was supposed to be a boy. My siblings, of course, having not suffered in a poor relationship as I, have moved out and have lives of their own. I am home helping my older parents with their house (the first they've ever owned and a fixer-upper) and am quite handy with power tools, projects, designs, gardening, and herbal healing. I, the second daughter, have achieved the ever elusive 'favorite son' status; guess they were right after all ;).

LOST THRONE

ARIN L. BLACKWOOD

Atlantis Rising Book One

My story doesn't start with a sordid tale of death, abandonment, and suffering. It's not some damn fairy tale. I mean it is, by the strictest definitions, but I wasn't some lost girl who just needed to be rescued and belong. I was happy—genuinely happy. If anything, I had too much curiosity and not enough fear. But that's hindsight for you.

I grew up an orphan. Now, don't start thinking that I was some lost little puppy who needed a family, my found family. I was adopted as a baby by a wonderful set of parents, and yes, they told me I was adopted as soon as I was old enough to understand. My parents were amazing, loving, and supportive—the best parents a girl could ask for.

They built me a sandbox and called it a "dig site." I spent hours unearthing bottle caps and fossils from the local rock store while they cheered like I'd discovered a lost tomb. I never once felt unwanted. I only ever felt... home.

History has always fascinated me. I love the mystery behind it, taking the little clues left to us and turning it into a story and a lesson. The dreams started at an early age. At first, I attributed them to a fanciful imagination after watching the animated classic movie with adventure and love. As time passed, though, the dreams became more vivid, and there were parts that felt so real that they hadn't been in any movie. And sometimes I woke up with sand under my fingernails. Once, seawater in my bed. I told myself it was sleepwalking, stress, anything else. But deep down, I wasn't sure.

Atlantis became an obsession for me, one that only my nearest and dearest knew about. I'd chosen my career path and didn't want my obsession with the lost city to negate my capabilities as an archaeologist. When I could manage it, I wrote papers on the topic, making sure I was discreet and professional, laying out the details and the evidence either debunking a current theory or analyzing old ones. I was careful not to reveal my interest—at least I thought I was.

But obsession is a hard thing to mask. And secrets have a way of slipping through the cracks, especially when they want to be found.

If I'd known what was coming—what those dreams truly meant—I might've run instead of chasing them.

I thought I was chasing stories in stone. Turns out, they were waiting for me.

Chapter One

"Where you off to this summer, Mattie?" I sat sideways in my favorite chair reading the latest fae fantasy smut, as he calls it, twisting the smooth lock of hair that lay just behind my ear. Mattie had walked into the kitchen, the smooth pop of the fridge door and the clink of glass my perfect sign that he had moved on to the celebratory beer, having finished his latest article.

"Nowhere, yet," he answered, twisting the metal cap off and tossing it in the sink with a clink.

I sat up, shoving the bookmark between the pages. "What do you mean nowhere yet? It's a little late in the season to not already be attached to a dig."

"I got a little sidetracked by this article. It's a big one, could open some significant doors for me. I missed the deadline for that underwater dig in the Mediterranean, it completely passed me by." He plopped his considerable form back onto the couch, taking a long draw from his bottle. By considerable form, I mean my bestie was whatever the blond version is of tall, dark, and handsome, sporting 200 pounds of lean working muscle. There wasn't one dig we've been on together where I didn't have to play-act his girlfriend to keep the ladies at bay. Not that he wasn't interested, they just weren't his type. Mind you, at this point, I'm not sure what his type is.

Also? He once carried me three miles uphill in a sandstorm because I sprained my ankle after ignoring his advice. Never lets me live it down. But that's Mattie. He shows up. Always.

"What about you?" He asks, and I start chewing on the nail of my pinky finger. It's my worst tell. Screams, I've got a secret. I don't answer, and if anyone knows my tells, it's Mattie. "Roorrry?" He says, elongating my name in obvious accusation. "You're keeping a secret. Spill, now."

I get up and rustle through the drawer on my desk. You know the one everyone has that all their important stuff goes into for safekeeping only to be lost in the chaos. Fortunately, or unfortunately for me (jury's still out on that one), the large manila envelope with the expensive lettering is still sitting right on top.

I'd check at least a dozen times in the last twenty-four hours just to make sure it hadn't vanished. Some parts of me expected it to melt away, dreamlike,

like so many other things that came in the night and left with the dawn. But no—there it sat. Solid. Real. And wrong. Something about it felt off, like I'd seen it before, but I hadn't. Had I?

I hand him the envelope, not daring to open it myself and risk more exposure to some kind of curse (because my luck is never this good), and sit back on my heels, chewing on my lower lip as he reads what's inside.

My stomach twists as I watch his eyes skim the page. What if it really is happening? What if this is the moment everything changes—and not in the good way.

"This is a joke, right?" He asks as he reads the contents of the main letter discussing a proposal to fund my research into the exact location of the lost city of Atlantis. When I say fund, I mean they're offering an exorbitant amount of money for me to lead an expedition.

"I don't know, honestly."

"You said no, right?"

I don't answer. Deciding to chew on the nail of my pointer finger this time.

My hands won't stay still. My brain won't either. It's like the words in that letter struck a chord I didn't even know was there, and it's still humming in my bones.

"You said no, Rory, right?" He asks again, more emphatically, like adding in my name is going to make me answer faster. I thought invoking names was only supposed to make someone appear.

"I haven't answered yet." I spit out as fast as my lips will let me, throwing my legs back out to rest my feet on the floor.

Mattie grabs at his forehead, tapping the stack of papers in his other hand on his knee. "Rory, you can't be serious. This can't be real."

"But what if it is?"

The words are out before I can stop them. And suddenly I want to cry, because it's not just a letter. It's the city. The one I've seen since I was a child, the one that's haunted my dreams like it's waiting. Like it remembers me.

He wipes his hand down his face, pulling at his mouth as he passes. "If it is, if you are fool enough to agree to this, I'm coming with you."

"Mattie, come on. This isn't even your area of expertise. You have other ambitions, and I can take care of any sleazeballs all on my lonesome. Don't get caught up in my crazy and potentially ruin your career."

I try to sound flippant, but my voice comes out too thin. The idea of doing this without him hits like cold water down the spine. I've gone on digs alone before. But this...this feels different. This feels like stepping into the unknown, and the only hand I'd trust to grab if I slipped was his.

"Ruin my career? What about yours? If word gets out that you took part in this and find nothing, no one will take you seriously. You'll be the crackpot of the field."

"My life, my choice."

"Ditto. I'm going with you. You need to have someone sane by your side."

"I haven't decided yet."

"If you do—"

The doorbell rings through our apartment, cutting him off. His long legs take him to the door much faster than mine. I always look like a chihuahua trying to jog to keep up with a Great Dane with this guy.

I follow, slower, nerves twisting like kelp in deep water. Something about the timing of that knock feels too perfect. Too rehearsed. Like a line hitting precisely on cue.

"Is Ms. Aurora Darling at home?" A very snooty-sounding British accent asks from somewhere on Mattie's other side. Yes, my parents were Disney fanatics, and yes, they thought it was a good idea to pair Aurora with Darling. A good chunk of my childhood was full of shoot-me-now moments of embarrassment. I've never liked hearing my full name spoken aloud. It always feels too sharp and expectant, like it belongs to someone I haven't become yet.

"Who's asking?" My overprotective best friend growls politely, using his entire body to not only block my view of our guest but also his view inside our apartment and therefore of me.

"Lloyd Blakely, Esquire. I'm here to inquire about a recent proposal that was sent to Ms. Darling. She has yet to respond, and time is of the essence. Ms. Darling," he calls to me over Mattie's shoulder like he knows I'm right behind him, not hidden by a 2-inch steel door.

The sound of my name again, spoken so precisely, sends a ripple down my spine. He says it like a summons. Like a memory I can't place.

"Do you have an answer? My employer is eager to hear your response and get the project in motion."

Mattie holds up a finger and closes the door. "This sets off so many red flags, I can't—just say no. I don't like this at all, Rory." He says in a hushed voice behind the door.

"I know. I know. But Mattie, what if he's just excited? This is a huge opportunity for me. I could end this once and for all and maybe the dreams will finally stop, my subconscious satisfied. They just want an answer now, not to leave now, I think." Even as I say it, something inside me itches. A wrongness I can't name. Like I've been here before, said these words before, and the ending didn't go well.

"No. The expedition is set to leave in a month from tomorrow. The ship will sail out of Barcelona." Mr. Blakely says through the door.

Mattie raises his brow in complete shock while I whisper-scream, "He can hear us."

"I assure you, Ms. Darling, I can hear you loud and clear. Your metal door does not block much sound at all," he says. "My employer is excited and eager to get this moving, as he believes you are correct in your research. It shows great promise."

I open the door again; there's no sense talking through it when he can just hear us anyway. "Who is your employer?"

"He wishes to remain anonymous at this time." He says, twisting an actual bowler hat brim in his hands.

"How convenient for him," Mattie says, attempting to mutter under his breath.

"Most assuredly," Mr. Bowler Hat remarks. "I do understand how challenging that can be, that he remains anonymous and you take all the risks of failure. However, he is confident you will not fail."

"If I say yes, will you leave? I can always change my mind."

"Indeed, pleasure to finally meet you, Ms. Darling. We will be in touch with the rest of the paperwork and your airline tickets. We will need a list of equipment you will require within the next week. Good day." He says, pats his hat back onto his head with a bow and starts back down the hallway toward the stairs, not the elevator.

"Wait," I call after him. "I didn't actually say yes." But he keeps walking like he didn't hear a word, like his leaving cements my yes. It feels like some invisible gate just slammed shut behind me.

"Well, fine! But Mattie's coming too!"

"I will add Mr. Matthew Beauregard to the manifest." He says and disappears into the stairwell.

"What the fuck just happened? How did he know your name?" I ask of Mattie. I'm not sure he hears me by the look of complete shock on his face.

www.ingramcontent.com/pod-product-compliance
Lightning Source LLC
Chambersburg PA
CBHW010647100726
47901CB00009B/2462